Praise for Playe

"Links Players has been waiting a long ti
journey with the multitude of great cl
And the wait has been worth it. You will enjoy the scenic journey through the highlands of Scotland and the Orkney Islands. But even better, you will discover another journey of the heart, through scripture and great minds of the past, all in search for the wisdom that God wants for us all. Colossians 2:2-3 states God's hope for us all, *"I want them to have complete confidence that they understand God's mysterious plan, which is Christ himself. In him lie hidden all the treasures of wisdom and knowledge."* Speaking for all the Links Players family and fellowships, we hope that you will find the treasure that is hidden in Jesus Christ. This book will help you do just that."

Jeff Cranford
President of Links Players International. www.linksplayers.com

Tim Philpot beautifully engages the Biblical story and our everyday struggles, through the feminine voice of wisdom. *Player's Progress* will capture your heart as you engage with the characters and imagery in this creative and enjoyable read."

Tracy Hanson
Retired LPGA Tour Professional and founder of
Tracy Hanson Initiative

"*Player's Progress* is a masterpiece of golf prose. After reading it, you will want to catch the first plane to Inverness and head north to discover the majesty of Royal Dornoch and the enchanting paradise of surrounding golf courses. You may even bump into a few of the characters like Mrs. Doubter or Mr. Niblick, and maybe catch a glimpse of Ben Hogan himself! It's an amazing blend of golf history and mystical golf characters who gather on the pages of the book."

Wally Armstrong,
Co-author of *The Mulligan* with Ken Blanchard,
PGA Tour golf pro, golf historian

"*Player's Progress* is an instant classic. I love reading good books, especially when you are inspired and remember the lessons being taught. This is a story of second chances which will especially connect with serious golfers. Tim is one of the few living authors I enjoy reading. You will remember this beautiful story forever."

Randy Wolff
Former PGA Tour player and author of *Our Daily Light*

"*Player's Progress* invites the reader to join a diverse foursome that highlights the best and worst in human nature. The players take on the challenge of playing "the greatest golf course in the world." Book your tee time now for an experience that will take you to the home of golf... and far beyond into eternity. It could be the most important round of your life!"

Steve Forrest
Past President, American Society of Golf Course Architects,
past "Golf Architect of the Year"

"Tim Philpot has created a golf course and story that needs to be played (read) by everyone who loves God and golf. Our great Creator God has gifted Tim with the imagination to create a wonderful tale of a life-changing trip to Scotland. Enjoy!"

Tom Heilbron
Founder of Keene Trace Golf Club,
home of the PGA Tour's Barbasol Championship in Kentucky

"My friendship with Tim has been packed with joy. Tim is an original, and so is his book, as he needed no photos to paint a panorama of some of the greatest golf courses in world. His humor is subtle and blended with great truth."

Jim Hiskey
Founder of Links Letter, mentor to PGA Tour players.

"*Player's Progress* shows us the sovereignty of God through an entertaining golf journey of eighteen holes and more. Tim's use of the great book of 'wisdom' provides insight into his love of golf and our Lord."

Dick Spybey
Retired Hall of Fame golf coach at the University of Alabama

"I met Tim Philpot on the first tee of the Old Course over thirty years ago. That day we prayed for Scotland. This book is an answer to those early prayers, linking the greatest sport in the world with the Creator Himself. Tim's book is about the journey of finding your true self in God. Read it and you may find your way too."

Pete Hiskey
Pastor to the golf world

"*Player's Progress* is fiction but filled with rock-solid truth. A cast of Biblical characters and golf luminaries either help or hinder the progress of the two main pilgrims, Lucas and ProV, on their walk through eighteen holes and more. The book is patterned after *The Pilgrim's Progress*, but with an entirely fresh and appealing approach. I think Bunyan would appreciate it."

Dr. Ed Robb III
Pastor Emeritus, The Woodlands, Texas U.M.C.

"On an obscure golf course in the Orkney Islands, the mysteries of golf, faith and the wisdom of the ages converge. For one golfer in desperate need of a clean scorecard in life – and maybe even for the reader — it's a life-changing journey of discovery and redemption. The allegory of *Player's Progress* is rich with colorful characters, meaning and insights for every reader, golf enthusiast or not. Bunyan would be proud."

Chris Tiegreen
Author of over twenty books,
including *The One Year Walk with God*

"Tim Philpot has taken his two loves, golf and Godly wisdom, and spun them into a mythical yarn that will delight your soul, dazzle your senses and quite possibly leave you both a better human and a better golfer. *Player's Progress* has unique twists and turns on every page. You won't be able to put it down.

Wayne Jacobsen
Author of *He Loves Me*, co-author of *The Shack*

PLAYER'S PROGRESS

A Golfer's Journey to Wisdom

a novel by Tim Philpot

PLAYER'S PROGRESS
A Golfer's Journey to Wisdom
By Tim Philpot

ISBN: 978-1-7359194-7-8

For information, contact the author:

Tim Philpot
PO Box 265
Loxley, Alabama 36551

admin@timphilpot.com
www.timphilpot.com
www.playersprogress.com

Published by:

Chilidog Press LLC
pbronson@chilidogpress.com

Chilidog Press
Milford, Ohio
www.chilidogpress.com

Illustrated by: Carter Quina
cquina@qgarchitects.com

Cover design by: Chad Crouch
www.Cre8tivegroup.com

Cover photo by: Carter Quina

Interior design and typesetting by: Craig Ramsdell
ramsdelldesign.com

Dedicated to the wisest women in my life:
my mother, Virginia Philpot,
and my wife, Susan Philpot.

Contents

Author's Note

This story has been a twenty-year journey in my mind.

The characters you will meet have become my best friends. The venues for the story are my favorite spots on earth. The pilgrims' journey and search for wisdom has been my own.

The ideas in this book all started when Titleist developed the revolutionary ProV1 golf ball in the early 2000s. It was an instant success.

I wondered, "ProV1. What a great abbreviation for Proverbs, the epic book of wisdom." My mind began to imagine a golfer, whose nickname was "ProV," searching for wisdom. I outlined eighteen themes from Proverbs and led a group of college golfers from Kentucky through a study for a few weeks.

But I also remembered the ancient allegorical novel, *The Pilgrim's Progress,* written by John Bunyan in 1678. Benjamin Franklin said you are not educated unless you have read this all time, best-selling classic, and I agree. Indeed, it is recommended that you read it before you open Chapter One of this story.

The style in this book is borrowed from Bunyan. Fictional characters have names that reflect their personalities. Multiple footnotes help make the book a teaching tool. And last, illustrations by Carter Quina, just as in *The Pilgrim's Progress*, help the reader see what my eyes have seen.

As a sign from the Almighty that I was on the right track, and just as I was finishing the final edits, a 1929 golf book by Chick Evans and Barrie Payne came across my desk. One of the funny chapters was "A Golfing Pilgrim's Progress," which began:

> *"Someday I intend to write a Golfing Pilgrim's Progress –*
>
> *Telling how the Golfing Pilgrim set out to reach the Celestial City of Par over a course called Difficulty.*
>
> *Describing his trouble on the first tee where he dubbed his tee shot into a creek known as The Slough of Despond..."* [1]

I smiled and knew that I was not the first crazy person who decided to write a Golfing *Pilgrims' Progress.*

As I was writing I also discovered that Proverbs was not enough. The great book of wisdom provides principles and quotable gems, but these ageless words are meaningless unless one can tap into the power of the Holy Spirit.

Living out wisdom every day is not the same as writing quotable material. Just ask Solomon and his 700 wives.

Attempts to live out the precepts of Proverbs without the One who created us is futile. So the story did not seem right without a caddie named Hollie—indeed, the Holy Spirit.

One final thought. The ancient wisdom in *Proverbs* (700 BC) and *The Pilgrim's Progress* (1678) seem to have the same vital ingredient: Time.

Time to grow old. Time to make mistakes. Time to read. Time to learn from sages of the past. Time to heal. Time to think. Time to remember.

[1] "Ida Broke: The humor and philosophy of golf," Chick Evans and Barrie Payne, E.P. Dutton and Co. Inc., New York, page 292 (1929).

Wisdom takes time. I am now retired, so I have time. Time to finally finish a metaphorical and pedagogical novel.

So here we go. To Scotland, to the Orkney Islands and beyond. Maybe even to eternity. Let your imagination run wild. Enjoy.

Tim Philpot
June 2022

Where have you gotten all these wise sayings?
Whose spirit speaks through you?...
These are just the beginning of all that he does,
merely a whisper of his power.
Who, then, can comprehend the thunder of his power?
Job 26:4,14

Part One
'On the Tee'

"No other links has quite the ageless aura Dornoch does. When you play it, you get the feeling you could be living just as easily in the eighteen hundreds, or even the seventeen hundreds. If an old Scot in a red jacket had popped out from behind a sand dune, beating a feathery ball, I wouldn't have blinked an eye."[2]

Dornoch Clubhouse, 2056

[2] Lorne Rubenstein, *A Season in Dornoch* (McClelland and Stewart, Ltd, 2001), p. 6.

CHAPTER 1
Royal Dornoch

"Good afternoon. This is Game number forty-two. On the tee, from Fresno, California, USA, Mr. Lucas Friend."

The Scottish brogue of starter Roddy McDonald was loud and clear.

It was 1:20 p.m. on the first day of the Carnegie Shield, the prized amateur event at Royal Dornoch Golf Club in Scotland. The date was August 12, 2056, the 150th anniversary of the first Shield tournament, when Andrew Carnegie from nearby Skibo had donated a trophy of priceless value to his favorite golf club in the world. Andrew had grown up around the small village of Dornoch, which would become *Royal* Dornoch when the King himself said so a few years later. Andrew's immigration to America for business fame and fortune never dimmed his love affair with life and golf and Dornoch.

The same could be said of Lucas Friend. Now seventy-two, he played in the high handicap division with fourteen strokes needed every round to fight with Old Man Par. Age itself had finally gotten the best of him. His glory years when he once played in the US Amateur in 2018 at Pebble Beach were long gone. He was just thirty-four then, and at the apex of a mediocre amateur golf career. The fact that he qualified for match play and lost six-and-five meant nothing now. After fifty years of work on Wall Street, he had retired and was now enjoying golf and family. Palm Desert in the winter and Scotland in the summer. Royal Dornoch was the highlight. He was one of hundreds of international members who made annual pilgrimages to the holy site.

Old Tom Morris had laid out the original modern course in 1892, but golf had been played on the links since 1616. And of course, the legendary Donald Ross had been the first greenskeeper and professional at Dornoch, learning all the nuances of golf at his beloved home course. One could say Dornoch was literally the home of golf, had St. Andrews not stolen the title. Dornoch's geography, sixty miles north of Inverness, made it difficult to locate in the age before cars and bridges and helicopters and airplanes. But now Dornoch had become a dream destination for nearly all golfers.

So, at 1:20 sharp, Lucas nodded a "play well" to his Scottish companions: Alistair from York in England, and Malcolm from Lossiemouth, a small village just around the corner from Inverness. Alistair and Malcolm nodded in return. Lucas hit his drive into one of the sneaky bunkers on the left, downwind, and off they went, taking their first steps into golf paradise.

After many decades of being among the top ten courses in the world (so said all the golf magazines), Royal Dornoch had finally arrived at the pinnacle—ranked consensus number one. Pine Valley, Royal County Down, Augusta and Pebble Beach were not happy about it. But decades of persistence and persuasion had finally convinced the golfing press that Dornoch was, in fact, by every available measure, the greatest golf course in the world.

How could a par 70 layout that plays less than 7,000 yards be called the greatest? The conversation around that question kept clubhouse bars busy for hours into the night, especially if the whisky was flowing.

It helped when Dornoch finally built a new clubhouse in 2030, and also helped when they built a new hole, the seventh, which became a signature hole in 2020. It was a 480-yard par four overlooking the entire North Sea. The hole had joined the fourteenth hole, known as "Foxy," on everyone's list of the greatest par fours in the world.

But the clincher was when the R&A finally, following the USGA's lead, put distance limits on equipment and golf balls in 2042. With one stroke of the pen, par 70 and 6,850 yards was back. The monsters of almost 8,000 yards were now seen as what they were, monsters. Golf sanity had been restored, and with it, Royal Dornoch had become the greatest golf course in the world.

Now it was 5:30 p.m., and Lucas sat at the scorer's table with a smile on his face. It was a polite smile from a veteran golfer. It could not cover up the pain of a triple bogey on the last hole or hide the torment golf inflicts on humans who try to hit a ball the size of a pebble with a stick four feet long into a hole made by rabbits. The Royal and Ancient governors of golf had decided in 1891 that all holes everywhere should be uniformly and exactly only 4.25 inches in diameter—and thus the knee-knocking, nerve-twitching "yips" were born. A lot can go wrong.

The weather had been perfect—mild winds and sixty-two degrees Fahrenheit. The greens had been perfect too, as usual. His playing companions had been lovely chaps to accompany him through paradise. The number on the card was barely relevant: 88.

"Nicely played," said Malcolm as he shook hands with Lucas on the eighteenth green.

Lucas had scored a net seventy-four, which meant he was now in position to qualify for match play for high handicappers, competing for the E.C. Fraser Cup. The nerves from the first tee had disappeared when he somehow parred the first hole from that fairway bunker. And his one-putt bogey at the famous par three second was even better.

Waiting to greet him was his young friend from America. Paul Victor Player was rumored to be a distant relative of Gary Player—a rumor he did nothing to discourage, although he had never been near South Africa. He had won the 2033 California State Amateur and even qualified for the Masters Tournament that same year when he finished runner-up in the US Amateur as a twenty-year-old sophomore in college. But he finally crashed and burned on the Q School garbage heaps. And now at age forty-three, twice divorced and behind on his child support, relieved to have his amateur status back, he was waiting near the caddie shack.

"So, ProV, you must be bored stiff to be out here looking for me," offered Lucas.

Paul had grabbed his nickname at Fresno State University, when he could really play. With his initials, PVP, his teammates started calling him PV, which soon became ProV when he quit school to turn pro. His sponsor, Titleist, was sure hoping he would make it, but like most kids with high hopes, the dream became a nightmare and ended with too many chips and three putts.

ProV, with his plus-one handicap, had teed off at 6:50 a.m. as one of the lowest handicaps in the field. His eighty in an early morning rain and wind was not what he had in mind. It was his first trip to Scotland, and he had not been ready for the bounce of the ball and greens with more slope than his brain could imagine. His thirty-seven on the front nine was actually fine until a bunker on the tenth hole did everything but eat him for breakfast. His six on a hole that played 157 yards was still munching on his heart just a few short hours later. If he could have forgotten about it and moved on, he might have survived. But that triple bogey fried his brain for an hour and led to four straight bogeys.

Lucas tried to empathize with ProV about his eighty, net eighty-one, but he was also still immersed in his own tragic triple bogey finish. The friends both had triple bogeys worth a sad discussion in the bar, sorrowful tales of bad luck. At the end of this day, Lucas was reasonably happy and Paul "ProV" Player was not.

But there is always tomorrow. And when tomorrow actually came, the highlands weather came with it. Teeing off at 8:40 a.m., Lucas would get the worst. His resulting ninety-seven, net eighty-three, meant the week was likely grinding to a halt. He would miss the match play in the high handicap division by two shots, with both of those shots sadly laying in the bottom of bunkers on the sixteenth and eighteenth. Perhaps he had made a mistake by not taking a caddie. He had pushed his own trolley and at age seventy-two, the final long hill to climb at the famous sixteenth had almost finished him off. Grinding to the finish when you are plus-twenty-four on the day is not easy. Breaking a hundred was his main motivation at the end.

When ProV finished in a late afternoon rain shower with another hard fought 80, it appeared the two American chaps would be going to Plan B, which was to play some of the northern gems of Scotland that most tourists never have time to locate and enjoy. But it was not entirely clear they had missed the match play cut. The weather had sent all scores soaring so, first, a stop in the bar would make sense to wait out the inevitable final tally.

"Okay, Paul," said Lucas, since it didn't feel right to call him ProV after two 80s. "What now? I have to presume we are done for the week. What's your preference? It would be four hours to St. Andrews. That's a good idea if this is your last trip here. Brora and Golspie are nearby. Both are fabulous. We can go to Castle Stuart, although beware the American greens fees. Nairn is great. Coul Links is next door but very private and not easy to access. Same for Skibo Castle. Malcolm says he'd be happy to host us at Lossiemouth, which is pure links."

"I never heard of any of these places, man," said ProV, who needed a drink.

Lucas had a very special golf course in mind, but he was not sure ProV was ready for it, so he changed the subject. "Poor Malcolm must have shot a hundred today." Lucas would wait to see if ProV would be open to his suggestions.

"The guy I played with was from Durness at the northwestern tip of Scotland. He swears it is spectacular," said ProV, glancing at the bar like a dog waiting on his treat.

"It is indeed, and the drive to get there is even more spectacular. Fortrose is breathtaking most days for views. But it's your call. I've been here forty times and this is your first trip, and who knows, maybe last trip. So what's your pleasure?"

"My pleasure would be a hot shower, a Guinness, and a psychiatrist to explain to me why I play golf."

"I can arrange the Guinness," said Lucas as he walked to the bar and offered the bartender his member's card to get the 15 percent discount.

As Lucas the teetotaler returned with the Guinness and his own hot tea, ProV continued the typical golfer's lament. "My preference would also be to know why anyone would vote this the greatest golf course in the world. I mean, really. I know what you think, Lucas, but seriously. Par seventy and less than seven thousand yards? Not even a lot of rough. Scenery, okay, I get it. And ambience, okay, I get it. But I'm sorry, this is not the greatest golf course in the world."

Lucas was listening patiently, realizing that his friend needed to vent.

"So, Paul, er ProV, Mr. former All-American, where else have you shot 80 two days in a row? Seriously, I remember when we went to Pine Valley on that two-day trip? You shot what? Seventy-two? Seventy-three? And even at Augusta you shot two seventy-threes when you played in the Masters. But I also know that if you played here a few more times, you might shoot a sixty-six on a nice calm day. So, I won't defend Dornoch. It does pretty well defending itself."

He shrugged and smirked and knew that after ProV had been back a few times, he would finally get it. The wounds inflicted by the razor blades of golf were too fresh now. They always take time to heal.

Within a few minutes, the final tally was in. Lucas Friend and Paul Player were not on the list of qualifiers. They would be free men for a few days.

Royal Dornoch had won again.

The conversation about the greatest course in the world continued into the night as ProV and Lucas gathered in the bar at the Dornoch Castle Hotel with other American fanatics who had come into town for the Shield. A sign over the bar declared it the Greatest Whisky Bar in the World, and therefore, the perfect setting for a liquor-fueled debate.

The debaters were all wealthy American men whose self-worth was wrapped up in their club memberships and myriad golf trips. No one could top anyone when it came to "Have you played blah-blah-blah?" and "Oh sure, but I didn't think it was as good as blah-blah-blah." On and on it went.

Tom from Sea Island, Georgia voted for Augusta, offering him the opportunity to tell how many times he'd been invited to play there by his good friend the chairman.

Jackson from Chicago made a serious whisky-driven plea for Chicago Golf Club.

Harvey from Louisville was sure that tradition trumped it all, meaning the Old Course at St. Andrews should be on top of his short list.

Pine Valley and Cypress and Pebble Beach got no votes.

Sandy Sutherland from nearby Golspie, a true Scot but now living in Palm Desert, California, put in his word for Coul Links, called "Embo" by locals—it was the "new" course built just four miles north of Dornoch back in 2030 after decades of government haggling over saving some sort of crawling creature that lived there. The thousands of pounds he had put up to be one of the exclusive members may have influenced his opinion about the Coore-Crenshaw design. He offered the concurrence of six-time major winner Jordan Spieth as proof certain. And the fact that Crenshaw contemplated having his ashes spread there when he passed away in 2042. No one was sure if it actually happened.

ProV just listened, half-drunk with disappointment about his two "snowmen" eighties more than the whisky. As he looked up at the bar, he wondered out loud to Lucas, "Have they misspelled whisky? Shouldn't there be an 'e' in there?"

Lucas smiled. "I know we put an extra 'e' in it back home, but I'd say when it comes to whisky, the Scots know what they're doing." He was otherwise strangely silent, listening with a satisfied smile to the conversation which finally and graciously ended. Lucas concluded the night's endless nothingness with the final word: "Dornoch, boys. Just that simple." With that parting word, he stood up and headed to his room. ProV followed like a faithful puppy.

As they returned to their rooms, ProV said, "Lucas, you were pretty quiet tonight."

"ProV, my man. You've been around me enough by now to know that inane conversation about nothing makes me crazy. Debating the greatest golf course is not much different from all the sports talk shows discussing who's the 'GOAT,' the greatest quarterback or basketball player or anything. It is useless talk which I choose to mostly ignore with a smile."

ProV was listening as the older man gave his friendly advice on their way down the narrow hallway.

"It's like discussing blonds versus brunettes at the Miss America pageant. I'd have preferred a conversation about why golf makes us so crazy. How a plus-one handicap can shoot eighty on a simple little six-thousand, eight-hundred-yard course with no water hazards, or why my hands tremble on the first green, or why it would even matter what a seventy-two-year-old has-been like me does with any game. Do old shuffleboard players choke? I'd have enjoyed a conversation with that psychiatrist you needed so bad today."

"I totally get it. See ya tomorrow," ProV said.

"And where are we going?" Lucas asked as a reminder to ProV that he was in charge of venue now.

"I think I will leave it in your hands. You've been here a lot and we only have four days. Your call. I trust you," said ProV, sleepy and half-dizzy from one too many Glenmorangies.

Lucas liked that answer. He knew exactly where they would go.

CHAPTER 2
Wake-Up Call

The only advantage to bad golf at the Carnegie Shield is that missing the cut means you miss the 6:00 a.m. wake-up call for a 7:30 tee time. Sleep was easy, and the warm bed was hard to leave for ProV.

He was in the middle of a nightmare when his alarm went off after 9:00, very busy in the underworld of golf dreams. When he groggily determined it was just a dream, he was so relieved.

ProV was the first alternate for the US Open in his murky netherworld. When some unknown someone didn't show up for his tee time at 1:06, his name was called to the first tee. He would be paired with C.Q. Wong from China, the greatest player in the history of the world, and an eighty-year-old Tiger Woods, making his ceremonial final appearance. It seemed to be Pebble Beach, but who knows?

The excitement quickly turned to panic as the name Paul Player was called to the tee. He had no clubs. He was at a urinal in the men's room in the clubhouse. He had lost his pants somehow. He was not sure how to get to the tee. His caddie was somewhere, but where? He panicked and asked everyone, "Where's the first tee?" Somehow, he found it, but no one was there. A marshal looked at the tee sheet and said Wong and Woods were teeing off on the tenth tee, which was two miles away.

So ProV, with no clubs, no caddie, no golf shoes and maybe even no pants (he was afraid to look), marched boldly through massive crowds trying to find the tenth tee. The march went through streets of concrete and a restaurant where nicely dressed people seemed offended that someone was barging through their fine dining lunch. He was flying in a helicopter at some point in his dreamworld, where the most bizarre things can seem perfectly normal.

And as he finally made it to the tenth tee, he looked at a giant clock that declared it was 1:39 p.m. His group was already on the eleventh tee, far ahead, and ProV had missed his tee time. How could he have been so stupid? And where was his caddie, Lucas Friend? The shame of this day would never leave him. He would be the laughingstock of all his friends and the Golf Channel would feature him as the idiot who couldn't make his tee time at the US Open.

Then the alarm started screaming. He hit the snooze button and awoke in a sweat, still reeling from his failure. And then relief. It had been a dream, a nightmare of epic proportions for any serious golfer.

This was proof indeed. Golf had made him crazy.

He showered and dressed quickly in his finest gray sweater, hoping no one would notice him today. He wanted to stay under the showerhead all day. The Scots had finally figured out American golf tourists would pay extra for a shower with lots of water streaming from the ceiling.

With breakfast shutting down at 10:00, he had to hurry, and that felt like the dream all over again. He hurried downstairs like he was running to the first tee. He made it just in time, at 9:52. Lucas was waiting. He'd been up since 6:00, an hour later than his normal.

Over a full Scottish breakfast of bacon, eggs, baked beans, tomato and more, ProV took a full ten minutes to tell Lucas about the dream. Lucas had had similar dreams for years. They were both hopelessly addicted to the personal successes and failures of a little white ball hit with a stick.

Lucas decided to push into the inner regions of ProV's fragile self. "ProV, it's a new day. Would you give me permission to dig a little into your psyche?"

"Oh, boy. Good luck with that. I had a so-called mental coach once. I read ol' Rotella and all the others. So sure, fire away."

"Here is what I see, man. You obviously have talent for golf, which must mean talent for many things. My experience says anyone who can play golf successfully, which you have done, may have an aptitude for success in all things. And other people see that. Super successful people who can't break ninety see a person like you and they'd give anything to be you." ProV nodded agreement. He had seen it happen in his sales job. Wealthy executives would have sold their souls to be scratch golfers.

"When I was on Wall Street," continued Lucas, "I had other brokers and finance guys who honestly believed I was competent simply because they had seen me win the club championship. Bad golfers, and the world is full of them, think a good golfer is a genius, not just on the course but everywhere. Men would call me for financial advice because I could break par."

ProV was still in a stupor but listening.

"But in your case, there is something missing. You have education. Now that pro golf is behind you, you have a good sales job with Titleist. You have personality, charisma. People like you."

"Yeah, except my kids and wives," said ProV with a rueful grin as he sipped black coffee. Lucas smiled and nodded agreement.

"Okay, man, but listen. Something's missing."

ProV looked straight into Lucas's eyes, suddenly alert.

"This may hurt, but one reason you don't appreciate Dornoch is that your spiritual side is numb. You do not comprehend some basics about links golf and places like Dornoch."

Lucas pulled out an old book, *A Season in Dornoch*. The pages were worn from many readings. "This was written in 2001, before you were born."

ProV had stopped working on his eggs to listen.

"Just one quote this morning from an old guy named Rubenstein. And then you can have the book to read as we go along.

> *"I made a list of things I liked about playing the game, to see if I'd been ignoring them.*
>
> *"I liked: playing alone on a course in the early morning or evening, hitting different shots according to what I saw and felt as I walked up to the ball; hitting the ball on the ground as well as in the air; playing not by yardages but by sight; playing with close friends; walking and carrying my own clubs; playing with a caddy and chatting with him as we moved along; playing in a soft rain; playing in cold nasty conditions while wearing layers of clothing; playing by the sea; hitting low shots into a strong wind; match play rather than medal play; playing worst ball, where the idea is to hit two shots each shot and then pick the worst result and play two balls from there—it's about the best practice one can get in; practicing at the end of the range in the evening; hitting every club in the bag to a green from the same spot; playing a full round with half a set, or even fewer clubs; standing in a bunker for an hour and hitting a variety of shots just to feel the spank of the club into the sand, the sand spraying and the ball popping out and rolling along the green; putting check on the ball from the sand; making a ball spin in various directions; hitting different shots from the same stance."*[3]

Lucas took a breath, looked up and found ProV staring back.

"And then, man, listen to this. He says, '*It became apparent to me that I'd ignored most of what I had enjoyed about golf.*'"

Lucas handed the book to his friend. "Now, my suggestion would

[3] Lorne Rubenstein, *A Season in Dornoch: Golf and Life in the Scottish Highlands* (McClelland and Stewart, Ltd, 2001), p. 132-133.

be, put that book in your suitcase and read it on the plane going home. But I've got some other things for you to consider first."

ProV was now fully awake. He put the book aside and went to work on a piece of toast. He also had his Royal Dornoch Course Guide sitting on the table. He had been analyzing both of his rounds in the Shield. He had duly recorded the numerous bad breaks that led to the twin snowmen. He marked comments in red ink on a scorecard. A good drive ended in an unplayable lie, an eight iron hit a hard spot and went 206 yards, and of course, the perfect nine iron on the tenth hole somehow spun left, leading to an encounter with one of Dornoch's bunkers and a nasty rake job by some "idiot," he had said, leading to the six.

Lucas slowed down the pity train by interrupting, "Now look in your course guide. You probably did not even notice that every hole has a short sentence written by the local minister at Dornoch Cathedral. A fine lady named Susan Brown was the pastor there from 1998 to 2021. What did she say, for instance, on the first hole?"

ProV was thumbing through the course guide and found the first hole, known simply as "First." He read:

> *"Number One—In the beginning, draw breath and enjoy a clean score sheet and all the possibilities that lie ahead. Choose now to take one step at a time and enjoy what that step holds."*

He looked up at Lucas like an altar boy confessing to a priest who might understand. "Okay, a clean score sheet," he said. "I wish I had seen this two days ago when I stood there. I was busy looking at the numbers, one hundred and nineteen from the edge of a left bunker to the middle. Two hundred and ninety to miss the bunker on the right edge near the green. The word 'enjoy' was not in my brain," a slowly humbled ProV admitted.

Lucas leaned across the breakfast table. "Here is what I think I know, keeping in mind I was sixty before I saw any of this, which means you may be twenty years away. Education. Good family. Professional success. These matter little if not combined with something I will call *wisdom*." He made air quotes as the word wisdom was emphasized. ProV instinctively repeated, "Wisdom."

Lucas continued. "And now are you ready? Dornoch is indeed *not* the greatest golf course in the world. I was just messing with those guys last night."

He paused and continued slowly. "I found wisdom a few years ago when I played the greatest golf course in the world. And if you'd like, we might even go there. That's *if* I can find it. I was there twelve years ago. It is in the Orkney Islands."

"And where is that?"

"Straight north about fifty miles, then over a ferry ride. Maybe more than one ferry, in fact. Quite the adventure."

"And what exactly will we find at this greatest golf course in the world?" asked ProV, the cynical man returning for an encore.

Lucas smiled and took his time answering, stalling to pour one last cup of coffee. Secretly, he had been hoping and wishing the day would come when he could return to that place where he found his soul. He had been afraid to go back. He had heard that to go back a second time might cost you everything. That scared him. It was not a tale one could tell at a typical bar or clubhouse locker room. No one told him to keep his days there a secret, but still, he had kept mostly quiet.

For one thing, no matter how much he thought about it, he actually was not sure it had really happened. It could have been a dream. It could have been a vision. He had had a heart attack twelve years ago and was in a coma for eleven days. It could have been the medicine. His wife had died that year as well. Maybe he was in shock.

But he remembered almost everything that happened. And now, could he do it again with his friend ProV? It was all very real. In his mind.

Lucas made it simple: "If you are ready for an adventure, you might discover that wisdom."

ProV stared at Lucas, paused and said, "Let's do it. But seriously, if this place is so great, why have I never heard of it?"

"I haven't even given you the name yet, so that's one reason you've never heard of it. And, honestly, I am not even sure I can find it."

"And the name?"

"Hokmah Golf Club. In the middle of nowhere on an island called Mashal. Orkney has seventy islands. Some are so small they just have some rocks and nothing else. No sheep, even. This particular island, Mashal, has no way there except a small ferry. The only thing on the island is this golf course, if I remember correctly."

ProV butchered the pronunciation. "Hokmah? Spell that, man."

"H-O-K-M-A-H. Obviously, you never heard of it," Lucas said as he downed his last sip of the bad Scottish coffee. The waitress was hovering about the dining room, wondering when the two Americans would leave so she could clear the table. Both men saw her angst and stood to leave as they finished the conversation. It was now 10:30.

"So, when do we leave?" ProV said. "To be honest, I'd like a day here to unwind. I was so serious about the tournament I haven't really even looked around the rest of Dornoch."

Lucas replied, "You might want to drive up to the Highland Games at Helmsdale. It is quite a Scotland experience. It would just be a thirty-minute drive up there. And tonight, the Pipe Band will be playing a concert, marching around Dornoch. Saturday is a good day to be around Dornoch in the summertime."

"Sounds like a winner," said ProV. "I've had enough golf for now."

"You're thinking straight. Let's get some rest today." ProV was nodding agreement. "ProV, you have already taken the first step, just like the course guide said. A clean sheet. No bogeys yet. Just the anticipation of a wonderful walk. I tell you what, clean up, relax and meet me in front of the hotel in half an hour. There is one thing I need to show you before we head north tomorrow."

ProV was not ready for more golf today. He needed sanity, not links golf. He was still beating himself up over two scorecards that reported 80. "Numbers do not lie," he had been told by all his coaches, and sadly he believed it. Peaceful tranquility on the golf course was still just a theory for him. He would need some more whisky today to get started with this adventure with Lucas.

CHAPTER 3
Follow Me

At 11:00 a.m., ProV was waiting with a coffee in hand on the sidewalk outside the hotel, just fifty steps from the front door of the famous Dornoch Cathedral.

"Follow me" is all Lucas said to his friend when he arrived five minutes later.

Lucas's name could not have been any more perfect. He was a true friend to many, especially right now to ProV. Lucas's mother obviously knew that his first name, derived from Luke, was in the Bible. He didn't claim to be a Bible scholar but he did know his mother's favorite verse was in one of the Timothy letters, *"Only Luke is with me."*[4] The Apostle

[4] 2 Timothy: 4:11

Paul said that about Luke when all his other friends had abandoned him in prison. Luke was Paul's only friend, or at least that was how he felt.

And now this modern-day Luke was being another, younger Paul's best friend.

They walked across the street to the cathedral, where a nice elderly lady seemed to be waiting for them, handing both Lucas and ProV a nice pamphlet with information on the history of the place. ProV skimmed the highlights and discovered the church had been built in the thirteenth century, during the reign of King Alexander II. The bishop had been Gilbert de Moravia, who became Saint Gilbert of Dornoch. The cathedral was burned to the ground during a clan feud in 1570. The Murrays and the MacKays didn't much like one another, and the feud led to a fire.

The church was rebuilt in 1616, coincidentally the same year golf was first played on the links of Dornoch. *Maybe the feud was decided by a big golf match instead of pistols and fires*, ProV enjoyed thinking to himself.

He remembered that Malcolm from Lossiemouth was a Murray. And the young assistant in the pro shop was named Lachie Mackay. He wondered with a smirk if these two young men knew they were obligated to hate each other for reasons unknown.

There was a lot more in the pamphlet, but ProV's attention span for church history was quite short. Lucas and ProV stopped in the side entrance area. On the right wall was a plaque, reciting the ninety-sixth Psalm, but only verses eleven and twelve in the original King James Version.

Lucas educated ProV that when they first played golf in Dornoch in 1616, it was just five years after the King James Version was published in 1611. Even the Bible itself had needed a rebirth.

ProV was impressed and never felt so uneducated. His three years at Fresno State were long gone. Lucas read slowly:

Let the heavens rejoice,
And let the earth be glad;
Let the sea roar, and the fullness thereof.

Let the field be joyful, and all that is therein.
Then shall all the trees of the wood rejoice
Before the LORD: for he cometh, for he cometh to judge the earth:
He shall judge the world with righteousness, and the people with his truth.[5]

ProV stared at the plaque. It was the first time in his forty years he had stopped long enough to think about any words in the Bible. Emotion surprised him but he avoided real tears by pretending to get a speck out of his eye. *What was that all about?* he thought to himself.

They wandered into the cross-shaped sanctuary. Even ProV, who had no vital spiritual roots, was in awe at the beauty of the stained-glass windows and the feeling that God might live here. It felt quite different from the Catholic masses he endured as a kid. The building itself seemed to be speaking to him – not words, just emotions.

Lucas suggested, "Let's just be quiet for five minutes. Don't say a word. Try not to even think. See if you hear anything. Just listen."

ProV nervously did as instructed. He found a hard bench in the third row. He ignored a couple of tourists wandering around pointing at the stained-glass windows. He did his best to think about nothing. After the full five minutes, Lucas hadn't moved from his spot on the front row. And then, from nowhere, or in his mind, or his imagination, from somewhere, startling enough to make ProV turn around and look for someone, a Voice rang out:

"There's a wisdom in the sand. There's a treasure in the darkness."

The Voice was clearly female. ProV turned but saw no one. Did she sound Scottish? Was this his grandmother Addie who had raised him since the age of nine? Was it his fourth grade teacher, an Irish nun named Sister Mustard?

How did Lucas know that a Voice might speak?

"Lucas, who was that?" whispered ProV as he stood and moved to the front near his friend, almost seeking shelter from whatever or whoever this Voice might be.

[5] Psalm 96:11-12 (KJV)

"Who was what?"

"You didn't hear a woman talking loud—almost shouting?"

Lucas feigned ignorance. "Don't go by me. I am 72, hard of hearing, survived a heart attack with a full-blown coma, and my wife used to always say I don't listen on purpose."

Lucas did a good job defending himself. But he knew what had happened.

He had been there before. "So, what did I miss?" Lucas was messing with ProV now.

"A woman. It felt like she was whispering in my ear, but at the same time it was really loud."

"And what did she say?"

"Something about a treasure in the sand and darkness. I'm not sure, to be honest. The only treasure I found in the sand was that bunker on ten when my ball buried itself in a bad rake job and I did well to one-putt for a six."

Lucas smiled, knowing ProV had heard the most important Voice in the world and yet he was still thinking about golf and his triple bogey. ProV was the proud owner of a memorable triple bogey, and was wearing it like a nametag at a cocktail party.

"So ProV, there's a treasure somewhere?"

ProV nodded and shrugged a maybe.

"Let's try this one more time. Sit down again. Give it just five more minutes."

ProV returned to his holy spot in the third row. And sure enough, the Voice returned.

"There's a wisdom in the sand. There's a treasure in the darkness."

ProV jumped up this time and hurried to Lucas. "Okay, man, you're messing with me now," he said, looking around to see who might be in on this joke, presuming now that a cameraman would jump out and the whole world would laugh at this crazed golfer in a cathedral hearing voices about a treasure.

But there were no cameras, no signs of a jokester. Just awesome reality that needed a response. Lucas jumped in to save the moment.

"Okay, man, relax. Just to let you in on a secret, I think I heard the same voice twelve years ago."

Now ProV was half glad that he might not be crazy, but half disturbed that his friend might also be a lunatic. Just to be sure, ProV asked Lucas, "And what exactly did you hear?"

He was still hoping Lucas would say it's all a joke, but instead, he simply said:

"There's a wisdom in the sand. There's a treasure in the darkness."

"That's it," ProV whispered, trembling like he had a three-footer to win a US Open.

As they got back to the hotel, ProV headed for the bar. It was not yet noon but the world's greatest whisky bar at the Dornoch Castle Hotel would be open for business. Lucas followed and when they sat down, still bloated from breakfast and the weightiness of the invisible female Voice, Lucas pulled out his phone. He sent a message to ProV, a poem he had written twelve years earlier, not long after the same Voice spoke to him.

"I'm sending you a poem I wrote when this happened to me. Dornoch and Psalm 96 inspired me to be a poet. Funny, huh?"

ProV opened his phone and, sure enough, a message from Lucas was there. He stared at Lucas, who just said, "Read it when you have time."

ProV had a local whisky in hand before noon and all the time in the world. He opened his phone and read slowly.

Lucas stayed quiet while ProV read silently. He walked off to find a pot of tea.

Heavens. Earth. Sea. Fields. Perfect for golf over the Links of Royal Dornoch.

"Let the heavens rejoice" (Look Up)

The views of the firth are so glorious

The clouds always moving in a beautiful disorder

The direction of wind always different

The portraits so awesomely changing

The shadows mean the sun is still there

The moon shines so bright on the back nine.

"And let the earth be glad" (Look Down)

The colors of green seem endless

The ground that we walk brings energy

The bounce of the ball lasts forever

The putts that we hole bring such joy

The balls that we lose seem so happy

The earth is the judge of a shot's real worth.

"Let the sea roar and the fullness thereof" (Look Out)

The smell of the sea invigorates the soul

The sounds of the sea are a symphony

The beach wants the ball when the wind is just right

The seagulls fly low like old vultures

The senses are all tuned to water's beauty.

The scenes of the sea paint a picture.

Let the field be joyful and all that is therein" (Look In)

The caddie's advice seems like nonsense

The caddie's approval means the ball will be found

The straight ball is not to be seen

The distance means nothing to clubbing

The score only matters in match play

The bogey will win most holes

The ghosts of the past ever present

The bunkers eat balls like kids eat candy

The rainsuit is baggy but perfect

The warmth of the fire is pure comfort

Then shall all the trees of the wood rejoice before the Lord.

The occasional tree seems majestic, so rare.

Instead gorse and heather and flowers galore. Indeed God Himself judges the earth called links golf. And He says, "It is good."

Since the land was not suitable for crops or food or production or buildings, it is only suitable for play. Or rabbits perhaps, or dogs on a walk. Or golf. A game where the ball must bounce, and a rabbit hole is the proper home for that ball.

And where pure righteousness and truth can be found. The player himself does not decide the outcome. The results are resolved by the earth itself, by the field of play, by the wind and the bounces, and the eyes of a caddie who find a ball that should have been lost. Ultimate truth is not a number on a scorecard. It is the exhilaration of a six-mile walk interrupted by a few swings, a few strokes, and the fresh air through the nostrils and lungs creating joy all the way to the feet walking the firm ground.

This land was not made for crops. It was made for joy. It was made for people and animals walking the beach, crossing the fairways with right of way. It was made for a threesome of two ladies and a collie. It was made for sheep and cattle and goats who share life with bogeys and birdies. It was made for wind and rain and sunshine, all within a moment.

Without even looking up, ProV continued the conversation. "So, you wrote this?" he asked, impressed that Mr. Friend was something of a poet. Lucas just nodded a yes and repeated, "Look *up*. Look *down*. Look *out*. Look *in*."

"Okay, Lucas, you've found something. I mean, your love for links golf is connected to some spiritual force, a connection between the land and the spirit. I am totally confused, but let's just say I am all ears, brother. If there's a treasure in the sand or darkness or whatever, let's go find it."

He smiled like he had already found a treasure. Perhaps he had. But he knew there was more.

CHAPTER 4
Ears to Hear

ProV was now warm from whisky and Psalm 96, the only scripture he had ever seriously considered. The morning cathedral experience had made him remember his grandmother's sincere attempts to make him a good Catholic. She had done the best she could.

He had gone to live with his father's mother, Grandma Addie, when his mother's alcoholism became dangerous for her little boy, the only child of a bad marriage between Paul Player Sr. and his wife Janie Whitworth. They had started as a nice country club "golf family"—club champions, in fact, in the same year—but it did not take long for booze and gambling to end it all.

Janie got custody of her son only because the father showed so little interest. The ink on the divorce was barely dry when Paul came to pick up his son for a weekend visit and found his former beloved drunk as a skunk on the couch with some so-called boyfriend passed out in a back bedroom.

But worse for the little boy than his mother being passed out was the lecture from his dad, who wondered aloud what Junior had done to make his momma drink like that. Why didn't you stop her, or some such question. He was nine.

ProV's father left the impression that keeping his mother sober would be his responsibility now that "daddy is gone." And gone where? He would never figure that one out.

Truthfully, neither parent wanted the kid, so Grandma Addie would be the answer, even though she had mostly failed raising her own son. Dad's new girlfriend sure didn't want little Junior messing up the new life she'd found with her new romeo.

Under Grandma's tutelage, ProV attended Catholic elementary school, Sunday School, confirmation classes, communion and even confession. Unlike most teenage boys, his confessions included stealing golf balls from the range. Lucky for him, the priest, known as Father Randy, was a golfer. All he needed for penance was a couple of "Hail Marys" when the padre found out the balls were just old Pinnacles.

But ProV was now mildly aggravated with his friend Lucas.

"So why did you wait until after I shot my two snowmen to give me this secret sauce," he asked, describing twin eighties in the lingo of the San Joaquin Country Club where he grew up. "What if I had known this three days ago? Maybe this new attitude and love for the links would have carried me to glory," said ProV, with just a hint of sarcasm.

Lucas laughed out loud, leaned over and touched ProV's ears: "You had no ears to hear, bro."

ProV just shook his head and sipped the whisky.

"In fact, don't you remember on the plane coming over? I tried to tell you about links golf but you were busy reading golf magazines about pronation and swing planes. You were busy looking at pictures of Hogan's swing. You didn't hear a word I said about the spirit of golf. Remember?"

ProV had been caught red handed, knowing he had spent thousands of hours in golf magazines and books and not a single minute seeking spiritual insight.

"Actually, I even sent you my poem on the links a few months ago when you told me you were coming on the trip. You told me you got it, but I could tell you never read it," Lucas said with a smile. "And now I have some assignments for you, if you are ready to learn."

ProV just said, "I am all in, bro. I get it."

"Okay. Your first assignment is to go back to Dornoch and just walk the course. The heavens, the earth, the sea, the links, the birds, the dogs, the wind. No clubs or golf balls. Take a five iron for a walking stick only. Just walk the eighteen holes. Stay in the rough, of course, so you don't interrupt the real players who qualified," said Lucas, knowing his comment would sting slightly.

"Ouch, that one hurts, but I get it."

"Not necessary, but perhaps take the course guide with you and read what Susan Brown said about each hole. That lady understood some things we need to know. You should know the word 'wisdom' is always feminine in the Bible. It is always 'she.' Maybe the cathedral voice is even Susan Brown's voice, who knows." [6]

"Lucas, I looked it up, the cathedral brochure says she'd be at least ninety-eight years old now. I sort of doubt it's her."

"It was someone." He knew Susan Brown was already on the other side. "Now, go walk the course. You should be back in a couple hours, get a nap, meet me for dinner at 6:00 and then off we go tomorrow at 6:00 a.m. The ferry leaves from Scrabster to Stromness at 9:00 and we need to be there an hour early."

ProV felt like the apostle Paul on the road to Damascus. He remembered the story from Sunday school since he had the same name. He had been knocked off his horse, seen a bright light, heard a loud voice, and Saul became Paul.

And now, he was going to play golf with no Titleists and only a five iron to steady his walk. His world was upside down. It was even drizzling rain, but it didn't stop him. He knew it would stop shortly. How could it be raining when he could still see his shadow? Perhaps a rainbow was on the way.

And sure enough, by the time he had finished the five-minute walk

[6] Proverbs 8:1-2 "Listen as Wisdom calls out! Hear as understanding raises her voice! On the hilltop along the road, she takes her stand at the crossroads."

from the hotel to the first tee, he was damp but happy. And indeed, a rainbow appeared as he neared the rough down the left side of the first hole. He carefully navigated the path that crossed in front of the first tee, staying left of the bunkers.

As ProV made his way around Royal Dornoch, five iron in hand, he saw some things he had never noticed before on a golf course of any kind.

With no scorecard to distract him, he could smell the sea.

With no clubs to carry, he could feel the wind.

With no balls to find, he could hear the birds.

With no holes to locate, he could hear a voice inside his head, bringing joy that was absent just yesterday.

"Where has this been my whole life?" he asked himself out loud.

As he approached the sixth hole, he stopped to watch a young man hitting backward away from the green from the front left bunker. He felt sorrow for the lad. Then he watched as the boy's older opponent missed two short putts that would have won the hole. ProV recoiled at the pain of tournament golf.

He quickly left behind the agony of competition and got back to the glorious walk. As he ascended the steepest climb at Dornoch to the seventh tee, he stopped to sit briefly on a bench halfway up, decorated with a plaque to remember some ancient member. He took time to look out over the ocean and course below. When he arrived at the top, he didn't need to throw up grass to notice the wind. He felt it in his face going out for the first eight holes and arrived at the ninth tee for the turnaround with red cheeks from the cool breeze that never stopped.

He realized the stretch of golf from the par three sixth through the par four eighth might be the greatest three holes anywhere, a fact that could only be appreciated when walking without a golf ball. In his mind only, he had parred every hole. Pars are good enough for a contented soul.

Clouds produced an odd array of light raindrops. His shadow came and went like a friendly dog following him.

He remembered three men he'd seen crossing the fifth fairway, returning from the beach with their bouncing and joyful dogs. "I wish I was as happy as your dog right now," he called to one of them. "What's his name?"

"Happy," was the answer.

"Of course," said ProV under his breath with a smile.

He went down on the beach to the left of the ninth hole, the first of only two par fives. The hard sand was perfect for a walk, and just twenty steps from the ninth tee. He saw a very old man throwing a stick for his yellow Labrador. When the stick snap hooked short of the ocean, ProV picked it up and threw it in. The dog splashed in and returned it to his new best friend, shaking so violently that ProV would need a shower just to clear the smell of the dog and the North Sea. He wished he could find the secret of a Scottish dog's joy.

Or maybe even the dog's owner, whose smile showed a glad heart. They stopped to chat. He learned the dog's name first, Barry. The dog's best friend was Graham Fairweather, 91, a former pastor who started a church in Dornoch many years ago. ProV learned that Graham's middle-aged son was now the pastor and a scratch golfer, having almost won the Shield a couple of times.

Graham was retired but came every day to the beach with his dog to see all of God's creation.[7]

It was remarkable how five minutes with the right person at the right time could make you consider believing in God. But that is exactly what happened. The old man genuinely listened to ProV's story of the voice in the cathedral and how he got to this beach on this day, then reached over and touched ProV's hand. "Son, I will be praying for you," he said in a Scottish burr as thick as morning fog. "Every day." And off he went with Barry and his stick.

ProV continued down the beach, wondering if he might also believe in the Almighty someday like that old man.

Indeed, the only stressed faces he saw were on the golfers he passed.

[7] Proverbs 12:10 "The godly care for their animals..."

The competition had turned them into serious men, even though golf had been taken up as a game to relieve the pressure of their careers as doctors or lawyers or tycoons. He felt sorry, for just a moment, for the poor guys who had qualified for match play and were back in the pressure cooker. Golf with a scorecard and a pencil is quite different from a nice walk around the links.

He stopped at the tenth tee for a hot chocolate with Baileys. Heaven was surely close now. The back nine walk was downwind and therefore seemed easier. The ground was giving him energy. The earth itself was producing joy. By the time he arrived at "Foxy," the fourteenth tee, he realized this was his first bogey-free round since a college tournament in 2032, when he shot 65 with no scars on his card. He was even par today in his mind. No reason to be greedy and ask for birdies. Pars would be just fine. All the way to the clubhouse.

He passed behind the fifteenth tee, now walking on a small path that separated the ocean and beach from the grand old lady called Royal Dornoch. At least 100 feet below was one of greatest beaches in the world, marred only by the view of dozens of pale Scots who had endured a cold and long winter. Across to the left in the east was the Tarbat Ness Lighthouse, and in front of him was miles and miles of ocean and linksland where humans had barely traversed, if ever.

To his right was the flag of the fifteenth green. Two men, along with two caddies, were doffing their caps and replacing the flag, finishing a match in the Shield. Someone has lost 4 & 3. A winner and a loser. Neither could have been as happy at this moment as ProV, although one man had some pep in his step and the other was slump-shouldered and despondent.

Eventually, golf would defeat all but one. And even his name would be quickly forgotten, just letters on a board in the clubhouse that would list winners of the Carnegie Shield.

He climbed the steep hill at the sixteenth, reached the green and headed right toward the clubhouse. The seventeenth hole would have taken him away from the clubhouse, and as much as he had loved this last two hours, he was ready for a nap.

As he got off the course, ProV opened his phone and noticed Lucas has sent a text: "Would you want to go play a few holes on the Struie?"

ProV was suddenly ready to play. He texted, "Yes."

Lucas responded, "Be there in ten minutes. We can play nine or more." Lucas was coming back to life after a wonderful snooze and was ready to go. He drove the one mile to the club, and sure enough, ProV was waiting on him, five iron in hand. ProV and Lucas had played the Struie two days before the Carnegie Shield. It was not like the world caliber championship course, but it was a wonderful links golf course with many of the same views and vistas.

"Let's go play with four clubs," suggested Lucas, who pulled his driver, pitching wedge, five iron and putter and placed them into his small carry bag. "You can just play with my clubs except for your walking stick there." ProV joined his own five iron with a three wood, eight iron, and lob wedge which doubled as a putter. The next two hours of golf with no scorecard and four clubs was the most fun ProV had had on a golf course since he beat Bruce Simpson and Charlie Barnhart out of a dollar in the sixth grade. The wind was howling and the course was empty so they could just skip around and make up holes, all led by Lucas who had done this before.

As they returned to the car park, Lucas announced: "Next assignment: I'm an old man and my back is killing me. I'm getting room service and going to bed. I have heard and seen the Pipe Band a million times, so I don't need any concert tonight. You might love it though."

ProV nodded agreement.

"But be sure to read the Susan Brown descriptions of the eighteen holes at Dornoch. Remember your walk with no bogeys and your five iron walking stick. Remember how good it felt to play the Struie without a card. Have dinner with the voice that spoke to you at the cathedral. And read Proverbs 30:1-5. You can find it on your phone. See ya at 6:00 a.m. Be checked out and ready to go."

They arrived back at the hotel and Lucas disappeared. ProV thought to himself, *He's actually looking old for the first time.*

ProV followed his friend's advice. He was not in the mood for bagpipes, as great as that sounded. He ordered room service as well, haddock and chips.

Thanks to his friend Lucas, Psalm 96 was now on his radar screen. He wanted to read it, but he had no Bible app on his phone and the Wi-Fi was down. However, lying beside the bed was a Gideon's Bible. He opened the Bible, and the pages fell open to Proverbs 30. ProV's eyes went straight to the first verse.

I am weary, O God;
I am weary and worn out, O God.
I am too stupid to be human,
and I lack common sense.
I have not mastered human wisdom,
nor do I know the Holy One.[8]

Psalm 96 would have to wait as ProV thought to himself, *Whoever wrote those words knows me quite well. I am tired, I feel stupid, I have no wisdom*. He was hopeful his friend Lucas had answers.

After the best fish and chips of his life, he laid in bed and read the counsel of the female reverend. The bagpipes started playing out on the streets in front of the hotel. He knew he was in Scotland for sure now.

"1st hole—In the beginning... draw breath and enjoy the clean score sheet and all the possibilities that lie ahead. Choose now to take one step at a time and enjoy what the step holds."

"Just what I need," ProV said out loud into thin air, "a clean scorecard." He turned the page.

"2nd hole—Small is beautiful—and testing. One word can build up or knock down. How can the little words we speak be more encouraging?"

He remembered the voice in the cathedral. Female. Small. But somehow encouraging.

[8] Proverbs 30:1-3

"3rd hole—The course opens up before you. Sea, hills, sweeping fairways. Pause to admire the natural beauty around you and appreciate what the Creator and humans can do together."

ProV remembered leaving the second green and walking to the third tee. He had seen virtually all of Royal Dornoch in front of him. The panorama took his breath away. So many different hues of green and blue. For lovers of golf, this was pure art.

But that was today with no clubs or ball. Yesterday he had made the same walk, fuming from a double bogey five on the tiny second hole. He had seen nothing but a 5-5 start on the scorecard. Indeed, it was even worse because he was keeping the card for young David Roberts from Brora, who had managed the 3-3 start he had envisioned for himself. ProV's obsession with a scorecard had caused him to miss one of golf's greatest landscapes. He read on.

"4th hole—The fairway slopes seaward and takes your ball with it. What are the things that pull you from the paths you should be taking?"

Oh, boy, that question could take all night, thought the tired ex-husband, lousy father and lonely man.

ProV fell asleep before he could think about it. The fifth hole and beyond would have to wait. He didn't want to sleep. He wanted this day to last forever. The emotions of the day, the voice at the cathedral and the smaller voices around Dornoch's links, had made him tired, even though this may have been the greatest day of his life.

He had played golf without a scorecard in hand. Maybe that was the key, he thought to himself. He blamed golf again for all the bad days he had suffered in his life.

But now it was over, and time to sleep without angst for the first time in many a year.

CHAPTER 5
A Clean Scorecard

ProV was ready to go at 6:00 a.m. sharp. He had sweet-talked a reluctant young waitress into finding him a "take away" Americano black coffee. ProV had lots of questions for Lucas as they headed up the A-9 highway toward Thurso. They would soon pass Golspie Golf Club to their right. The temptation to stop and play the James Braid layout was strong after Lucas had raved about the place.

"It is links mostly, but then the middle six holes make you think you're at Pinehurst," reported Lucas, pointing to a patch of pine trees down by the sea. "Too bad there is no time for good courses today. We are trying to find the greatest."

ProV said simply, "I understand."

Two miles up the road, overlooking the North Sea, was arguably the greatest castle in Scotland, called Dunrobin Castle. It was a source of tourist income for locals but also a reminder of the Clearances, a historical travesty which still haunted the memories of many locals.

The land-owning Sutherlands, who owned Dunrobin, had evicted the local tenants, which led to starvation and worse. The Duchess still came there at times to check out her property. It all happened before 1850, but the pain was not forgotten.

But no time for castles and history today.

Just four miles further north was Lucas's personal favorite, Brora. He had been a member there for twenty years. He spent eight weeks every summer in an older apartment overlooking the eighteenth green. At least eighteen cows and more than 100 sheep grazed on the course and "managed" the rough. They were hated by locals and the greens crew, but loved by American tourists.

Lucas's favorite local rule of all time was on the back of the Brora card: *"Fresh excreta from animals shall be played as temporary water."* He always smiled thinking about a stuffy old rules official being asked to decide what is "fresh."

Brora was another James Braid layout and had been on Tom Watson's favorites list. Five-time Open champion Peter Thomson had come there often and was an honored member with his own room of memorabilia.

And then they had the North Sea views for thirty miles on the A-9 all the way to Wick, another classic links course, but simply too far out of the way for most rational golfers. Somewhere between Brora and Thurso, ProV was ready for some answers.

"Ok, pal, where are we going?"

"I told you, I wish I knew for sure. We go to the Isle of Mashal. We find Hokmah Golf Club. The only other time I was there I was accompanied by my second cousin Andrew. He died last year, but honestly, one reason I am nervous about all this is that I genuinely cannot be sure we will even find this place."

ProV was doubtful. "I found a map of the Orkney Islands. It lists all seventy islands. Twenty islands have humans. The rest are just birds and sheep, apparently. And Mashal was not on the list."

Lucas already knew that. He had been looking at maps for twelve years.

"Faith, brother. We just keep going. You gotta believe," he said with a smile. "Maybe I have misspelled it. Or more likely, just forgotten the correct name."

"And this cousin who led you there is now dead?"

"Yup, my cousin Andrew Evangel led me there. Dornoch, up to Thurso, on the Scrabster ferry, and once we arrived in Stromness, it was all a blur. I do know it was not easy. It involved at least one more ferry. But Andrew seemed to know what he was doing. He saw things I was missing. I was just following him."

ProV dozed off for the final thirty minutes until he heard, "Wake up, big boy. We're at Scrabster Ferry Terminal. You missed the exciting four-minute drive through Thurso. We will be loading up in ten minutes, enough time to grab a coffee."

That sounded like heaven to the caffeine addicted ProV. "And how long is the ride?"

"Less than two hours. We should roll in to Stromness around 10:30. That's if we make it. You may not remember one of these ferries went down in a storm in 2032. Killed everyone on board. I forget how many."

ProV was suddenly wide awake.

Lucas handed ProV a brochure about life in Stromness, a seaport with houses and shops all built from local stone, and really old. During the seventeenth century the town was an important part of the war between France and England. Now it was just the first point of entry for tourists in the summer, and a few hundred men who still tried to make a living as fishermen. Stromness was a small village, but still the second largest town in the Orkney Islands, where only 20,000 people lived.

As the large ferry carrying tourist buses and cars got moving, ProV found a comfortable seat, ordered a black coffee and pulled out his course guide from Royal Dornoch to read again some of the comments of the Reverend Brown. The ride north would be smooth today with an unusually calm sea.

Putting a spiritual touch into the course guide was a first for ProV. God had never been a serious thought for his first forty-three years. His grandmother's hopes never took root. When she couldn't afford the Catholic school any longer, he became a product of California public schools. His god was himself and his golf ball. Since his parents had shown little interest in loving him, he presumed God was the same. Beyond an agreement that there must be a God or gods somewhere, he was neutral. But now he found the comments of the reverend soothing.

As the ferry left shore, ProV picked up where he had fallen asleep the night before. He barely remembered the third and fourth holes because they were both par fours going the same direction, but also because he had made routine pars with no trainwrecks to help him remember all the bunkers and problems. It had been down the middle and onto the green, boring and beautiful golf.

He continued his reading.

> *"5th hole—Looking down from on high, think about a highlight in your life. As you walk to your tee shot, tell your partner what for you, is one of the moments you have felt most 'blessed.'"*

ProV took the suggestion literally and found Lucas, sitting in the breakfast area of the ferry, sipping his coffee and checking texts and emails. "Lucas, I am on the fifth hole," pointing to the booklet, "and this Reverend Brown says I should tell my partner one of my most blessed moments. Well," he stammered, "that blessing was yesterday. And this trip. And you."

He pretended to get something out of his right eye, hiding another tiny tear or two. Lucas did what he had never done before with ProV. But now was the perfect time for no words, just a hug.

ProV got another coffee and went back to his seat, wiping more tears. He opened the course guide again. The sixth hole was 150 yards or so of sheer terror with bunkers left and a vicious hill right. The tiny green was ten steps from left to right and required a perfect shot. Lucas had told him on the plane coming to Scotland it might be the best par three in the world. He had agreed when he made a two during their only practice round. A perfect eight iron to a foot.

"Sixth hole—Be warned! A bunker with a magnetic draw awaits you. Choose your club carefully and think of the choices you have made in life. You have to live with the consequences!"

Now this preacher lady was getting personal. ProV moved on quickly, not ready to think about all the bad choices he had made that put him into life's pot bunkers. He remembered with a smile the guy yesterday hitting backward from the same bunker.

He turned the page and pushed his anguish deeper into his psyche where not even Dr. Freud could find it.

"7th hole—A wide and straight fairway greets you. Yet this hole is stroke index 2.... Sometimes it's when life appears straightforward that we find ourselves surprised by troubles. Who is it you return to at such times? Now turn around and look behind you, and be stunned by the view."

He remembered the view from the seventh tee, and remembered thinking, *There has to be a God.* He had only seen that view yesterday when he walked the course without a golf ball. During the tournament he had seen nothing but bogeys, and his only reference to the Almighty had been under his breath when a good drive ended up in a sandy divot. Tournament golf had taught him to "focus"—not the best advice for seeing the supernatural.

He couldn't wait to see what the next page had for him, since he loved the eighth hole. He had birdied it both days in the tournament.

"8th hole—Focus on Dunrobin Castle in the distance—but don't forget the drop! A reminder for people of faith that they have not to be so heavenly minded that they are of no earthly use! Keep your eyes open to who and what's around you."

Good advice, he thought. He loved the hole because either a big drive or the second shot is down a slope so steep that snowboarders would love it. And the green was in a bowl, so mediocre shots could get a bounce to it. In short, it was fun. But Lucas might disagree, having managed an eight on this same eighth hole, proving every shot at Dornoch can be a challenge if the winds and the bounces go wrong.

The ferry seemed to be getting close to shore so he decided that finishing the front nine was enough for today.

"9th hole—Stand for a moment and listen. What can you hear? Soak up the sound and let it re-energize you as you approach halfway."

ProV remembered his magnificent walk on the beach at the ninth hole yesterday. He remembered the old pastor who promised to pray for him every day. He remembered how much he loved the dogs and the sounds and the smells of the sea. This was as heavenly as a memory can be. He swore to himself that when he got home, he would get a dog. A female dog. One that would follow him on the golf course. She would ride with him on a golf cart, retrieve his ball. Maybe even retrieve the TV remote control when he couldn't find it. He would name her after his first girlfriend in sixth grade, Ginger. She would be his only female friend. He was done with women.

ProV closed his eyes. He tried his best to imagine again the beauty of the course left behind at Dornoch. His soul was bathed in temporary peace while he dozed off.

Lucas jostled him awake a few minutes later. "Hey, man, you need to peek out the window on the right. The Old Man of Hoy needs to be seen."

"What's that?"

"It's an odd formation that comes out of the sea, created by thousands of years of erosion."

The outside deck was full of touristy types as ProV arrived and took pictures like all the others. When the ferry landed safely in Stromness, he breathed a small sigh of relief. There would be no headlines tomorrow about a ferry sinking in a raging sea off the Orkney Islands.

As for Lucas, the pressure was building. Where to begin? What now? How to find Hokmah Golf Club? His plan was to go to the

Stromness Golf Club and just ask. Surely the golf pro would know.

Every small seaside town in Scotland has a links course. If you're lost, go to the sea. Usually there are plenty of simple signs.

The street that led through Stromness was a claustrophobic, single lane with traffic going both ways. Cars were parked where no one should ever park. Shops left and right, dogs on leashes galore, baby buggies being pushed by mothers. Creeping along, Lucas had to pull over and even back up once to make room for a small mail truck. Everyone knew the deal and seemed so patient. The town was built long before cars, when narrow streets shared by animals and people were normal. Cobblestone all the way. Obviously, there must be a better way to the golf course, ProV gently reminded him. The scene could have been romantic, but Lucas was on a mission.

Sure enough, within ten minutes they were there. Green grass and a sign welcomed all to Stromness Golf Club. Two middle-aged ladies were sitting outside eating a sandwich, trolley and clubs by their side, appearing to be ready to tackle the golf course. "Good morning, ladies. Where's the pro shop?" Lucas asked. They looked like they should know, dressed in short sleeves for summertime despite the fifty-two degrees.

"Aye, good morning. There's a wee shop around the corner but you don't need to check in. Just put your money in the box and off ya go." ProV and Lucas glanced at each other, unsure what to say. "Oh, we can't play today, just looking for some information."

"Sure, well, go inside the door around the back. I think I saw Alexander go in there just now. He keeps things going around here," offered the lady who looked like she could win an Orkney arm wrestling contest.

There were only two cars in the parking lot on this sunny summer Saturday. The flags were limp and the links looked inviting in the rare Orkney sunshine, but no time today for a quick eighteen.

Inside, they found an older man behind the counter, sitting on a stool and shuffling papers. He looked exactly how an old pro should look in Scotland. More hair than needed in the ears, and a mustache that needed attention. No more than five foot six, with a gray sweater and grayer hair and a shape that said he had eaten too many pork pies. He barely looked up, not too thrilled about two Americans showing up to test his links and ask annoying questions. The shop was so small it was now crowded. No clothes or clubs for sale. Just a counter for Alexander and enough room for a few logo ball markers, scorecards and pencils.

"Can I help you?" he finally grunted as ProV looked at the ball markers, thinking about how his friends back home would ask about the strange logo and name.

"Good morning, Alexander," Lucas said. The nametag said "Alexander Skeptic, PGA."

"I am Lucas Friend. Paul and I have been down to Brora and Dornoch for a few days. I sure wish we had time to play here but we are on a limited schedule and looking for another golf course and, frankly, we are lost. Hoping you could help us find the place."

"Aye, what ya looking for?" Alexander smiled as he saw ProV reaching for his wallet to buy some ball marks.

"Hokmah Golf Club. I know it's in the Orkney Islands. I was there twelve years ago and I just cannot remember where it is."

Skeptic's face turned red, changing like a chameleon, the grumpiness back suddenly.

"You know, this happens quite often here. Maybe once a month some lad comes rolling through here asking about this place called Hokmah. I grew up on this island. I was a golf professional for over forty years, mostly down in England at Woburn. I am now back home for the last couple of years, helping the boys keep this place going after I retired." He paused to light a cigarette. Whatever laws applied to smoking were ignored by the only man available to enforce such a rule.

"I promise you, the Hokmah Golf Club does not exist. Someone is scamming you Americans. I hope you didn't pay green fees in advance because if you did, you've been suckered."

Or at least that is what Lucas thought he said. The Orcadian accent was thick and quick.

Skeptic continued. "I suggest you catch the next ferry back to Thurso. If you're looking for the greatest golf course, go back to Dornoch."

"But the course is supposed to be on Mashal Island. Maybe I am mispronouncing the name."

"Aye, I have heard that too, and believe me, there is no Mashal Island. You are not mispronouncing anything. These places don't exist."

"I was there twelve years ago."

"Dear sir, you had too much whisky in Dornoch. Sorry I canna' help ya."

ProV pulled his wallet and handed over ten pounds for some logo ball markers, with a "Keep the change, pal," to end on a good note. Skeptic nodded and off the two pilgrims went. Into the Orkney Islands with no clue where Hokmah might be.

CHAPTER 6
Go to Pappy

As he walked back to the car, Lucas heard a female voice in his head: *Go to Pappy. Go to the Narrow Way.* It sounded much like the voice he had heard in the cathedral twelve years earlier. He said nothing to ProV.

He was not sure about this voice. Was this some version of wishful thinking or the voice of reality? Was he just talking to himself? *Everybody does that*, he thought to himself.

Still, though, doubts can be overwhelming at certain moments. Even John the Baptist had once doubted his cousin Jesus was the Messiah.[9] He knew better, but he doubted anyway.

Go to Pappy. Go to the Narrow Way. And then Lucas remembered the club was definitely on a road called Narrow Way. It was all his feeble mind could recall. So off they went, traveling north on A-965, the radio blaring some BBC news, happy to be on this great adventure. They passed the Rings of Brodgar; they passed signs for the famous prehistoric village Scara Brae; they ended up at Birsay Bay, turned east toward the Bay of Firth and then, wondering if they were lost, saw a sign that said "Stromness: 4 Miles." They had circled back to Stromness, more lost than ever.

Lucas had to admit he was clueless. It was time to ask for directions. His wife would have been scolding him by now, but ProV knew to just

[9] Luke 7:18-23

be quiet. There was no Narrow Way in sight. And no "pappy" either. Maps were no help. Even the sweet British lady on the GPS was hopelessly stumped and confused.

Lucas wondered out loud if the answer would be found in Kirkwall, the largest "city" in the islands. Just twenty minutes eastward, the two pilgrims headed for the town whose name meant "church bay," or so ProV had read in a brochure. The center of the town, population around 9,000, was dominated by the magnificent St. Magnus Cathedral, which took three hundred years to build, starting in the twelfth century. This now sleepy village had been a thriving metropolis more than 800 years ago.

They parked on the street and wandered around Kirkwall for the next hour, asking shop owners and café waitresses if they knew of the Hokmah Golf Club or the Narrow Way.

Everyone politely said no. Several old timers mentioned there had been a golf course in Kirkwall many decades ago, but it had closed due to a general lack of interest. Apparently, the course was not good enough to attract tourists, and the weather was simply horrendous. Life was hard enough for the locals without bogeys and worse to ruin a fine day.

Lucas was not frustrated yet. He knew most Scots loved to help lost tourists, especially Americans. But as he told ProV, "They are usually really bad at giving directions. They know where to go but they've been there so many times they have never had to think about what to do to get there. So the words get all mixed up with things like, 'Go up this road a ways, and when you see the hill on the left, you'll be getting close, and then you may see a church to your right, and when you see that you turn up down around a corner'—and on and on until your head spins."

ProV smiled, since he had already figured that one out. Even though they had received no help yet, he could tell the local Orcadians were as upset about not knowing as the visitors themselves.

A young lady, no more than 20, finally offered sound advice. "Can't say I've heard of such a place. Check down at the tourist center. If anyone will know, it would be my aunt Sally—Sally Helpful. She's the expert around here on the Orkney Islands. She could even organize a tour if you like."

The boys found a local fish and chip place that had people standing in line at the Saturday lunch hour. It was perfect. Just the right amount of grease. And obviously fresh fish, eaten on a newspaper at an outdoor table. Just fifty-eight degrees was cool for the Americans in their turtlenecks and sweaters, but the locals basked in the sunny short-sleeved weather.

After lunch they located the Visitor Centre. Sally knew nothing. She speculated that Narrow Way could be on the northernmost island, called North Ronaldsay, just 2.7 square miles, known for its historic lighthouse, migratory birds, and unique breed of sheep that eat seaweed. "The island has a population of thirty," she said.

Lucas asked her, "Is there a place called Pappy?"

"Of course, Papa Westray, but all the locals just say Pappy," said Sally. She found a brochure. "There also is a Papa Stronsay, but only a handful of monks live there." So far, Sally was not as helpful as her name.

"If you really want to go to Papa Westray, find your way to Westray by ferry, and then, just to say you did it, take the world's shortest commercial air flight. Loganair has two flights a day on a six-seater from Westray to Papa Westray. Flying time is ninety seconds. The cost is twenty-nine pounds." ProV didn't say it, but a flight on a tiny plane was making him nervous now.

Sally shook her head: "But, there's definitely no golf course in Papa Westray, although this brochure says Westray has a nine-hole course. To be honest I have never been to Westray or Pappy. Not much reason to go that far north."

Lucas remembered he read in a brochure that the third hole at Westray was the longest hole in Europe. "It's a seven-hundred-and-eighty-yard par six," he told ProV. "I'm sure it must play over a thousand yards into the winds of Westray."

Like a typical Orcadian, so serious about helping visitors, Sally continued to look in booklets and speculate about Hokmah. "You know, I really should figure this out. I've had at least a dozen people here in the last few years looking for this place. Loch Ness is less a mystery than this Hokmah."

She gave them brochures of other sites in the Orkneys, handing them to Lucas as consolation for missing Hokmah. He felt like he had brochures for the entire archipelago of seventy islands. She especially emphasized Burray, population 350, for amazing views over Scapa Flow to spot seals, otters or birds.

And there were ruins of another cathedral that should not be missed. But ProV did not come to Scotland to see cathedrals. Dornoch Cathedral was it for him.

And despite the summer sun which almost never sets, it was getting late. Lucas nodded to ProV, it was time to move on. The voice in his head was louder than ever: *Go to Pappy. Go to the Narrow Way.*

He said, "Sally, you have been just like your name, so helpful. I have always wanted to go make that ninety-second flight to Papa Westray, so with or without Hokmah, we will go to Westray and check off the world's shortest flight from our bucket list. I think if we catch the ferry we can check into the B&B you mentioned and be ready for the flight tomorrow morning." And off they went.

A quick Google of Papa Westray showed it to have a population of only twenty-five hearty souls, down from a peak of ninety in 2011.

The pilgrims arrived at the Kirkwall ferry terminal at 4:45 p.m. There were no signs of life, no cars in the lot or in line to board a ferry. Lucas located what he thought was the right queue for cars, then got out to find someone who knew what they were doing. Inside the terminal there were no signs of life, just a sign that declared tickets could be purchased online or onboard the ferry.

All questions were answered when the ferry pulled in right on time. Two older men dressed in brown monk-like garb exited on foot before a handful of vehicles followed.

Lucas stopped the monks and, just to be sure, asked, "Is this the ferry to Westray?"

"Yes indeed. You are in the right place," said the aged monk with an

English accent, offering a smile. "Welcome to Orkney. What brings you to the islands?"

"Oh, we're just tourists, trying to find a golf course on a remote island here. It is called Mashal Island. I don't suppose you know about it? Or a course called Hokmah."

Both holy men looked quizzically at each other and shook their heads. "Never heard of it."

Introductions discovered they were speaking to Father Stephen John, from Birmingham, England, and a much younger Brother Victor Joseph, from Denver—an American.

Lucas asked, "What is the name of your order?" remembering monks come in as many flavors as Baskin-Robbins ice cream.

Father Stephen answered, "Sons of the Most Holy Redeemer."

Lucas blurted, "Me too. I am a Son of the Most Holy Redeemer."

The monk seemed puzzled. "Are you Catholic?"

"No, but I do have a rosary which Mother Teresa blessed when she came to California over fifty years ago."

ProV was happy to avoid the question about being Catholic. Technically, he was, but that was his little secret.

The monk seemed impressed, so Lucas shared his story of Mother Teresa's gospel. "When a priest in California thanked Mother Teresa for doing so much good, she said quietly, 'I'm not good.' Then she turned her eyes to heaven and softly said, 'Jesus.' Or at least that is the way my sweet Protestant mother told the story. She was standing just a few feet away. It became my mother's short version of the Gospel, straight from one of your saints."

Both padres smiled polite approval, still not sure it was so simple.

Father Stephen finished with an invitation. "We just came into Kirkwall to visit one of our sick brothers in the hospital. Our order owns a very tiny island known as Papa Stronsay. We live there at the Golgotha Monastery. Maybe you can visit us someday. We will be back there in a day or two, so any time would be fine."

Lucas thanked them for the invitation. "Maybe the next time, father. Thanks for your help."

"We will pray you find your golf course," said Father Stephen, surely the first time in his life to offer such a prayer.

Lucas and ProV were pretty sure they were on the right road to Papa Westray, but Lucas now wondered to himself, *Maybe we have the wrong Papa. Are we supposed to go to Papa Stronsay*?

Twenty minutes later, the Kirkwall ferry to Westray left on time. The only other vehicle was a huge cattle truck, headed back empty to the island after taking some unsuspecting cows on their final boat ride.

ProV used his phone to look up the order and found out their day started with prayer at 3:15 a.m. and included Latin Mass and a lot of manual labor all day long.

The website, updated in 2050, said that seven monks now lived on the 180 acres of Papa Stronsay. And it showed their mission statement which had not changed since 1998 when they started:

> *Fundamentally, our message is this: Remember O Christian soul that time passes quickly and you too must soon die, be judged and enter into your eternity of heaven or hell. You have only one soul to save; that is your chief, nay your only work. For what does it profit you if, by your work, you gain the whole world which must soon end, and lose your immortal soul in an eternity of sufferings that will never end. What exchange can you give for your soul? There is none. At all cost then, save your soul.*[10]

ProV pondered its magnitude and showed it to Lucas, who thought out loud that it must answer questions that underly all human beings. It explained religion of all kinds, both true and false. Surely everyone wonders about the universe and God and eternity.

Lucas said, "I am not sure how living in a monastery in Orkney accomplishes that goal, but I must say they sure got me thinking."

ProV just nodded. The words echoed in his mind. *At all cost then, save your soul.* But how?

Lucas booked the Loganair flight and the Doubter's Bed and Breakfast

[10] https://www.papastronsay.com

while on the first hour of the ferry ride. They got the only two seats available for a flight the next day. The bed and breakfast brochure touted a satisfied customer: "Watched seals out of the window over a fantastic breakfast." Lucas was more interested in a shower with real water pressure than watching seals over breakfast. But for one night it would be just fine.

They arrived safely on Westray after a ninety-minute, rainbow-splashed journey through the islands. The drive from the ferry dock to the B&B in Pierowall was fifteen minutes. Mrs. Doubter greeted the tired Americans as they rang a bell to announce their arrival. She led them to rooms 1 and 2, the only guests for the night.

"And what time would ya' like breakfast? If you're catching the flight to Pappy it won't matter. They don't leave until noon. Sleep as long as ya' like tomorrow. I'm here all day no matter what, except for church at half ten."

Lucas told her the flight was at nine. "No sir, Mr. Friend. Tomorrow is Sunday and they only run once on the Lord's Day. Noon. That's it."

Exhausted, both Lucas and ProV were happy they could sleep in.

"So, we could do breakfast anytime?" offered Lucas. "Those tomato and mayonnaise sandwiches on the ferry were not much. We missed a real dinner somehow in all the travel to get here. We will need your full breakfast."

"Of course, whatever you want and whenever you want. Just ring the bell when you're ready."

"Thank you. You are so kind. Now, one last question. It's a longshot but do you know any road here called the Narrow Way?"

Mrs. Doubter frowned in thought, then said, "Well, this island is so small we don't need road signs. I haven't been down all of them, but there are certainly a couple that could be described as narrow."

Lucas felt hope rise in his heart. "Could you perhaps give us directions to them in the morning?"

"Sure. Now, find your rooms and get some sleep. The room to your left is bigger but the room on the right has a better view."

And with that, Lucas headed with his bag to the largest room down the hallway. He threw his clothes over a chair and crawled into bed with one of the booklets on the Orkney Islands. He was asleep before he could even turn a page.

Meanwhile, ProV took his suitcase to the smaller room which supposedly had the best view. But he cared little about any scenic views of oceans or seals or sheep.

He was quickly in the bed, but wide awake. The room was colder than he wanted but he found a heavy down blanket, pulled it over him and located his Royal Dornoch Course Guide again. Surely reading would put him to sleep.

He turned to the tenth hole, his triple bogey nightmare.

> *"10th hole—'Fuaran' is Gaelic for a well or a spring. Did you notice it? You passed a little river that otters tumble down in the early morning. Now you are at the halfway house—take (or buy) a drink and think of the simple joy of being refreshed."*

He remembered and could even taste the hot chocolate. He also remembered his one-putt six. He moved on quickly.

> *"11th hole—A long hole with a chance of a seat at the end! How important is rest and relaxation? Be at peace—no matter the score!"*

Okay, thought ProV, that would be a new experience. The only time he had ever had peace about a score had been something under par. But now he was indeed peaceful on this Saturday night in the middle of God knows where. He was half-asleep when he reached over and flipped the lamp switch down. The darkness was never even noticed.

CHAPTER 7
Time to Go

Sunday morning was raining "cats and dogs," an old Scottish term that was now universal for a downpour.

Indeed, the heavy rain plus anticipation for what today might bring had woken ProV early. He heard Lucas next door stirring as well. The ancient ticking alarm clock said 6:00 a.m.

He stayed in bed, pulled out the course guide and remembered he had made it into the back nine.

> *"12th hole—A path crossed the fairway. Reminisce and share with your partner how the path of your life crossed with a significant other in your life. Think of how wonderful is the gift of love."*

He thought about the only loves he could ever remember: Mary Ann and Mary Lou, his two ex-wives. He apparently had a weakness for women named Mary. He decided maybe he should do as instructed and converse at breakfast with Lucas about his "gift of love." Mary Ann was for sure the only true love of his life. The other Mary had come along at just the wrong time, at the wrong place, wearing the wrong skirt. He was distracted for a moment thinking about the first time he had seen her in a bar at a golf course. He quickly moved on.

"13th hole—Run up to the top of the dune behind the tee and look out over the sea and beach. Psalm 46 talks of roaring seas and shaking mountains, but whether the sea is wild or calm, think of the beauty and fragility of the natural world. How can we enjoy and care for it?"

ProV remembered he had indeed gone to the back of the thirteenth tee and seen the majesty of the ocean view. He made a mental note to ask Lucas about Psalm 46 later. He also remembered he hit a seven iron to eight inches on the second day of the Shield. The sweet feeling of a perfect iron shot, drawing with a right to left wind to a back left pin, was still in his hands. But he needed to move on.

"14th hole—Rough, no bunkers but a double dogleg. For many this is Royal Dornoch's signature hole. Let the challenge excite you—and rise to it. Life is too short not to have times when you push yourself to your limits."

Good advice, thought ProV. Just as the fourteenth hole had pushed him around, resulting in two bogeys, so it was time for him to push himself to know more about the Voice, which he now capitalized in his imagination, and this place called Scotland. He had birdied the hole in his one practice round, and Lucas had warned him not to think it was easy. He agreed in his mind it was one of the great par fours in the world.

"15th hole—The easiest hole on the course—if you play it well! Select your club and know as you do that this hole, like life, is what you make of it."

Indeed, he had made a mess of the fifteenth on day two, nearly driving the green, then putting up a steep hill but not hard enough as the ball returned to his feet for an ugly bogey. Using the putter four times is never a good memory. But on day one he had hit a nice little wedge to a foot for one of his few bright spots, stopping his string of bogeys that followed his triple.

And he thought of his life, all the ups and downs. No one's fault really. Just his own choices.

"16th hole—Onwards and upwards! From sea level at the tee, take yourself over to the bench at the left of the green and enjoy the panorama. It puts your golf into perspective and brings to mind Psalm 8, which talks of all God has made and asks the question: what is mankind that you are mindful of them?" [11]

ProV thought, *I need to ask Lucas about Psalm 8*. He also remembered that honestly this might be the only hole at Dornoch that was not much fun. Uphill holes with a blind shot to the green can be tedious. But even still, the views at the top of the hill are worth the pain of getting there.

"17th hole—From the heights to the depths! But you emerge onto a green that's big and welcoming. As you head for the final hole, you meet those only just beginning their round. Wish them well as you continue on to the eighteenth tee."

This touched him in a spot he didn't expect. Every golfer who comes off the seventeenth green at Dornoch passes players waiting or driving off the third tee.

Typically, kind words are exchanged. Something like, "Be careful, the greens are really fast today," or, "Where ya' from?" if the golfers are obviously American tourists with caddies.

ProV was thinking deeper already. He knew he was just getting started in life, even at age 43. Lucas had mentioned this back at the hotel, that symbolically the younger ProV was on the third tee of life, and the older and wiser Lucas was walking off the seventeenth green, encouraging him all the way. He sensed the love of Lucas in a way he had seldom known.

What a great thought. A friend who has most of life behind him, trying to help someone with most of life in front of him.

[11] Psalm 8:3-4 "When I look at the night sky and see the work of your fingers ... what are mere mortals that you should think about them, human beings that you should care for them?"

"18th hole—As you prepare to tee off, think of the number of people in the last 400 years who have stood where you are. Regardless of your round, be grateful for the energy to play and for the company and the scenery. Take a deep breath. Swing slow and true and give thanks for the exercise of body, mind and spirit."

Even though he was still in his snuggly bed, ProV stopped in his mind near the eighteenth tee, remembering that on his walk with a five iron he had paused for a twosome who were still battling their match down to the last hole. The tension of match play was thick on the tee. He began to meditate on the Reverend Brown's words. Golf had literally saved him so many times.

He thought about the fact Ol' Tom Morris had stood on that eighteenth tee.

Harry Vardon had been there often. James Braid. Ted Ray.

Not to mention more modern heroes, such as Watson, Norman, Nicklaus and, of course, his own beloved namesake, Gary Player. And he remembered that while he was playing those two days at Dornoch, he had felt none of this spiritual emotion. He was wrapped up in his own pity party over shooting eighty. He cursed himself quietly.

ProV finally crawled out from under the warm comforter, an aptly named feathery, a necessity in the northern regions of Scotland, even in the summer. And sure enough, the shower was a disappointing drip-drip. When he finally dressed and made it to breakfast, it was 7:00 a.m. Lucas was halfway done with the full Scottish breakfast.

"So, Lucas, I finished the course guide. That lady preacher got me thinking."

"Yeah, it is pretty good. I've always wondered why more courses don't do something similar."

ProV heard Mrs. Doubter coming behind him. He almost complained about the cold room and the shower that barely got him wet, but quickly remembered the last words he had read, to *"be grateful for the energy to play and for the company and the scenery."* He said "Good morning" with a huge grin. A yellow cat wandered in.

"Tea or coffee?"

"Black coffee please, and lots of it!"

"And what else this fine Orkney day?"

"Whatever he's having. Lucas always leads me right."

"Very well. A full Scottish breakfast. And you want your eggs the same? Poached lightly?"

"Perfect! But make it three eggs please. I don't remember a real dinner last night. But before you leave, what do you mean by 'fine Orkney day?' It's pouring out there."

Mrs. Doubter dove into a speech she had delivered many times about the weather in Scotland and especially the Orkney Islands. Even though no one in Orkney speaks Gaelic, she was originally from the western islands of Scotland where Gaelic was common. She had moved to Westray with her husband many years ago and brought some of the odd language with her. She agreed raining "cats and dogs" was very Scottish, but not to be confused with "chucking it down," which is heavier. Or "yillen," which is merely a shower of rain with wind. Or "uplowsin," which is a heaving rain. Or "goselet," which is a drenching downpour. Or "drookit," where the person is totally and utterly soaked to the bone. Or a "sump" of rain that comes with gusto and great strength.

She was just getting started and ProV began to wish he had never asked. The cat yawned as if he'd heard it all before.

"But the worst for me," she said, "is 'plowetery,' which is just a shambles really, rainy, showery, grimy, damp. You don't feel like you'll ever get dry again." She took a breath.

"Oh, and don't forget the 'pish-oot,' which is an intense downpour when it's just 'pishing it doon.' But no problem, the rain is just God's way o' cleanin' the coos, which is how we say that every cloud has a silver lining."

ProV reached over and touched her arm, "Three eggs, lightly poached."

She finished by saying today could be just a "smirr," a fine rain drizzle, by the time the sun got high in the sky. She also warned that the "haar" could be coming, a notable mist which glides in from the east mysteriously.

"So, what's your main take away from the guide?" Lucas asked after Mrs. Doubter went back to cook breakfast.

"Too many to count. But let me ask about the only one I am thinking about today." ProV pulled out the guide and read the parson's advice from the twelfth hole: *"Reminisce and share with your partner, how the path of your life crossed with a significant other in your life. Think of how wonderful is the gift of love."*

"So, partner," he paused and looked straight at Lucas, "my only two 'significant others' have left me." He put air quotes over the term, which he hated.

"I messed up. They fell out of love. And the gift, whatever it may have been, was gone. You know most of the story. Two Marys. Both gone. And when I did as the reverend told me to do, and thought about the wonderful gift of love, all I got back in return was one lonely thought." He paused.

"I have no idea what love is."

Lucas poured himself another cup of tea with milk and took his time to answer. "So let me guess. Mary Ann was your real love. You have two children with her. Mary Lou was a passing fancy, not love at all. Am I close?"

"You nailed it. In fact, Mary Lou has already moved on. I was number three for her. She got married again in Vegas last month to sucker number four. If I could move the clock back a few years, Mary Ann would be my wife again."

"So, love," said Lucas. "Honestly, it may be the number one mystery of the universe. Love." His eyebrows raised to emphasize no one had a perfect answer. "But part of the answer is found in language itself. English is very inadequate at this point. We love golf. We love ice cream. We love our kids. We love a woman. Mrs. Doubter even loves this cat. So it shouldn't be a shock that we don't understand love."

ProV was not satisfied.

Lucas continued, "Let's do this. If we can find this golf course today, we will find love with a capital L. That much I can promise you. So let's take it one step at a time. For today, let's forget love and find Hokmah."

They finished breakfast but the rain continued. The plane did not leave until noon, presuming the rain stopped long enough to take off and land ninety seconds later. So Lucas suggested they stay awhile, read, rest some more and wait for the rain to stop.

This sounded perfect to ProV, who truthfully needed another hour of sleep. Before retiring back to their rooms, however, Mrs. Doubter offered more confusing directions about the "Narrow Way" and said her goodbyes, telling them she would be going to church. It was Sunday morning. She never missed services at the Westray Baptist Kirk, where twenty people would listen to a sermon from an 82-year-old pastor who never ran out of great stories about his many years as a missionary in Congo.

"Don't worry about locking the door when you leave. There are no thieves on Westray," she said. "We have no police, no crime and, truthfully, no laws to even break. We all just get along."

Back in his room, ProV pulled out the Royal Dornoch guide again but dozed into another golf dream. Instead of the nightmares of the past, this time he was making every putt and winning some tournament by double digits.

Lucas stayed wide awake, hopeful that Mrs. Doubter had helped him find the Narrow Way.

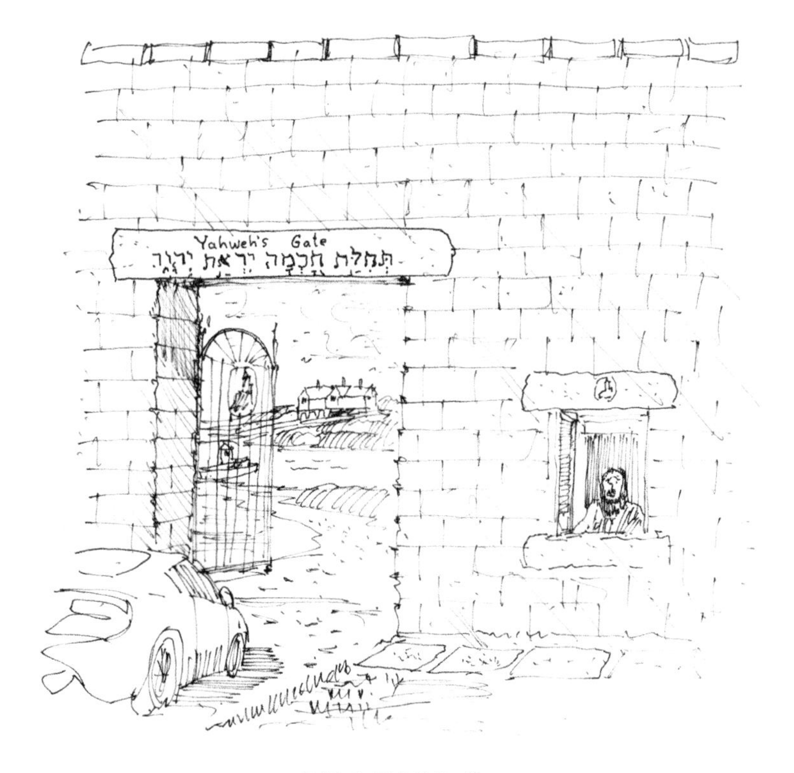

CHAPTER 8

The Narrow Way

ProV set his alarm just in case. It went off as scheduled at 10:02 a.m. He sprung to his feet as he heard Lucas knocking on the door with, "Time to go, man." It was back to the real world—if you call being at a bed and breakfast in Westray in the Orkney Islands looking for a golf course named Hokmah the real world.

He quickly grabbed his bag, met Lucas at the car and off the two pilgrims went in search of the Narrow Way. Plane reservations were secure for noon to cross the Papa Sound to Papa Westray. Lucas had called Loganair again and confirmed there was one flight only on this Sunday.

But first they would seek the Narrow Way. And they had ninety minutes to kill. Mrs. Doubter had confirmed they could see the whole island in that time. A serious "haar," the misty kind, had appeared so the scenery was limited.

Mrs. Doubter's last words were simple: "Good luck, but I doubt you'll find it, and if ya' do, there'll be nothing there. My memory tells me it could be ten minutes up the north highway, just past the golf course and the Noltland castle."

Sure enough, the boys were lost in no time. They stopped for five minutes to check out the Westray Golf Course. No cars in the parking lot. No pro shop. Just a barn that kept some equipment, some old balls lined up for people to play with and scorecards in a box near the gate beside a putting green. A sign said visitors could pay twenty pounds to play all day by going to a website. This was interesting but definitely not the Narrow Way to Hokmah.

ProV and Lucas got back in the car and headed westward on a narrow road indeed. GPS was no help. ProV was navigating from scribbled notes from Mrs. Doubter, while Lucas was now just hoping his friend would not lose heart for the journey. He knew, deep inside, that this was worth the effort and confusion. He had found wisdom at age 60, and now he wanted his friend to find it at age 43. It could save him decades of heartache and misery, not to mention eternity.

And then, as suddenly as a deer might emerge from the forest, there he was. ProV saw him first: A man was standing by the side of the road pointing toward a one lane road: "Narrow Way." He looked homeless. His hair was down his back, matted from what looked like years in the Orkney weather with no comb or barber. His beard was halfway down his chest. His clothes were rags. It was a cold day for American types, but this strange man seemed comfortable in shepherd's clothing like a Middle Eastern nomad. He was young, no more than thirty or so. And he was yelling like a madman, "Follow the Narrow Way, turn here!" He pointed the pilgrims toward a right turn to the north.

So turn they did. As they looked back, he barely moved, seemingly satisfied that someone listened to him.

"Lucas, we gotta stop and talk to this guy," shouted ProV. This was, without any doubt, the oddest moment of ProV's life, topping the Voice in the cathedral. He was seriously questioning his own eyesight and sanity. What was going on here?

Lucas backed up slowly as ProV nervously rolled down his window. He was nervous. Was it a dream? Had he watched too many reruns of *The Twilight Zone*? "So, good morning, my good man. We may be lost."

The odd character just smiled and nodded. He pointed to the small sign in faded letters.

"And you are?" ProV tried again.

"Goo' morning," he said with a clear Orkney accent. "John's the name."

"I'm Paul. This is Lucas."

"Sure, I know. I remember Lucas from the last time. And I'm sure he told me he'd be back, probably with a friend."

ProV looked over at Lucas to see if this was a big gag. He again looked for cameras in the gorse bushes. Had Lucas done all this just for a laugh?

But no, Lucas just raised his eyebrows and the haunting young character seemed serious.

"So," continued ProV, "tell me, who are you anyway?"

"Some say I am a voice crying in the wilderness.[12] Others say I am just a friend of the bridegroom, the so-called best man at a wedding.[13] Either one fits fine, although to be technical, I am just the son of Elizabeth and Zechariah.[14] I am here to point people like you to the Narrow Way. As you can see, not many find it."

Now that he had spoken, Lucas remembered this strange man. Indeed, he said to ProV, "We found the right place." John was not done. "So, go. You're on the right path. Enter through the narrow gate. *For wide is the gate and broad is the road that leads to destruction, and many enter through it. But small is the gate and narrow the road that leads to life, and only a few find it.*" [15]

[12] Matthew 3:1-6

[13] John 3:28-29

[14] Luke 1:57-60

[15] Matthew 7:13-14 (NIV)

ProV had no idea what he had said.

Lucas put the rental car into gear and slowly took off. When ProV looked back, the man was gone. An angel maybe? Confusion and excitement mixed with fear was the recipe for a Sunday that would never be forgotten.

Lucas headed down a single lane, not uncommon in Scotland's wild northwest. "What do we do if traffic comes at us?" ProV asked anxiously. Native highland grasses had not been mowed lately, maybe forever, and rose above the car, bending with the winds and making the road feel even more narrow.

"To be honest, I am not sure. But I do remember that ol' Andy Evangel told me it would seem all wrong. He said, '*There is a way that seems right to a man, but its end is the way of death.*' [16] He reminded me millions are headed for disaster, but the narrow way leads to life."

This narrow way was straight as a string. After just a mile, a large structure appeared in the distance. Within seconds, an enormous wall with a smaller gate appeared. The huge thick wall, more than twelve feet high, disappeared both left and right into a forest of yellow gorse. A sign hung over the door. Pro V read it out loud as they approached, "Yahweh's Gate." But what is that writing on the bottom of the sign?[17] "No idea," said Lucas, "but it looks like Hebrew."

The wall was too high to climb over and too long to go around. Lucas knocked on the small window near the gate. No one answered. He knocked again. He heard some rumbling and shuffling from the other side. A jovial middle-aged man with a reddish beard peeped through and said, "Knock and the door shall be opened," [18] laughing at his own bad joke.

"So boys, I suppose ya' wanna play golf today," he said, leaning on a ledge that reminded ProV of the ticket counters at baseball stadiums.

[16] Proverbs 14:12 (ESV)

[17] Proverbs 9:10 "Fear of the Lord is the beginning of wisdom..."

[18] Matthew 7:7

He looked like many old Orkney men—in need of a barber for his eyebrows and ears more than his bald, round head. He could have passed for Alexander Skeptic's brother.

"Yes, sir. I haven't seen a sign but I presume this is Hokmah?" said Lucas.

"You found the right place, gentlemen. But let me make this easy on you American types. Let's speak plain English. The club's name in English is Wisdom Golf Club. 'Hokmah' is just the best Hebrew word for wisdom."

"I didn't catch your name, sir."

"Shallum[19] Niblick. I've been watching this gate for many years now, along with a few of my friends. Some days not a soul comes through. Other days I never get to sit down. I'm glad you came early because it will take another hour or more to get through to the course." He looked at his watch. "Time is movin' on, so I will call the starter and make sure you get a tee time around noon if it suits you."

The window door closed and ProV was forced to wait again. A moment later, Niblick reappeared with the good news.

"Boys, they will be expecting you on the first tee at 11:52. Caddies are arranged."

"Thank you so much. So, seriously, Mr. Niblick, where are you from?" ProV asked.

"Dornoch. Surely you've heard of it. Magazines say it's number one now. That's only because they never heard of Hokmah Golf Club," he said with a twinkle in his eye.

"Oh, Dornoch. We just left there. The only reason we're here is we both failed to qualify for match play in the Carnegie Shield."

"Aye, you're not the first nor the last. Let me guess. You were doing just fine until you made an eight on one of the easy holes," he almost giggled. Lucas remembered with a smile his two lost balls and subsequent eight on the eighth.

"Now, first some simple paperwork." Niblick gave ProV a form to

[19] 1 Chronicles 9:17-19

fill out and shut the window. The questionnaire for first time visitors had three questions under a bold headline:

Welcome to Hokmah (Wisdom) Golf Club.

For temporary daily membership, please fill in the following with a Yes or No:

1) Do you agree that Someone designed Hokmah Golf Club?

2) Do you desire to upgrade your life and golf game?

3) Do you agree to try to return someday with a friend to show them what you will learn today?

A golf pencil with the club logo, a lighthouse, was provided.

As ProV filled out the form, another car screeched to a halt. It was the latest model BMW electric. It stopped in front of the gate and out popped a red-faced character who looked like another American tourist. A younger blond waited in the car, fixing her lipstick.

"You in line here?" the guy said to ProV, obviously miffed at the delay.

"Yeah, the guy will be right back. You might as well relax, this seems to take a while. He has forms to fill out."

"I've got a tee time in less than an hour, and we need to hit some balls and warm up, so would you mind if I go ahead?"

"Suit yourself, pal."

Wearing the latest golf attire, the slightly overweight 50-ish man knocked on the window, then banged on the gate, then the window again.

Looking around to try to see how he might get through without passing through the main narrow gate, he noticed to his right, at the far end of a small car park, a broad path which appeared wide enough for maintenance equipment. Lucas and ProV had not seen it.

"Look, tell them I couldn't wait," he said with a thick New York accent.

Lucas answered, "Sir, have you been here before?"

He shook his head.

"Then, I am pretty sure they will not let you play without Niblick stamping your hand or ticket or something. I was here a long time ago and I still remember a guy being sent away."

Clearly perturbed, the guy talked super slow, and even pointed his finger in Lucas's chest: "Apparently, you don't know who I am. I am Arthur Arrogant. I could buy this place if I wanted. I am only here because a guy that works in my firm claims this is the greatest golf course in the world, and I am checking off my bucket list. Frankly, I don't believe it, but I have an extra day here with my girlfriend. So look, I am going over here to the broad way and head on in."

His hair jostled in anger as he spoke. As Arrogant headed around the gate, Shallum Niblick returned, smiling. He had heard the entire exchange. "Poor guy thinks he has a tee time. Convinced that the world revolves around him. He will find out soon enough."

Lucas shook his head. ProV handed over the form after checking Yes to all three questions.

Niblick continued, "Yeah, I didn't answer Arrogant because I knew exactly what would happen. He would have answered 'No' on all three questions."

The doorkeeper glanced at ProV's form. He had passed. He didn't know who the creator of Hokmah might be, but every course has someone. Crenshaw or Ross or Nicklaus or Baird or even Ol' Tom Morris—or just nature itself as the creator, along with the winds and the weather of Scotland over many centuries.

ProV said, "One more question. What or who is Yahweh? This gate looks like it's been here since Braveheart."

Niblick smiled. He loved that question coming from a golfer. "You will find out today. But let me give you a hint. You probably dreamed of playing in the British Amateur or the US Amateur, right?"

ProV responded proudly, "Actually, you will be impressed to know that my friend here," pointing to Lucas, "played in the US Am at Pebble Beach many years ago. Me too a few years later." He decided to feign humility by not mentioning he had finished as runner-up.

"Okay, so you get the reference. Yahweh is not the British Am or the US Am. Yahweh's real name is 'I Am.'"

Confused, ProV asked, "I am? I am what?"

As the old man opened the gate, he looked at ProV and said, "Just 'I Am.'" [20]

Lucas and ProV got in the car and drove very slowly through Yahweh's Gate, which was narrow indeed, with only inches to spare around the car.

"I Am" said ProV again. 'I am who?"

"Later, ProV, let's get to Hokmah first," said the best friend in the world.

[20] Exodus 3:14 "God replied to Moses, 'I AM WHO I AM.'"

CHAPTER 9

The Listening Ferry

Within moments, the straight and narrow road reached a wide river which led into the North Sea. Across the way, perhaps half a mile into the open ocean, they could see a small ferry which seemed to be headed their way. A land mass could barely be seen in the misty morning. It was less than a mile across to the Isle of Mashal.

The ferry seemed too small for cars at first, but as it got closer they could see two cars on board. It reminded Lucas of the ferry from Cromartie to Nigg, just below Dornoch. Such a ferry was needed to get to Fortrose to play golf so this was a familiar sight to Lucas.

A small sign near the water simply said:

> *"Wait here kindly. Maximum two vehicles per trip. Typically, this ferry leaves every thirty minutes from 8:00 a.m. until sundown. Ferries run daily at the sole discretion of the ferryman."*

The ferryman was standing at the rear of the ferry as it cozied back onto shore, ready to guide the two cars backing down off the small boat. A concrete embankment made it easy to pull back off the ferry.

The muscled ferryman had a dark beard and a sunburned nose and was young enough to handle any problems.

Out from the cabin came a fuming Arthur Arrogant. He had been upstairs with the pilot, threatening lawsuits and countermeasures for his poor treatment at Hokmah. He climbed into his BMW, joining his blond beauty, who was too cold in her mini-skirt to get outside into the cool Orkney breezes.

Apparently, his bid to play at Hokmah had been denied.

On the other hand, an older Scandinavian couple crawled into their shiny silver Toyota. They waved to the ferryman with huge smiles, happy to have had a perfectly fine experience. They offered a tip that was quickly refused, and then backed out safely once the back door was down.

They stopped in the turnaround area, giving a nod to Lucas and ProV, who were now poised to drive onto the ferry. But first, of course, Arrogant had to exit. He gunned his BMW in reverse, causing the ferry to bob in the water and scraping his rear-end on the concrete landing. When Arrogant saw Lucas, he couldn't help himself, screaming through his window, "This place is a joke!"

Arrogant was quickly in the rearview mirror as Lucas slowly pulled up the small ramp onto the ferry. They were the only vehicle for this 15-minute adventure. There were, however, a handful of people who climbed aboard. How they got there was a total mystery but there they were. Maybe workers?

"Wow, what a trip that guy was," said ferryman James Lesser, whose nametag made it clear who was in charge. "Now first, hand me your keys. Don't need problems like this last guy."

Lucas complied quietly.

"My name is James. Your pilot this morning is Zechariah.[21] He is upstairs piloting this vessel. Please do not attempt to speak with him. He is deaf and prefers to stay silent. That was his son John out by the road today, pointing the way."

[21] Luke 1:5-25 "Meanwhile the people were waiting for Zechariah...."

Lucas vaguely remembered James from the first trip.

"Now, here are your instructions. We put them in this little booklet just so I don't have to talk too much."

Lucas and ProV stood outside in the fresh air as the ferry slowly began to move. The document made the rules clear:

We are crossing the Listening River which leads into the North Sea and across to the Isle of Mashal, home of the Hokmah Golf Club. You have passed through Yahweh's Gate and agreed you want to become a better golfer and person.

The first key is to listen. Therefore, remain silent on this short journey across the river. You must say nothing. Nothing.

One who cannot listen cannot learn. The temptation to speak will be enormous. People will ask your opinion. Others may politely ask how you're doing. Don't answer. Just listen. Especially listen to older people, perhaps one who is the age of your parents or more.

You may hear voices in your head. These could be the voices of your spouse or mother. They could be the voices of some mentor or sage. Don't stop the voices. Just listen.

One last and serious warning: If you fail this small test and speak, you will not be allowed entry to the Isle of Mashal or Hokmah Golf Club. This seems harsh. But it is essential.

Lucas had forgotten this part. He glanced at ProV who was, thankfully, speechless with eyebrows raised.

Two minutes into the trip a nice lady came over. "Good morning. I'm Miss Busybody. That's my boyfriend over there, Mr. Talkative, chatting away with the young lady. Beautiful weather today, eh? Would you like a tea or coffee?"

Lucas grabbed ProV by the arm just as he was getting ready to say, "Of course. Black coffee, please"—words that would have doomed the trip. He motioned with his hand to his mouth to "zip it up."

Another well-meaning lady, sounding English, strolled over and said, "Hello, men. My name is Chit Chat, a nickname from my childhood. You guys are surely American. So, what do you think about your President? The news we get seems to be pretty bad for him."

Lucas grabbed ProV's arm again, bringing him back from the brink of defending his country and President. Both of them realized they would need to go to the other side of the ferry to get away from people who wanted to talk about weather, sports, or politics. Or even worse, themselves.

Instead, they heard the sounds they needed to hear. Seagulls chirping. Waves splashing. Winds moving. Seabirds calling. And then, the voices from the past.

ProV heard his dad's voice. At first, painful insults that no little boy should have to hear. But then telling his buddies at the golf club how his son shot 65 that morning. What a feeling of pride from a father to a son, a voice which never goes away.

And then he heard his grandmother Addie's voice, forgiving him when his life had turned into disaster, all his own fault. Encouragement and forgiveness, good words to hear. Sadly, his mother's voice could not be heard. She was silent still.

But there was a third: a loud stranger's voice begging for attention. It was accusatory, a voice that never let him forget he should be at home with his wife and kids right now, getting ready for a high school baseball game, reminding him of the bankruptcy, divorce and too many three-putts.

This evil voice was trying to get through, telling him he was "a no-good bum," a "failure," a "basket case," a "loser." His college coach was an old-school guy who thought golf coaches should be like football coaches. It never worked, but the coach's voice had never gone away completely, telling him he would never make it.

But after a few minutes, with each sound of the waves and seagulls squawking, the negative voices were losing their steam. The birds and wind and waves were winning the day.

As the ferry coasted into shore, James Lesser came over and gave a short benediction. "Men, you can speak now. But first, hear me:

"All who listen to me will live in peace, untroubled by fear of harm.[22] Fools think their own way is right, but the wise listen to others.[23] If you listen to constructive criticism, you will be at home among the wise." [24]

ProV was listening, a good next step. "You need big ears when you arrive at Hokmah Golf Club," offered James with a smile.

As Lucas and ProV opened the door to enter the car, they noticed that the three other passengers were gone already. Where had they gone? Were they angels sent to weed out the pretenders and tempt poor souls to speak?

It didn't matter. They had passed the test.

As Lucas started the car, he noticed Zechariah descending the steps from his navigational perch above. Mr. Z, as he was often called, gave the boys a thumbs up, but also a hand gesture asking them to wait just a moment. He was much older than James—perhaps an uncle or other kinfolk.

He handed them a card which he had printed out for all his passengers.

> *Many people have felt sorry for me because I am deaf. But believe me, it is a blessing. I can hear the Voice of the only One that matters. And because speaking is difficult for me, I keep silent unless I have something really important to say. And by staying silent, I have a lot of friends! So, pay close attention to what you hear. The more you listen, the more understanding will be given to you—and you will receive even more.*

Mr. Z was smiling as Lucas drove slowly off the ferry. Indeed, Lucas and ProV were both speechless at that moment. They had arrived at Hokmah Golf Club. The drive onto the property felt like holy ground. Silence made perfect sense.

The road from the ferry to the clubhouse was like driving through

[22] Proverbs 1:33

[23] Proverbs 12:15

[24] Proverbs 15:31

one of the famous French manicured gardens, Versailles perhaps, only more colorful. They pulled up to a small sign that said, "Bag Drop." A young man with olive skin came out quickly to assist. The name tag said "Epaphras." [25]

Lucas and ProV both looked up at the clubhouse as they emerged from the car. It looked like the Royal Calcutta Golf Club, thought ProV. He had been there once, when he spent six miserable weeks playing an Asian minor league tour. Calcutta was reputedly the second-oldest golf club in the world, so said golf historians who had never heard of Hokmah.

One could see the hidden beauty in a building that needed some paint and a few million bucks to bring up to code. But at this moment, to Lucas and ProV, it was breathtaking.

ProV could see the pleasure on Lucas's wrinkling face and agreed with a simple, "Lucas, my man, this is a step back into time."

"It looks ancient because it is," said Lucas.

Epaphras gave some simple instructions. "Gentlemen, welcome to Hokmah Golf Club. We will have your clubs down at the practice range. Your golf shoes and other items you may need will be in your lockers inside the clubhouse to the left. Your names will be on the lockers. Hiram in the pro shop is aware of your arrival and you can check in there."

With some time to spare, Lucas and ProV gave themselves a tour of the clubhouse. The simple dining area looked out over the North Sea. Below was the huge eighteenth green. The bar area nearby was small, with room for no more than twenty people. A bartender was cleaning glasses.

"Good morning, men. Welcome to the Galilee Bar. Might be a bit too early for a drink? But we have sandwiches and a full bar menu if you like. Also, coffee or tea."

"Thank you. Maybe later. What's your name?" asked Lucas.

"Cana. Cana Galilee. We specialize in the best wines in the world.[26]

[25] Colossians 1:7 "You learned about the Good News from Epaphras..."

[26] John 2:1-11

The world's greatest golf course needed the greatest wines," he said with a knowing smile. Lucas got the point, while ProV was barely listening, gazing out the huge window and trying to figure out what the eighteenth hole looked like.

The tour continued through a door that read "Men's Locker Room." Inside were about sixty lockers, all made of old Scotch woods. Golf spike marks from what seemed like 150 years ago dotted the floor. There had been no effort at modernization. The closest thing to modern were the showers, which Lucas always checked out first. Sure enough, they were the latest and greatest showerheads, straight from the ceiling, a full fourteen inches across. He tested the pressure with a twist and a rush of water strong enough to heal whatever might ail you came flooding out. No drip-drip here. He knew a post-round shower was in his future.

The locker room attendant was standing behind his counter, busy polishing white shoes but also talking to a man sitting down to tie his brown golf shoes. Lucas and ProV were in awe and shock when they recognized the small man sitting down.

Was this really Ben Hogan? Had he not died in 2010 at about age ninety? He looked to be fifty. The guys overheard the conversation.

"Rufus,[27] it's been a long time since I first came here. When was that? You'd remember." Rufus indeed would remember.

"Sir, my calling has been to serve here any way possible since the first day I heard about this place. That was so long ago I can't remember it. My daddy, Mr. Simon Cyrene,[28] brought me here when I was fourteen years old and I sort of never left. But if I'm not mistaken, your first visit here was 1952, right after your accident. This place may have saved your life, or at least your career."

Hogan gave a small affirmative nod. "No doubt about it," said Ben.

Lucas and ProV were mesmerized as he marched out of the locker room, headed for the course or range. The sound of golf spikes clanking made it feel indeed like 1952, and no one stopped him. Hogan nodded

[27] Romans 16:13

[28] Mark 15:21

back with a small smile, not really looking at the guys, but acknowledging they were there. ProV was having his best golf moment ever. Ben Hogan had noticed him. Nodded in his direction.

They found their lockers: 111 for Mr. Friend; 112 for Mr. Player. They put on their golf shoes, thanked Rufus for helping them and tried their best to do it all fast, hoping now to have a chance to go watch Ben Hogan hit golf balls, an experience that already was surpassing all of ProV's expectations. Lucas promised him a special day. If nothing else happened, it was all true. Even if Hokmah was not the greatest course, it was certainly the greatest locker room.

CHAPTER 10
Leave Everything Behind

The pro shop was small. A retail marketing man would be appalled at the lack of logo memorabilia. No hats. No shirts. No ball markers or green-repair tools that said Hokmah. No list on a wall showing the world's greatest golf courses with Hokmah in bold letters at or near the top. Music was playing softly through the ceiling. Lucas recognized the instrumental playing as they walked into the shop. It was some heavenly orchestra performing "How Great Thou Art."

Behind the counter was an older man with the name tag "Hiram." [29] He had overseen the pro shop for a long time. He got the job because of his dear friendship with the designers and builders of the club. His family had provided much of the infrastructure and manpower to build Hokmah. He was not a golf professional, but he sure looked like one standing behind the counter. He had become an expert at smiling and handling troublesome members or visitors.

As Lucas walked in, Hiram was helping two other customers, so he waited patiently to check in.

"ProV, man, you go on. I will take care of this. You need to go find

[29] 1 Kings 5:1 "King Hiram of Tyre had always been a loyal friend of David."

Hogan. He's probably on the range beating balls. You don't want to miss it."

"Thanks," said a grateful ProV, who scurried out the door and down a few steps toward the range. His hope for Lucas to cover the green fees had come true. He would help with the caddie tips.

Meanwhile, the pro shop was in tension.

"What? Are you serious?" said a young and handsome man with a Greek accent. "You cannot possibly be serious?" he raised his voice in a controlled temper tantrum.

Hiram said, "Mr. Demas,[30] I am very sorry you didn't understand the fees here. As I told you, if you are not satisfied at the end of the day, a full refund will be given. But the upfront payment is a requirement."

"We traveled two days to get here. You guys need a website to explain this better. I know I was told, 'If you have to ask you can't afford it,' but I presumed my sponsor was just kidding. I cannot sign that paper."

His companion, Alexander "Gus" Coppersmith,[31] asked Demas, "What's the problem?"

"This guy wants me to sign a paper giving Hokmah everything I own to play here. This is insane." Gus curled his lips and raised his eyebrows in shock. Demas had invited him as a guest.

Hiram said, "Again, Mr. Demas, I am sorry. This place is surely not for everyone."

"Let's go," Demas said, muttering curses in his native Greek. "If we leave right now we can be back in Greece by late tonight. You can be back in your factory on Monday morning. And I will be back at my desk in Thessalonica." As they walked out, he called his pilot who was waiting at the tiny Westray airport. This reminded Lucas that he had forgotten to cancel the flight to Papa Westray. *Oh, well. Just happy we found Hokmah,* he thought to himself.

While the drama with Demas was unfolding, Lucas was busy scanning the scorecard. Sure enough, his first trip to Hokmah had not been a dream. He now remembered every hole.

[30] 2 Timothy 4:10 "Demas has deserted me because he loves the things of this life."

[31] 2 Timothy 4:14 "Alexander the coppersmith did me much harm...."

One of the signs of a great course is the ability to remember holes when the day is done. After only one day at Hokmah twelve years ago, his memory of every single hole came flooding back. He not only remembered the holes. He remembered his caddie. The only thing he didn't remember was his score. It didn't matter.

Every hole had a name. The first hole was "Trust."

Lucas stepped up to the counter. He already knew the deal. His host Andrew Evangel had paid the green fees twelve years ago and never regretted it for one minute. Lucas knew this was the perfect way to start the last few years of his life. At 72, it was time. Time to give it all.

Hiram greeted Lucas warmly despite the problem pair walking out the door. "Sir, the green fees are simple. Just sign this document. Read it carefully. You are signing over everything you have to the club. I know it sounds extravagant, but we do offer a full money back guarantee if you're not satisfied. Nothing to lose. And full payment allows you one guest for free."

As he signed, Lucas paused to tell Hiram, "My cousin and friend Andrew brought me here last time. He told me about these outlandishly expensive green fees. When I politely tried to stop him, he told me Jesus said, 'Leave everything behind and follow me.'[32] Andrew told me that, in his view, most people who call themselves Christian now do just the opposite. He said, 'They *keep* everything and ask Jesus to follow them.' That stuck in my head for these last twelve years."

"I like that," Hiram smiled, "and I presume Mr. Player knows what a gift you are giving him?"

"We will see. Right now he just wants to see Hogan."

"Head on down first to the caddie shack. The caddie master will be waiting for you. He will be wearing his familiar kilt."

Lucas left the pro shop with a net worth of zero.

Sure enough, the caddie master had the traditional kilt in the special colors of Hokmah. Red and green mostly.

[32] Luke 5:11 "As soon as they landed, they left everything and followed Jesus."

"Good morning, Mr. Friend. You can call me Adam. By the way, sir, kilts are not an Orcadian tradition, but I wear this in honor of all our Scottish friends down south. Visitors seem to expect kilts and bagpipes," said the caddie master with a huge smile.

"Sure, Adam, I was here a dozen years ago," offered Lucas with a smile.

"Indeed, and I've been here from the very beginning," [33] said Adam with a chuckle. "We have two very fine caddies for you today. You will be with Sophia Spiritos, but everyone calls her by her nickname, Hollie."

"I was with Hollie the last time," said Lucas, happy to know she was still around.

"Most people remember her. She's been here from *before* the beginning."

"*Before* the beginning," Lucas repeated, pondering the depth of such a statement.

Adam looked at his starter's sheet and continued, "Mr. Player will be with Mr. T, whose real surname is Tulloch. Mr. T is shy so he will not say much except with hand signals, but no problem. Hollie will be there to give advice. They will both be down at the range with your clubs." Lucas thanked Adam.

"Your foursome is nearly the only one playing this afternoon, so take your time. We paired you with a young chap who showed up this morning looking for a game, as well as a member who may show you a few tips."

"Sounds fine," said Lucas.

"You will love playing with Mr. R.W. Wright. You won't be wasting any time looking for his balls. He keeps it in the short grass."

Sure enough, the caddies were at the range where ProV was sitting on a bench, mesmerized, watching Ben Hogan hit five-irons. Ben turned to talk to ProV.

"If you wanna know how you're really hitting the ball, hit your five iron. The driver and short irons will lie to you," he said as he hit a small fade into the light Scottish breeze. The temperature was ideal:

[33] Genesis 2:3

64 degrees on a mostly sunny day. The caddie was a young college kid name Kris. She threw him another ball. ProV was too nervous to speak to Hogan. He just nodded and watched in awe.

Lucas was spellbound as well, not just by Hogan's swing but the entire setting. He looked around and saw the typical beautiful triangular mountains of golf balls stacked everywhere. Unlike most courses in Scotland, Hokmah had a practice range supreme. And every ball on the range was a Titleist Pro V1.

Most Scottish courses, even Royal Dornoch, have a net near the pro shop. Warming up is frowned upon. Beating balls like Hogan was doing is not well understood. After all, golf was about getting a ball near the hole, no matter what it takes. How much does a pretty, repeatable swing help with that? In links golf, you need low, high, hooks, fades, bounces, feel. Hitting balls on a range with perfect lies and no slopes could never help with those shots.

Hollie and Mr. T waited with golf bags. Mr. T seemed especially pleased to carry a bag with a name on it. "Paul (ProV) Player" was in bright red letters. It was all a leftover from the days when ProV was going to be a star and Titleist was his sponsor.

Hollie Spiritos was the only regular female caddie at Hokmah. "Good morning, sir, you may remember me. Everyone just calls me Hollie."

"Of course, Hollie. How could I forget you?" said Lucas with a smile. He hugged Hollie like she was his long-lost daughter home from college. "You look exactly the same as last time. Do you not age at all?"

"Not here, sir. It's the ocean breezes I suppose."

Mr. T presented himself to ProV with a strong handshake.

Hollie explained Mr. T would be mostly silent. "Pleased to meet you, Mr. Player. Mr. T is excited to go around with a good player. They tell me you're a 'plus one.' Believe me, we get some weak slices around here. Looking forward to a great day. In fact, maybe the greatest day of your life."

"Hollie, thank you. You can call me ProV. Mr. T is not the only one with a nickname," he said as he reached into his bag for a golf glove.

He shook hands again with Mr. T, establishing the caddie/player bond that sometimes bears great fruit.

ProV would have been happy to watch Hogan all afternoon, but it was now half past eleven with an 11:52 tee time. It was time to work out the travel legs before suffering the pressure of the first tee. He took a few swings and chipped a few balls with a wedge. ProV could hardly contain his pure joy of hitting Pro V1 balls on a range. They didn't even say 'Practice' on them. They were all numbered seven.

I'm so tempted to steal a few balls, he thought. In fact, he remembered, when he was fifteen back in Fresno he had done just that. "Father Randy, I have sinned, I stole a dozen practice balls off the range at the country club yesterday." Thank goodness Father Randy was a five handicap and forgave all his sins.

Hollie offered her first piece of wisdom for the day. "The greatest book in the history of the world is arguably Proverbs. Thirty-one chapters full of wisdom. Today will not only be a wonderful journey around the greatest golf course in the world. It will also be a study in Proverbs."

ProV raised his eyebrows in confusion on that one. He was more worried about his own game than the book of Proverbs. But he was here, and ready to learn.

Smart caddies know a golfer's favorite subject is usually themselves and how good they used to be. Hollie asked ProV, "And how did you get your nickname, sir?"

"That's a good one. My initials are PVP. Bottom line, I used to be pretty good. So, the name stuck one day with my college buddies. But that was a long time ago. Today, let's hope we can break eighty."

"No worry there, sir, you will definitely break eighty. We will play the member tees. This is friendly golf and a lovely walk."

ProV thought about how far away from home he was and wondered, *How in the world did this happen?* The journey to the first tee at Hokmah had been a long one. Fresno to San Francisco, to New York, to Edinburgh, to Inverness, to Royal Dornoch, to the Dornoch Cathedral, to the Orkney Islands—all to see what this course might offer.

ProV knew he needed some wisdom. His failures in golf had led to failures in finances and family. One bankruptcy. Two divorces. Two teenagers he didn't see very often. Indeed, now he was missing another whole week with the kids over the summer holiday to go to Scotland and play golf. His kids and ex-wife were not impressed. Everyone who knew Mary Ann agreed she was the sweetest and most forgiving woman in the world, but even she had her limits. She sarcastically had started calling him her 'ProV 1X, with an emphasis on the X."

Even Lucas had gotten a phone call from Mary Ann just before he got on the plane for this trip: "I can't believe you would be complicit in this loser missing another summer of being a dad. And spending money for Scotland when he's behind on child support. My lawyer will get the next call." Lucas still felt guilty. She had hung up before he could explain anything.

But he knew this day was, without a doubt, the most important day of ProV's life. Either it would turn everything around, or he was doomed. Lucas had not been able to tell Mary Ann he was taking a prodigal father and husband to a land where wisdom might change his life. Only time would tell.

They left the main range and the caddies made a detour to a short teaching center. ProV and Lucas took the chance to warm up the short game with chips and pitches.

Neither had ever seen such a sight. Some of the greatest teachers of all time were there. Was this real?

Butch Harmon was working with a kid who looked like he could have been Tiger Woods' grandson.

David Leadbetter was at the end of the range with a young Asian girl.

Bob Toski was helping an older man who was still looking for a swing. ProV overheard him tell Toski, "I think I found something last night on the range." He had to have been ninety.

Wally Armstrong was surrounded by a group of eight kids with a "hula hoop" and other gadgets galore. He seemed to be having more fun than the kids.

Moe Norman was hitting drivers on a string for someone with a video camera.

Brian Fuqua, the famous putting guru, was on the green showing drills to an eager college kid with a bag that said Kentucky.

Hank Haney was helping some young guy with the driving yips, telling him to look at his cap instead of the ball.

ProV stared at the lineup, then looked at Lucas, whose raised eyebrows said, "I told you this place was special."

It was now 11:45. "Time to go," announced Hollie as she led the guys over toward the first tee.

"There's a small putting green next to the first tee where you can hit a few putts. And if you're worried about lunch, we will be stopping at the turn for seafood pot pies only served here. It's all set up. Snacks on the tee if you need something."

ProV's stomach was growling already.

"And waiting for you on the tee is one of our hostesses, Lady Wisdom.[34] She will have a word for you as you get going."

Sure enough, a modestly dressed older lady was stroking putts on the tiny green just steps off the first tee. She had been ladies club champion too many times to count, and now took a role of ceremonial starter when the weather was good. Hollie introduced her to the California pilgrims. "Gentlemen, meet my sister, Lady Wisdom. Some people call her Madam Insight." [34]

"Good day gentlemen. It is a pleasure to welcome you to Hokmah. Unlike many of the members here, I live on the Isle of Mashal all year long, even in the cold dark winters. Many years ago, I built a nice home just around the corner in a nearby neighborhood. I live next to Sanity; and Knowledge and Discretion live just down the street.[35] We have the most peaceful neighborhood in the world. Perhaps you will find time to visit my home before you leave."

ProV couldn't resist thinking to himself, *Sanity. Wouldn't that be nice for a change. A peaceful home. I cannot even imagine.*

Lady Wisdom continued, "One quick thought and we will be on

[34] Proverbs 8:1 "Listen as Wisdom calls out!"

[35] Proverbs 8:12 (The Message)

our way. The Creator of Hokmah asked me to convey a message as we get started."

ProV and Lucas leaned on their putters and listened to ancient words:

My child, listen to what I say, and treasure my commands.
Tune your ears to wisdom, and concentrate on understanding.
Cry out for insight, and ask for understanding.
Search for them as you would for silver; seek them like hidden treasures. Then you will understand what it means to fear the Lord, and you will gain knowledge of God.
For the Lord grants wisdom!
From his mouth come knowledge and understanding.
He grants a treasure of common sense to the honest.
He is a shield to those who walk with integrity.
He guards the paths of the just and protects those who are faithful to him.
Then you will understand what is right, just, and fair, and you will find the right way to go.
For wisdom will enter your heart, and knowledge will fill you with joy.
Wise choices will watch over you.
Understanding will keep you safe.
Wisdom will save you...[36]

With that, Lady Wisdom smiled and headed back to the clubhouse where she had scheduled lunch with her pleasant companion and brother, Knowledge.[37] Hollie thanked her and said, "Let's go, gentlemen. I hope you were listening. Wisdom will save you."

ProV and Lucas had finally arrived. Into a new world. Looking for a treasure in the sands of the links of Hokmah on the islands of Orkney. Into their future.

[36] Proverbs 2: 1-12

[37] Proverbs 2:10 (The Message) "Lady Wisdom will be your close friend, and Brother Knowledge your pleasant companion."

Part Two

The Front Nine

"Long ago on a golf course that was no longer there, he'd told me to open my eyes and see the glory of the world. The way to heaven, he said, is heaven." [38]

Hokmah Golf Club
The Isle of Mashal
Orkney, Scotland KW17 2DW
+44 1856 777777
www.HokmahGolf.com

Hokmah Golf Club

"Wisdom in the Sand. . ."

Hole	Par	Hdcp	Name	Proverbs	Professional	Member
1	4	7	Trust	3:05	407	360
2	4	1	Truth	12:19	472	422
3	4	5	Eyes	4:25	468	408
4	4	9	Prudence	27:12	340	290
5	4	3	Integrity	10:09	460	416
6	3	13	Patience	16:32	240	204
7	5	15	Temper	17:27	590	510
8	3	17	Tongue	18:21	120	115
9	5	11	Heart	22:17	660	545
Out	36				3757	3270

[38] Dodson, James, Final Rounds, (London. Arrow Books, 1996), p. 254.

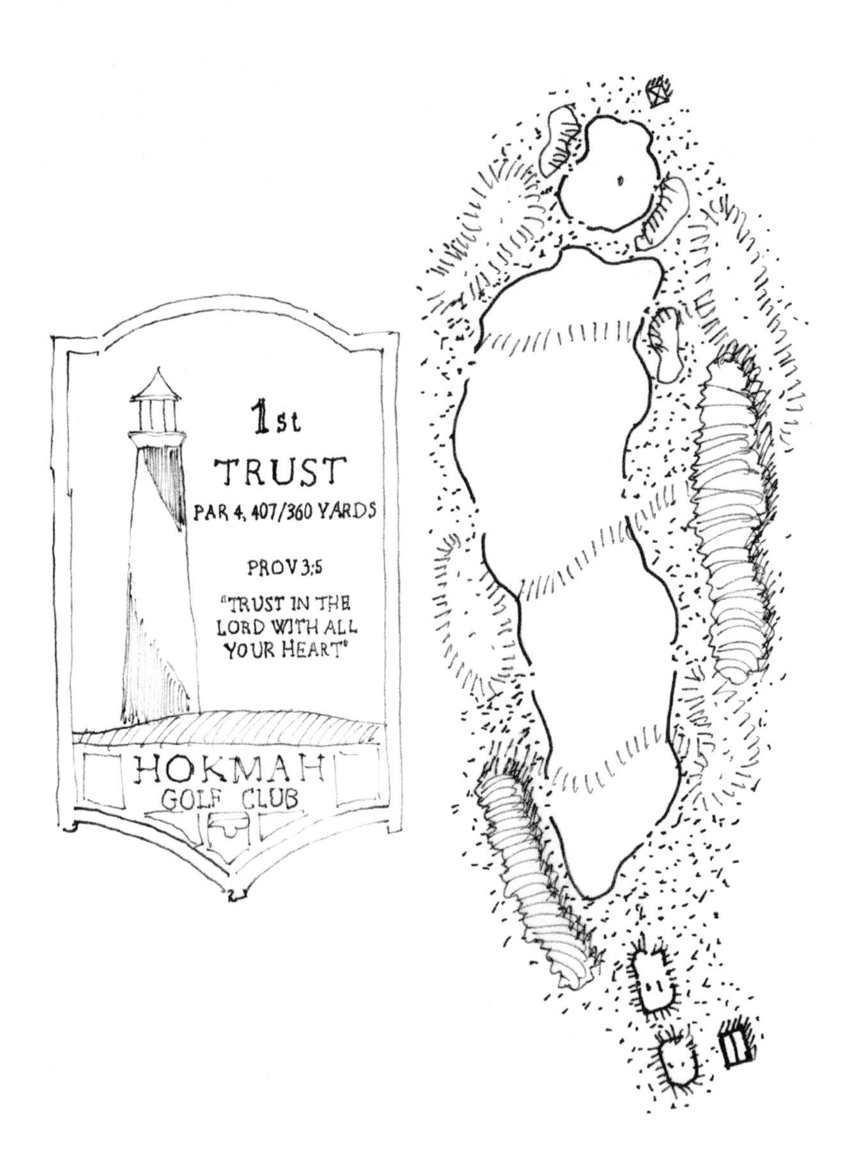
1st
TRUST
PAR 4, 407/360 YARDS
PROV 3:5
"TRUST IN THE LORD WITH ALL YOUR HEART"
HOKMAH
GOLF CLUB

1st Hole – Trust

PAR 4, 407/360 YARDS

"Trust in the Lord with all your heart..."

Proverbs 3:5

Lady Wisdom had spoken. It was time to play golf.

The first tee marker announced the number of the hole and gave it a name, a common custom on Scottish courses. But this one had a verse to follow.

"TRUST," it said.

"Trust in the Lord with all your heart..." was in green letters on a white background.

The caddie master, Adam, doubled as the starter. In his kilt he made the perfect person to get the round going. He was also the first and only superintendent of Hokmah.[39] He knew every blade of grass.

ProV and Lucas were paired with two other gentlemen who were hurrying to the tee, so they had a moment to chat. Lucas asked, "So,

[39] Genesis 2:15 "The Lord God placed a man in the Garden of Eden to tend and watch over it."

Adam, you were here in the beginning. What was this like before the course was built?"

A huge smile came across Adam's face. "It was a magnificent garden.[40] Hard to believe since there is not a single native tree on any of the Orkney Islands. Not one. But believe me, the place was paradise. Perfect for a golf course. The Creator really just came in, rearranged a bit here and there, and was smart enough not to mess with the perfect environment for a golf course."

The conversation was cut short when their companions for the day arrived with their caddies and it was time to play. R.W. Wright offered a friendly smile with a handshake and a simple, "Welcome to Hokmah." He pronounced the name with a clear Orkadian accent, the 'H' starting in the back of his throat.

Following close behind was another American visitor, who simply nodded to the small assemblage of players and caddies on the tee as he fumbled in his bag for balls and tees. He had missed the opening speech of Lady Wisdom.

The first hole at Hokmah was a reasonable par four of 360 yards from the member tees. No out of bounds. No real trouble. Indeed, the hole offered a great opportunity for a par or even a birdie. But still, any first hole is the opening scene to a four-hour mini-series drama, with plenty of heroes and bad guys and an uncertain ending.

Adam announced the group as if it was a US Open. "On the tee, Mr. R.W. Wright."

The honorable Mr. Wright was a good player and a founding member. His caddie, Barnabas, handed him a three metal. The head cover had the Hokmah logo, the lighthouse which is seen from nearly every vantage spot on the course. His practice swings were smooth and rhythmic.

Mr. Wright was even at Hokmah during the sad years when the course had been shut down. Yahweh's Gate was locked and weeds grew up through the fairways and greens. Like everyone else, he had been

[40] Genesis 2:8 "Then the Lord God planted a garden..."

forced to leave through an eastern gate.[41]

Hollie whispered to Lucas as Wright approached the ball. "Watch R.W. He knows there is a good player inside of him. He's looking down the fairway as he prepares to hit the ball but he is also looking inside himself, looking for the 'good guy' who lives there and can be trusted. That 'good guy' is hard to find on the first tee."

Lucas examined Wright. He had a good routine. He seemed to actually see the shot before he swung the club.

Hollie continued, "You see, Wright has a healthy respect for the course but also of the Creator of the course. He knows he will not be in control of everything that happens today. He knows planning a round of golf is as absurd as planning your life when you are twelve years old."

Wright made a rhythmic swing and the ball sailed silently through the mid-day sun. Straight down the fairway with the smallest of draws. He turned and smiled: "This will be fun. You never know what a day like today will bring. One shot at a time."

Adam announced, "On the tee now, from Sodom Valley Golf Club in Arizona, Dr. W. D. Deadend." His caddie pulled the cover off the latest and greatest driver, following his man to the tee for some solemn advice.

On the edge of the tee, Lucas whispered to Wright, "So who is your friend Dr. Deadend?

"Oh, we're not friends. I came along to help out because you're all guests today. This guy showed up this morning and wants to be a member. He says he is a scratch golfer." His eyebrows went up as he said, "He checked the right boxes to get here, so we will see."

Dr. Deadend was dressed in the latest golf attire, but seemed too short for his lavender pants. "Good morning, men. Many friends call me 'Dubs,' for my initials, or 'Doc.' I brought my own caddie. Meet Eddie Mocker." [42]

Lucas and ProV smiled and nodded politely. "Mocker has helped

[41] Genesis 3:23 "So the Lord banished them from the garden of Eden."

[42] Proverbs 14:6 "A mocker seeks wisdom and never finds it."

me plan this round. Planning is the key to everything. We know exactly where we want every shot to be hit."

Wright stepped forward and said, "Dubs, can we talk?" He took Deadend to the side for a quiet, friendly warning. "I've heard about Mocker. He thinks careful planning can avoid all the trouble out there.[43] Then when things go wrong, he blames the course designer."

"Indeed, he does. And that is why I have hired him for the day. I have not broken ninety in a long time and I am confident Mocker will help me."

Wright looked puzzled. "But you said you were a scratch golfer."

"Well, my handicap is eighteen, but I don't think scores tell the story. I've made many pars and even birdies over the last few years which surely should count for something. It's just a matter of putting it all together, and I am sure Mocker will help me do that. Today is the day."

R.W. quietly stepped away, knowing he was talking to a fool.

Dubs turned to his caddie. "Mocker, what do we do here?"

"Three wood down the left side gives a perfect angle into the right pin placement on this first hole," Mocker answered. The caddie had actually never seen Dubs hit a ball. All he knew was that the gentleman from Arizona was supposed to play par golf.

Dubs approached the ball like a hunter stalking his prey and finally prepared to swing just as the ball fell off the tee. "That's one," he joked. He replaced the new Pro V1 666,[44] a special order with his company logo, snuck up on it and hit it so far right that dunes and knee-deep gorse and heather were in play.

So much for plans. Dubs shook his head and gave Mocker a frown. "Shoulda' hit driver, my best club," he mumbled.

And then it was time for Lucas to hit. Hollie told him to relax and let it go. "Nothing to fear. *Fearing people is a dangerous trap, but trusting the Lord means safety*." [45]

[43] Proverbs 16:1 "We can make our own plans, but the Lord gives the right answer."

[44] Revelation 13:18 "Wisdom is needed here. Let the one with understanding solve the meaning of the number..."

[45] Proverbs 29:25

With Hollie's words ringing in his ears, Lucas sent his ball down the fairway. "Nice shot, sir," affirmed Hollie.

Hitting last, ProV hit a nervous three wood toe-hook that stayed out of trouble. He handed his club to Mr. T and off they went. Why had an experienced golfer like ProV been so jittery?

As if reading his mind, Lucas said, "Golf exposes you, doesn't it? The ball just sits there. No one can help you. All alone. It would almost be easier if all you had to do was react to a curve ball. In golf, you have to create your own reaction. Not that easy."

ProV nodded. Yes indeed.

"So, Hollie, tell us more about this place," Lucas said as they walked down the perfect links fairway—not soft and sluggish like courses at home, but with the optimum bounce that invigorates the walk.

"This first hole is called Trust because that is the opposite of fear. You can't play golf if you are afraid. And yet, just as fear is unhealthy, there is another healthy version of fear. It is godly fear.[46] Some just call it Awe or Respect. God is God and we are not. The Hebrew sign over Yahweh's Gate tells us that this 'fear' is just the beginning. It is nowhere near the end. But you have to start with this Awe or Respect. It will add years to your life.[47] In fact, see the old man sitting up behind the green? He is living proof of what I am telling you."

With each step, the vague figure came into view. He looked comfortable, sitting in a simple lawn chair with an umbrella over his head to keep the sun away. He wore a gray tweed flat-top hat with glasses.

On their approach shots, Lucas, ProV and R.W. all got to the green with reasonably short irons. Dubs should have chipped out to the fairway and worked on a good bogey. But after two aborted attempts to hit a seven iron from four-inch rough, he was already at five when he got to the green.

Finally, ProV recognized the man behind the green. "Is that Byron Nelson?"

[46] Proverbs 9:10 "Fear of the Lord is a foundation of wisdom (*Hokmah*)."

[47] Proverbs 10:27 "Fear of the Lord lengthens one's life."

He looked like the epitome of joy in the flesh.[48] He watched as the group putted out. Three pars and Deadend's two-putt triple bogey. Byron was having a friendly chat with a balding older man whom no one recognized.

Wright led the group over to meet Byron—all but Dubs, who walked away briskly toward the 2nd tee, cursing about the unfairness of such a starting hole.

Mocker shouted, "Come on, boys. We don't have time for small talk with every old man we see along the way."

Byron heard them but seemed to understand.[49] "Boys, there will always be guys like that around golf. Pay 'em no attention. They probably had a bad childhood. I just pray for them. I used to pray for Hogan, although he beat me so many times, maybe I shouldn't have," he offered with a chuckle.

"Mr. Nelson, you are way too humble," stammered ProV. "You won nineteen tournaments in one year. Eleven in a row in 1945. I've been trying to imitate your swing for twenty-five years. This is a great honor to meet you." He wondered if this was a dream. Hogan, and now Nelson?

"Well, I was a fair striker of the ball at one time. It's true I won eleven in a row once," Nelson said in a Texas drawl. "But truthfully, a lot of good players were off to war. They were the real heroes, not me. I was just a golfer and a rancher. If I'm proud of anything it would be my beloved Louise. And then the good Lord allowed me a second love, Peggy, after he took Louise to heaven. Love should not be underrated. And one day you will realize even love starts with a healthy fear and awe of the Lord. *'Don't envy sinners, but always continue to fear the Lord.'*[50]

"You boys have a nice day. But before you leave, meet my friend Larry Nelson here. His locker is right between mine and Nicklaus's at the

[48] Proverbs 16:20 "Those who trust the Lord will be joyful."

[49] Proverbs 15:33 "Fear of the Lord teaches wisdom. Humility precedes honor."

[50] Proverbs 23:17

Hall of Fame. We've tried our best to figure out if we might be related, but apparently not," said the old pro with a smile.

"Hello men, just call me Larry," offered the humble soul sitting with a five iron which he now used for a cane. "I come to Hokmah just to soak in Byron's wisdom at least once a year."

Neither Lucas nor ProV recognized the lesser known Nelson, who won three majors in the 1980s.

"Was that really Byron and Larry Nelson?" ProV asked. Hollie answered quietly, "Doesn't matter. You see what you see and you hear what you hear. Listen and learn." ProV kept quiet, except for the talk in his head. *What's with this place? Ben Hogan and Byron Nelson. A range full of pros long gone. Names like Lady Wisdom. This has to be a dream.*

As he walked to the second tee, ProV was still thinking about Byron and his two wives. He also had been married twice, but what a contrast. His were ex-wives, and the memories were not good.

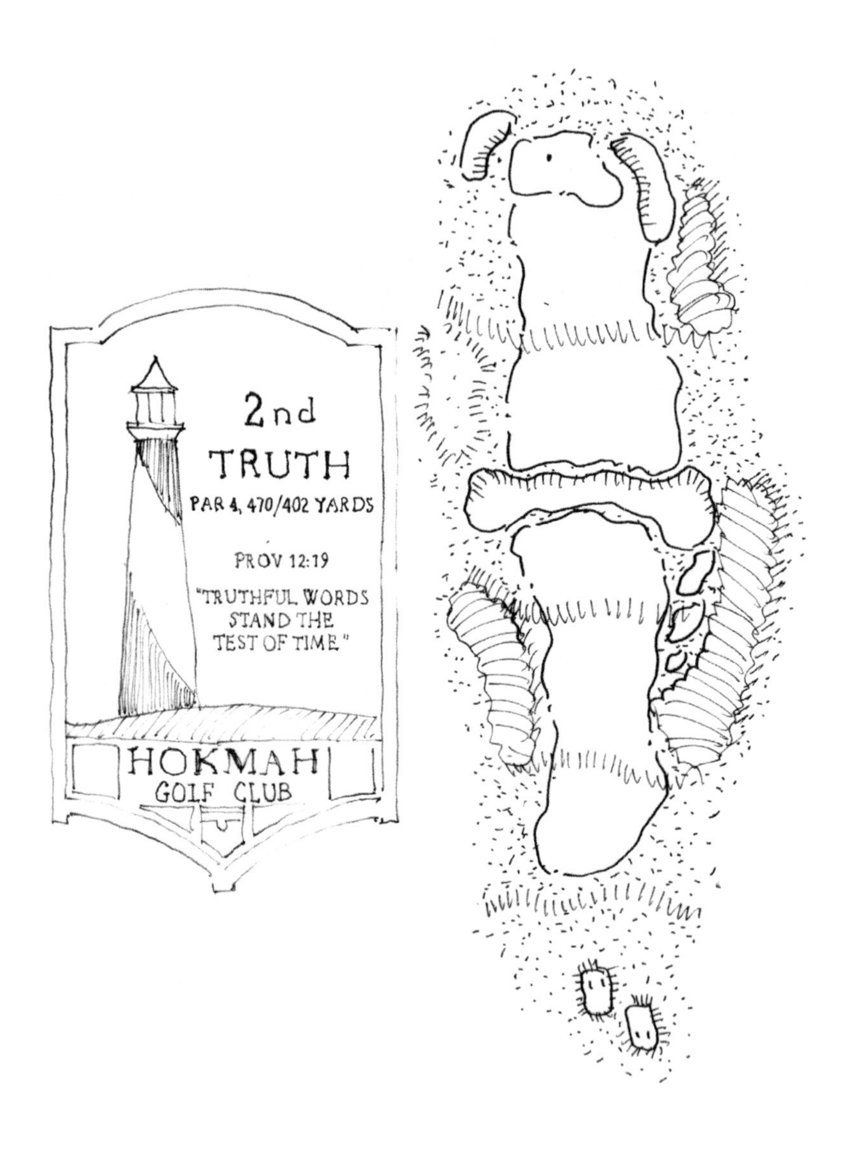
2nd
TRUTH
PAR 4, 470/402 YARDS
PROV 12:19
"TRUTHFUL WORDS
STAND THE
TEST OF TIME"
HOKMAH
GOLF CLUB

2nd Hole – Truth

PAR 4, 470/422 YARDS

"Truthful words stand the test of time."
Proverbs 12:19

"Ok, Hollie, remind me. What do we have here?" said Lucas as they climbed three steps to the second tee. Before she could answer, an odd character appeared from a small shed behind the tee. He was wearing a long black robe and a British wig seen on solicitors and judges in courtrooms all around the United Kingdom.

"Hello, gentlemen, you can call me Bigwig," he said. He explained to the pilgrims he had earned the nickname as a Scottish judge in Inverness, but was now retired, and came to regale Hollie and the Americans with his standard speech on the truth.[51]

Wright said, "Glad to see you again. How's everyone in your world?"

"Thanks, R.W. All is well."

Lucas shook hands with the judge, "My caddie tells me this is your hole."

[51] Proverbs 12:17, "An honest witness tells the truth; a false witness tells lies."

"Well, I have been here a long time. And being in courtrooms for many decades, I do know a lot about truth, and even more about liars," said Bigwig with a knowing grin.

"I have always marveled at your wigs," Lucas said.

"I suppose it seems odd. The term 'bigwig' came from the fact that the higher the judge, the bigger the wig." He smiled.

"For over three decades, every day, I asked people to put up their right hand and asked one question: 'Do you swear to tell the truth, the whole truth and nothing but the truth, so help you God?'" [52]

ProV's only court experience had been his first simple and quickie divorce, but he remembered the uneasy feeling of swearing to tell the truth or else.

Bigwig cleared his throat and began, "We all forget, do we not, that the truth has many levels. There is the raw truth itself, or the correct recitation of the facts. But if you don't tell the *whole* truth, those facts can actually operate as a lie.

"Or some people will tell the truth, but *add* just enough fiction to turn it into a lie." He paused. "Even on a golf course, you need to tell the truth about yourself. For instance, I am a fifteen handicap with a version of the chipping yips. That means I putt a lot from off the green. If I forget my truth, I am in trouble."

ProV nodded understanding. Big Wig continued.

"And of course, the last element is often forgotten, 'so help me God.' If there was no God, would truth even exist? Not really. When we speak it might be smart to remember the Creator of the Universe, including this golf club, is listening and evaluating the truth in us."

Aha, ProV thought, *the Creator is listening and paying attention.*

"So, with that in mind, Lucas," offered Hollie, "let me answer your original question. What we have here is a par four. Long. It's about four hundred and twenty yards from our tee. It helps here to understand the truth about yourself. Not many people can hit it over the cross bunkers in the fairway."

[52] Proverbs 14:25 "A truthful witness saves lives...."

The elevated tee pointed at the North Sea. To the right were gorse bushes and three hidden bunkers Lucas could not reach. And it was tight. A massive cross bunker was the main visual, splitting the fairway at 250 yards. The scorecard said par four but that was pure fiction for most golfers. It was the number one handicap hole. But Hollie stayed positive.

"Lucas, you need to know the hole, but more important, you also need to know yourself." She was already pulling the cover off a three wood. "Lay up with a three wood and then you have a good chance to get near the front of the green with a long iron. ProV, same advice, although you've probably got a five iron into the green if your layup is perfect."

Mocker jumped in, "Come on, guys, you gotta be kidding. This is a long and difficult hole that requires a long tee shot." He remembered Dubs had said his driver was his best club, reached into Deadend's bag for the big stick and asked, "Dubs, how far can you hit it?"

"I hit a drive three hundred yards about a month ago," he said, failing to add it was downhill and downwind, bouncing on desert hardpan.

"OK, then, I like this play. It's a driver for sure, no problem," Mocker said.

Wright, ProV and Lucas laid up. All down the middle, although ProV still had his toe hook working with his three iron.

Now it was time for Dubs. He flushed it. He posed. It was as good as he had, and he knew it. It bounced at about 220 yards and rolled out toward the deep cross bunkers. The last roll creeped into the bunker like a teenager slipping into his room half-drunk after midnight. He now would be faced with escaping from Hell's Bunker, after which the St. Andrews bunker on the fourteenth hole was named.

As they left the tee box, Hollie said, "Is that North Sea not gorgeous? We get rainbows almost every day, and they're all different. Be sure to take time to look up and look around as you play links golf."

ProV did not need to be told. He was mesmerized.

At Lucas's ball, Hollie said, "I know you don't wanna hear this, but the shot should be a hybrid that leaves you just short of the green. You might even be able to putt it from there. Anything more is just asking for trouble."

She answered his frown with, *"An honest answer is like a kiss of friendship."*[53]

Lucas relaxed and took the hybrid.

Sure enough, he flushed it but came up twenty yards short of the green. Hollie handed him a putter before he could even think about it. Only then did she point out bunkers so deep left and right that a coal miner would get lost. But he thought, *I wish I had known I would hit it so solid. I could have gotten there with a three wood.*

Mr. T pulled a five iron out of the bag for ProV, but after seeing the shot by Lucas, ProV reached for his three wood. Ignoring the wise counsel of the caddies, he remembered the three wood he hit in the Masters on the fifteenth hole when he was twenty years old. He could still hear the applause as he walked up the fairway to find his ball within inches of the hole.

But this time, his toe hook had not left him yet, and he landed in the deep left bunker that Mr. T had hinted was there. His first double bogey at Hokmah would sting.

Meanwhile, Wright had also left his ball ten yards short. "Looks like ProV is finding out what the name of this hole is all about," he said to Hollie. "He forgot he's not a college kid anymore."

Hollie had seen it all and knew that was the truth.

Meanwhile, Dubs had arrived at his ball which was last seen off the tee headed to the cross bunker. This hole was so difficult the club provided forecaddies. Working today were Larry Liar and his cousin False Witness, experts on the "nudge of the foot."[54]

The regular forecaddies were always given the weekend off, which meant a two-day Sabbath of Saturday and Sunday. That was good for Ananias and his wife, Sapphira, who were super religious and never missed any services but had a sad reputation for not speaking the truth.[55]

[53] Proverbs 24:26

[54] Proverbs 6:13

[55] Acts 5:1-4 "...You weren't lying to us but to God!"

The forecaddie's job was to not only locate balls hit into trouble, but when possible—often for an expected tip—improve the lie, with either a small toe or a big toss.

Liar had already found Dub's ball in the bunker, lying under the rake on a downslope with nothing ahead but thirty yards of sand and scruffy weeds. Magically, Liar had managed to get both the rake and the ball out of the bunker so it looked like the rake had stopped the ball from going to its sandy grave.

"Good break, sir," said False Witness, whose job had been to tell Liar when the coast was clear to do his magic. "The ball was headed for sure into that bunker when the rake stopped it. You must be a monster. I've never seen anyone long enough to get to this bunker into this breeze. You deserved this break." Mocker slipped the boys a ten-pound note.

But there is a limit to what lying forecaddies can do for a delusional man like Deadend. His topped second shot went back into the bunker and Liar and False Witness just wandered away muttering to themselves how hard it can be to help some people. They had done their best.

Deadend hit multiple six irons from the bunker, until finally one hit the lip and popped out. When he finally arrived at the green, he putted out and said, "Six."

R.W. and Lucas made uneventful fives, while ProV fumed that his legitimate six from the deep sand had been matched by Dubs' pencil six.

Hollie told him, "*The godly hate lies.*[56] Relax, men, '*a false witness will be cut off.*'"[57] ProV was starting to dislike Deadend and showed it. "So, Dubs, what was that?" holding a pencil and scorecard in hand, pretending not to hear when he had mumbled something about a six. Dubs ignored ProV and stopped to talk to a man sitting behind the second green. It was quite a sight. He was now speaking with arms flapping to help him explain something to a man sitting on a throne.

The middle-aged, dark-haired man was dressed like a Roman soldier from AD 30, with a blanket wrapped around him for comfort. Hollie

[56] Proverbs 13:5

[57] Proverbs 21:28

waved to ProV and Lucas to keep moving up the hill to the next tee. When they arrived, they looked back down the hill where Dubs and the soldier were just breaking up their conversation. Dubs had been telling him about his "six." The soldier was listening intently, nearly convinced that indeed it had been a double bogey, even though he well knew the antics of Liar and False Witness. As Dubs walked off, Lucas and ProV could hear the soldier declare loudly, *"What is Truth?"*[58]

"He says he is Pontius Pilate," offered Hollie. "I really don't know. I've stayed away from that man. I suggest you do the same."

ProV could see this was going to be a day like no other.

[58] John 18:38

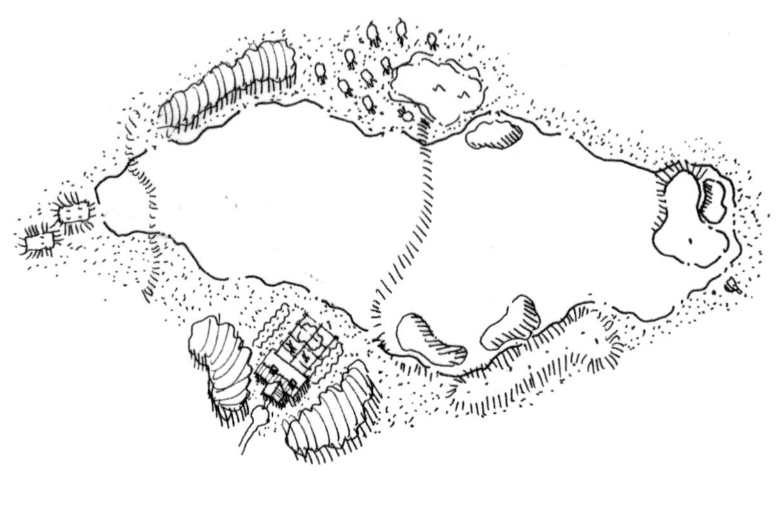

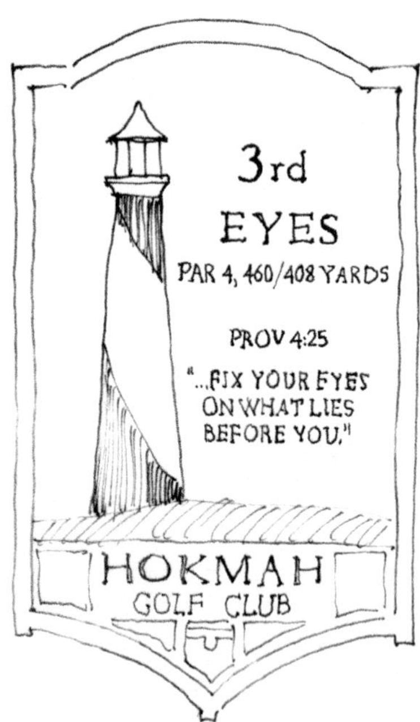
3rd
EYES
PAR 4, 460/408 YARDS
PROV 4:25
"...FIX YOUR EYES
ON WHAT LIES
BEFORE YOU."
HOKMAH
GOLF CLUB

3rd Hole – Eyes

PAR 4, 460/408 YARDS

"Look straight ahead and fix your eyes on what lies before you."
Proverbs 4:25

Playing with Wright was already a special treat. It was like having a second caddie. Just watching him swing was helping Lucas's tempo, and ProV's toe hook had disappeared completely by the third tee, when he hit a perfect high draw down a wide fairway. The wind helping from the right made him comfortable. He had followed Hollie's advice to keep his eyes on the fairway.

Hollie had warned them all approaching the tee, "Look straight ahead, and fix your eyes on what lies before you. Mark a straight path for your feet. Stay on the safe path. Don't get sidetracked." [59]

[59] Proverbs 17:24 "Sensible people keep their eyes glued to wisdom, but a fool's eyes wander to the ends of the earth."

As ProV was picking up his tee, Deadend came stumbling up to the tee box and loudly proclaimed, "Wow, would you look at that!"

Everyone's eyes were drawn immediately to the left rough where a herd of angry looking boars were grazing near a small loch, a very real water hazard. As they stared, the boars seemed to multiply, dozens of them grazing in the mid-day sunshine. Lucas mentioned the demoniac named Legions whose pig story had made him infamous, but ProV had not heard the story and it could wait for another day.[60]

But then Lucas heard Hollie gently whisper, "You ain't seen nothing yet." And to the right, across some white OB markers was a beautiful mansion, complete with a glass covered swimming pool and models who were doing a shoot for an upcoming sports magazine. All of a sudden, the boars were not so interesting to the eyes of the pilgrims.

Hollie got everyone's attention to explain this was a long par four, 460 yards from the back tees. The fairway was as wide as the opening hole at the Old Course at St. Andrews, about eighty yards. But, boars left and swimsuits right. Not to mention deep sandy bunkers left and right as well. Hollie jumped in once again: "Gentlemen, this is one of the major obstacles you will face your whole life. You need to focus on this hole. Take your eyes off the things of this world that will cause you to stumble. Both fear and pleasure will distract you. ProV, look down the fairway. What do you see?"

"Wild beasts and bikinis," said ProV.

"Wrong answer. Your ball will go to what you see. The ball will even go to what you think about. You absolutely must look at the fairway and the fairway only. It's actually a wide fairway down there. But the more you look at the distractions left and right, the narrower the fairway gets."

Mocker was shaking his head in disagreement and Hollie just let him go, knowing she would be wasting her breath to stop him from doing what he did best—mock.[61] "Ridiculous. Nothing wrong with

[60] Mark 5: 1-20

[61] Proverbs 9:7-8 "Anyone who rebukes a mocker will get an insult in return... So don't bother correcting mockers; they will only hate you."

taking in some scenery. This game is about the swing, not the eyes. Never saw anyone hit a ball with his eyes."

Hollie responded, "But I also never saw a blind man who could get to the green without a lot of help."

Mocker grumbled, "Don't listen to this woman. What woman can understand the mind of a man?"

Her response was quick. "Actually, as you well know, I am not saying anything original. I am quoting a man, who said profoundly, *'Death and destruction are never satisfied, and neither are human eyes.'*" [62]

Lucas and ProV focused on the fairway and found it with good enough drives, leading to routine pars.

Wright drove it straight, followed with a six iron on the green and eventually birdied the hole. Hollie said to Lucas, "Watch R.W. If you don't see the hazards, the hole is actually very simple. Fairway. Green. Hole. Thanks very much, and on to the next tee."

Deadend found himself, predictably, OB right, away from the swine and close to the distracting models. As the group putted out, he was nowhere to be found. Mocker came struggling down the hill to the green. "Sorry, men, Dubs said to go on without him. We will catch you later. Please go ahead."

Sitting behind the green was a poorly dressed, humble man with a Labrador sitting quietly by his side. "Bartimaeus[63] is usually here," said Hollie. "He is completely blind but loves to sit and listen to the birds and the seals and otters."

Wright walked over to speak to the blind man. "G'day, Bart. How's your day?"

"Wonderful, R.W. I am taking today off from the clubs, just enjoying nature's beauty. I must get back to work tomorrow. The blind championship for Hokmah is coming up this Friday. I need to get ready."

"And who's your competition this year, Bart?"

[62] Proverbs 27:20 (NIV).

[63] Mark 10:46 "A blind beggar named Bartimaeus (son of Timaeus) was sitting beside the road."

"Well, once again, I'm the favorite." He paused and smiled. "No one else is playing!"

Blind Bartimaeus laughed at his own joke along with everyone else. "You know, I love to come sit behind the third hole, 'Eyes,' because the big advantage I have over you folks is that I can't see all the trouble on this hole. Hollie lines me up and tells me where the fairway is, and I just swing. No negative thoughts. As I told Hollie the first time she caddied for me, 'If there's any trouble out there, I don't wanna know about it, just tell me where to go, not where not to go.'"

"Blessed is the blind man who has '*ears to hear and eyes to see—both are gifts from the Lord,*'" said Wright.[64] "Jesus had actually healed Bart at one time. He could see for several years. In fact, after playing golf without sight for many years, his touch and feel for the game in his hands became amazing. Then, when he could see, the touch was still there and he actually became a really good player. He even made it to the semifinals of the Carnegie Shield once upon a time. It was quite a story when it happened."

Hollie nodded and said, "But the blindness returned. And this time, he refused to ask for healing. He had discovered a peace in blindness that was not there with full eyesight. Quite a story."

Bartimaeus offered a final word: "Jesus had *mercy on me*.[65] That's all I needed."

ProV was listening. And learning. He was developing "ears to hear." Now he needed eyes to see.

[64] Proverbs 20:12

[65] Mark 10:47

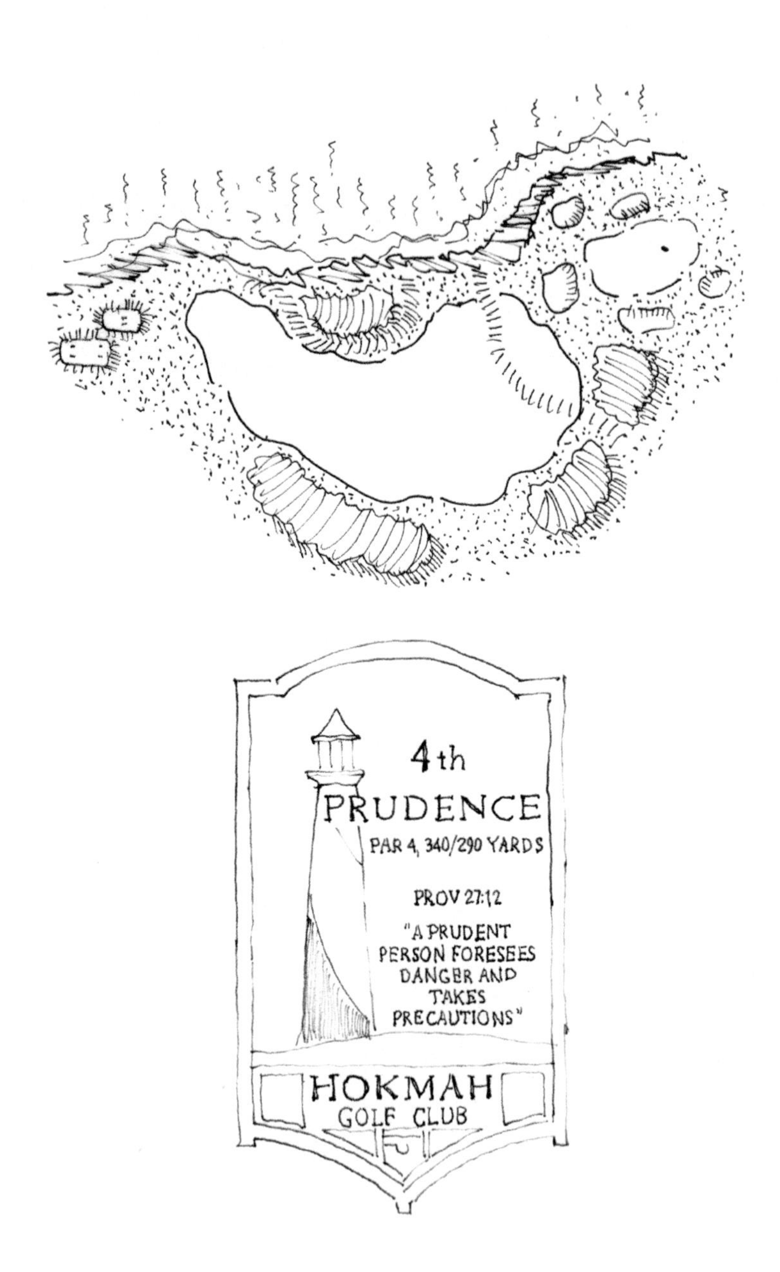
4th
PRUDENCE
PAR 4, 340/290 YARDS
PROV 27:12
"A PRUDENT PERSON FORESEES DANGER AND TAKES PRECAUTIONS"
HOKMAH
GOLF CLUB

4th Hole – Prudence

PAR 4, 340/290 YARDS

"A prudent person foresees danger and takes precautions"
Proverbs 27:12

As the small covey of golfers and caddies walked to the fourth tee, back toward the sea, one of Scotland's purest moments happened. A cloud had come out of nowhere to create a three-minute shower. As soon as it came, it went. And then, as if on cue, a rainbow. And not just any rainbow. A double rainbow from earth to earth. ProV had missed more than one rainbow at Dornoch during the Carnegie Shield, thanks to self-absorption with his golf game and bogeys. Now his eyes were alive to God's creation.

The fourth was a drivable par four for bold golfers, just 290 yards from the member tees. But trouble lurked everywhere in the form of bunkers, plus the prickly and beautiful yellow weeds known as gorse or whins. The left dogleg had nasty bunkers on the right side, plus the rocky beach on the left. Seals and otters waited for lost balls. Thieving seagulls were often seen snatching nice white golf balls from the green.

The postage stamp green at Royal Troon was modeled after the fourth at Hokmah. Only a fool would go for this green from the tee.

The hole was so full of trouble, the club had a full-time forecaddie on the hole. Dewey Diligence came in each day from his home on the Isle of Forethought.

"Prudence[66] is required on a golf course, and this is the perfect example. Four or even five iron down the fairway, wedge on the green, move along," said Hollie. "Pars and birdies when you do this prudently."

Wright laid up with a hybrid. Lucas followed suit, both in the middle of the fairway.

ProV was next and overheard Wright whispering about the time he had seen a one on this hole. ProV knew the excitement of "going for it." His hero as a kid had been Roy McEvoy in *Tin Cup* who always went for it, no matter what.

The adrenaline rush was like a kid stealing candy from a grocery store. He could not resist the temptation; he ignored Mr. T's offering of a five iron, and pulled a head cover off the driver. He had already forgotten what happened on "Truth" just a few minutes ago.

Hollie came closer and gently warned: *"Wise people think before they act."*[67] She was kind in her tone but relentless.

And reluctantly, ProV listened, put the driver back, accepted the offered modern version of a mashie and split the fairway.

"A prudent man," Hollie nodded as the ball was in the air.

As the group approached their balls in the fairway, they heard a loud yell from the tee. "Fore!!" screamed Mocker. Deadend's stopover on Eyes had not been as exciting as he hoped, so he had rushed to the fourth tee, driver in hand, ready to go for the green on the short par four. His drop kick drive got lucky and went straight, which meant his ball landed near ProV's five iron. This made Dewey Diligence smile. The sight of four balls in the fairway was a rarity.

"The good Lord keeps His eye on fools sometimes, protecting them from themselves," said Wright.

[66] Proverbs 14:18 "The prudent are crowned with knowledge."

[67] Proverbs 13:16

The pin was tucked in a far back left position which Hollie suggested they ignore: "Center of the green. Don't even look at that flag. It's a sucker pin."

Lucas and ProV both hit the center of the green from 100 yards, thirty feet from the pin, while Wright was able to get a little closer.

Dubs, however, was going for the stick. His best shot of the day—"perfect," he called it—finished long in the deepest bunker on the course. He would have never found his ball if not for Dewey Diligence watching it plug into the face of the sandy abyss. "Lucifer's Cave" had been named after the evil one himself on a visit in the beginning, many years ago. Dubs took four stabs to escape, complaining that not only did the ball plug but he had also been in a footprint, failing to mention it was his own. As Dubs was completing another epic meltdown, Hollie whispered in ProV's ear, *"The prudent see danger and take refuge, but the simple keep going and pay the penalty."* [68]

She then pointed to Wright, who had quietly two-putted for a routine par. "Notice your friend here. He is keeping mostly quiet."

Wright said, "I know 'going for it' is exciting stuff. But one of the most satisfying moments in golf is knowing you have been prudent. Fairway, green, nice putt and a tap in. You walk off the green feeling pretty good about yourself."

ProV knew they were right. Again.

"A person without self-control is like a city with broken-down walls," [69] said Hollie as they watched Dubs argue with Mocker.

Lucas was reminded that the word "prudent" comes up often in his world of Wall Street and financial advisers. "The Prudent Investor rule requires a fiduciary to invest trust assets as if they were his own," he said.

Hollie nodded and said, "You need to pretend your golf ball is valuable. Pretend it is worth ten thousand dollars. It would make you think twice about what chances you'd take."

"Or what if the rules of golf required that you play with only one ball. What if a lost ball was a disqualification," offered Wright.

[68] Proverbs 22:3 (NIV)

[69] Proverbs 25:28

ProV laughed. "There'd be a lot of seven irons off the tees." Then he asked, "So, prudence. I have never used the word. It means laying up all day?"

Wright replied, "No. Sometimes you need to go for it. But for me, it is just the ability to govern yourself by the use of reason—caution or circumspection as to danger or risk." He pointed to an older man sitting quietly with four dogs reading a book overlooking the sea.

"See that man? He is the famous theologian Thomas Aquinas. No one knows it but he is a twelve handicap. He spends the month of August at Hokmah, recharging his energy. Wonderful man to listen to over a meal. He says he loves this hole for the views but also because the hole is a teacher. The hole is 'pedagogical,' he calls it."

Lucas and ProV were both ignorant of such a large word.

"You may have heard of his four cardinal virtues. Prudence, temperance, courage and justice. Notice first on the list was prudence. We need to keep moving but let's stop for just a moment to chat with him."

Wright enjoyed introducing the famous moral philosopher to his new friends. Four dogs were mostly napping at the feet of their master Thomas.

Lucas did what everyone wanted to do, pet the dogs and ask their names.

"Oh, this is Prudence, Temperance, Courage and Justice. My four best friends and my cardinal virtues!" he said with a friendly chuckle.

R.W. dove right into the subject. "I know you'd rather talk on the subject for eight hours, but can you help us in eight seconds? What is prudence and why is it important?"

"My best definition is 'wisdom concerning human affairs, or right reason with respect to action.'[70] Many golfers think it means always laying up, being cautious, never going for it. Not at all. But it does mean using common sense on when to go for it."

Thomas finished with, "The world is full of people with no prudence," nodding toward Dubs who had moved on without stopping to soak in

[70] Shawn Floyd, "*Thomas Aquinas: Moral Philosophy*", Internet Encyclopedia of Philosophy 2005, https://iep.edu/aq-moral/.

wisdom from the older man. "They are usually loners, making decisions without wise counsel." He looked at ProV and said, "You, sir, seem to have some good friends here to help you make this one of your virtues," nodding toward Lucas and the caddies.

"Very true, sir. Thanks for your time," said an enlightened ProV, as they marched off to the next hole.

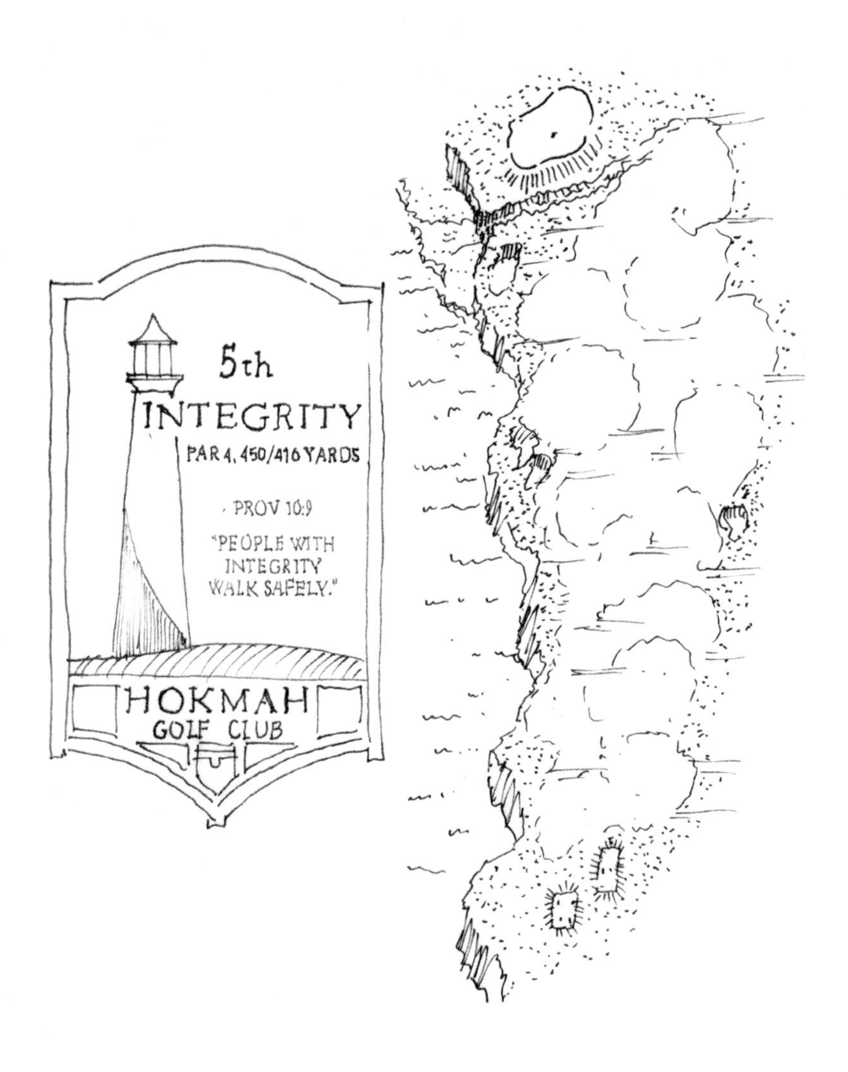
5th
INTEGRITY
PAR 4, 450/416 YARDS
PROV 10:9
"PEOPLE WITH
INTEGRITY
WALK SAFELY."
HOKMAH
GOLF CLUB

5th Hole – Integrity

PAR 4, 450/416 YARDS

"People with integrity walk safely."

Proverbs 10:9

The fifth tee was set in a deep and darkish valley near the sea. Huge dunes separated the waves below from the tee box. As ProV walked the path to the tee the light was disappearing, as if it was dusk in the middle of the day, or a partial eclipse of the sun. He and Lucas arrived at the tee just in time to see Barnabas hand R.W. a driver.

"This is the most difficult hole on the course, although one would never know it by the scorecards turned in," said Hollie as she likewise handed Lucas his driver. "We call this hole Integrity." [71]

Lucas had worked enough on Wall Street to understand. Hollie continued, "It is an honesty which goes way deeper than just telling the truth. It runs deeper than appearances, goes to the heart of who a person is in private. Honesty is just the beginning." [72]

[71] Proverbs 2:7 "He is a shield to those who walk with integrity."

[72] Proverbs 20:7 "The godly walk with integrity."

The hole had troubles all around: bunkers and gorse and whins, not to mention the "wee burn" fronting the green. It was only eighteen inches across, but a steep slope at the front edge of the green sent mishit or spinning balls into the water fifteen yards below the elevated green.

Hollie explained why the hole was so hard. "You should not play this hole without your best man stepping forward. The hole is hard for a lot of reasons, the most obvious one being no one can see you play this hole. Your score is completely based on your integrity. I will not be with you. It is a long par four, downhill all the way to the burn which fronts the green, through this Valley of the Shadow of Death. You must carry your own clubs on this one hole. I will meet you on the green after you've holed out. Be sure to putt out. No gimmes."

She saw the anxious look on ProV's face and reassured him, "Don't worry. You'll know what to do when it's your turn to hit."

Off she went. Mr. T and Barnabas followed, leaving the entire group to carry their own clubs and play alone. Deadend insisted, however, on keeping Mocker by his side and was already on the tee, taking honors away from Wright's routine par on the previous hole.

Sure enough, each player who stepped to the tee found himself all alone. No one saw Deadend top his ball into the gorse in front of the tee, or Mocker put another ball on the tee and say, "Hit another one, sir. No one saw that." His next ball was thankfully airborne.

No one saw Wright's perfect drive down the left side of the fairway, funneling to the bottom of a steep hill into an old divot.

No one saw Lucas hit a weak fade that trickled into a right bunker and a footprint.

No one saw ProV boom his best drive of the trip, well over 300 yards, so far that it covered a small hump in the fairway which hid the final bounce dead left into a hidden hellish bunker.

Fifteen minutes later, after each man had holed out, it was if the lights had come back on. The mist had lifted. The clouds had been so thick and dark that Moses could have been coming down off the mountain with the Ten Commandments. They were all shaking their heads over the somewhat frightening experience. Each had a story to tell.

This was always fun for Hollie and the caddies, listening to the wild stories of how players dealt with Integrity. The Creator set this hole up to test everyone.

Mocker reported that Deadend made his first par of the day. Two drives, three to escape a bunker, one penalty shot in the burn, plus a three-foot putt which became a two-foot putt after marking the ball creatively—all added up to a "four." Mocker didn't even blink.

Wright not only hit out of a divot, but carelessly addressed the ball and caused it to move from a horrible lie into an even worse one. But that was a stroke. What should have been his second shot was now his third, and by the time he holed out he scored a sad but honorable triple bogey. He counted them all.

Lucas also survived the integrity test, taking his medicine in the bunker footprints and relieved to hole an eight-foot putt for a five.

ProV had not done so well. He always prided himself on playing a game of integrity, where players are their own referees and call penalties on themselves. He grew up watching *The Legend of Bagger Vance* and loved the final scene when Junah Randolph calls the penalty on himself while trying to beat Bobby Jones and Walter Hagen.

ProV loved to be seen by others as a really "good guy" who played by the rules.

But the real ProV was not averse to a small cheat. Especially when he clearly was the victim of a bad break. In this case, as he followed his perfect drive down the middle of the fairway, he was already planning a nine iron or pitching wedge for a short second shot to the green.

When he did not see his ball in the fairway, his heart began to race. He felt the temptation to cheat even before he knew he might need to. He searched for a full five minutes, desperate to locate the ball which had mysteriously disappeared. Finally, twenty yards to his left was a hidden bunker that had gobbled up his ball like a hungry dog. It was under a rake in the bottom of the bunker. He cursed. And not under his breath. No one was around, so why not. He used some old words he thought he had conquered.

As he carefully removed the rake, the ball changed position. Was this a penalty or not? He wasn't sure, but who cares. No one is watching. He wedged out sideways. A smart shot, he thought. His next shot was a perfect nine iron, or a "niblick," as Hollie would call it. It came up four inches short of the green, and slowly rolled backward, finding the wee burn in slow motion like a dramatic fumble in "slow motion" replay in a football game.

After his perfect drive and his perfect nine iron, he was at least four in the middle of what Americans call a creek. With another two-stroke penalty for not replacing his ball in the bunker, the four was now a six. Or was it an eight since he took five minutes to find the ball? Or what does happen when you play a ball which should have been declared lost? His head was spinning.

He took his drop back on the line of entry, pitched on the green fifty feet too long, and after three sloppy putts had no idea what he made. As his ball dropped into the hole, Lucas appeared from the mist and asked, "So, how'd you do?"

ProV shook his head, speechless.

"I get it," echoed Lucas, having no idea what a nightmare ProV had just experienced. "But I need a number." He had the scorecard out and pencil in hand, waiting.

"Just give me a six," mumbled ProV, conveniently forgetting his three putts. It was at least a nine, maybe eleven or twelve. ProV was now operating on the same level as Deadend.

With no one to watch or keep him honest, he found himself just as short on integrity as Dubs, maybe the creepiest guy he'd ever met. And worst of all, no one knew how dishonest he had been except himself.

He had now met the biggest cheater he had ever known—the man in the mirror that he never wanted to be.

Behind the green was a bespectacled young man, seen chatting with a foursome who had stopped to talk. The group apparently had been in front of Lucas and the boys, unseen until now. They were now waving the pilgrims to play through. The foursome had decided to stop and chat with this unfamiliar figure.

"That's Bob Dickson," said Hollie. "Great guy. He won both the US Amateur and the British Amateur in the same year, 1967. Not easy to do."

Lucas wanted to hear more. "So, what's he doing sitting behind a hole named Integrity?"

"In 1965 he was leading the US Amateur in his hometown at Southern Hills Country Club in Tulsa, Oklahoma. It was medal play then. During the third round, he looked in his bag on the second fairway and found a fifteenth club. No one needed to know the mistake, but he immediately called a penalty on himself, four shots, and lost the tournament by one. It was not even his club. Someone had put it there by accident."

ProV knew he could never have done that. He would have kept a towel over the club, hoping no one saw it. *What a stupid rule,* he thought. *If you never hit the extra club and if it was not intentional, what's the harm?*

The foursome speaking to Dickson included an older man with a beard like old Tom Morris, dressed in pitiful clothes, certainly not appropriate for a golf course. And the other three were dressed in the finest and latest Nike wear, looking like tour players. ProV once again looked to Hollie as they walked toward the sixth tee. "So, Hollie, who were those other guys? I hadn't even seen them in front of us."

"That group teed off an hour in front of us. The older man is actually Job,[73] known throughout the history of the world as 'a man of integrity and upright.' If we have time, I can tell you quite a story about him later. I caddied for him many years ago when he was the greatest golfer in the universe."

Wright knew the story. "Satan himself got permission from God to take away everything Job owned. He was living proof that being rich and upright is possible, an unthinkable thought for most people who presume all rich people are unrighteous crooks. Ol' Job had it all. Then, even when he lost it all, he never lost his integrity."

"So who are the other three guys?" asked ProV.

[73] Job 1:1 "Job was blameless—a man of complete integrity."

"Oh, those are Job's three friends. Eliphaz, Bildad and Zophar. With friends like them, who needs enemies? I see them a lot here hanging around the range, telling everybody what they are doing wrong. I heard them all telling one poor guy early this morning, 'With a swing like that, you really should quit.' They all have nicknames. Eli, BD, and Mr. Z, we call 'em. They love to hang around Job because his problems seem bigger than theirs. Job should have told them to leave long ago but he is too nice a guy."

Lucas and ProV seemed interested in chatting with Dickson but he was busy with the other group, who turned and waved to Hollie to play through. She led the pilgrims toward a path where a bright light was shining toward the next tee. As they walked on, a somber sense of regret emerged in ProV's spirit. He wasn't sure what the test of the fifth hole had been about. All he knew was he had failed it.

6th
PATIENCE
PAR 3, 240/204 YARDS
PROV 16:32
"BETTER TO BE
PATIENT THAN
POWERFUL"
HOKMAH
GOLF CLUB

6th Hole – Patience

PAR 3, 240/204 YARDS

"Better to be patient than powerful."
Proverbs 16:32

Hollie and Mr. T were waiting on the sixth tee. They could tell by his slumped shoulders and hanging head that ProV had not passed the integrity test.

"Okay, time to forget the last hole," Hollie said. "It's over. So now we need patience to get back on track. This is a long par three. Hit to the front edge of this huge flat green with whatever club will carry one-eighty to one-ninety and bounce on, then hope for two putts, take your par and move on. The troubles here are left and right, pin high and long. Stay short and patient[74] and you'll be fine." She handed a four hybrid to Lucas, who waited now since Dubs had claimed the honors after his 'par' on the last hole.

Mr. T presented a six iron to ProV like a waiter with a bottle of fine wine. But ProV shook his head. Laying up on a par three was against

[74] Proverbs 20:22 "Wait for the Lord to handle this matter."

every bone in his body. He stood quietly, waiting to hit last, the only spot he was comfortable with after his meltdown on the fifth.

Deadend said, "Mocker, whaddya think?"

Mocker whispered, "Sir, that woman has lost her mind. This green is huge. Last year someone had a hole-in-one here. Just take your three wood, even driver if you think you need it, and go for it. Put a nice smooth swing on it."

Dubs pulled the cover off his driver. "This is no time to sit back. Never up, never in."

Dubs offered up his version of a smooth swing—with a jerky, decelerating follow-through. His ball sailed right, into a wee pond Mocker had forgotten. Hollie had not mentioned it either, knowing to stay positive. "Saul's Pond" had grabbed many a wayward or careless ball over the years.

Lucas took Hollie's advice and laid up nicely—not easy to do on a par three, but he was learning. ProV, however, was having a hard time, still reeling from seeing his thorny soul in the mirror on Integrity. He reached into his bag and grabbed a three iron. He was still fuming and thought, *I am not laying up with a six iron on a par three with a big ol' green.*

But this time he got lucky. His quick swing resulted in a chunk with top spin that hit way short but rolled and rolled and rolled until it stopped on the green, twenty feet left, pin high. "The Lord is so good to fools on occasion," whispered Hollie to no one in particular.

Wright hit to the front edge and managed to two-putt with a lag to eight inches, while Lucas made a four, hitting his first putt too hard. Lucas was smiling though after the three-putt, knowing that perhaps the most difficult part of links golf was two-putting from long distance.

ProV's putt fell in a side door, proving God was not against him just because he was a cheater. His birdie was pure art, as is every two on a scorecard.

Dubs, meanwhile, was busy looking for his ball in the Widow's Pond, sure he would find it with the help of the forecaddie Persistent

Widow.[75] She told him exactly where it had rolled in. "I hate to lose a ball," said Dubs, who had enough money to buy the club but was now worried about losing a five-dollar golf ball.

Persistent Widow was quite a lady. As they walked off the green, Hollie explained she was the same woman who got her petitions answered, but only after patient and persistent pleas to an unrighteous judge. "Patience and persistence are valuable virtues," said Hollie.

Gathered behind the green under a large shed was a large group of adults and children who appeared to be having a family reunion of some sort. Strolling slowly from the shed was an older gentleman, probably in his eighties, who some might call pudgy or plump. He sure didn't look like a champion golfer. He was smiling and said to ProV, "Nice putt, young man. Wonderful two!"

"Thank you, sir. I didn't know anyone was watching."

Wright jumped in to introduce the pilgrims to Billy Casper. ProV had never heard of him. Lucas only remembered from the history books that Casper overcame a seven shot deficit to win a US Open from Arnold Palmer in the '60s.

"Guys, Billy loves this Patience hole because it symbolizes the way he played his golf. He won fifty-one PGA Tour events, five Vardon Trophys, two US Opens and the 1970 Masters, all while being considered too short off the tee. How did he do it? Patience. He beat people like Nicklaus and Palmer quite often, using clever course management skills and patience. In fact, the 'Big Three' of Palmer, Nicklaus and Player should have been the 'Big Four' if you went strictly by the record book."

Billy loved the compliments. "Oh, my friend R.W. here is very kind, but the point is simple. In golf, you have to let the game come to you. No way to force anything. Even when I made up all those shots on Arnie on the back nine at the Olympic Club, I didn't push the panic button. I patiently waited for the breaks to go my way."

ProV was curious now. "So, Mr. Casper, how did you get this patience?"

[75] Luke 18:1-8

"Well for one thing, see the bunch over there around the shed? That's my family. I had eleven children and seventy-one grandchildren," he said with a shake of the head. "God taught me patience through some tough days with them."

Wright jumped back into the conversation. "Men, we need to be moving along, but one final point. You may remember Zach Johnson. He was here recently and told me the whole story of how he won the Masters in 2007 and the Open at St. Andrews in 2015." Lucas nodded, knowing the story himself from his history books.

"He played the Old Course with such patience the locals marveled that he must have been born in Scotland. He understood you cannot push the Old Lady around. You have to be patient with her."

Billy added, "Golf has a mind of its own. You cannot force anything to happen. Just one shot at a time with the exception that it is okay to think about your *next* shot, such as where do you want to play from. And be willing to wait. But don't wait for bad things to happen. Stay positive and wait for good things to happen. For the putts to fall. For the wind to be at your back. A layup is not surrender. It is more like a punt in American football. Be patient and expect the good breaks."

"Zach laid up on every par five in his Masters win," said R.W., "even though he had the firepower to get there in two with a wood."

ProV had never had this virtue. He had never liked to wait for anything in life. He quit school early. His first divorce was a lack of patience. He couldn't wait for change, in either Mary Ann or himself. The marriage counselor they saw told him it would take a whole year to work through the issues. He didn't have patience for that.

Billy left them with one last word, "ProV, great to meet you. I know you're here looking for wisdom. Looks to me like the birdie you just made on this Patience hole is a sign from heaven. You're in the right place!" [76]

[76] Psalms 27:14 "Wait patiently for the Lord. Be brave and courageous. Yes, wait patiently for the Lord."

As the golfing pilgrims marched on toward the next tee, Dubs was still grumbling and looking around the edge of Saul's Pond. He had no patience to stop and talk to another old guy he had never heard of. "Let's go," said Hollie. "We can't wait on Deadend. He will find us later."

7th
TEMPER
PAR 5, 590/510 YARDS
PROV 17:27b
"A PERSON WITH UNDERSTANDING IS EVEN TEMPERED."
HOKMAH
GOLF CLUB

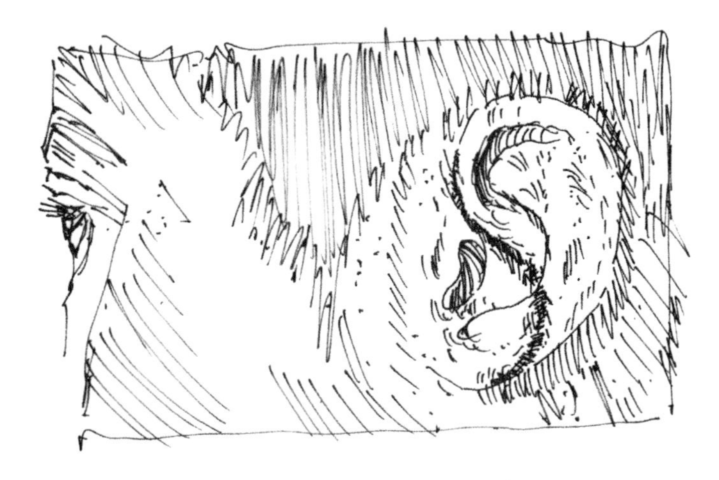

7th Hole – Temper

PAR 5 590/510 YARDS

"A person with understanding is even tempered."
Proverbs 17:27b

Hollie was full of advice as the foursome came up to what seemed to be a beautiful and playable par five with little trouble—not counting the North Sea on the left. "The main obstacle here is yourself," she said.

ProV's birdie two had cleared his head after the disaster of his fictional "six" on Integrity. "Hollie, my obstacle has always been me," he said shaking his head and recovering his sanity.

"Then this hole will be quite the challenge," said Hollie.

Lucas and Wright chatted amiably as they walked slowly to the tee through gorse bushes turned yellow as in the Orkney spring, even though it was the middle of August. They had really hit it off, two peas in a pod who were further along in their spiritual journey than ProV or Deadend. Three-putts and bogeys seemed to be acceptable. Contentment was a good word to describe them both.

The seventh hole was one of the most stunning holes in the world. It was played eighty yards above the sea, near crags occupied only by the sea birds. Puffins nested on the cliffs below. "Watching birds fly *below* you is one of God's most awesome sights," observed Hollie as she was describing the hole to the players. The hole itself was straight and easy to reach in two when downwind. The fairway was so wide it would take a horrible shot to end up in the ocean with the seals and otters. Deep bunkers on the hole were the only thing to avoid. No obstacles were hidden.

Looking out across the sea, Hollie pointed out the largest lighthouse in Orkney on the neighboring island. It was the model for the club's logo. The only person on that island was a lighthouse keeper whose ship had ignored the lights and wrecked there decades ago. He decided to stay as the keeper of the lights.[77] He was known as "John the Beloved," named after the apostle, although no one knew his real name. Legend said he never slept, watching all night for wayward ships. No one had ever actually seen him.

Hollie loved to tell John's story but sadly, many golfers paid no attention, too mired in self-doubt and anger because they had not brought their best game to Hokmah. They looked inward at the demons of golf, and upward, cursing God Himself under their breath for all the bad breaks on the first six holes. Tempers often flared by this seventh tee.[78]

"Six holes is actually an interesting spot in a round of golf," said Hollie. "The golfer's dream of a memorable scorecard is usually gone. Scratch golfers may already be six over. Professional golfers may be over par, still looking for their first birdie. High handicappers have already used almost all of their strokes."

Wright added, "Yes, when the fact sets in that this round has been and will be a disappointment, anger emerges from the depths of false expectations."

Deadend was stuck on his temper tantrum from the lost ball on the last hole and heard nothing of Hollie's wisdom.[79]

[77] 1 John 1:5b "God is light and there is no darkness in him at all."

[78] Proverbs 19:11 "Sensible people control their temper; they earn respect by overlooking wrongs."

[79] Proverbs 12:16 "A fool is quick tempered, but a wise person stays calm when insulted."

The group was being held up by a tall bearded solo player in the right rough.

"Where'd this guy come from?" shouted Deadend to Mocker.

"No idea, sir. He must be lost. And I don't recognize his caddie either."

Hollie said, "This guy is almost always here. He plays the first few holes and everything seems fine, then he gets to the seventh hole and his temper gets the best of him and he takes an hour just to finish the hole. I've seen him hit balls into the ocean until he runs out of balls."

Mocker shook his head. "And this fool has a name?"

"He insists we call him King. His real name is Saul. Not sure if that's his first or last name. The pond on six is named after him, when he nearly drowned there one day," said Hollie. "And one of his problems is he takes out the same caddie every day, an angry fellow named Cain.[80] These guys are a bad combination. Fights.[81] Always in trouble. Mostly just foolish stuff." [82]

While waiting on the King, Hollie explained the hole. "Some might call this our signature hole. Four bunkers protect the right side off the tee, nothing but rocks and ocean and seals below the left rough. The good news is the wind is usually off the sea, keeping balls on the golf course. Your best option is to aim out over the North Sea and let the wind bring it back."

R.W. and Lucas did as they were told and landed safely on the fairway. ProV gave in to fear and pushed his ball into the right rough, lucky to miss the bunkers and not too bad, since Mr. T signaled "safe."

Deadend was last to hit. The wind gusted as he swung and carried his ball into the first bunker guarding the right rough. The forecaddie was pointing to the ball when they arrived, simply stating, "That's a decent lie for this bunker."

Mocker handed his man a wedge to get out, but he shanked it dead right into the angry gorse. As he reached into the bush to grab his ball,

[80] Genesis 4:5,8 "This made Cain very angry..."

[81] Proverbs 15:18 "A hot-tempered person starts fights."

[82] Proverbs 14:17 "Short-tempered people do foolish things."

thorns cut his wrist and fingers, and then ripped his new cashmere sweater. He broke his wedge over his knee and threw it into the whins.

Mocker dropped a ball in the fairway and handed him a three wood, hoping it would survive the tantrum.

He topped the three wood which also took a ride through the air, luckily down the fairway this time. *He finally hit a fairway*, thought Mocker, not wanting to get fired just yet.

ProV started to actually feel compassion for Deadend and said, "I think I better go try to calm Dubs down. Poor guy has lost it."

Wright made it plain, "Stay away. *Don't befriend angry people or associate with hot-tempered people.*" [83]

Hollie agreed: *"Hot-tempered people must pay the penalty. If you rescue them once, you will have to do it again."* [84]

So ProV left Dubs in the hands of his only friend and his worst enemy, himself.

The experienced forecaddie was a balding middle-aged man. He had located ProV's ball in the right rough and pretended to look for Deadend's shank as he stomped through the abyss of gorse for a full three minutes before declaring the ball lost. Deadend cursed the poor chap for not finding his ball.

"Right here, sir," the forecaddie said as ProV approached his ball in three inches of rough. He smiled and sang, "I once was lost but now am found." His own joke made him laugh out loud.

"Thank you, man," ProV said. "And who exactly are you?"

"Well, I am just a man who loves the sea. Simon's my name. They gave me this assignment because of my affinity for the sea and my temper. At one time my hot temper got the best of me. I thought righteous anger was a good thing until I cut off an ear and realized my temper was about to ruin me."

ProV wasn't sure what to make of that introduction.

"You boys have a good day," Simon said. "Stay calm."

[83] Proverbs 22:24

[84] Proverbs 19:19

The hole ended with a glorious birdie by Lucas when he holed a chip from just short of the green. Wright seemed happy with his bogey after missing a short putt.

ProV was satisfied when he wedged out, then hit a three wood third shot onto the green and two-putted for a surprising par.

Deadend had not even attempted to finish the hole after his sixth shot on the hole ended in the ocean, scattering puffins along the way. He was so angry that Lucas worried his head would explode.[85]

Simon and Hollie chatted as they walked calmly up toward the green, chatting like the old friends they were. Behind the green sat another soldier, who stood and hugged Simon like a long-lost friend. Meanwhile, Dubs was headed toward the next tee when Simon stopped him.

"Mr. Deadend, sir," Simon said, waving him over toward the soldier. "May I introduce my friend Malchus."

"Pleasure to meet you, sir," Malchus said, extending his hand to the red-faced, furious Dubs. "I hope you have enough clubs to finish." Everyone laughed but Deadend.

"You see, I am here as living proof that a hot temper does you no good. Simon, who appears to be so calm and cool, was once so ill-tempered he took a machete and cut off my ear," turning his head to show a small scar. "And now we are best of friends."

Deadend took a closer look at Malchus. "You must have had a good surgeon."

Malchus and Simon smiled at each other, then looked into Hollie's eyes. Malchus said, "Indeed, the best. The very best." [86]

Hollie explained the story of Simon and Malchus to ProV as they marched to the next tee. ProV was "all ears."

[85] Proverbs 29:22 "An angry person starts fights–a hot-tempered person commits all kinds of sins."

[86] John 18:10 "Then Peter drew a sword and slashed off the right ear of Malchus, the high priest's slave."

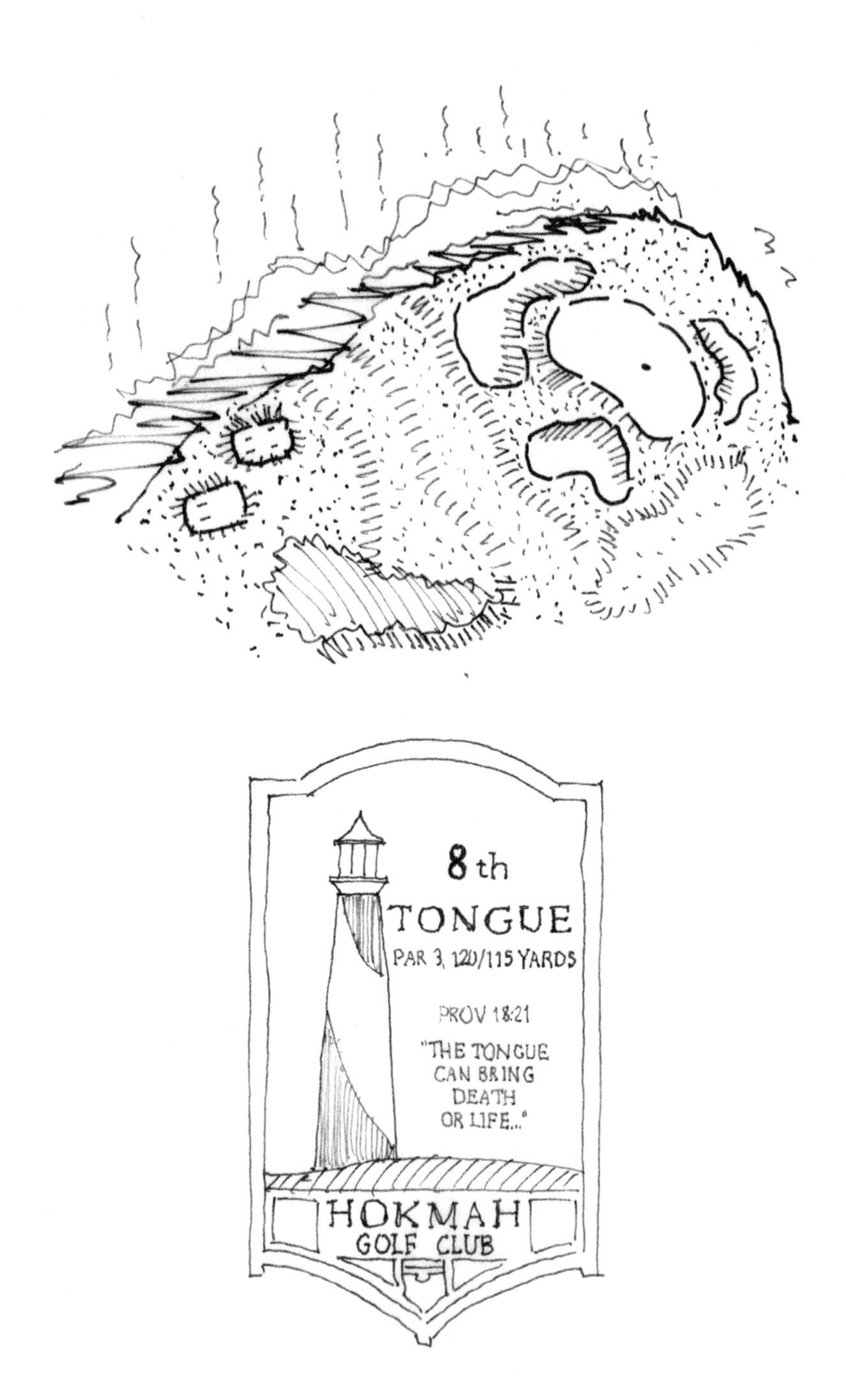
8th
TONGUE
PAR 3, 120/115 YARDS
PROV 18:21
"THE TONGUE
CAN BRING
DEATH
OR LIFE..."
HOKMAH
GOLF CLUB

8th Hole – Tongue

PAR 3, 120/115 YARDS

"The tongue can bring death or life..."
Proverbs 18:21

A couple was waiting on the eighth tee to greet them: Larry Loudmouth from Loose Tongue, a small village on an island nearby, and his girlfriend Gabby Gossip.[87]

Loudmouth loved to talk with Gabby or anyone who came through his path.[88] His favorite subject was himself. His mouth never stopped with name dropping, criticisms, bragging and the latest gossip around the club, usually preceded by, "Don't tell anyone but..."

Whenever Larry took a breath, Gabby jumped in to tell anyone who would listen all about their baby, little one-year-old Rumors.[89]

Deadend felt like he had finally met a friend, and found great comfort in the scathing remarks by Loudmouth. He nodded assent and "amen" with Larry's assessment that "anyone who thinks this is the greatest golf course in the world needs their head examined."

This shortest hole on the course was perched at the end of a small

[87] Proverbs 11:13 "A gossip goes around telling secrets."

[88] Proverbs 17:4 "Wrongdoers eagerly listen to gossip."

[89] Proverbs 18:8 "Rumors are dainty morsels that sink deep into one's heart."

peninsula. It looked a lot like the much photographed seventh hole at Pebble Beach.

Hollie gave some interesting golf history about the tiny hole to the two Californians. "Few people would know that Douglas Grant, the co-designer with Jack Neville of the Pebble Beach links in 1920, visited Hokmah in 1910 while living in England. I caddied for him one fine day. He was a really good player. Douglas left for California when World War One broke out in 1916, winning the California State Amateur in1918, all of which led to his invitation to help design an epic course around the Monterey Peninsula." Lucas and ProV were genuinely interested in this connection between the holy ground of Hokmah and their native California.

R.W. politely asked Loudmouth to be quiet for a moment as he offered sound advice from the tee box.[90] "This is the smallest hole imaginable on a championship golf course. It's downhill to a green that will not receive anything but a perfect shot. The wind keeps the green firm and fast."

ProV was listening.

"The wind is usually a crosswind from the left, like today, the worst possible scenario for a downhill wedge shot. It is impossible to keep it under the wind because you are already up on the elevated tee. Two front left pot bunkers are the best of several bad options. Right goes down a steep hill with an impossible pitch and the grass just long enough to eliminate putting up the bank. Long is in the ocean or rocks. Short is safe, but how do you justify laying up on such a short hole? This might be the hardest approach shot on the course."

Hollie added, "Just like your tongue, this hole is small but causes all sorts of problems."

ProV hit a sweet, chippy eight iron, kept as low as possible, that spun left to four feet. Deadend was so unfamiliar with such a purely struck shot that he let out an audible "Oh no" when the ball left the clubface. Less than 1 percent of the golfing world could even contemplate such

[90] Proverbs 10:31 "The mouth of the godly person gives wise advice."

a beautiful shot. The sound of the ball squeezed just right. The flight of the ball like a sea bird looking for fish. The bounce to the left with the perfect spin. ProV nodded a "thank you"' when Hollie said, "Now that's a proper golf shot." He almost felt like he belonged on a Scottish links. When he later made the putt for the two, he simply said, "I feel like I just skipped a hole." Two twos on the front nine were rare at Hokmah.

Lucas and Wright were not so lucky. They were happy to get out with fours from the front left bunker and the right-side grasses, respectively.

Deadend's seven iron never had a chance. He unleashed another flurry[91] of expletives as his tee ball went long and right into the waves below. He blamed his caddie and hit two more balls in the ocean before declaring it the worst hole in the world. Loudmouth was quick to agree with his new friend.

Even after bogeys, Wright and Lucas were smiling, quietly aware they had experienced the thrill of playing one of the great holes in the world with a wind that made par unusual. And they rejoiced with ProV over his birdie.

On a path that led to the next tee was young James Lesser. He had learned the value of silence as a boy from his uncle, the ferryman they had met crossing the Listening River. Long ago he had written, *"The tongue is a small thing that makes grand speeches. But a tiny spark can set a great forest on fire. And among all the parts of the body, the tongue is a flame of fire. It is a whole world of wickedness, corrupting your entire body. It can set your whole life on fire, for it is set on fire by hell itself."*[92]

Sitting with him was a young girl named Miranda. Nearby was the one and only Miss Gossip who had walked down the hill with the players.[93] Even though she was dating Loudmouth, she loved to gossip about him and his whole family, especially Larry's mother, Loretta Loudmouth. And since Miranda was a listener, she was a perfect target

[91] Proverbs 4:24 "Avoid all perverse talk; stay away from corrupt speech.

[92] James 3:5-6

[93] Proverbs 25:23 "As surely as a north wind brings rain, so a gossiping tongue causes anger."

for Gossip. Miranda seldom said anything. In fact, she only said, "Don't forget, guys. You have the right to remain silent. *Watch your tongue and keep your mouth shut, and you will stay out of trouble.*" [94]

James added, "My uncle taught me well—if you keep quiet, people presume you're pretty smart. When you open your mouth, your tongue often confirms the exact opposite."

Dubs heard the young man's sermonette. He pointed his finger in James's chest and said, "I have half a million followers on Twitter. The whole world wants to know what I think. I do a video every day telling people how to invest their money. My tongue makes more money in five minutes than you make in a lifetime." He stormed off to the next tee, still yapping at Mocker about the wrong club.

James shook his head and stated the obvious, *"People can tame all kinds of animals, but no one can tame the tongue. It is restless and evil, full of deadly poison.*[95] *The tongue can bring life or death, those who love to talk will reap the consequences."*[96]

[94] Proverbs 21:23

[95] James 3:7-8

[96] Proverbs 18:21

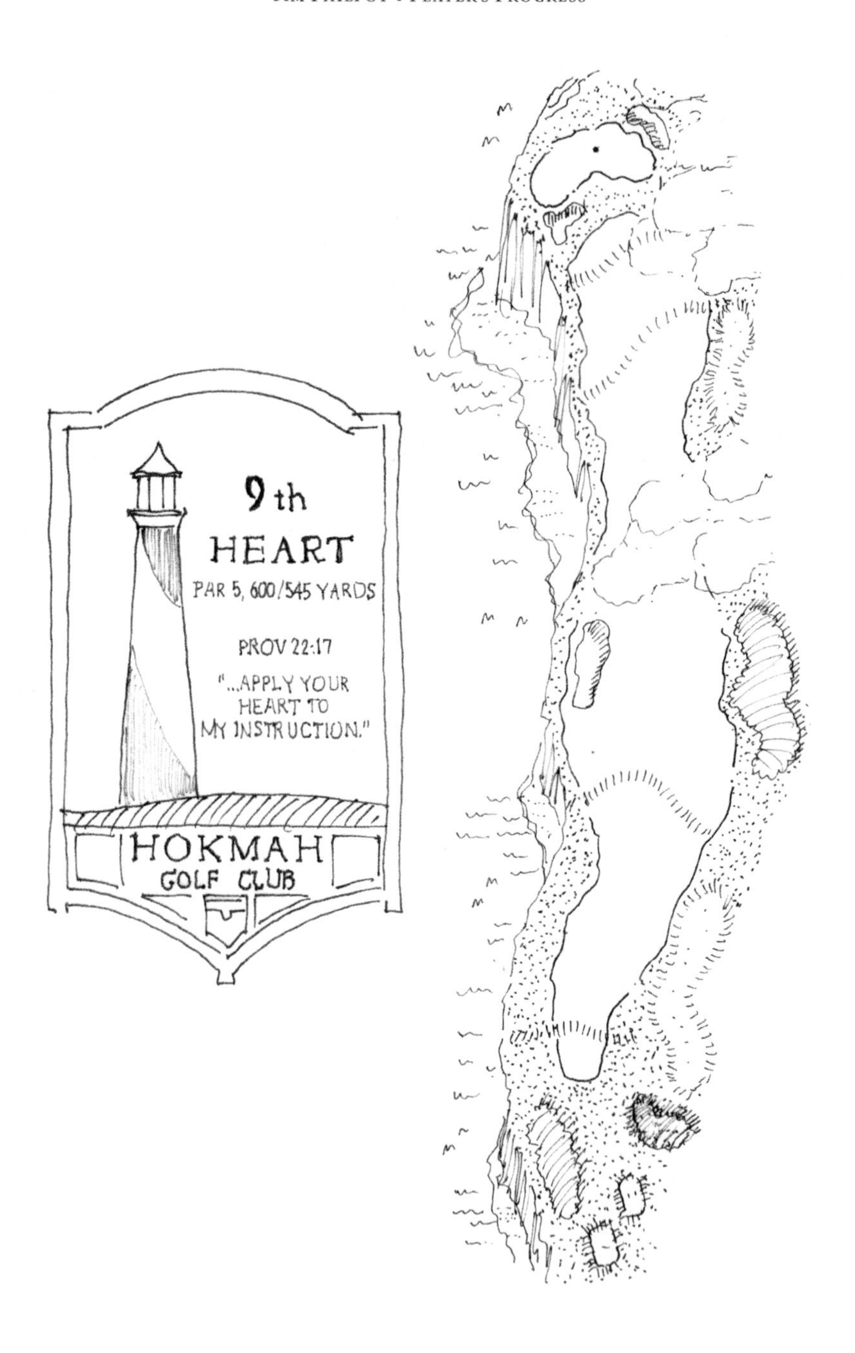
9th
HEART
PAR 5, 600/545 YARDS
PROV 22:17
"...APPLY YOUR
HEART TO
MY INSTRUCTION."
HOKMAH
GOLF CLUB

9th Hole – Heart

PAR 5, 660/545 YARDS

"...apply your heart to my instruction."
Proverbs 22:17

The ninth was uphill all the way, finishing not only at the farthest point from the clubhouse but also the highest point on the course. The green was located at the foot of a mountain whose top was almost always in the Orkney clouds. The hole was often played into a cool damp wind that swirled off the mountain. It played like a par six for most golfers. Left of the fairway were the same cliffs on the seventh and eighth holes, reminding ProV of his days as a junior playing at Torrey Pines in California.

Hollie handed Lucas a driver and invited him to hit the ball with his heart, not just his hands and clubface. She explained her "heart" admonition by quoting scriptures with a poetic Orkney brogue, pausing after each sentence to let the words sink in.

"Wisdom is enshrined in an understanding heart.[97]

"My child, if your heart is wise, my own heart will rejoice![98]

"Though good advice lies deep within the heart, a person with understanding will draw it out.[99]

"The crooked heart will not prosper.[100]

[97] Proverbs 14:33

[98] Proverbs 23:15

[99] Proverbs 20:5

[100] Proverbs 17:20

"For wisdom will enter your heart, and knowledge will fill you with joy.[101]

"People may be right in their own eyes, but the Lord examines their heart."[102]

Lucas made his best swing of the day and the ball sailed into the mist coming in off the mountain and the ocean from the left. ProV and Wright followed suit, down the fairway. Just like the previous two holes, it was distracting to play this ninth hole with the North Sea and cliffs to the left, sea birds large and small playing in the Orkney summer winds, the lighthouse on the adjoining island, and then a majestic mountain behind the green.

This hole was a cathedral, designed and built by the Creator Himself. Instead of a pipe organ, the hole's music was provided by the crashing waves below. It was a golfer's version of the "Hallelujah Chorus."

As the pilgrims marched ahead on the long par five, Deadend was nowhere to be found.[103] He had turned back toward the eighth hole, continuing to argue with James Lesser about the virtue of tweeting and letting people know what you think.

Hollie chatted all the way up the fairway about the heart, saying some things ProV had never heard. She said a pure heart was possible.[104] She called it an undivided heart.[105] Behavior could never be perfect, but God's perfect heart could live in us.

Wright seemed to know what she was talking about. Lucas didn't really understand but knew he should listen and believe anything that came from Hollie. ProV was clueless about this perfect heart. The word "perfect" was throwing him.

Hollie compared it to golf. "Consider this. Many shots in golf are

[101] Proverbs 2:10

[102] Proverbs 21:2

[103] Proverbs 6:14 "Their perverted hearts plot evil, and they constantly stir up trouble."

[104] Psalms 32:11 "Shout for joy, all you whose hearts are pure!"

[105] 2 Chronicles 19:9 "You must always act in the fear of the Lord, with faithfulness and an undivided heart."

'perfect,' in the sense that the strategy and the execution are exactly right, the club hits the sweet spot, the ball flies as intended, and when the ball lands three feet from the hole, both the player and the caddie say 'perfect.' The putter is handed to the player and a beautiful walk to the green follows. By some people's thinking, it was not perfect since the ball didn't go in the hole, but I say it was indeed perfect. The mind and the body and the soul all came together into an undivided heart. Old timers like me call it a perfect heart."

Sure enough, the trek to this green was long and difficult. ProV hit a "perfect" five iron for his third shot and made par while Lucas and Wright made routine bogeys, realizing not every six is evil.

Deadend had hurriedly returned to the group. His ball had come rolling between Wright's legs onto the putting surface after he hit the greatest three wood of his life. He apologized with a prideful "I didn't know I could get there into that wind."

Behind the green was the ominous mountain, and Hollie pointed to a man walking down from a path toward them, dressed like a shepherd. "That's King David," she said, "a *man after God's own heart*."[106] By now, nothing surprised ProV or Lucas.

As the group putted out, Hollie introduced the great man who had taken down Goliath but failed with Bathsheba. "He was a supreme sinner but also a saint. How is that possible? The heart. It's all about the heart."

Hollie finished, "*Whoever loves a pure heart and gracious speech will have the king as a friend.*[107] Let's go say hello."

R.W. whispered to Lucas as they left the green, "David was a typical male in so many ways. Good at fighting battles with other men. Weak at handling women."

Hollie loved to stop and chat with David. Often his harp was on his knee and he was writing a new song, just for today. Sometimes it was a guitar, or a violin. He even hummed on a harmonica at times. He

[106] 1 Samuel 13:14

[107] Proverbs 22:11

was often dancing with joy, sometimes alone but often surrounded by children and family or friends.

He seemed to know who was coming and would write a song for the new folks.

Today he was sitting with a Scottish friend from Perth. "Meet my friend Ian White.[108] He took many of my Psalms and put music to them. I am especially fond of Ian," said the King as he hugged Ian.

"We are working on a new tune today from Psalm Ninety," said Ian, who strummed and hummed a new tune that made the King's face light up. "This song is in honor of David's seventieth birthday." [109]

King David was not as handsome as ProV would have thought. His face was weathered and tired. His seventy years had been full of battles and caves, not just palaces. He greeted them all with a hug, even Deadend, whose best shot of the day had him in high spirits approaching the green with a putter in hand.

"Man, what a great shot up the hill and onto the dance floor," King David said.

Dubs enjoyed the compliment and looked into the eyes of the first man to ever hug him. He nervously responded, "Yeah, on the dance floor but not very close to the band."

David loved to call the green his dance floor because he used it for that very purpose, dancing with joy in the presence of his God. The ninth green was the biggest one on the course, similar to the eighteenth green at St. Andrews, with even its own version of the Valley of Sin, a place where David would often weep in memory of his failures. Hollie was whispering to Lucas and ProV, "He cries a lot, not only in pain for his foibles but in joy for God's mercy. Tears are such a wonderful creation—useful for both joy and sorrow. Many of his songs reflect those tears."[110]

That made sense to ProV, who cried when he qualified for the Masters and cried the same tears when his first wife left him. Hollie

[108] www.littlemistymusic.com

[109] Psalm 90:10 "Seventy years are given to us. Some even live to eighty."

[110] Psalm 139:1-24

continued, "The King often remembers with tears of thankfulness the voice of his mentor, Samuel, who had chosen him to be the King. The Lord had spoken to Samuel and told him to keep in mind *'the Lord doesn't see things the way you see them. People judge by outward appearance, but the Lord looks at the heart.'*"[111]

The King loved Hollie. She could tell his story better than he told it himself. It was easy because she knew him better than he knew himself.

"He was the youngest and least likely to ever be a king. But God saw his heart and chose him to defeat Goliath and become the king. Don't expect to understand in these few minutes how a man like David could be so revered. His failures were obvious—Bathsheba and the murder of her husband, just for starters." ProV did not remember that part of the story but kept quiet. He would ask Lucas later.

"David also weeps on the mountain or in the valley over his children, even the ending for Solomon, who penned much of the Proverbs. The Bible record tells us *'The Lord was very angry with Solomon—for his heart had turned away from the Lord....'*[112] And it was not Solomon's behavioral sins, it was his heart that disappointed the Holy God he claimed to worship."

"The heart!" Lucas found himself repeating.

For today, David had composed and was singing a song, *"God is my shield, saving those whose hearts are true and right."*[113]

"*My heart is glad and I rejoice*,"[114] he sang with exuberant joy. Ian joined him in the background.

Then the great King offered an invitation to the sojourners who were now halfway through Hokmah. "Can I offer some wisdom from my seventy years on earth?"[115]

[111] 1 Samuel 16:7

[112] 1 Kings 11:9

[113] Psalm 7:10

[114] Psalm 16:9

[115] 1 Chronicles 29:28 "He died at a ripe old age, having enjoyed long life, wealth, and honor."

"Of course," said Lucas, who knew this would be good.

"I hate to quote myself, but I've never heard it any plainer," King David said with a smile. He prayed with his eyes wide open and hands lifted high.

> *"O our God, we thank you and praise your glorious name! But who am I, and who are my people, that we could give anything to you? Everything we have has come from you, and we give you only what you first gave us! We are here for only a moment, visitors and strangers in the land as our ancestors before us. Our days on earth are like a passing shadow, gone so soon without a trace."* [116]

The King hugged everyone and headed with Ian down a path toward the sea.

Lucas meditated on the fact that he was now seventy-two, and his own days were numbered.[117]

Hollie motioned for the men to follow her up a small hill to a coffee shop at the foot of the mountain. Lunch was waiting—a chance to relax and gain strength for the back nine adventure.

Lucas and ProV followed dutifully, while R.W. stayed behind to try to convince Deadend to come with them. Despite his fine shot to the ninth green, Dubs seemed set on turning back. This climb up a mountain was too much for him. He told Mocker to call the helicopter pilot to see if he could be picked up on the wide ninth fairway. He had had enough.

[116] 1 Chronicles 29:13-15

[117] Psalm 90:12 "Teach us to realize the brevity of life, so that we may grow in wisdom."

Intermission

'THE MOUNTAIN TOP'

"Jesus took Peter, John and James up on a mountain..."
Luke 9:28

The ninth green was three miles from the clubhouse, a typical links layout: Nine out and nine in, with small variations. The green was high above sea level with a dramatic cliff on the left, steep enough to cause acrophobia. While it was the highest point on the golf course, it was not the apex on the property.

At the far end of the links stood a striking mountain formation. The peak was usually in the clouds, even on an otherwise clear day. Pointing into the clouds, Hollie said simply, "There are no mountains in Orkney, except this one place, which many would call just a large, rocky hill. Welcome to the Mountain of Threes."

Deadend would miss the mountain. He and his "scratch handicap," with help from "the greatest caddie in the world," had shot at least fifty-four on the front nine, and that was with a fancy pencil.

His chat with King David should have encouraged him, but instead had just aggravated him. The King had told Deadend the worst sinner he had ever met was David himself. Murder, adultery, pride, arrogance, greed. He said it to give the man hope for himself but Dubs walked away thinking this David guy must be a bad dude, feeling thankful he was not that bad.

Hollie explained it was customary for visitors to walk all the way to the top. The monster back tee on the tenth was there, for one thing, even though no one actually played from there. The view of all of the Isle of Mashal was worth the six-minute ascent if the clouds cooperated.

First, though, free lunch and drinks would be served at the ultimate halfway house, just a few steps off the ninth green. Coffee or hot chocolate was available. Or a sip of a favorite whisky, just a sip, to warm the body. Or the best mountain water right from the streams of Hokmah. Plus the promised seafood pot pie and chips to remember forever.

The group sat around picnic tables that looked like they had been there for centuries. "Hello Rhoda,"[118] said Hollie with a smile as a young lady appeared with food and drinks for all.

"Good afternoon, Hollie. What a great day you have arranged for our guests. Again. You never fail," said the girl, who obviously knew what she was doing. Rhoda disappeared back to the small kitchen.

Hollie declared, "We are better off now as a threesome. My old pro called it a triad. The most powerful unit in the world.

"There was a man all alone," she quoted Ecclesiastes 4. "Solomon was the richest man in the world but knew about being alone.[119] This is the most fundamental problem faced by mankind. It has even been proven in scientific studies with rats, but we know it is true—being alone is a death march."

[118] Acts 12:12-15

[119] Ecclesiastes 4:8 (NIV)

"Even golf alone is not much fun," added Wright.

Hollie nodded, "Ecclesiastes said it, *'Two are better than one.'*[120] In golf, it always helps to have a playing companion. You learn a lot by watching the other person's ball. And of course, a caddie for sure," reminding them it was unthinkable to not have a caddie when golf was first played. "In the beginning, before mowers and fancy greenskeepers, golf was a two-person sport. One person hit the ball and the other person found it!"

Lucas could not resist, "There is nothing better than golf with a great caddie!" looking straight into Hollie's brown eyes.

She continued, "And three is even better. *'A cord of three strands is not quickly broken,'*[121] says Ecclesiastes. A threesome is better for golf but also, in life situations, a third person in the room helps two people resolve disputes. Or makes conversation on difficult topics easier. You can speak to one person while pretending to talk to someone else. Parents do this all the time. They speak to someone else but hope their kid is listening."

Lucas chimed in, "Even an animal works as the third party sometimes. My father used to talk to our dog, Birdie, hoping I was listening!"

"The power of three is quite real," agreed Hollie with authority.

Lucas nodded approval. He giggled as he remembered an old quote from English golf commentator Henry Longhurst: "There's nothing quite so lovely as threes on a card," having seen twelve consecutive threes on a Scottish Open card at Gleneagles. *Three sure looks good on a scorecard,* ProV thought.

Wright added, "Even God is a threesome." He winked at Hollie when he said it.

Hollie continued, "So, this is the Mountain of Threes. Some call it the Mount of Transfiguration, in honor of Mark, the ninth chapter.[122]

"You will see some of the greatest threesomes ever. Put on a jacket. It

[120] Ecclesiastes 4:9 (NIV)

[121] Ecclesiastes 4:12 (NIV)

[122] Mark 9:2-13

will be colder walking up the mountain. Mr. T and Barnabas and I will stay here. You need to do this for yourselves. We will wait for you on your tenth tee, which you will pass in about twenty steps," said Hollie as the group polished off the seafood pies and found their jackets. "You'll be gone about thirty minutes, max."

A serene and holy mist now covered the mountain as ProV, Lucas and R.W. began the ascent. Wright's presence offered comfort that this short climb would end well. He would be a guide for the two American pilgrims.

As they passed the tenth tee, ProV looked below and could barely make out the golf course. Then, through gaps in the clouds, he could see it all, even the clubhouse three miles away.

Just past the tenth tee was a fork in the road. Two paths looked very similar. ProV and Lucas were both glad R.W. was there to lead them. To the left was a small sign and a group of three religiously garbed men. The sign pointed with an arrow to "Mt. Sinai." The three finely dressed men were poring over a thick scroll full of words and laws. The chief priest was Farah C. Rules. He had lived on the mountain for a long time. The three men looked up at the golfing pilgrims and beckoned them with promises of life eternal.

It almost made sense to ProV, who was by now getting accustomed to following some very unusual orders.

But as ProV took one step in that direction, R.W. grabbed his arm and pulled him toward the other path, which seemed more treacherous and narrow.

"There is a way that seems right.[123] That path leads up a secondary mountain called Sinai," Wright explained. "Moses was there once upon a time. He received the law there—the so-called Ten Commandments, which by the time the lawyers got through was more like seven thousand laws. And all you have to do to get this eternal life, they promise, is keep them *all*."

"All?"

[123] Proverbs 14:12 (NIV) "There is a way that appears to be right but in the end it leads to death."

"You heard me right. Metaphorically speaking, just shoot fifty-four every day and you're fine," said Wright. "They have a rules committee that loves to find people doing something wrong. They love to call penalties."

ProV told R.W. about a six-shot penalty in a college tournament. "This official loved giving out penalties. He got me for a combination of slow play, improperly marking my ball while taking a drop from a hazard, and moving an object in the hazard. It was a ten on the scorecard which I have still not forgotten. That guy loved his rules."

R.W. smiled. "So you know the type. Believe me, climbing Mount Sinai will do nothing but get you killed. You will fail, and the wages of failure is death.[124] There is a cliff over there which no one survives."

He pointed at the huddled men reading the scroll. "Besides, those guys are really good at keeping score but can't break a hundred on their best day. They know the rules of golf and life but it doesn't help them play the game."

A soft, misty rain began to fall. Fortunately, there were small shelters along the narrow route. Sitting in one of the shelters, looking content to wait out the brief shower, were three golfers dressed like it was 1922.

Fifty-year-old Harry Vardon was showing his grip to a younger Francis Ouimet, while Ted Ray was lighting a pipe and wiping his mustache all at the same time.

The great triumvirate from the 1913 US Open did not seem to notice the pilgrims. The moment seemed sacred, and Wright motioned they should keep going. The sun came out and shadows appeared within seconds. ProV was now groggy from so many characters of the past—or was it the sip of whisky below?

Wright led the pilgrims up the winding and narrow path. Rounding a corner, they quickly came to another famous threesome.

They were sitting on a tee box in front of what looked like the clubhouse at the Royal and Ancient in St. Andrews. It was still 1922. ProV had seen enough golf pictures to recognize the scene. Gene Sarazen was showing his new invention, a sand wedge, to Walter Hagen while

[124] Romans 6:23 "For the wages of sin is death, but the free gift of God is eternal life through Christ Jesus our Lord."

Bobby Jones spread out drawings for a new course in Georgia. Hagen was busy opening a bottle of the best Scotch from the north of Scotland, waiting his turn to give them putting tips.

Wright kept the Americans moving, not even stopping to try to say hello.

Pretty soon, a small rusty sign appeared, "Welcome to Ft. Worth, Texas." It was just off the path on the left and led to a small pro shop. Cowboy hats were hanging on a wall, and they could hear the clanking of metal golf spikes as they watched three little boys, perhaps ten years old, sneak into the locker room of a public course in Ft. Worth.

ProV was mumbling, "What the heck is going on here? St. Andrews is nowhere near Texas on any map I've seen."

R.W. overheard. "Keep in mind it is still 1922. That's Hogan, Nelson and Snead. Notice Sam has no shoes. Ben is the little bitty guy with a black eye. And of course, Byron is the tall, clean-cut kid."

ProV was shaking his head.

The three boys left the locker room and almost ran to the first tee on the hardpan, baked-out Texas prairie that was thirsty for rain and green grass. They each carried three hickory clubs. The boys hit quickly. Snead with no shoes finished in perfect balance. The young Hogan half topped his ball and scowled, knowing he would probably lose today. Byron was smooth, smiling as he turned his back to the ball and released it into the dusty sky. And off they went.

A few steps farther up the mountain, they turned to their right and R.W. said, "It's 1970 now." A television in the background was showing men walking on the moon. The "Big Three" of television's first experience with golf were sitting on a veranda, wearing green jackets, laughing and smiling at what had to be Augusta National Golf Club. Azaleas were in full bloom.

Arnold Palmer was autographing hats and flags, politely complaining about the faulty pen he had been handed. He liked his autographs to be legible.

Gary Player was dusting himself off after fifty pushups on the lush green grass.

And a thirty-year-old Jack Nicklaus was surrounded by his wife and several small blond children, his family. It was evident he was not just the greatest golfer of all time—everyone knew that, including Jack. He was also a great dad.

But the threesomes were not done yet. At their next turn in the trail was the final group. Tiger Woods sat with the other two players who had come up short of the Nicklaus record for major wins. Ben Craig from Aberdeen, Scotland had won seven Masters, passing Nicklaus' six, and Sam Hwang from Korea had passed Tiger and almost caught Jack with his seventeen majors. He was a god with a small 'g' in Korea. This was especially miraculous since he had been born in Pyongyang in 2015 before South and North Korea united in 2037. Golf had been an evil "capitalist" sport when he was growing up in North Korea.

ProV's head was spinning and his heart was shivering. It was so cold that he later told Lucas he thought he saw snowflakes.

Two threesomes at the apex topped them all. Moses was there, white beard and all. Elijah looked younger than his 3,500 years. And sure enough, Yeshua was there. Jesus Himself had joined the two great prophets to form the greatest mountaintop threesome in human history.

Lucas reached over to touch ProV's hand, just to make sure he knew it was not a dream. "Jesus with Moses and Elijah," he whispered reverently. All were dressed for a winter day in Jerusalem in the year AD 30.

Standing nearby was another threesome of onlookers, young men who looked even more confused than ProV.

Peter, James and John were there by invitation from Yeshua. Peter was younger than the man they had seen on the seventh hole. The disciples were full of both confusion and joy. It was the kind of joy people know who are invited to the inner sanctums of the holy—insiders to the ways of God.

That included Wright. And now, that included Lucas too. And maybe even ProV. He was getting there. He was becoming an insider to the sacred.

Down below at the tenth tee, Hollie just smiled. She knew what was happening. She had been here before. Before the beginning.

In fact, when Jesus had left the earth, more than 2,000 years ago, He mentioned Hollie would still be around to handle problems and comfort souls. She was doing her best.

R.W., Lucas and ProV were unseen bystanders. No one had noticed them yet.

Yeshua, Moses, Elijah, Peter, James and John were sitting around a picnic table with a light lunch of brown Scottish bread with butter, and a heavenly red wine. Peter recalled with a laugh the time he suggested giant statues of Jesus, Moses and Elijah—until the voice from heaven made it clear, *"This is my Son, listen to him."*

It took some effort, but Peter had listened to the voice.[125]

R.W. whispered to Lucas, "Let's just listen in for a moment. But we can't stay long. They're waiting down on the tee." Lucas nodded.

They heard Jesus say quietly,

> "If any of you wants to be my follower, you must give up your own way, take up your cross, and follow me. If you try to hang on to your life, you will lose it. But if you give up your life for my sake and for the sake of the Good News, you will save it. And what do you benefit if you gain the whole world but lose your own soul?" [126]

"This is the same Yeshua who, when he was only twelve years old, *grew in wisdom and in stature and in favor with God and all the people,*"[127] said R.W. ProV remembered some of this story from his Catholic schooling.

R.W. continued, "Jesus once said, *'Wisdom is shown to be right by the lives of those who follow it.'*[128] He knows more about wisdom, about

[125] Mark 9:7 "Then a cloud overshadowed them, and a voice from the cloud said, 'This is my dearly loved Son. Listen to him.'"

[126] Mark 8:34-36

[127] Luke 2:52

[128] Luke 7:35

'Hokmah,' than all the wise men in the world combined. It's pretty simple. Wise men seek Him."[129]

ProV could not take his eyes off Jesus. He was not handsome as some think of the term. But the look in his eyes toward his friends was compelling. ProV wanted to know this person.

Jesus then turned and looked at ProV, then Lucas. They were face to face with a man who knew everything about them. The energy left ProV's body. Lucas was not much better. Wright was quite comfortable in the holy presence of this Yeshua, who said only three words: "Listen to Hollie."

Then ProV heard another voice from above and behind him: *"This is my Son. Listen to Him."* He looked around to see who it was, and when he looked back toward Yeshua. He was gone, along with the others. A holy and heavy mist covered the scene.

R.W. stated the obvious, "Boys, it's time to go."

ProV gave Lucas a glance. And then he had a thought: *I think I believe.* Little did he know Hollie was listening as he talked to himself. He smiled inwardly, *How stupid would I be to* not *believe—I've just met Jesus. Face to face.*

Walking back down the hill to the tenth tee, Hollie, Barnabas and Mr. T were waiting with one final threesome—the Morris clan.

Ol' Tom, of course, plus young Tommy. It was obvious who they were, since the white beard of golf's patriarch was unmistakable, and young Tommy was wearing the British Open championship belt he had retired by winning three straight years beginning in 1872. Tommy had died on Christmas Day, 1875, just three months after the death of his wife and son in childbirth.

Sitting with Ol' Tom and young Tommy was the lesser known brother, James Ogilvie Fairlie Morris, known as "Jof," who tied Tommy's record over the Old Course in 1887 with a seventy-seven. In those days "hockey sticks" with hickory sticks was quite a good score.

Hollie knew the history. "Tom had more misery than most. He was famous in his day but also no stranger to suffering. All of his children

[129] Matthew 2:9-11

died before he did. In fact, his oldest son was not the famous Tommy we know. His first son was also named Tommy and died at age four. The custom back then was that if a young child died, the next son born would have the same name, and thus, there were actually two Tommy Jr.'s. His youngest son John died at age thirty-four after living in a wheelchair all his life. Jof lived longer than anyone, just fifty. Tom's dear wife died in 1876, not long after young Tommy's tragic death." ProV had never heard any of this.

Wright was also familiar with the great man's faith. "Not many knew that the source of his strength was his suffering and the faith in God which just naturally comes with it. In 1780, he was made an elder of Holy Trinity Kirk, a center point of his life. No pain or disease could stop him, though. He died falling down some stairs at age eighty-seven in 1908."

ProV found himself staring at the old pro, thinking about the seventy-three he shot at age seventy on the Old Course with clubs and balls that made par at least eighty. Thinking about all the courses he designed. Thinking about how he had changed the game forever.

Hollie nudged ProV, "Look at the book he's holding." Sure enough, it said Holy Bible, and it was open and filled with handwritten notes. He knew featheries and niblicks and spoons, but he also knew the One who made it all happen. The Creator of St. Andrews. The Creator of Hokmah.

The sights and sounds of the mountain from twelve years ago were so stunning that Lucas's brain could not contain them. He had forgotten too much. And now, he was jumping through his skin as he remembered. *How could I have forgotten this?* he thought.

Hollie offered advice: "One of the keys is to remember what you should remember and forget what you should forget. God is always telling us to 'remember' the right things. Most people do the opposite."

ProV was now fully aware he should listen to Hollie, just as he had been instructed by Yeshua on the mountain. Hollie's endorsement from the Man Himself was extraordinary indeed.

Now that ProV had met Yeshua face to face, he would follow his advice. Listen to Hollie. And believe.

Part Three
The Back Nine

"When the game is at its highest level it creates confusion in our minds. It's not just hit the ball in the air and land it on a dime on the green knowing it will stay there. The sharpest course designers put some wickedness into the holes. They want you to stand over the ball and wonder what will happen if it hits that hump..."[130]

Hokmah Golf Club

Hole	Par	Hdcp	Name	Proverbs	Professional	Member
1	4	7	Trust	3:05	407	360
2	4	1	Truth	12:19	472	422
3	4	5	Eyes	4:25	468	408
4	4	9	Prudence	27:12	340	290
5	4	3	Integrity	10:09	460	416
6	3	13	Patience	16:32	240	204
7	5	15	Temper	17:27	590	510
8	3	17	Tongue	18:21	120	115
9	5	11	Heart	22:17	660	545
Out	36				3757	3270
10	4	10	Knowledge	18:15	520	477
11	4	18	Discipline	1:07	330	248
12	3	12	Wine	20:01	180	152
13	4	4	Money	10:02	510	413
14	5	2	Women	6:26	780	780
15	4	6	Work	24:30	476	410
16	3	16	Pride	8:13	190	165
17	4	8	Love	21:21	474	388
18	5	14	Wisdom	8:01	560	507
In	36				4020	3540
Total	72				7777	6810

[130] Lorne Rubenstein, *A Season in Dornoch* (McClelland and Stewart, Ltd, 2001), p. 44.

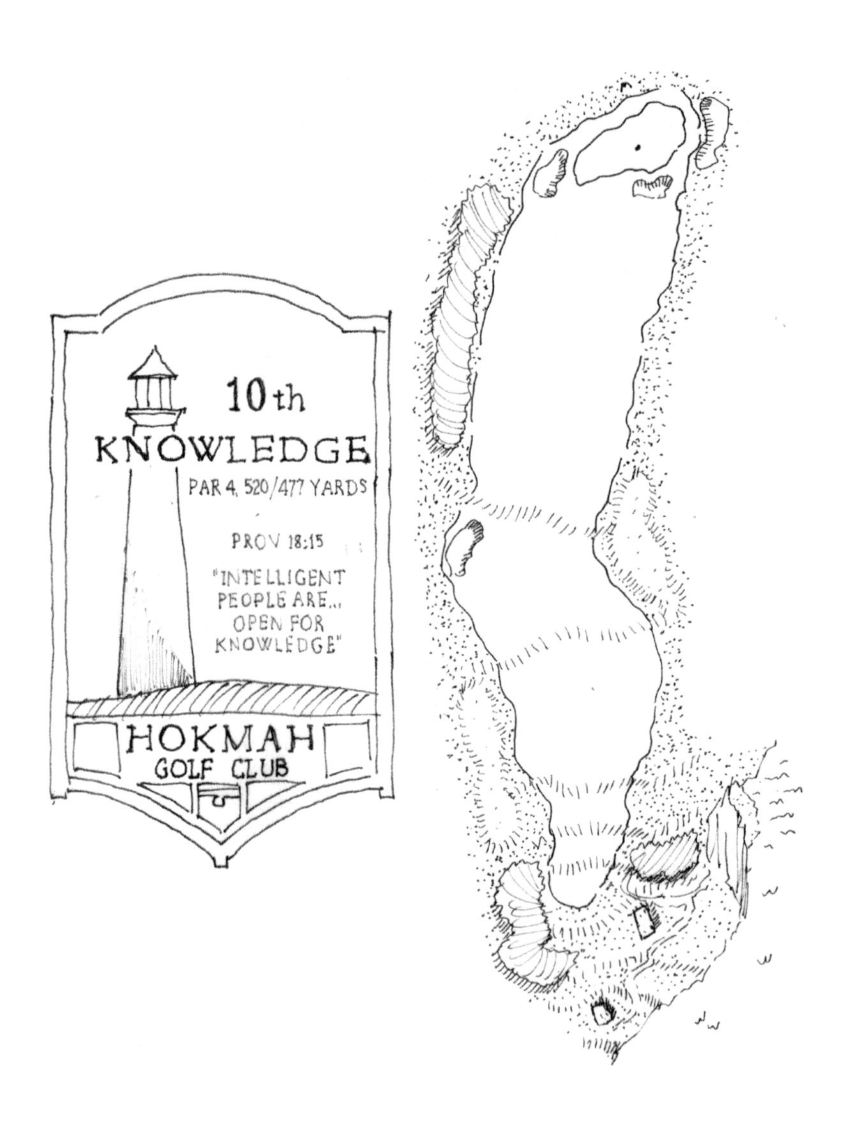
10th
KNOWLEDGE
PAR 4, 520/477 YARDS
PROV 18:15
"INTELLIGENT
PEOPLE ARE...
OPEN FOR
KNOWLEDGE"
HOKMAH
GOLF CLUB

10th Hole – Knowledge

PAR 4, 520/477 YARDS

"Intelligent people are... open for knowledge."
Proverbs 18:15

The back nine started with a dream hole everyone loved. Downhill off the mountain, usually downwind, with a wonderful view not only of the flight of the ball sailing into the distance, but also John's lighthouse to the right and yellow spring gorse bushes on both sides. A white speck in the distance was the clubhouse. Somehow, the bushes stayed yellow and flowered all summer in this Hokmah version of Eden.

The fairway was wide enough to hit an exhilarating driver with little fear of losing the ball. Most players would leave Hokmah talking about the longest drive of their life off the tenth tee. It was like shooting adrenaline into their souls. The combination of downhill, downwind, plus the energy of the Halfway House and the memories of the Threesomes on the Mountain—it all created a "high" that could not be duplicated anywhere in the world.

The hole was called Knowledge. The length made it appear to be a difficult hole on the scorecard, but in reality it was one of Hokmah's birdie opportunities. Four-hundred-yard bombs off the tee were routine.

The Morris boys loved to watch and shake their heads, remembering when they could only blast an old featherie about 190 yards.

ProV was still living in the glory of the mountain adventure as they arrived at the tee box. "So Hollie, what's this Knowledge hole about?" He was listening now. He seemed to have "ears to hear and eyes to see."[131]

"Knowledge. Not to be confused with wisdom, which is deeper and more important than mere knowledge. But nevertheless, it is still important to *know* some things," she replied.

ProV knew more than when he entered the gates of Hokmah. But he wanted to know a lot more.

Standing on the tee to greet each player was young Bobby Longball, who not only won the World Long Driving competition ten times but also won two tournaments on the regular PGA Tour, making him the only person to do both. He modeled his game and his brain after Bryson DeChambeau. When yardage books were banned on the PGA Tour, Bobby responded by memorizing the yardages for every PGA Tour course. He knew the yardage and average barometric pressure from the left fairway bunker on the eighteenth hole at Augusta, or any PGA stop for that matter. He seemed to have a photographic memory. The hole called Knowledge was his favorite because it summarized the secret of his success: "Knowledge is power."

Plus, this hole was for bombers, and Bobby had brute power developed mostly in the gym, like his hero.

Naysayers feared his ridiculous length off the tee would ruin the game. But four-hundred-yard drives could not answer all the questions that golf asks a player.

Hollie greeted Bobby with a friendly nod and asked him to brief the players on the tenth hole.

[131] Proverbs 20:12 "Ears to hear and eyes to see – both are gifts from the Lord."

"Downwind, as usual," he said. "The fairway is forty-five yards wide. No reason to do anything here but hit the longest drive of your life!"

ProV was pumped up. The front nine was behind him. He had just met Jesus Himself and polished off a seafood pot pie. He was ready.

But sadly, he overswung and hit a toe hook that just would not stay up in the cool breeze. When the ball stopped rolling, it was "only" 370 yards away. Lucas and Wright followed with well struck drives that seemed to stay in the air forever, finally coming down near ProV's ball. They would all be only 150 yards to the center pin position.

Bobby decided to walk the hole with the threesome. When ProV asked the obvious question, he said, "Oh yeah, I've driven this green many times. Almost every day actually. Even did it with a three wood a couple of times."

Hollie turned to Lucas as ProV and Bobby walked ahead of them, talking about how barometric pressure affects a golf ball.

"Bobby has always understood knowledge is important. Proverbs has a lot to say on the subject. *'Choose my instruction rather than silver, and knowledge rather than pure gold.'*"[132]

Lucas responded with something he had read from Proverbs: *"Knowledge will fill you with joy."*[133]

Hollie was impressed Lucas knew some Scripture. "Lucas, you are a learner. For some reason, many people hate this kind of knowledge."[134]

Just as she said that, sure enough, they heard Deadend and Mocker screaming "Fore!" from the tenth tee. They had changed their plans. The mist was too thick for their helicopter to safely depart. Plus, the pilot had one drink too many. He had planned on a couple of more hours to sober up. So, Deadend had decided to go ahead and play the back nine. Mocker told him the back nine would suit his game better.

The comfortable threesome was now interrupted again by the fourth man and his Mocker.

[132] Proverbs 8:10

[133] Proverbs 2:10

[134] Proverbs 1:29 "For they hated knowledge and chose not to fear the Lord."

Dubs had somehow hit the best drive of his life. His ball was rolling past the other three balls in the fairway. All the caddies and players looked back to see if this was really Deadend. Surely not. For years to come he would brag about his 375-yard drive.

ProV was embarrassed to hit first behind two older gentlemen and a hacking fool. But his nine iron from 150 was perfect, offering him a birdie chance. Lucas and Wright followed with nice shots as well, both within thirty feet.

Deadend, out of breath from hurrying to catch up, strutted to his ball and took a nine iron from Mocker for the 140-yard downwind approach shot. A cold shank brought Mocker and his man back to reality. Deadend looked at Mocker as if he been handed the wrong club. He examined the face of the club carefully. Obviously, something was wrong beyond his control. His third and fourth were shanked as well, and by the time he reached the green, laying five in a right-side bunker, his demeanor was back to normal.

Behind the green was the familiar figure of Jack Nicklaus. It was an older version of the Golden Bear, barely able to stand and greet the guys, not the younger man they had seen on the mountain.

Jack also had loved the long ball. And he had invented the yardage book. He knew knowledge was king. He used that extra knowledge to win more majors than anyone in history.

While waiting on Deadend to stumble his way around the green, ProV and Lucas greeted Nicklaus. ProV shook his hand and said simply, "It's an honor to meet the greatest player ever."

Jack just nodded. "Pleasure to meet you as well. Nice shot there, young man."

Sitting with Jack in two old wooden chairs was an older gentleman who Jack introduced. "Men, this is my friend Ivor Young. He was one of my secret weapons, a real friend."

"Good afternoon, men," said Ivor. "Hanging around Jack for a few minutes will be worth your time. It sure has been for me."

Hollie interjected quietly but for all to hear, "See, ProV, everyone needs an older friend," nodding in Lucas's direction, "even Jack

Nicklaus." ProV responded with an understanding nod and a question for the Golden Bear.

"So, Jack, sir, they have always said you were the first golfer to actually keep yardages in a book. Is that correct?"

Jack gave credit to another older friend, Deane Beman.

"In nineteen-fifty-nine I won the US Amateur on sheer power and talent, not really knowing how to play proper golf. Then in nineteen-sixty-one, I showed up at Pebble Beach for the US Amateur. I was twenty-one. I had almost won a couple of US Opens already, but in practice rounds at Pebble Beach, the blustery winds gave me fits on approach yardages. I mentioned this to Deane, who said, 'Why don't you measure them like I do?' He was the first person I ever met who, along with his caddie, would walk a course in advance and step off yardages. We were all just playing by visual estimating. Taking Deane's advice, I found that the more yardages I paced off, the more greens I hit and the closer I got to the cups. By the time the championship began, my confidence was as high as my spirits."[135]

"So you won?"

The Bear smiled. "Oh yes, my second US Amateur on my favorite course. Knowledge of the course created confidence for me."

ProV then finished with, "And of course you won the US Open there, too. Nineteen-eighty-two. I've read all about it."

"Yes sir, with the same little book. But can I tell you something even better than knowledge of the golf course?"

"Sure."

"Go putt out first. I'd love to see a birdie. Bobby can tell you we get a fair number of birdies on this hole."

Lucas and Wright made routine two-putt pars. With Nicklaus watching, ProV was the most nervous he had been all day. He brought Mr. T in for a read. Left lip, five-footer. He always joked that if he went to hell it would be a steady stream of left to right five-footers.

He closed his eyes. Visualized the break. Used all the knowledge of

[135] Jack Nicklaus, *Jack Nicklaus: My Story- An Autobiography (Ebury Press, 1997)*

Mr. T on the greens and sure enough, the ball dropped in for a birdie three. He was thrilled to hear a solitary handclap from the greatest player in the history of golf.

Lucas and ProV walked back to the great Nicklaus. R.W. said, "Men, take your time. You don't want to miss this."

Hollie stood to the side.

Jack introduced his buddy. "Ivor and I grew up together at Scioto Country Club in Columbus and became dear friends. He helped me build Muirfield Village and was even the first 'captain' of the club. He actually located the land for the golf course."

Ivor was proud to be sitting with the Golden Bear. "Yeah, you should know I beat Jack two-and-one in a junior club championship at Scioto in the nineteen-fifties," interjected Ivor, who paused and then delivered the punchline. "Of course, I was seventeen and Jack was ten at the time!" Everyone howled as usual.

"So," continued Jack, "everyone needs an older friend, someone to follow and even imitate. I want Ivor to tell you just a little bit of his story."

"Well, men, thanks in part to being one of Jack's best friends, I found a lot of success in everything I did. Plenty of money, flying with Jack on international trips, sharing a house with him at the Masters. I was blessed also with a sweet wife and great kids. I was well known as a good and honest businessman."

He paused to put on a jacket as a cool breeze blew through.

"But when I was in my forties, a friend shared with me some spiritual things I needed to hear. Stuff like 'No one is good enough' for heaven. I was taught heaven is a perfect place for perfect people. But the problem is that perfection is not possible. And then he said something strange but wonderful. He looked straight at me, knowing how much I loved and respected Jack, and said, 'Not even Jack Nicklaus has ever birdied every hole, shot fifty-four. Nobody is perfect, not even the greatest.'"

Nicklaus was listening to a story he had heard often.

"This friend then said even a good man like Ivor Young needs a Savior. He said it with such a loving smile and demeanor that I was not offended. Indeed, it was like the Holy Spirit"—he paused and glanced at Hollie— "reached into my heart and made me realize that instead of being perfect, or great, or even good, all I needed to enter the gates of Heaven was Jesus Himself, who died and forgives all sins, especially the sin of thinking we are good enough—called pride."

Jack smiled every time he heard the story again.

"So, Ivor," said Lucas, "some people are saved from their sins, and some are even saved from their goodness?"

Ivor nodded. "That's a great way to think about it. I had a lot of both, frankly."

Lucas understood.

Ivor continued, "So, don't underestimate knowledge as a basic platform for anything in life. But instead of just knowledge, seek wisdom, a treasure which all my good deeds could not bring. I was saved, not just from all my sins, but from my human reliance on my brains, knowledge and goodness. There is a verse I really like which says it succinctly."

Ivor pulled a small New Testament from his pocket and read:

"Paul said in Colossians, concerning Jesus, *'In him lie hidden all the treasures of wisdom and knowledge.'*[136] I like the way he said that."

Being a smart man of quiet faith and few words, Jack knew the pilgrims needed to move along, so he stood up, signaling it was time to go. "Now you guys run along. You've got some more birdies to make."

As they walked quietly to the next tee, Hollie reminded them what the hole was all about, *"Intelligent people are always ready to learn. Their ears are open for knowledge."*[137]

[136] Colossians 2:3

[137] Proverbs 18:15

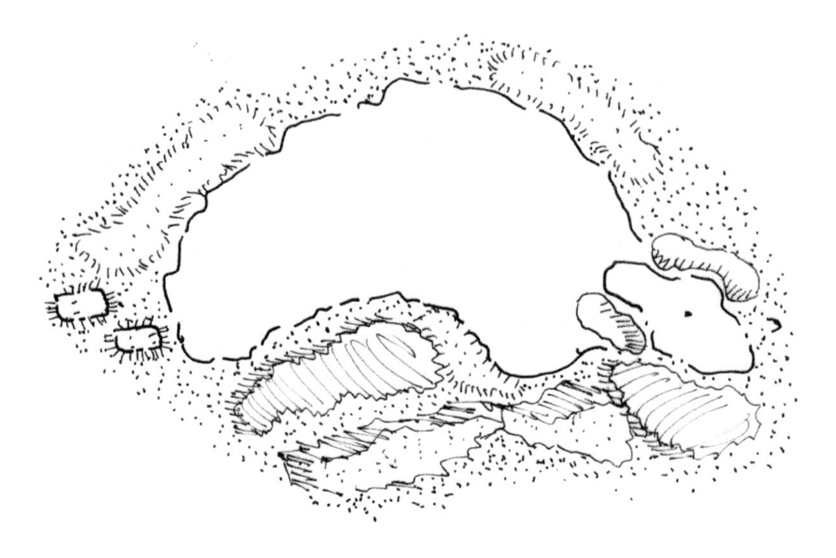

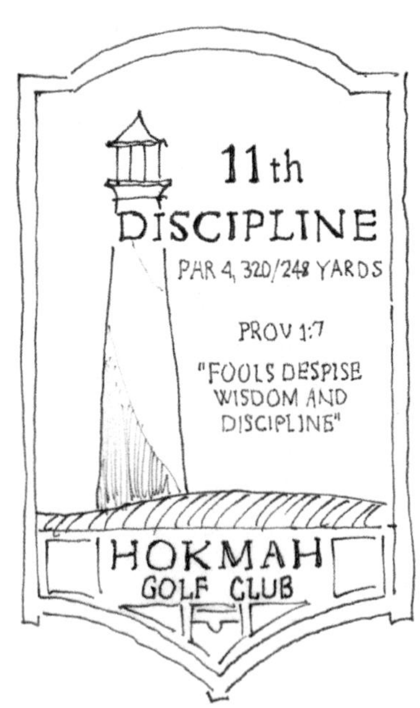
11th
DISCIPLINE
PAR 4, 320/248 YARDS
PROV 1:7
"FOOLS DESPISE
WISDOM AND
DISCIPLINE"
HOKMAH
GOLF CLUB

11th Hole – Discipline

PAR 4, 320/248 YARDS

"Fools despise wisdom and discipline."
Proverbs 1:7

The sign on the eleventh tee simply said "Discipline," a word that made ProV wince. If he had discipline, he might have multiple PGA Tour victories. Instead, he was nowhere. In golf. In life. In love. In short, discipline was not his strong suit. He said to himself, *Ouch.*

Hollie began quoting Proverbs as if she was announcing the next golfers at a British Open.

"People who accept discipline are on the pathway to life." [138]

"To learn, you must love discipline." [139]

"If you reject discipline, you only harm yourself; but if you listen to correction, you grow in understanding." [140]

Wright noticed ProV was anxious and reminded him not to be too hard on himself. "The word 'discipline' has a double meaning," he said.

[138] Proverbs 10:17

[139] Proverbs 12:1

[140] Proverbs 15:32

"First, it relates to parenting. *'Those who love their children care enough to discipline them.'*[141] And *'a wise child accepts a parent's discipline.'*"[142]

That got ProV to thinking. His dad was never around to discipline him properly. He just got yelled at when it was too late to change anything. He had to answer a lot of stupid questions, such as, "Why did you hit that club?" Or, "Why did you go out with those guys?" Or, the worst one, "How can you be so stupid?"

And he remembered what he thought each time: *Maybe I am just like you?* He could never say those words aloud, so he buried them deeper than a coal mine. As he got older, those words had become a buried lie in Hell's bunker.

Wright continued, "But second, for us adults, the key is to discipline ourselves, meaning to develop regimens of mind and body which lead to successful and healthy lives."

ProV beat himself up in his mind even more. *I never practiced like I should have, never ate right, basically did whatever I felt like doing most of the time. No discipline.*

Waiting on the tee was Bernhard Langer. His greeting was warm and welcoming, especially for a man whose personality could be uniquely direct. He was the greatest senior player of all time. He was even "Player of the Year" at age sixty-four back in 2021. This hole would provide some of his secrets.

Hollie encouraged the guys to chat with Bernhard while the caddies tossed up grass and otherwise figured out the distance and clubs necessary for the upcoming tee shot.

"ProV, perhaps you will recall we met in 2033 at Augusta?" said the two-time Masters champion. ProV was stunned that Bernhard would know his name and remember him.

"Well, Bernhard. You have an amazing memory to remember a nobody like me. Of course, I remember meeting you. Sadly, I was a cocky and overrated kid back then, but you were so genuinely interested

[141] Proverbs 13:24

[142] Proverbs 13:1

in me. I still remember our conversation. You told me to keep working hard and find a good routine for life. I was secretly laughing at it all, thinking all I needed was my talent. Work and discipline were for people like you. I was such an idiot."

Bernhard smiled. "ProV, I am really happy to see you again. You have come to the right place!"

Hollie then delivered the facts of this short par four. "It is playing just over 240 yards today, although a crow would only fly 220 yards to make the green. The tees could be set longer but the greenskeeper wanted to tempt the players today. To the right is a steep ravine. Balls hit there will only be found at the risk of one's life. But the left has plenty of room."

Indeed, disciplined golfers would lay up short and left. The design had created plenty of nice green fairway so a simple mid-iron would leave an easy pitch and a possible birdie. In some minds it was just a long par three.

Hollie loved to tell the story of Bobby Jones playing the hole that way, adding, "If Bobby Jones lays up, why are you going for it?" No one ever had a good answer, but few single digit players laid up either. For ProV, it was hard not to grab a hybrid or three wood and swing away.

Lucas turned to the great German champion for advice from one of the greatest ball strikers of all time. Langer's iron play was impeccable. His ball danced around the hole as much as any in history. "Bernhard, should we lay up here?"

His German accent had been Americanized by decades in Florida with his American wife and family. "This is the hardest shot on one of the hardest courses in the world—if you go for the green," he replied. "The green is small and dangerous. Anyone should be satisfied with a four here. Hit a middle iron to the widest part of the fairway, hit a pitch shot, one or two putts and move along." In other words, he agreed with Hollie.

Deadend was already hitting out of turn. He and Mocker had been quietly mimicking the German's speech. His tee ball with a driver sailed to the right—gone in the deep ravine.

Langer smiled, shook his head and whispered to Hollie, "He wants nothing to do with Discipline."

ProV had a three wood in hand, but after watching Deadend take off into oblivion, he went back to his bag and grabbed a six iron, hit it nicely left and was actually close enough with the bouncy turf to think about putting from twenty yards short off the firm links fairway.

Lucas and Wright both pulled five irons and hit perfect layups.

Bernhard smiled and said he would walk the hole. He had been the all time winningest senior golfer in history. He was disciplined in exercise, practice, food, balance, family, God… everything.

Lucas asked: "Bernhard, what's the number one key to your success?" He expected the answer to be discipline, since this was his favorite hole. But Langer surprised them all.

"Jesus Christ," he said clearly, without hesitation. After the mountain experience, ProV was all ears for this Jesus talk.

He then told them the short version of how hard work and practice had resulted in being a Masters champion in 1985 at age twenty-six. He was in such shock that when the chairman Hord Hardin asked him in the Butler Cabin to explain what had happened out on the course, he had casually said, "Jesus Christ, I can't really explain what happened."

"Unfortunately, Jesus was just a curse word for me in those days. I was driving from Augusta to Hilton Head on the Monday after the Masters. It should have been the greatest moment of my life. But for a reason I could not understand, I felt empty. I wondered to myself, 'Is this all there is to winning the Masters? Why do I feel so empty?'

"I had no sense of spiritual need while I was working my way up the PGA ladder. But now I was on top, even ranked number one in the world—but I felt no inner peace. And just as I was asking myself these questions, Bobby Clampett and I were playing a practice round on Tuesday morning. He invited me to the tour's Bible study that night. I went. A man named Larry Moody was there and taught about a man named Nicodemus, who was told he needed to be born again."

Bernhard used air quotes as he said "born again."[143]

"I had never heard that term in my life. I went back to the Tuesday night studies for many months until finally, after talking a lot with Larry Moody and Larry Nelson and many others, I surrendered my heart and life to Jesus Christ. As it turned out, nineteen-eighty-five was the greatest year of my life. I won at Augusta and found eternal life all in one year."

Hollie never got tired of introducing people to Bernhard because she knew he would be faithful to honor the name of Jesus.

Bernhard continued, "And now, here I am, helping guys like you. In fact, you may get to meet Nicodemus later today. He hangs around Hokmah quite often. He has become one of my best friends."

Mocker and Deadend had gone straight to the twelfth tee, not even bothering to look for the lost ball in the ravine. They wanted no part of discipline or speeches from Langer or Hollie. The remaining threesome all made routine fours, which Bernhard complimented: "Never be disappointed with a par."

Behind the green were two odd looking fellows who stood no more than five feet tall. They were singing softly and tenderly. At first, ProV wondered if it was Ian Woosnam but no, it was definitely not the wee Welshman.

Hollie encouraged them to stop for a moment. "That's John Wesley and his brother Charles who wrote over 6,500 hymns. They can give you another side to this discipline question. We've got to keep moving but a couple of minutes with these guys is worth a chat."

Lucas asked, "So, who are you and why are you here?"

In a beautiful English accent, John said simply, "We are here to make sure you understand that discipline is never enough. Discipline is necessary but will not save you."

He had sought to find God in obedience and a disciplined life as a young Anglican clergyman, even thinking that being a missionary to the heathens of Georgia would save his soul. But he discovered all

[143] John 3:3 "I tell you the truth, unless you are born again, you cannot see the Kingdom of God."

his discipline meant nothing without God living inside him. "I cried out to God on the ship coming home from America. 'God, I went to Georgia to save souls, but who will save me?'" said John.

Wright smiled because he loved this story.[144] So did Bernhard, often remembering that both his story and John's story had a Georgia connection, two hundred years apart.

Wesley finished his story, "When I returned to London, I went to a simple gathering at a place called Aldersgate. As the scripture was being read, my heart was strangely warmed. I knew Jesus had saved me, not based on my good works and discipline but upon the mercy of God alone.

"We will hope to see you around the clubhouse," he said as Charles began singing again. "Oh, for a thousand tongues to sing, thy great redeemer's praise..." The Wesley voices trailed off as the group of pilgrims marched on to the next hole.

[144] John Wesley, *The Works of John Wesley, Volume 1,* Third Edition Complete and Unabridged, Volume 1, 14 vols. (1738; repr., Baker Book House Company, 1978), 103.

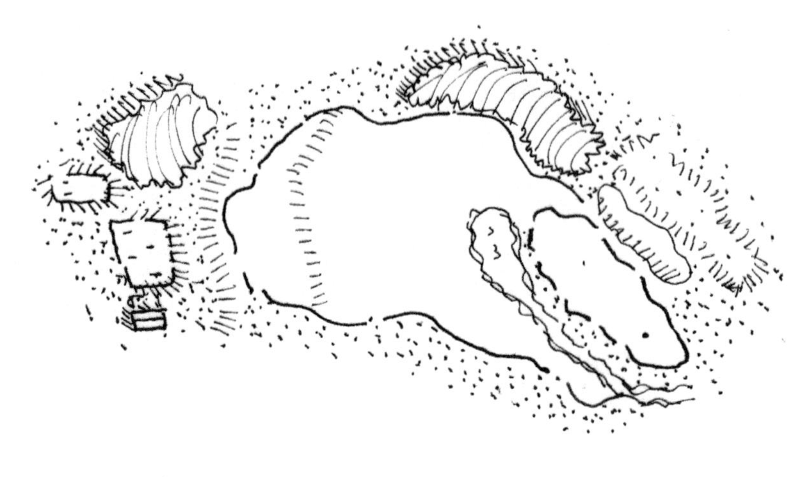

12 th
WINE
PAR 3, 180/152 YARDS
PROV 20:1
"THOSE LED ASTRAY
BY DRINK
CANNOT BE WISE"
HOKMAH
GOLF CLUB

12th Hole – Wine

PAR 3, 180/152 YARDS

"Those led astray by drink cannot be wise."
Proverbs 20:1

A friendly bartender was waiting behind a bar on the twelfth tee. "Good day, gentlemen," he said to Deadend and Mocker, who didn't stick around for Langer or the Wesley brothers. "My name is Jack. Jack Daniels." Mocker had told Dubs he would love the twelfth hole.

Jack poured drinks from his very own bottle for Dubs and his caddie. He loved to discuss with great passion how his hero John Daly won the Open at St. Andrews in 1995. He pulled a book from under the bar to quote his old pal who shared his initials and once famously said, "My best friend in those days (early tour days) was Jack Daniels. Had been since I was nineteen. Most of the time I was drinking Jack like you wouldn't believe, a fifth a day, sometimes more... Back then, JD and JD were quite a pair—practically inseparable."[145]

[145] John Daly, My Life In and Out of the Rough (Harper Collins Publishing 2005), p. 4.

Jack liked to imply that he should be credited with Daly's two major wins.

Mocker[146] and Deadend had been sitting at the bar for nearly twenty minutes, listening to Jack's tales, when the other pilgrims finally made it up the hill. They were sitting with one of the regulars, Albert Alcoholic,[147] discussing who knows what. Albert lived like a rich man but basically had nothing.[148]

Jack was rumored to be on his last leg. His liver was almost gone. A bartender was not supposed to drink, but that rule was broken every day.

He continued to laugh and read from Daly's own mouth, "I was having what had, over the summer, become my usual triple Jack Daniels on the rocks, no water, three at a time... I was taken to the hospital because I'd passed out with my eyes open and the guys I was drinking with thought I'd had a stroke or something. The next day I shot two under."[149] That sentence brought hoots and hollers of joy.

Deadend and Mocker agreed that Daly was indeed a worthy hero for them.

R.W. and Barnabas avoided the bar, which was easy to do on the largest tee box at Hokmah. The hole was a virtual replica of the twelfth at Augusta, with a beautiful stream fronting the par three, an elevated tee, and tricky Hokmah winds to overcome. It played 180 yards from the tips, but only 120 on many days. The greenskeeper set up the course with a tricky wind in mind. The tee was elevated so winds could never be avoided and disasters were always waiting to happen.

Hollie also ignored the bar, leading Lucas to the tee markers. The pin was tucked back right. Today's member tees were at 152 into a small breeze. Hollie handed Lucas a club. "It is a perfect six iron into the middle of the green. Don't even look at that bar or that pin."

[146] Proverbs 20:1 "Wine produces mockers; alcohol leads to brawls. Those led astray by drink cannot be wise."

[147] Proverbs 31:6-7 "Alcohol is for the dying, and wine for those in bitter distress."

[148] Proverbs 21:17 "Those who love wine and luxury will never be rich."

[149] Daly, Ibid at 3-4.

As soon as he hit it, he thought to himself, *Yes. Nothing quite so tasty as the sweet spot on a six iron*. He would gladly settle for a two-putt from thirty feet.

R.W. did the same with a five hybrid after a swirly breeze came up suddenly.

ProV had the honors but he had stopped to talk to Jack Daniels about his old hero Daly. A small Guinness seemed like a good idea to commemorate the moment.

He had already forgotten that Jack Nicklaus and Ivor Young had him crying on the tenth green. He had forgotten he had birdied the hole with the Golden Bear watching. He had forgotten the Langer speech on discipline and Jesus. And he forgot that John Daly didn't deserve to be discussed in the same breath with Jack Nicklaus.

Wright and Lucas, along with Hollie and Mr. T, sat down and waited. The view was so glorious that waiting was not a problem. North Sea right, a beautiful stream below near the green, and best of all, two pretty white specks in the middle of the Hokmah green.

"Where else would you want to be than right here?" Lucas said to no one in particular. There were no clocks on the back nine at Hokmah. Time had disappeared.

ProV finally ambled over, "Well, guys, how far?"

Mr. T signaled 152 with his fingers as he motioned with his hands that the wind was in their face.

ProV's shot of whisky that followed the Guinness had just kicked in. Mr. T's selection of a seven iron, presented once again to ProV like a waiter offering fine wine in a five-star restaurant, was rejected. "Give me the eight. My adrenaline is pumping." Alcohol had lied to him again.

As he reluctantly handed over the eight iron, Mr. T looked toward Hollie with a raised eyebrow. She shook her head, knowing what would surely happen.

The eight iron was struck perfectly, despite the alcohol. It was only six inches short of perfect, which meant the ball was now comfortably settled into the wee pond which fronted the hole. But instead of settling for the drop zone at eighty-five yards, ProV wanted to prove the eight iron was the perfect club. Every drink takes a few IQ points away from the golfer, and ProV was not only losing golf balls but his mind as well. Another ball hit toward the toe was baptized.

As ProV dug in his bag for a third ball, Dubs took the tee and deposited two balls in the watery grave. Dubs now thought he and ProV were tight. "Well, ol' buddy, we just don't have it today. Hard to be great every day. But that Jack Daniels. What a great guy."

ProV stared at his new drinking buddy and realized he had sunk back to the bottom from his moments of redemption with Nicklaus and Langer.

The forecaddie was a gentle soul named Sonny Sober, who waited patiently beside the green. He was a man of limited talent who had beaten JD and Alcoholic out of a lot of money over the years. Being sober was worth at least three shots a side, and twenty IQ points when it came time to make the bets.

The idea that alcohol cured the yips and calmed the nerves over three-foot putts had been debunked long ago.

As ProV left the twelfth green with a seven, Sober whispered in a loving tone, "So, friend, did we learn anything here today? Maybe alcohol has not been kind to you and your family?"[150]

Lucas nodded a thank-you to Sober and took ProV's arm to lead him to the next tee. Alcohol indeed had been the ruin of ProV's father, and it was a major cause of his failures as well. His parents had met in a bar. Went home together that night and stayed together long enough to produce Paul Jr. It had been an alcohol-fueled love story, and when the fumes went dry, so did the love. All that was left were memories of screaming and arguing, and a vow to "never be like him," while at the same time trying to make him proud.

Typical teenage and college drinking adventures eventually became midtwenties alcoholism for him too. Heredity is quite real, especially when it comes to flaws and foibles. And alcohol.

[150] Proverbs 31:4 "Rulers should not crave alcohol."

The "high" coming off the Mountain of Threes had evaporated into the cool Orkney air. Lucas put his arm around his friend. "Let's go, buddy. Time to move on."

Hollie quoted Proverbs 23 as they moved away,

Who has anguish?

Who has sorrow?

Who is always fighting?

Who is always complaining?

Who has unnecessary bruises?

Who has bloodshot eyes?

It is the one who spends long hours in the taverns, trying out new drinks.

Don't gaze at the wine, seeing how red it is, how it sparkles in the cup, how smoothly it goes down.

For in the end it bites like a poisonous snake; it stings like a viper.

You will see hallucinations, and you will say crazy things.

You will stagger like a sailor tossed at sea, clinging to a swaying mast.

And you will say, "They hit me, but I didn't feel it. I didn't even know it when they beat me up.

When will I wake up so I can look for another drink?" [151]

As they left the twelfth green, ProV thought he saw a viper under his feet. He jumped, fell down, hit his head and sobered up.

[151] Proverbs 23:29-35

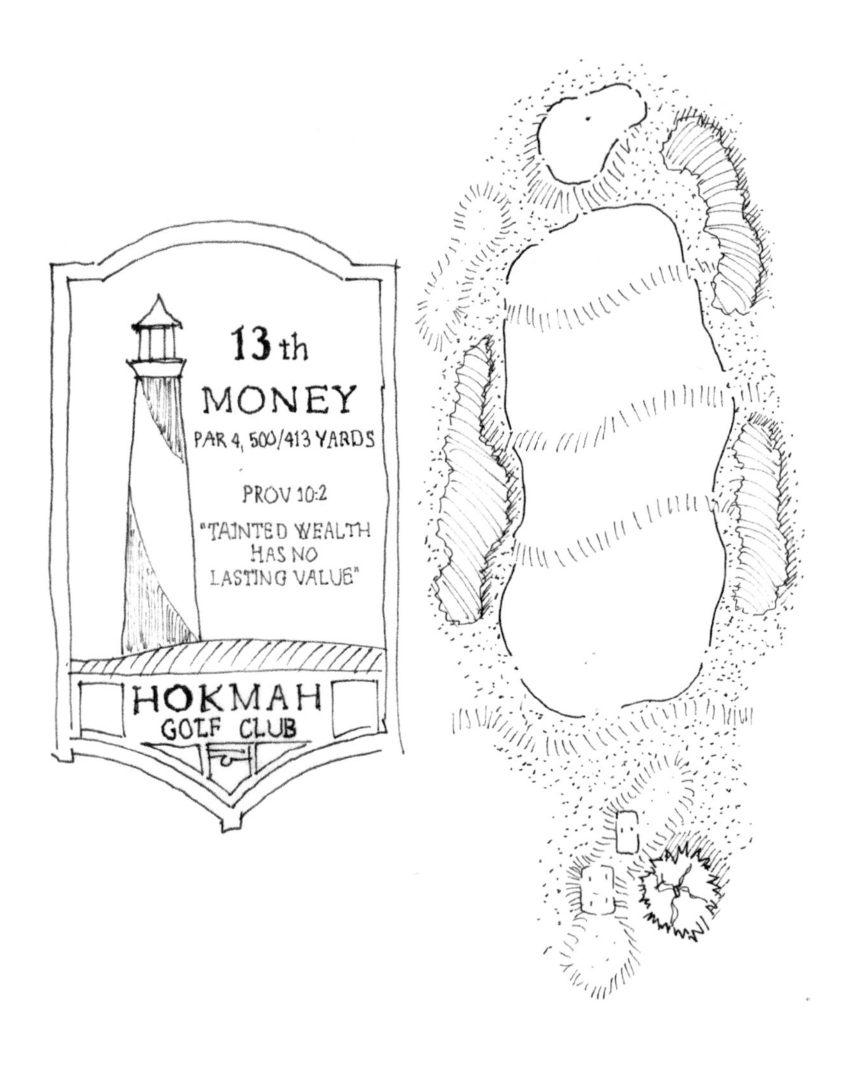

13th
MONEY
PAR 4, 500/413 YARDS
PROV 10:2
"TAINTED WEALTH
HAS NO
LASTING VALUE"
HOKMAH
GOLF CLUB

13th Hole – Money

PAR 4, 500/413 YARDS

"Tainted wealth has no lasting value."
Proverbs 10:2

The long thirteenth hole had been the ruin of many golfers. It was the only hole on the back nine which turned around and went back to the north, into the wind and toward the Mountain of Threes. The hole was long enough and usually into the wind, so the designer had made this the only hole without any bunkers. It was hard enough.

The tee was elevated on a sand dune, with a lonely dead tree just a few steps to the right. ProV and Lucas were shocked to see what appeared to be a man hanging from the tree.

Wright told them, "His name was Judson Judas.[152] He was a CPA, a treasurer for a big company. He's been there as long as anyone can remember. Some say it was nineteen-twenty-nine. Some say much longer."

[152] Matthew 27:5 "Then Judas threw the silver coins down in the Temple and went out and hanged himself."

Hollie chimed in, "Don't worry. The image you see is just a mirage. A reminder that power and prestige and wealth will never satisfy."

On the tee was a handsome young man who greeted Hollie and her pilgrims with apologies for being in the way. Hollie knew the routine. This guy played this same hole every day. He loved it. He was just teeing off, a long straight drive down the right side, when ProV, Lucas and R.W. walked up.

"Just sit tight a moment, guys. He will be gone very quickly," said Hollie.

The man and his caddie, Greedy Green, trotted down near the right rough where many a ball had disappeared into an eternal grave. ProV asked Hollie, "That handsome kid has a good golf swing. What's his name?"

"No one knows. He is here almost every day. He seems to have enough money to do whatever he wants, but he loves hanging out with all the famous and not-so-famous golfers. He lives in a big mansion on Lucre Island, east of Westray. A helicopter brings him in most days."

She pointed behind the tees where a helicopter pad had been constructed just for him. "As you can see, the hole is a paradise to the eyes. Beautiful view of the North Sea across to the left. The hole sits up high enough to see the sea. The shadows and the contours of the hole make it a piece of art. He spends a lot of time on his phone checking and rechecking his accounts, counting his money. All we know is he is rich and young and claims to be a ruler of some kind, perhaps an earl or a viscount with a snobby British accent to match his title."

ProV didn't know what to make of it all. A quadruple bogey mixed with alcohol was still stinging him. Some rich kid in the fairway was the least of his worries.

Wright had the honors coming off a nice par, and his drive on this "money hole" needed no forecaddie—right down the middle. ProV and Lucas followed suit.

Richie Rich and Poorest O'Poore, the forecaddies, were glad they could relax. They both had grown up in New Debt City, a huge metropolis most people had visited often. Both suffered from the same disease:

love of money.[153] One had too much, and the other had too little, but their malady was the same.

"Interesting how they can be so similar," said Wright. "Poor people are sure that their unhappiness is caused by the lack of money. And people with plenty of money are also sure their unhappiness is because someone has more than them."

Deadend, meanwhile, was still reeling from too much time at the twelfth tee bar. And since he clearly had more money than the other three men combined, his eyes lit up when he saw the sign for this thirteenth hole. "Finally, we get to my hole."[154]

He had gotten uber rich overnight. A Ponzi scheme had turned his small fortune into a gigantic one. He was halfway to becoming a billionaire "with a B," as he loved to say.[155] He counted his money every day. The net worth number at the bottom of the page controlled his moods. For him, it was way more than just black ink on a white piece of paper. It was the only scorecard that mattered.

Mocker handed him his driver and said, "Hit this just like the one on number ten. This is the number-four handicap hole, into a breeze, with trouble left and right." Mocker whispered, "Be careful, we're running out of balls." Two dozen should have been plenty, but they were down to their last sleeve.

Even Mocker thanked the Lord quietly when Deadend's drive found the fairway. It was not pretty, but the drop kick had straightened out the clubface and landed him 200 yards down the middle. As they walked off the tee, Deadend bragged about his "high net worth."[156] Hollie could have told him his entire portfolio would go to zero within two years. But she knew he would not listen.

[153] Proverbs 22:2 "The rich and poor have this in common: The Lord made them both."

[154] Proverbs 13:11 "Wealth from get-rich-quick schemes quickly disappears; wealth from hard work grows over time."

[155] Proverbs 21:6 "Wealth created by a lying tongue is a vanishing mist and a deadly trap."

[156] Proverbs 23:4-5 "Don't wear yourself out trying to get rich. Be wise enough to know when to quit. In the blink of an eye wealth disappears, for it will sprout wings and fly away like an eagle."

As the foursome approached their tee shots, Richie and Poorest were chatting. They had Googled the players and wanted to talk to Deadend, who was listed in *Forbes* magazine near the top of one of their lists. Richie's own millionaire status was depressing him. He wanted to see if Deadend could offer any tips to gain more wealth and happiness.

"Great drive, sir," offered Richie. Sadly for him, Deadend was only interested in his next shot. Mocker handed Dubs his three wood with, "Straight to the flag. All you got," and backed the golf bag right into Richie to signal, *That's enough, kid.*

Deadend topped his ball, cursed God and started walking, throwing the three wood back in Mocker's general direction. Richie admired that and looked forward to the day when he could be rich enough to mistreat caddies and employees.

Poorest O'Poore had wandered over to chat with the two Americans. His dream was to live in the USA where everyone, it seemed, was prosperous. He lived in a caravan with his eighty-seven-year-old mother, surviving on a government check and a few tips from golfers. His love affair with money was more fantasy than reality, since he was virtually penniless, thanks to a mindset of poverty.

As he approached, Hollie handed Lucas a three wood. He needed all of it for the long uphill approach. ProV followed suit with a solid four iron. Wright was the only one who actually made the green's surface, smashing his three wood up the bank and onto the green. But all three were close enough to the green to experience one of golf's sweetest feelings—a 200-yard walk with a putter in hand.

As they all marched toward the green, Hollie told the young forecaddies what she always did: "Young men, follow me. You're wasting your life down in this valley of money. I know it's comfortable here, but you are missing some unspeakable joys—even eternal life itself."

The forecaddies paid no attention. They just shook their heads and wandered back to the comfort of their conversation. They were busy planning a trip to Arizona to visit Deadend, with a stop nearby to experience the joys of Vegas.

Up by the green, the young man who had teed off in front of them had stopped. This would be his only hole today. Indeed, he had played the hole a half dozen times today while checking his accounts on his phone.

Hollie dropped Lucas's bag next to the young man and chatted while the group putted out.

Almost whispering, the rich young man with no name said, "Look Hollie, we've had this conversation too many times. You told me I would have to sell everything I have to follow you out of here. Why would I be so crazy? I've got it all here. And how do I know eternal life even exists? You're just like that rabbi I talked to awhile back. He knew I had kept all the commandments my whole life. But for some reason which I will never understand, he acted like that was not good enough. Well, I disagree. I am good enough. This valley suits me just fine. I love this hole. Play on."

Wright was on his way to a routine par, if you call a drive and a three wood and two putts from fifty feet routine. ProV had sobered up and also made a par, while Lucas seemed perfectly happy with a bogey five. Deadend told Mocker to give him a five, which was very generous since he had hit the ball six times and picked it up once.

Wright was always disturbed by the young man whose name was unknown. He knew money and wealth had a grip on this young man, especially since he had inherited the money.[157] It all seemed like such a tragedy, missing out on the experience of being a personal disciple of the Rabbi because he was obsessed with money.

"It would indeed be better to be poor, don't you think?" offered Wright to Lucas and ProV as they walked to the next tee. "Peter, James and John were blessed to be relatively poor. We know their names because they said 'Yes' when Jesus said '*Follow me.*'"[158]

Behind the green, sitting at a picnic table, was a tiny lady dressed in white. She was alone. "Is this the famous Mother Teresa?" asked ProV.

[157] Proverbs 20:21 "An inheritance obtained too early in life is not a blessing in the end."

[158] Matthew 4:19

"No," said Hollie with a smile, "although the resemblance is staggering. She's the widow Mite. She's the same woman who gave all she had to Jesus once. Stop and talk to her for a few minutes. It is always worthwhile. Her story is so powerful that we call her Dinah Mite."

The widow Mite was chatting amiably with an older gentleman named George Generosity.[159]

"And the man with her may even be better," Hollie said. "Absolutely the happiest man you've ever met. He gives away ten times more than he lives on every year, and still seems to have plenty.[160] He claims God just keeps replenishing his barns."

Lucas and R.W. walked straight to the older couple for a friendly hello. Lucas asked them about the handsome young man, knowing they must know him well. "What's that dude's name?"

The widow Mite knew him all too well. "We just call him Nameless. Odd, I know, but how sad his case truly is."[161]

She explained, "His story is told in the Bible.[162] He had an offer from Jesus to be one of His twelve disciples, and to have treasures in heaven, but he turned it down. He was too busy. Too proud. Too addicted to his stuff. Too much in love with himself."

As they all finally turned to leave, the tiny widow Mite handed each player a poem about the young man.

We are not told his name—this "rich young ruler"
Who sought the Lord that day;
We only know that he had great possessions
And that he went away.
He went away; he kept his earthly treasure
But oh, at what a cost!
Afraid to take the cross and lose his riches—
And God and Heaven were lost.

159 Proverbs 22:9 "Blessed are those who are generous."

160 Proverbs 11:25 "The generous will prosper."

161 Proverbs 11:28 "Trust in your money and down you go!"

162 Mark 10:17-22

So for the tinsel bonds that held and drew him
What honor he let slip—
Comrade of John and Paul and friend of Jesus—
What glorious fellowship!
For they who left their all to follow Jesus
Have found a deathless fame,
On his immortal scroll of saints and martyrs
God wrote each shining name.
We should have read his there—the rich young ruler—
If he had stayed that day;
Nameless—though Jesus loved him—ever nameless
Because—he went away.[163]

ProV's countenance changed as he read the words. Nameless left him speechless.

[163] Mrs. Chas E Cowman, *Springs in the Valley (1939); repr., Zondervan Publishing Company, 1997, 269.*

14th
WOMEN
PAR 5, 780/780 YARDS
PROV 5:18
"REJOICE IN THE
WIFE OF YOUR
YOUTH"
HOKMAH
GOLF CLUB

14th Hole – Women

PAR 5, 780/780 YARDS

"...rejoice in the wife of your youth."
Proverbs 5:18

Greeting the players just left of the fourteenth tee was a well-dressed older man who introduced himself as Dr. Hugh Utter Fool.[164] "Welcome, men," he said, "you will love this hole. Let me suggest a stop at my cottage down the left side there. We call it Folly's Cabin, in honor of my beautiful daughter. She'd love to meet you."

Hollie was quick to grab ProV and Lucas and move them to the other side of the tee, away from Hugh. "Ignore him. He is harmless if you ignore him," said Hollie.

"By far the scariest hole on the course," offered R.W., knowing such negative talk was not normally good for golfers who need to know

[164] Proverbs 6:32 "But the man who commits adultery is an utter fool, for he destroys himself."

where to hit the ball, never where *not* to hit the ball. A golfer needs to play without fear. But this was not just any hole.

Hollie was keeping quiet. She knew the macho mind and the fourteenth hole at Hokmah but she would let R.W. handle the counsel on this hole. Wisdom in the Bible was always in the feminine gender. "Always a 'she,'" she would say with a smile. And part of that wisdom was knowing when to let R.W. speak for her. She was wise enough to know most men would not take advice from her about other women.

R.W. recommended the group stop, take a moment, and look down the fairway. Not all of the trouble was so obvious. Indeed, the female forecaddies, Jezebel and Eros, were beckoning from the fairway to just "Come on down." They were wearing attire more suitable for the beach, despite the cool temperatures.

The hole had only one set of tees, set at 780 yards. No shorter tees for older men. This hole was a monster. For even the longest of hitters, it was four or five shots and played as a par six or seven, even if played perfectly. The scorecard said par five, but that was a fiction. Double-figure scores were common.

Some never finished the hole, living out their lives in the arms of women who won the battle of the sexes.

Wright pointed at the slightly downhill tee shot and explained: "To the left you can see some trees, a forest really. These are the only proper trees on the course, not native to Scotland. They were shipped in and planted in about eighteen-sixty when the first Open was being played. We now call them simply Folly's Forest.

"The forest is full of wildlife. Stags caught in traps, oxen going to slaughter, birds flying into snares.[165] Even tigers have lost their way in these woods. It is a dangerous place."

Lucas and ProV noticed a huge female pig with a gold ring in her snout[166] coming out of the woods. On the other side, far away from

[165] Proverbs 7:22-23 "He followed her at once, like an ox going to the slaughter. He was like a stag caught in a trap.... He was like a bird flying into a snare..."

[166] Proverbs 11:22 "A beautiful woman who lacks discretion is like a gold ring in a pig's snout."

the temptations of the left rough, was a graceful and beautiful doe.[167]

R.W. continued his warning, "Actually, millions have been lost there. No, billions. Solomon himself is still the king in those woods. Very sad. His one thousand wives and concubines are there somewhere. Ironic, indeed. He was acclaimed as the wisest man on earth. And yet, at the end of his days, he was no better than the rest of you boys, maybe worse." ProV didn't know what a concubine might be but part of him wanted to find out.

"Down the left side, separating the fairway from Folly's Forest, is a river of death known as Samson's Stream. The falls and the fast-moving stream are deadly. Any ball hit in there should be abandoned. It appears to be a gently shallow stream, but in fact is filled with fury."

ProV heard the warnings. But still, part of him wanted to go see the forest creatures. Or experience Samson's Stream. What is it that draws a man to such danger? Temporary insanity? He found himself saying he'd like to talk to Solomon the king. But what he really wanted was to see those wives and concubines. Maybe even help Solomon with his kingly "duties."

Mr. T handed ProV his driver, pointing down the middle. ProV put his draw on the ball, secretly hoping for the exotic forest. The ball stayed straight down the middle.

Hollie applauded, "Nicely done, sir." He feigned satisfaction.

Lucas and Wright had been listening well. They hit three-woods, making it at least a five-shot hole. Each found the fairway.

Deadend got advice from a mumbling Mocker, who was hoping his man would hit it left. He got his wish and the pair disappeared into the forest. They found his ball in the backyard of a lovely little home with smoke coming from a chimney. It appeared to be a safe and cozy haven. Little did Dubs know, *"...her house is the road to the grave. Her bedroom is the den of death."*[168]

[167] Proverbs 5:18-19 "...rejoice in the wife of your youth. She is a living deer, a graceful doe."

[168] Proverbs 7:27

A sign at the edge of the fairway warned, *"Don't wander down her wayward path. For she has been the ruin of many; many men have been her victims."*[169] They ignored it.

Wright, meanwhile, was talking to Lucas and ProV as they left the tee. "Good play, men. Now, you've usually got to hit four monster shots. Sort of like real life. The drive is just the first survival test, like being a teenager with all the hormones flying. The second test is early adulthood, when marriage or a faithful girlfriend is wonderful but not usually enough to keep the other women out of your mind.

"Then the third shot, when you just get tired of seeing the same ol' face and hearing the same ol' voice day in and day out. Your beautiful bride can turn into a quarrelsome wife[170] after a few years. The eyes can wander to younger women.

"And just when you've survived all that, old age comes roaring in as the fourth and final shot. You think you've survived all the big tests. The woods and river of death seem behind you. I presumed at age seventy everything would cool down and women would not bother me anymore. But no, that fourth shot is a tough one. Indeed, the fairway narrows over the last fifty yards, and Samson's Stream comes across the fairway, finding balls hit too short of the green. It's called Walter's Burn in honor of Hagen, who hit three balls into the burn on October 6, 1969, when he was seventy-six years old. He was never seen again."

As Wright finished speaking, the young lady Folly appeared from the left woods.[171] She greeted each golfer with invitations to join her for some *"stolen water and secret food."*[172]

She was the oldest daughter of Hugh Utter Fool, loud and hard to forget. Too much makeup did not stop men from looking twice or

[169] Proverbs 7:25-26

[170] Proverbs 27:15 "A quarrelsome wife is annoying as a constant dripping."

[171] Proverbs 9:13 "The woman named Folly is brash. She is ignorant and doesn't know it."

[172] Proverbs 9:14-17

even three times at her ample cleavage. Hollie warned the guys, *"Her guests are in the depths of the grave."* [173]

She was walking with a handsome couple, both with long flowing hair. "Samson and Delilah," shouted Hollie loud enough for all to hear. Apparently, Samson[174] had survived his trip into the stream which carried his name. But Delilah was leading him by the hand, perhaps to a nearby barber.

All three players had survived the first three shots, but were still well over 200 yards from the green. Deadend had disappeared into Folly's Forest, not likely to be seen again.

The three made their way toward the green after their fourth shots landed safely across Walter's Burn which crossed the fairway fifty steps from the front edge. They were still nowhere near the hole. A nice breeze was now helping the golfers. Three putts later from short of the devilish green, all three agreed they were just happy to survive this testing fourteenth hole.

"I heard a good one long ago. Ninety-nine percent of a man's problems are in his pants," offered Wright. He pulled out his wallet to demonstrate. "Money and sex. They cover almost all temptations and sins for men."

Behind the green was a crowd of females. Four groups of ladies were obviously avoiding each other. The first group, chatting around a picnic table with a big umbrella, were modestly dressed in Middle Eastern Biblical garb. Hollie went to join them for a short visit. She stayed just long enough to give greetings to each one who stood to give the traditional kiss on both cheeks.

Lucas had to ask Wright, "So who are these ladies?"

"That is Lydia, Anna, Deborah, Phoebe and two ladies named Mary. Often there are more, but some of the ladies had to work today. Martha is almost never there, busy working, but several others join

[173] Proverbs 9:18

[174] Judges 16:4-22

when possible. They call themselves the Proverbs Thirty-One Ladies.[175] They play a few holes on Tuesdays. Lovely ladies who never keep score."

Lucas knew a bit about Proverbs Thirty-One women. His wife, now gone ten years, had been such a saint. His heart was still breaking. Every day.

A second pair of just two ladies seemed preoccupied, talking about their husbands. "I honestly don't even know these women," said Hollie as she picked up Lucas's bag to move on to the next tee. "Mrs. Nagger and Mrs. Complainer are not much fun. Their husbands play a lot of golf. It's a vicious circle. These women complain about how much their men play golf, which of course in turn makes the men want to get out of the house for anything, especially more golf. And then the women talk even worse. The Naggers own a lovely home on a nearby island, but he often spends the night here in an attic.[176] Mr. Complainer lives in the desert all alone most of the time."[177]

She pointed, "See the third group over there? They come up out of Folly's Forest just to cause trouble. You can see by the way they are dressed that their intent is to lure men into their webs, like spiders. Their main weapons are cleavage, bright lipstick and dyed blond hair." ProV was definitely watching.

"And don't be fooled. These are not just prostitutes. These are professional women—lawyers, business ladies, social workers, famous media types... all seductive in their goal to find men." Folly and Delilah had joined the small party. They often sat on the front porch of Folly's little cabin and lured men into the bedroom.

Hollie stopped to chat with the fourth and final group of ladies who were assembled on the path to the next tee. They gathered around Hollie as if she were their loving grandmother, which in some ways she

[175] Proverbs 31:10-31

[176] Proverbs 21:9 "It's better to live alone in the corner of an attic than with a quarrelsome wife in a lovely home."

[177] Proverbs 21:19 "It's better to live alone in the desert than with a quarrelsome, complaining wife."

was. They all were modestly dressed and had a radiance that was hard not to notice. Their beauty came from within. They all hugged Hollie and said, "See you later this week. We will be here."

"So, Hollie," said Lucas when they caught up to her, "who were those last three ladies?"

"Undoubtedly the happiest women in the world. You can't know how good it is to be virtuous unless you once lived in the darkness and forest of sin. They were able to break away. Those ladies were stuck down there for quite a while, until God gave them the key to escape."

"Names?" asked Lucas.

"The oldest lady is Rahab.[178] She was a prostitute who ended up being one of Yeshua's great-grandmothers. Isn't she beautiful?"

Lucas agreed. She was ancient but beautiful.

"The second lady, standing by the well, is Sam, short for Samaria Sychar.[179] Just a nickname. She met Yeshua one day and He told her about the five husbands and the man she lived with at the time. Poor thing. Not a prostitute but didn't think she could live without a man. Almost worse in a way, allowing any man to hang around without so much as one denarius coming her way."

Sounds like my mom, thought ProV with anguish in his heart. He had a couple of half sisters he barely knew in California somewhere.

"Believe it or not, Sam is the first person to whom Yeshua revealed he was the Messiah. He revealed his deity to a single woman with five ex-husbands. She believed in Jesus as the Messiah even *before* the disciples!"

Hollie continued to walk and talk. "And the third lady may be the most special of all. Mary Magdalene was a wild woman who met Yeshua, received forgiveness and healing for all her sins, and began to follow Him everywhere. She received the honor of being the first person on earth to see the risen Christ."

[178] Hebrews 11:31

[179] John 4:7-26

ProV knew none of this. He stared at Hollie to see if she was kidding. She was not.

"And best of all, Yeshua spoke her name. She only recognized him when he said, 'Mary.'[180] He knew her name."

Hollie added a postscript for ProV: "Paul Player, the same One knows your name. Keep listening for the Voice. You will hear it."

As these profound words sank into the bottom of ProV's shoes, Lucas turned to his friend, "ProV, think about it. Jesus picked two wild women to hear and see the good news first! Sam heard he was the Messiah. Mary found the empty tomb." ProV scratched his head in wonderment.

As they continued toward the fifteenth tee, a rainbow appeared in the sky, just across the vista of the North Sea. Lucas said, "You know, Hollie, even that rainbow was stolen from us a few decades ago by people who worship sexual perversion."

"Yes, believe me," agreed Hollie, "I know all about it. This is not just about casual and improper sexual relationships between men and women. This is a full-blown revolt against the Creator, the God of Heaven who created us male and female to love and replenish the earth through loving each other."

Hollie stopped Lucas in his tracks with a final statement on the subject. "This is all out war by the evil one against God and His creative powers. When he stole our precious rainbow, it was his final battle cry."

She paused and looked Lucas in the eye, "But his time is short."[181] She smiled.

ProV had been listening to it all, knowing he had had enough of chasing women. He wondered for the first time, *Maybe Mary Ann and the kids would take me back?* It was doubtful. Mary Ann was not truly a Proverbs Thirty-One lady. Not yet. But he knew she could be.

Deadend had finally appeared. He was wet and claimed he had been

[180] John 20:16

[181] Revelation 12:12

chased by a tiger, then tripped and fell into a narrow well deep in Folly's Forest.[182] "I was lucky to survive that one." No one asked for details, even though he was shaking like a Labrador coming out of the surf.

[182] Proverbs 23:27 "A prostitute is a dangerous trap; a promiscuous woman is as dangerous as falling into a narrow well."

15th
WORK
PAR 4, 466/410 YARDS
PROV 24:30
"I WENT PAST
THE FIELD OF
THE SLUGGARD..."
HOKMAH
GOLF CLUB

15th Hole – Work

PAR 4, 466/410 YARDS

"I went past the field of the sluggard..."
Proverbs 24:30

Samuel Sluggard was lying down on a bench near the fifteenth tee. He had shown great promise as a youth. His uncle Slothful had put a golf club in his hands at age two and the game came easy. He imitated his uncle's sweet and smooth swing. He could break ninety by age nine. He was a plus-two handicap by age sixteen. He nearly captured the British Amateur at seventeen. He would have been the champion with a trip to the Masters but he missed a three-foot putt on the thirty-sixth hole.

For Sluggard, the game was easy. Too easy. No reason to practice. No reason to work.

But now he was old and looked even older. He was part of the maintenance crew at Hokmah. His only job was this fifteenth hole. But while the first fourteen holes had been beautifully maintained, Sluggard's fifteenth was sadly grown up in weeds, a maintenance disaster.

Bunkers had not been raked. Fairways were rarely mowed. Hollie was ashamed but she knew the Creator kept Sluggard around, hoping he might change.

She told Lucas, "Leave him alone. Believe it or not, that old guy with the gray stubble won the British Boys in 2022. He was gonna be the next Rory McIlroy. Now look at ol' Sam. Sad."

Sam slowly stood up and swaggered over to Wright.

"Nice to see ya again, R.W. You're not gonna play this misery of a hole are ya?"

R.W. nodded with a smile that said, "Of course we are." He joked, "You know Hollie. She's teaching a couple of visitors some things they never heard."

Sluggard frowned. "Oh, Hollie. So full of herself. So sure she knows it all. Pity the poor soul she's baggin'."

The fifteenth hole was indeed hard work. It required mental strength. It required a long and difficult walk up the largest hill on the back nine. The ground was softer than the other holes, making it seem even more difficult than it was. Both sides of the fairway were guarded by thorny bushes with briars. There were thousands of balls in them, since going in to look was unthinkable.[183]

Sluggard said, "If I was you, I'd skip this hole. Too much hard work here. Golf is supposed to be fun, like when I won the British Boys." To his disappointment, nobody took the bait and asked about his victory just thirty-four years ago.

"Plus, see those lions[184] down in the fairway? Scary creatures, I promise you. I've seen 'em eat a man alive."

ProV and Lucas looked but saw no such creatures. Hollie whispered, "Sam is always coming up with excuses to not do his job. No one else has ever seen these 'lions' but he swears they exist and make it impossible for him to mow the fairways or green, or otherwise care for the hole."

[183] Proverbs 15:19 "A lazy person's way is blocked with briers, but the path of the upright is an open highway."

[184] Proverbs 22:13 "The lazy person claims, 'There's a lion out there!' If I go outside, I might be killed."

R.W. knew better. The first time he met Sluggard, he had to let three groups play through as he stopped politely to hear about the 2022 British Boy's Championship, which sounded like a major by the time Sluggard got through.

Sam singled out ProV this time. "Well, since you seem interested, I had never hit a practice ball in my life. Just a few warm-up shots when time allowed. I qualified with no problem, and my first match was against Lee Westwood's son. I dispatched him six and five.

"I really never had any trouble until the finals against Nick Faldo's grandson, who had worked way too hard to get there. And of course, along the way I beat some boy from Germany who fancied himself another Bernhard Langer, practicing all the time. Work, work, work. All a waste and I proved it in that tournament."

Lucas overheard it all. Hollie cautioned, "Stay away. He's contagious." Sluggard went back to his bench.

All four players hit mediocre drives down the fairway and as they walked, Hollie quoted Scripture from Proverbs.

> *"I walked by the field of a lazy person... I saw that it was overgrown with nettles. It was covered with weeds... A little extra sleep, a little more slumber, a little folding of the hands to rest—then poverty will pounce on you like a bandit; scarcity will attack you like an armed robber."* [185]

The hole was a par four, but all seemed happy enough to be on the green in three shots, avoiding unraked bunkers, prickly thorns and gorse left and right. ProV had not avoided a huge divot which found his golf ball. Mr. T. shook his head at the bad luck, but the so-called fairway was in poor condition, thanks to Sam's lazy bones. When they all two-putted for bogeys, even Dubs, Hollie reminded them, "Nothing wrong with a bogey on this monster."

Joseph from Nazareth was behind the green. Lucas looked at Hollie. "*The* Joseph of Nazareth?"

[185] Proverbs 24:30-34

"Yup. Stop and chat. Always worth the time. Think about it. The man chosen to be a father to the Savior of the world must be worth some time."

Lucas stuck out his hand and felt a calloused hand engulf his own. "So, Joseph, what a pleasure. We know so little about you. Why are you sitting here on this hole named Work?"

That got a huge smile from the middle-aged man. "Well, as you well know, I am a carpenter. Not easy work. Only get paid for what we produce. So being lazy is not an option. Talent is not as important as hard work."

That rang a bell with Lucas who remembered what one of his old golf teachers had tried to teach him fifty years earlier. "Joseph, I think you would agree with something I still remember from the old days. It was for a bunch of lazy, irresponsible kids on a golf team, but I found it helpful on Wall Street, too."

Joseph put down his tools, wiped his brow and sat on a chair that was almost finished. "I'm all ears."

Lucas pulled a laminated card from his wallet and read, "Ten Things That Require No Talent: One, being on time; two, making an effort; three, being high-energy; four, having a positive attitude; five, being passionate; six, using good body language; seven, being coachable; eight, doing a little extra; nine, being prepared; ten, having a strong work ethic."

"Excellent," Joseph answered with a smile. "No one knows this, but my son Yeshua had no talent for carpentry. He was terrible. But now that you mention it, he had all of the above. Nobody outworked my boy."

Lucas and ProV looked around to make sure they were not holding anyone up. They wanted to stay and talk to Joseph for a while.

"So why were you chosen to be his earthly father?" asked Lucas.

"I have no answer for such a profound question, but consider this, I worked with my hands. I was basically poor. I had no wealth. Yeshua would not be raised in a home of privilege, not even a white-collar home of a politician or lawyer or rabbi. It was a humble home of a blue-collar worker like me."

"So our Savior would have calloused hands," said Lucas, thinking a thought he had never considered. Joseph opened his hands to show Lucas his own callouses, paused, and then reminded the pilgrims, "Callouses. Yes. But nail scars too." ProV was listening to the entire exchange with his jaws dropping.

Hollie knew it was time to go but finished with, "Men, do you realize what Joseph is saying? The Savior did not prepare for saving the world by going to a seminary or Bible school. He prepared by going to work every day! He learned what hard work was. He learned what it was like to produce a product, a good product. He learned what it felt like to get cheated by a customer, not paid sometimes. He learned more about human nature by working with his hands and selling a product or service than he ever could have learned as a full-time student rabbi."

Hollie concluded with, "Work brings profit, but *mere talk leads to poverty.*[186] *Lazy hands make for poverty.*"[187] She gazed back at Sluggard who was now engaged in an argument with Mocker, who had stopped him to complain about the divot Dubs had landed in. Even Deadend and Mocker seemed to know laziness was a sin.

[186] Proverbs 14:23

[187] Proverbs 10:4 (NIV)

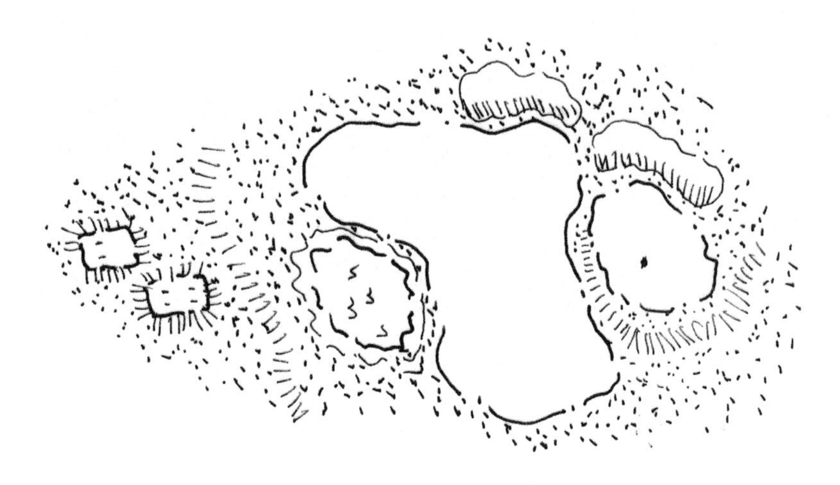

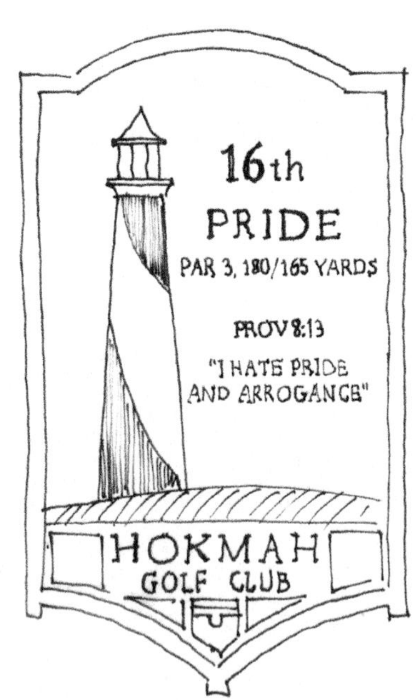
16th
PRIDE
PAR 3, 180/165 YARDS
PROV 8:13
"I HATE PRIDE
AND ARROGANCE"
HOKMAH
GOLF CLUB

16th Hole – Pride

PAR 3, 180/165 YARDS

"I hate pride and arrogance."
Proverbs 8:13

Nimrod Narcissus was waiting on the sixteenth tee. His sole companion was a large mirror, similar to the ones used by golf instructors to show players what's right or wrong in the setup. Nimrod was multitasking, looking at himself in the mirror and taking a selfie with his camera.

"Who is this guy, Hollie?" asked Lucas.

"He comes from here in Orkney, a small and strange island called Itsallaboutme on the eastern coast, on the way to Scandinavia. He claims Norwegian roots. Nimrod was once a wonderful golfer. He was also, as you can see, quite a handsome fellow. His blond flowing hair and good looks meant many people, both men and women, would fall in love with him. Women wanted to bed him. Men wanted to be him."

This reminded ProV of the weeks following his appearance in the Masters. He was the center of attention in his college golf world. And that attention became ProV's addiction, or so a counselor had once told him.

Hollie continued, "Tradition says Nimrod treated those admirers with contempt. He became quite famous for using the people around him. But he finally messed with the wrong woman."

Sounds like me, thought ProV with sadness.

"A beautiful woman named Naomi Nemesis figured out how to exact her revenge. She led Narcissus to a still pond just twenty yards in front of this sixteenth green. It's not really much of a water hazard. Just clear and cool water from a spring. Seldom does anyone hit a ball bad enough to land in the water. Narcissus saw his own reflection in the pool and immediately fell in love with it. He was so fixated by his reflection he was unable to leave it, and eventually his powers wilted away. Over time, no one really loved him at all—except himself."

ProV shook his head and confessed, "Both my wives accused me of having narcissistic personality disorder. I don't really think I did, but I did have an exaggerated sense of self-importance. I called it confidence, but it was over the top."

Lucas nodded. "Pal, I must say you were pretty bad, especially after you played in the Masters. Your ego was working overtime."

"Not an excuse, but let's face it. Everybody I knew was telling me how great I was. Getting dates was easy when you just played in the Masters. My golf teachers kept pounding it into me that you have to believe you're the best. Confidence and a huge ego seem to be necessary for big-time golf."

Hollie said, "I doubt you had a clinical condition. Probably just a typical issue of too much pride. Being proud is not attractive. But here's how to tell the difference, ProV. The actual clinical condition affects half of one percent of the population. The effects are devastating for the people around the person."

ProV pondered several loved ones hurt in the wake of his ego. Remorse was overtaking him as Hollie continued. "Here's a small seven-point test to see if you have it now or ever did." She spoke slowly to give ProV time to think.

"One, lacks empathy. Two, hogs conversations. Three, charming. Four, manipulates relationships. Five, needs control. Six, blames others. Seven, thinks rules are for others only. In short, not a good guy to be. And not a good guy to be around either. Also, about three times more likely to be male."

Hollie just smiled after her last point. "So how many of the seven fit the old Paul Player?"

"Looks like I get an A-plus. Seven out of seven."

Lucas disagreed. "I'd say you get an A-minus, six out of seven. You were never that charming."

ProV smiled with his friend on that one, a sign he was already better, and changed the subject by asking Hollie, "What's up with this beautiful par three? I've had two twos already today. I am going for the trifecta."

"There's my man, no shortage of confidence," said Lucas shaking his head, knowing confidence is good but pride is dangerous.[188]

Nimrod returned to his pool and ignored the peons on the tee.

Hollie answered with the facts, "Mid-iron. Smallish green. The pond is really not in play. It is there just for Nimrod to hang out. He stays there most days just cleaning it and making sure it stays crystal clear so he can see himself well. He goes back and forth between the pond and the mirror."

She handed Lucas a six iron. Mr. T offered a seven iron to ProV. "Middle of the green, boys," finished Hollie, not even mentioning the deep bunkers left and steep sand dunes right which needed to be avoided.

R.W. had already struck a nice six iron on the front of the green, just thirty feet from the center hole location.

ProV was still thinking about Hollie's test as he hooked his ball into a left bunker. The feel in the hands and the sound of the ball was all wrong.

Lucas made a smooth, sweet swing and the slight breeze hit the ball just right to land six feet from the hole.

[188] Proverbs 15:25 "The Lord tears down the house of the proud."

It was Deadend's turn to hit, but the group had to wait while he finished gazing at himself in the mirror. He said to no one in particular, "They should have one of these on every tee."

All day he had talked and talked about the golf course he was building back in Arizona. Not even Mocker was listening by now.[189]

Finally, Deadend thinned his five iron, skipping the ball four times across the Nemesis Pond, nearly hitting Nimrod in the head as the ball finally ended up on the other side of the pond. Nimrod was so busy looking at himself that he never even noticed the ball miss his head by a yard. He was only upset that the ball had caused pond waves which interrupted his self-gaze.

He looked up and gave Deadend a dirty look. And naturally, Deadend didn't take it well. Within moments, the two egomaniacs were[190] shouting insults at each other. Mocker stepped in to move his man along.

Meanwhile, ProV dug into the greenside bunker and splashed the sand perfectly, then watched the ball crawl into the hole for this third two of the day. Lucas sadly missed his birdie, while Wright made another routine par. Deadend hit the ball five times and said, "Four."

Behind the green were two humble but distinguished old men.

Hollie said, "Surely you recognize the guy with the white beard. You met him on the mountain not long ago. You will want to meet him."

Wright led the guys over and introduced them. "Gentlemen, this is our dear friend Moses, the most humble man who ever lived. Or so says the Bible."

Moses threw back his head and laughed. "Guess who wrote those words in the Bible about how humble I am?" He paused. "Me!"

He laughed even harder. "What kind of fool would call himself the humblest man in the world? Probably the least humble man in the world. I was a mess."

Hollie advised, "That's why you need to be careful about quoting the

[189] Proverbs 16:18 (NIV) "Pride goes before destruction, a haughty spirit before a fall."

[190] Proverbs 13:10 "Pride leads to conflict; those who take advice are wise."

Bible. And remember, pride has always been the main sin. If you had to describe one great sin, with a capital P, it would be Pride. Lucifer[191] gave up the glories of Heaven because he could never be the center of attention. Many people would rather fail doing it their way than succeed doing it God's way—even die their own way than live doing God's way."

Moses then introduced his companion, "So now let me introduce you to my friend here. Agur is a most interesting guy. He might be the smartest man around here. He is the author of an entire Proverb that made him quite famous at one time. He loved his lists. He put them into foursomes. People used to pay a lot of money for his seminars. He was a guru of gurus."

Lucas and ProV had never heard of him.

"His lessons were things such as, *'The four things that never say enough'*—meaning they will beat you every time—*'the grave, the barren womb, a thirsty desert and a blazing fire.'* Stuff like that."[192]

"Or the one he got a lot of attention for was, *'The four things I don't understand: how an eagle glides through the sky, how a snake slithers on a rock, how a ship navigates the ocean, how a man loves a woman.'*"[193]

ProV grinned a knowing smile. "Exactly," Lucas said. "Who can explain all that?"

"But what made Agur unique was his humility. Despite his apparent wisdom, he truly didn't think he knew anything. He started his proverb with this:

I am weary, O God;
I am weary and worn out, O God.
I am too stupid to be human,
And I lack common sense.
I have not mastered human wisdom,
Nor do I know the Holy One.[194]

[191] Isaiah 14:12

[192] Proverbs 30: 15-16

[193] Proverbs 30: 18-19

[194] Proverbs 30:1-3

Before Agur could even finish his recitation, ProV remembered this was the exact Proverbs 30 he had opened in the Gideon Bible back at the Dornoch Castle Hotel. *Coincidence? Maybe not,* he thought to himself.

Agur shook hands with ProV and said, "Okay, ProV, three questions from my Proverb. This will show if there is any hope for you or not. First, are you weary?"

"Oh my, yes. I am sick and tired. And frankly, I am also sick and tired of being sick and tired."

"Second, are you feeling stupid or smart?"

"Stupid almost every minute of every day. I used to joke that I watch *Jeopardy* just to remember how stupid I am." Agur had no idea what that meant but he continued.

"And my guess is your first two answers would have been a lot different when you were twenty-one years old?"

"Of course, I thought I was king of the world."

"So, you passed the first two tests," said Agur. "You have enough humility to know you are tired and ignorant on most days. Now the big one." Agur took a deep breath. "Last, do you know the Holy One?"

"Well, I am sure the right answer is to say I do, but hey, you know full well that would be a lie. I absolutely do *not* know the Holy One. In fact, even after all I have seen here today, I have no idea who you are really talking about. God, I guess. But I don't know. So even if I flunk your test, the answer is no."

"ProV, your instinct to fake it and say yes is what most people do. But your honesty to admit that you don't know the Holy One means you have passed the test of humility. God said he will indeed reveal himself to the *humble and contrite hearts who tremble at my word.*"[195]

Agur said, "Only the humble can appreciate the obvious truth of my words long ago.

Who but God goes up to heaven and comes back down?
Who holds the wind in his fists?

[195] Isaiah 66:2

Who wraps up the oceans in his cloak?
Who has created the whole wide world?
What is his name—and his son's name?
Tell me if you know!" [196]

"When you admit you know nothing compared to the Creator with a capital 'C,' you have taken the first tiny step toward God," Hollie said.

"Will we see you guys again?" asked ProV.

"Hope so," said Moses as he and Agur walked back toward the clubhouse. They had walked out to the sixteenth just to meet the pilgrims.

Hollie summarized: "Agur says simply, 'I am tired. I am stupid. I do not really know the Holy One.' Pride, especially religious pride, says 'I am full of energy. I am smarter than you guys. And I know God better than you do.'"

ProV remembered some religious types and realized why they were so unattractive to him.

[196] Proverbs 30:4

17th
LOVE
PAR 4, 454/388 YARDS
PROV 21:21
"WHOEVER
PURSUES...
UNFAILING LOVE
WILL FIND LIFE..."
HOKMAH
GOLF CLUB

17th Hole – Love

PAR 4, 454/388 YARDS

"Whoever pursues ... unfailing love will find life..."
Proverbs 21:21

Ninety-year-old John lived near the seventeenth tee, overlooking the North Sea. He was not the young man who was seen on the mountaintop with Peter and his brother James. It was John the beloved, age unknown but obviously full of years. He was sometimes called the *"one whom Jesus loved."* [197] Those who live long enough become "beloved." He had disproved the theory that the good die young.

His tiny cottage was just thirty steps from the seventeenth tee, overlooking the North Sea and the lighthouse. He spent most of his summer days in prayer and thanksgiving on his back porch, but also

[197] John 20:2

was responsible to care for the mother of Yeshua, who lived with him. The one and only Mary.

Peter and James had been martyred, given their life for the sake of their Lord. Only John had been left to get old and ponder the deep things of God.

Hollie pointed to the Beloved: "See the old man wandering over here? That's John. He wrote the gospel of John, plus his three letters to churches which we just call 1st John, 2nd John, and 3rd John. And of course, Revelation, written when he lived on the isle of Patmos. He did what many people hope to do—leave something behind for people to read."

Hollie never wrote anything herself, but she inspired all sixty-six books of the Bible.

R.W., who was now a dear friend of this older John, said, "Surely it didn't hurt that Mary was there to pray and talk with him. He knew the whole story."

ProV stared at the old man in awe as R.W. continued, "John had plenty to say if anyone would listen. He not only spent three years with Jesus, night and day, including being at the cross as Jesus died, but he then heard all the stories from Mary over the next many decades."

ProV's head was spinning. And it didn't help that the sign on the tee box said "Love." If there was an exam on that subject, his grade every year since the fourth grade would be "F."

Hollie said, "We have played sixteen holes to get to the most important two holes. Hole seventeen is 'Love.' What a poor word in English."

The seventeenth had another stunning view. Ocean and beach to the right, bunkers to be avoided on the left, but a wide fairway and often downwind, making this par four hole a delight on most days. A small river, just ten yards wide, fronted the green and ran into the ocean's bay. Salmon jumped if you caught it on a perfect day. The left edge of the clubhouse in the distance was the perfect aim point off the tee. The finish was in sight.

John the Beloved hung out around the member's tee. Perched up on the back tee were three older balding men with a desk and writing utensils of antiquity, quietly debating. Socrates, Plato and Aristotle were discussing love. The debate had been going on for nearly 2,500 years. They were oblivious to anyone below. They had no interest in speaking to anyone except themselves. John called them "the three smartest fools in the world."

John was the world's greatest expert on love, keeping it simple with "God is love," but what did that mean? Hollie decided to keep it light-hearted by turning the conversation to golf as the men waggled their drivers on the long par four.

"A major step to good golf is simple. You have to love it," exclaimed Hollie. "As you swing this time, say aloud on your backswing, 'I love this game!'"

It seemed to work as the entire foursome all hit decent drives downwind, even Deadend. Thanks to his relative youth and latest technology, he caught a good one that slipped past everyone, even ProV.

The fairway was crowded with multiple forecaddies. John followed the foursome down the elevated tee as Hollie shouted, "Let's meet the forecaddies. All Greeks." It looked like a convention down in the fairway. There were six forecaddies on this hole.

"Why so many?" Lucas asked.

"Because love has so many definitions. These ladies and gentlemen spend a lot of time arguing about who is the 'true love.' No one has answered the question yet. They are the worst forecaddies on the course. They lose balls frequently because they aren't paying attention at the right times."

Hollie was pointing out Eros, Philia, Storge, Ludus, Pragma and Philautia as they walked off the tee.

John followed along, using an old hickory mashie for a walking stick. It was a gift from Bobby Jones. He walked and talked with R.W., as he did many days. Today he was speaking on his favorite subject:

"In the beginning the Word already existed. The Word was with God, and the Word was God... So the Word became human and made his home among us. He was full of unfailing love and faithfulness." [198] R.W.

[198] John 1:1, 14.

had heard it all before, but it was soothing to hear it again from the great 'beloved' one.

"This 'Word' was the Greek 'Logos,' well known to the whole Greek world as the Divine force, power and wisdom that is in all of creation. Indeed, how wonderful it was for me and the other disciples to walk and talk with this Logos for three full years. Power, reason, logic, creativity and wisdom, all wrapped up in a person, fully God and fully human."

Meanwhile, Hollie was introducing the pilgrims to each forecaddie. R.W. needed no introduction. He simply hit his second shot and headed straight toward the green with his friend John, saying, "Guys, I will be waiting at the green. Take your time."

First was Eddie Eros, pursuing Folly, who had followed the group from the fourteenth hole, into the left rough. He was supposed to be watching for balls off the tee, but he seldom saw anything but skirts and cleavage. Hollie explained, "Eros just means sexual or romantic love, or love of the body. I hate to say it but when Solomon said he was in love, that's what he meant. Eros does not make a great partner."

Philip Philia was hanging out with family and special friends, having a picnic in the right rough that overlooked a wonderful vista of the ocean and islands in the distance. Lucas spoke up since he knew a lot of about Philia. "This word describes what we have for each other," he said to ProV. "You know Philadelphia is the city of brotherly love? The word comes from this idea. Love for a brother or dear friend."

ProV almost teared up when Lucas came over with a big smile, hugged him and said, "ProV, I '*philia*' you."

"Stevie Storge is hard to pronounce and even harder to explain," Hollie said, pointing to a young forecaddie eating an ice cream cone near ProV's drive. She spelled his name phonetically for her pupils. "S-T-O-R-G-A-Y, with emphasis on the first syllable. He says he is the real love because he is so common. If you love ice cream, that is storge. If you love a certain football team, that is storge. If you love math, that is storge. Storge is almost everything not covered by these other folks."

Hollie continued, "I love this seventeenth hole. To me, it is the greatest golf hole in the world. There is Faith and Hope, but no doubt, the greatest of these is Love." Storge wrongly presumed she was talking about him and puffed up like a frog.

Phyllis Philautia walked over confidently to chat briefly. As she approached, Hollie explained, "Philautia is a self-love which we all need to be healthy, but be careful because it can move quickly into narcissism."

"Hello, Phyllis," she said to the upbeat young lady. "We ran into your cousin Nimrod Narcissus a few minutes ago. What a guy!"

"Yeah, sorry about him. We keep praying for him. It is healthy to love yourself, but there is a fine line you never want to cross. All I really do is try to remember God loves me, so I should love myself too!"

R.W. nodded an amen. "The Apostle taught a lot about this when he called himself the 'one whom Jesus loved.' I used to think such talk was arrogant, but no more. He was right."

Phyllis started to sing an old children's tune, "Jesus loves me this I know. For the Bible tells me so...." She smiled and said, "Enjoy the day, guys."

Hollie kept them moving down the fairway, "See the gray-haired couple holding hands and walking slowly over near the beach?"

"Sure," said ProV.

"That's Paulina Pragma and her beloved. She stands for a love that is long lasting, forever. There is nothing erotic about it. Pragma is permanent." She waved to the old lady, who grinned and shouted back, "Hello, my dear Hollie. Can't stop to talk today. I am busy with my beloved." She loved long walks on the beach.

Also on the beach, playing in the sand, was a young lady named Lucy Ludus. Her friends called her Lulu. She had forsaken her forecaddie duties to hang out with her first boyfriend. Hollie described Lucy, "She is only thirteen years old. Ludus love doesn't last long. Lots of flirting and teasing. She will be back soon."

ProV remembered being pursued by such girls long before he reciprocated the interest.

"Some poor souls never get beyond Ludus, even at forty," Hollie said.

They had met six Greek forecaddies, and ProV was more confused than ever about the meaning of love. He knew he loved golf at one time. He thought he loved his wife Mary Ann at one time. He loved his kids, although he confessed he seldom thought about them, probably because he knew he had caused them so much pain. He was realizing the closest love he actually possessed was an obnoxious self-love. And when that goes wrong, life gets messy.

John the Beloved offered wisdom, "ProV, do you remember the first time you told Mary Ann you loved her? Well, what you really meant was, 'I love the way you make me feel.' Not many twenty-year-olds have any concept of love."

ProV and Lucas both hit their second shots into greenside bunkers. Just three hours ago, ProV would have cursed himself, at least quietly, but now he was slowly finding some peace with his golf game.

Deadend, on the other hand, was not learning much. He had followed Eros and Folly into the left rough and no one was sure if he would survive or not.

R.W. and John the Beloved were standing on the green chatting. Behind the green sat three women. Hollie made her most interesting comment of the day, a big statement in light of all that had already happened. "Lucas. ProV. See those three ladies sitting behind the green?"

Both nodded a yes.

"These are the three most important women in the world, unless you count me," she smiled humbly.

"And they are?" asked Lucas.

"The younger lady is Agatha Agape. She is the perfect picture of God's love. When the New Testament was written, there was no good word for the love of God in Greek, so we needed a new word. We came up with 'agape' to try to convey this love of God. The Greeks could not even imagine such a perfect love. It is used in eighty places in the New Testament. God is agape. For God so 'agaped' the world...."[199]

Lucas noticed that Hollie seemed to imply she was involved in writing the New Testament. He was now fully aware that his caddie had a supernatural glory.

[199] John 3:16

"And the two older women?"

"The lady on the left is a sweet Hebrew lady, Helen Hesed.[200] Maybe my favorite person in the whole world. Her name has no perfect meaning. It is often translated as 'Lovingkindness.' It is found over two hundred times in the Old Testament. With no perfect English translation, we have words which we associate with hesed. Loyalty.[201] Kindness. Unfailing. Faithfulness. Reliable. And of course, God's love for us."

ProV was listening carefully. He knew he needed to find love, whatever it may be, not just some Greek or Hebrew word that defined it.

Holly continued with her love lesson. "The best definition for hesed may be this—when the person from whom I have a right to expect nothing gives me everything."[202]

ProV knew instinctively that he was not ready to give that kind of love. Indeed, he was not even prepared to receive it. He thought about the women he had met at Hokmah, the way they were changing him and Lucas one conversation at a time.

Hollie. Then the Widow Mite. Now Agape and Hesed. *Wisdom is indeed female*, he thought—a new paradigm for him on this bright and sunny Orkney day.

"Lucas, who would have thought when we were having breakfast with Mrs. Doubter just this morning that I would ever agree that wisdom is female. But as much as it hurts to say, I think it's true."

Hollie smiled. "And to Helen's right is Ava Ahava. Some people think Ava and Helen are twin sisters but actually they are quite different."

ProV and Lucas stole a glance with each other as they listened. "Ahava represents the most basic concept of affection found in the Hebrew world. When you read about Abraham's love of his son, Isaac,

[200] Proverbs 3:3 "Never let loyalty and kindness ('hesed') leave you! Tie them around your neck as a reminder. Write them deep within your heart."

[201] Proverbs 20:6 "Many will say they are loyal friends, but who can find one who is truly 'hesed?'"

[202] Michael Card, *Inexpressible: Hesed and the Mystery of God's Lovingkindness (Intervarsity Press*, 2018), 5.

the word is Ahava.[203] Or when Isaac later says he loves food, it is Ahava.[204] It often covers a man's love for his wife.[205] Ahava also can describe the wrong kind of love—as in *'you love evil more than good.'*[206] Delilah used the word to lay a guilt trip on Samson, *'How can you tell me 'I love you' when you don't share your secrets with me?'*"[207]

Hollie led the men over to meet the three simple ladies.

After the introductions, Lucas said, "Helen, they tell me you are unexplainable, which might be true for every female, actually."

She smiled back with an understanding face and nod of the head. "Indeed, Lucas. God's love is beyond human language. It leaves us all speechless. If you are using words to describe the love of God, you are falling short. It is so much more. Look out over that view to your right. The ocean, the clouds, the rainbows we see every day, the island and the lighthouse across the way, the seabirds chirping, the sounds as well as the sights, the fishing boat going out with just one man adjusting the sail, the rocks below us...." Her voice tailed off to a whisper.

Lucas and ProV were listening to love.

"But now take one more step. This is why people can still have this love no matter what. You could be in prison or a nursing home right now and have this same inexpressible love. Close your eyes. What do you see?

"Lucas, do you see your mother and father smiling as they talked about you? Do you see your Angelina as she forgave you for your failures? Do you see your friend who gave you blood in the hospital not long ago?"

Lucas had entered another world. He was not on the Isle of Mashal now. He was in the world of hesed.

"And ProV, do you see your grandmother who should have been too

[203] Genesis 22:2

[204] Genesis 27:4

[205] Ecclesiastes 9:9

[206] Psalm 52:3

[207] Judges 16:15

busy with her own life to take in a child like you? Or do you remember the kind and loving fourth grade teacher, Mr. Coleman, who knew your troubles at home and would often make sure you got to your ballgames? You remember your neighbor lady, Mrs. Ferrell, who had you over for Christmas dinner more than once, even after you threw a baseball through her back window and lied to her?"

ProV and Lucas kept their eyes closed as they remembered many situations of hesed love that had been forgotten.

Hollie closed with, "Hesed does not care what wrong has been done, what sin has been committed, what trust has been violated. Hesed keeps coming and giving. Always."

The conversation ended and the men walked off to putt out for bogeys that were no longer a tragedy. Golf scores were secondary now. Love had appeared. *Agape. Hesed. Ahava. What a threesome. They should have been on the mountain,* thought Lucas as they walked away.

As the group marched to the eighteenth tee, Deadend was nowhere to be found.

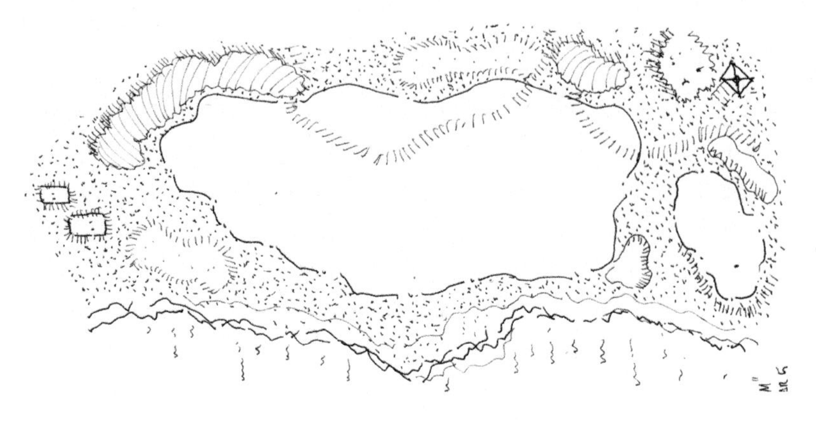

18th
WISDOM
PAR 5, 540/507 YARDS
PROV 8:1
"LISTEN AS
WISDOM
CALLS OUT"
HOKMAH
GOLF CLUB

18th Hole – Wisdom

PAR 5, 540/507 YARDS

"Listen as Wisdom calls out..."
Proverbs 8:1

The eighteenth hole offered an opportunity for a grand finish. Eagle threes were possible if the wind was just right. Birdies were common, which always made the post-round drink or lunch taste better. Even a disappointing par was suitable in the cozy atmosphere of Hokmah's bar with the fireplace crackling.

The ocean on the right was just for the view. The Creator didn't want golfers losing balls and strokes on this benediction hole. He wanted everyone to finish well.

Hollie explained, "It's appropriate that the final hole is Wisdom.[208] Since wisdom is mostly female, she needs time," she said with a huge smile. "You must finish the whole course before God's true wisdom makes sense. And realize we are not talking about human wisdom."[209]

[208] James 1:5 "If you need wisdom, ask our generous God, and he will give it to you."

[209] 1 Corinthians 1:21 "Since God in his wisdom saw to it that the world would never know him through human wisdom..."

Standing on a high spot to the left of the back tee were two tall and older ladies. Lucas recognized Carol Mann, leaning comfortably on an old bullseye putter which looked like it was made for her hands. The Hall of Fame golfer was always there, according to Hollie, nodding politely to each person who arrived, whether golfer or caddie.

But the other lady was even taller and more prominent. "You remember Lady Wisdom from the first tee," said Hollie.

The older lady pointed with a smile which said, 'Look at this,' indicating the sea, the cliffs, the mountain and far off islands. It was as if she owned them. The lighthouse in the distance was barely noticed with so much of God's original artistry to capture the eyes.

No one would call Lady Wisdom beautiful, but it was difficult not to gaze at her.

She and Carol waited patiently for the whole group to arrive. All but Deadend stopped to listen. He and Mocker showed up late and marched ahead thirty yards to the front tee markers and were ready to end the day.

"Gentlemen," said Carol, "You have finally reached the last hole. And this is the grand lady of the club. We simply call her Lady Wisdom.[210] You met her on the first tee, and she has been hoping to see 'new men' arrive at this eighteenth tee."

Lady Wisdom took a bow, as Carol continued: "Her father was the Duke of Mashal, who helped found the club in the beginning. She is invited to every meeting here. She is a good person to have in the room when any subject is discussed, and since this final hole belongs to her, she loves to get in the last word on Hokmah. We ask visitors to pause for just a moment here to listen to her."

Hollie added quietly in a whisper to Lucas, "Lady Wisdom also loves to visit with John, Agatha, Ava and Helen. They are all dear friends. Even Mary comes down on occasion. They pray together, laugh together, cry together. It is a major lovefest most days."

[210] Proverbs 1:7

Lucas and ProV both found a bench to rest their weary bones. The adrenaline of the day was coming and going, and at this moment it was trending downward. The wooden bench was actually a pew from the Holy Trinity church in St. Andrews, donated by Ol' Tom Morris long ago.

"Oh, and by the way, she doesn't look it, but she is really old," whispered Hollie with a smile.

"Really? So how old is she?" whispered ProV, knowing that asking a lady about her age could be dangerous and futile.

"Just listen, she may let you know."

It was time for Lady Wisdom to perform. It was dramatic. It was loud. It was poetry.

"The Lord formed me from the beginning,
before he created anything else.[211]

She had been around in the beginning. Like Hollie. And now she offered wise words for her children.

And so, my children, listen to me,
for all who follow my ways are joyful.
Listen to my instruction and be wise.
Don't ignore it.
Joyful are those who listen to me,
watching for me daily at my gates, waiting for me outside my home!
For whoever finds me finds life and receives favor from the Lord.
But those who miss me injure themselves.
All who hate me love death."[212]

Deadend and Mocker could hear it all from the forward tee. Deadend muttered, "I just hate old people like her. Think they know something we need to hear."[213]

[211] Proverbs 8:22

[212] Proverbs 8:32

[213] Proverbs 1:32 "Fools are destroyed by their own complacency."

He hit his drive and moved ahead without his playing companions, unwilling to wait. Joining Mocker and Deadend was Freddie Foolish, who would be their personal forecaddie on the hole. He was captain of the Fool's Club.[214] The club was set back in a valley just two hundred steps from this eighteenth tee, in a small area known simply as "Eden East," a popular dive for locals who complained about almost everything.

Freddie said, "You think you got it bad listening to the old lady today. What if you had to hear her nonsense every day of your life like me?"

Mocker nodded agreement as Freddie said, "Mr. Deadend, sir, follow me. This last hole is a disaster. It will lead you to the clubhouse where all the so-called 'wise men' hang out. You will hate it. We've got an alternate club I think you will love." He pointed out a path to the left leading into a dark valley, just past the second tee.

Hollie explained, "When Hokmah was re-opened by Noah and other patriarchs long ago, the Creator decided there needed to be a place for these fools to hang out. They were uncomfortable in the main clubhouse. They were always criticizing Lady Wisdom and others who ran the club." Lucas knew the type from his many years of living around country clubs.

"They even tried to build a tower at one point.[215] Fools love skyscrapers. They honestly believe the man with the tallest building is the winner in some sort of game. Thankfully, the sands of Mashal are not friendly to multiple stories."

"Makes sense," nodded Lucas.

"These fools were not only miserable themselves, but they made other members and guests miserable just being around them. So, the Creator authorized the Fool's Club in a barren and rocky valley where no vegetation would grow. He also gave them access to the golf course on certain times and days."

[214] Proverbs 1:7 "Fools despise wisdom and discipline."

[215] Genesis 11:1-9

Lucas was curious. "Why would the Creator allow such nonsense?"

"The Creator was really big on one principle—free will. The Trinity had a huge discussion on this very point which lasted for a long time. Father, Son and Holy Spirit discussed this for eons, and we finally reached a decision," said Hollie.

Lucas and ProV had "ears to hear" and noticed Hollie was now speaking of the Trinity in the first person.

"We should never force anyone to do anything. Our greatest gift to mankind will be their free will. Every person must choose for themselves. Love and Wisdom cannot exist unless every person is free—free to choose otherwise, free to go to the Fool's Club. Otherwise, people would all be robots. Love cannot exist without the freedom to reject it. Wisdom cannot exist without the option to refuse it. And the rejection of Love and Wisdom defines a fool."

R.W. offered some backup for Hollie's eternal words. "For me, believe it or not, I had trouble believing all the God talk. But I made a decision. I made a choice to believe. I told myself, even if it's not all true, I choose God over no God. That choice opened the door to true faith." ProV was seeing the same door.

"It isn't that complicated. *'Don't live like fools, but like those who are wise,'*"[216] said R.W. "Now, let's see what wisdom we might find on this last hole."

They all hit solid drives, the wind at their backs, down a wide fairway. Reaching the green with a big second shot would be possible. "Well done," said Hollie.

ProV was walking with R.W., who said he had heard Lady Wisdom many times. "But the thing I love about her is that she almost never gives the same speech twice. She has so much to say. When you are in her presence, the best thing you can do is be quiet—shut up—and maybe ask her some questions. I wish we had more time with her. Maybe later."

ProV asked the obvious question, "Wisdom. How do I find it?"

[216] Ephesians 5:15

"It almost always has one key ingredient. I will leave you with one word which is usually needed. And you may not like this answer." He paused. "Time. It is as basic as the idea that a chocolate cake needs time in the oven. Wisdom needs *time*."

For ProV, this meant he might have to wait a while. But he also saw the positive side. He was only forty-three years old. There was hope and time for him.

R.W. continued, "Time to grow old. Time to make mistakes. Time to read. Time to learn from sages of the past. Time to heal. Time to remember. Wisdom takes time."

"Well, R.W., you're pretty wise yourself."

"Maybe. Now that I am retired I have time to think. Time to play golf. Time to listen. Time to hang out with wise men older than me. Time. It is a great gift."

Lucas was also getting it, "Now that I am over seventy, I totally understand and agree. Take knowledge, mix it with experiences over time, and wisdom comes out the other end, especially if you mix in the ageless thoughts of Lady Wisdom and her female friends like Hollie."

"You boys are messing with me now," ProV said, shaking his head. "To be honest, you seem to be telling me that the people with the most wisdom in the universe are likely to be older women. I have spent my whole life so far ignoring older women. But now that you mention it, I am quite sure I wouldn't be here if not for an old woman named Grandma Addie, who saved the day for my whole family. There was not a single person in my entire family with any sense at all except her. I wish she was living so I could thank her."

"You can see her again, ProV," offered Hollie with a reassuring touch of his hand.

ProV said, "Really?"

"And maybe sooner than you think."

ProV wandered away down the fairway, now wondering if this meant his life was nearly over.

All three golfers reached the final green in two giant downwind strikes. What a pleasure to hit a par five in two shots. ProV had reached with just a five iron. No one was near enough for an eagle three, but by this time, scores meant nothing. Wright was just as content with his three-putt par as Lucas was with his two-putt birdie. ProV charged his eagle putt and now had three feet for a final birdie.

His lifelong habit of knowing how he stood was hard to break. Only he was aware he needed this three-footer to break eighty. He felt nerves like he was back at the US Amateur with a putt to go to the Masters. Just three feet of perfect green grass stood between him and a four-inch hole in the ground.

ProV's putter was shaking like Barney Fife waving his pistol, and when the final tap in wobbled into the hole for a birdie, caps came off and no one ever knew how nervous he had been. The contented threesome hugged like a happy family. Hollie, Mr. T and Barnabas joined in the celebration.

Part Four
The Treasure

"I have failed, Bagger. Here on this field and in all else in my life. I know you've brought me here deliberately, and I know it's out of love for me. Love I can't seem to understand or return. Help me, please. Show me.

I am ready at last to see." [217]

The field of battle

[217] Steven Pressfield, *The Legend of Bagger Vance,* (Avon Books, Inc. 1995) p. 175.

CHAPTER 1
The 19th Hole

It was four o'clock—too late for lunch and too early for dinner. Plenty of time in the Orkney summer for more golf with a setting sun at 10 p.m., but ProV and Lucas needed time to let the majesty of Hokmah sink into their souls.

R.W. led them to an outdoor patio which overlooked the sea. The small sign read "Loaves and Fishes Bar and Grill."

Deadend was long gone. The group was just sitting down on the patio when they heard the engine roaring, looked up and saw his helicopter taking off.

Mocker was left behind, shaking his head and cursing the copter over the cheap tip that hardly made the day worthwhile. Dubs had tipped him with a dozen ProV1's with his 666 logo—not the hoped-for thousand pounds. At least Mocker knew where another two dozen balls and a couple of drivers were scattered around the property.

Before Dubs' departure, Freddie Foolish managed to get him into the Fool's Club for a quick drink and a chance to meet all the mockers and fools who gathered to tell their lies and exaggerations.

The place was full of laughter, but not the kind that was pleasing to the ear. More like the laughter of demons who haven't figured out they are trapped in a bad spot for a long time. Members of this club never played the eighteenth Wisdom hole at Hokmah. It was against their "religion."

The pathway to the Fool's Club smelled like dog vomit[218] but somehow was a fragrant aroma for the fools. The dirt path was crowded with thorns so those who visited would often be bleeding by the time they walked in the front door,[219] especially if alcohol had been part of their day. It was a noisy place, with loud voices clamoring for attention. Tempers would flare and fights were common.[220] Much of the conversation ended with agreement that the fools' parents had been too hard on them.[221] Leaders who had plotted incredible evil would proudly proclaim to their buddies how they accomplished their dastardly plans.[222] Each month they would honor one of their own for some outstanding achievement in this world of fools.[223] The ceremony was like the Oscars or Emmys, with red carpets and pretend media all around, celebrating themselves. Social media was always well represented, especially since newspapers had become extinct twenty years ago.

As Hollie presented all this to the pilgrims, they were genuinely glad to have missed all the "fun."

ProV followed R.W. into the bar and ordered an Arnold Palmer tea. Lucas followed his friend with, "I'll take the same." He had a scorecard and a pencil in hand. He was accustomed to analyzing every round with greens and fairways hit, plus the number of putts and birdies. He calculated that, sure enough, his putt on eighteen gave him a seventy-nine—if he graciously gave himself a double bogey on "Integrity"

[218] Proverbs 26:11 "As a dog returns to its vomit, so a fool repeats his foolishness."

[219] Proverbs 26:9 "A proverb in the mouth of a fool is like a thorny branch brandished by a drunk."

[220] Proverbs 14:17 "Short tempered people do foolish things."

[221] Proverbs 15:5 "Only a fool despises a parent's discipline; whoever learns from correction is wise."

[222] Proverbs 30:32 "If you have been a fool by being proud or plotting evil, cover your mouth in shame."

[223] Proverbs 26:8 "Honoring a fool is as foolish as tying a stone to a slingshot."

instead of the eleven that a tournament card would record. His three twos would never be forgotten.

While knocking off some Scottish chips and the Arnold Palmers, R.W. continued answering questions from ProV and Lucas. He was full of good answers but also clarified, "The older I get, the more questions I have." He called it "exploding ignorance" explaining that in his search for answers, he always ran into ten more questions.

"The quest for wisdom never ends," he said. "Indeed, people who have all the answers all the time make me nervous. Wisdom is knowing what you don't know. Fortunately, Hollie is around to help."

"Speaking of Hollie, where is she?"

"She was called to help comfort a dear soul who had lost her husband. But she will be back tomorrow."

"Men," said R.W., "let me suggest you spend one more day here. Dinner tonight. Tomorrow morning at seven there's our Mulligan Monday Meditation in the Valley Room. The leader this week is someone you will recognize. Paul Tentmaker. And after that, you can play another round. There is a second eighteen holes here, known only to insiders, to the members. We call it Segullah, an old Hebrew word for treasure. It is the Treasure Course."

ProV looked to Lucas for guidance. Lucas seemed excited, knowing he had not played a second course on his first visit. Or if he did, the memory was gone. Lucas asked, "So where would we spend the night?"

"Oh, you'd stay at the Dormie House," R.W. pointed at a small white building at the edge of the sea, surrounded by rocks and seagulls with puffins flying in for the night.

"The Dormie House has two bedrooms en suite. You'd be the only ones there tonight."

"And the cost?" Lucas asked.

R.W. reminded them, "Oh, don't you remember? You've already paid all you have. This is included in the deal if you want it."

"And why do they call it the Treasure Course?" ProV asked.

"Simple. There is a treasure on the course. Not everyone who plays here finds the treasure. Some do and some don't. But it is there. I found it myself many years ago. In my view, Segullah is better than even Hokmah."

"So why didn't someone tell us about this sooner?" ProV complained.

"You cannot play Segullah without first playing Hokmah. You find Wisdom first. Then you can seek the Treasure."

It was an easy decision to stay. Especially since ProV again remembered the Voice: *"There's a treasure in the darkness."* One more day made perfect sense.

A bellman appeared with a name tag "Philemon," already carrying their luggage. The five-minute walk to the Dormie House was as scenic as any hole on the course. The pathway was just inches away from cliffs which dove to the sea itself. A handrail kept Lucas and ProV feeling safe.

Philemon chatted all the way about his father in faith, Paul Tentmaker.[224] He was working at Hokmah because of Paul's admonitions and wise counsel. "I owe that man my very soul, so when Paul asked me to come and be in charge of the guest rooms here at Hokmah, it was an honor." He was genuinely excited because the pilgrims would meet Paul and hear him speak on Monday morning.

The pilgrims passed a mammoth putting green reminiscent of the greens found in many Scottish town centers. Eighteen little flags wound through hillocks more severe than anything on the course. Having the time of their life, if laughs and high fives tell a story, were a young man and his wife with two little boys who seemed ready to be addicted to the great game of golf. ProV remembered when he was ten years old and discovering the beauties of the game. He looked at Lucas and said simply, "Hey, man. Have I thanked you yet for this trip? This day? If not, it is because I am speechless."

Lucas checked into the Ol' Tom Morris Room. ProV was next door in the Young Tommy Room. Philemon unloaded the luggage, left a key, refused all attempts at a tip, and said, "Mr. Wright told me to let you know dinner would be back at the clubhouse at seven."

[224] Philemon 1:4 "I always thank my God when I pray for you, Philemon."

"Thank you, Philemon," Lucas said. It was already 5:00 p.m. and the pilgrims were ready for a short nap. "Can you make sure we are awake at six-thirty for dinner?"

"Of course, sir. I will knock on your door. With pleasure."

ProV was in a stupor when the knock on the door startled him. Lucas opened the unlocked door and found his friend barely moving and groggy. "Let's go, man. Dinner time. Philemon saved me from oversleeping, so I understand."

ProV's muddled mind tried to remember where he was and why he was sleeping while the sun was still shining through a huge window overlooking a giant sea. Was he at Pebble Beach? Was this a dream? No, he quickly remembered. He was with Lucas Friend at Hokmah Golf Club in the Orkney Islands. An old fashioned clock on the wall said it was 6:45 p.m.

"Okay, man, give me ten minutes." He was an expert at a quick shower and out the door in eight minutes, so ten was plenty.

Lucas said, "Just come on over to the dining room. I'll mosey on over."

Sure enough, ProV was headed that way at 6:58.

When ProV walked into the clubhouse, he was greeted by the host and hostess wearing nametags: Abraham and Sarah. Lucas and Wright were already chatting with them. They had prepared an amazing dinner of roasted meat—a tender calf served with yogurt and milk.

At first ProV thought it sounded awful, but later he had to agree it was the finest meal ever, pure Mediterranean style with vegetables and seasonings one could not soon forget. Abraham and Sarah were the servers, politely letting Wright and his two guests digest not only their food but the sounds and sights of Hokmah. They had a corner table with a view. No one else was dining this Sunday evening.

There were lots of laughs during the meal about the amazing day, many at the expense of poor ol' Dubs, one of the richest fools in the world. Wright never did give an adequate explanation for how he even got on the course. By now, he was back in Inverness, probably screaming at his pilot to get him back to his island home below Malta. It had been especially funny to watch him squirm when his wife called him as he was coming out of Folly's Forest.

"And the highlight so far?" asked Wright, implying that something better could still be waiting.

Lucas said the entire threesome experience on the Mountain with Jesus was his highlight. ProV didn't disagree with his friend, but he was still talking about meeting Hogan in the locker room. Watching him hit balls had been an amazing start.

After dinner, Abraham returned and invited the three to retire to a comfortable sitting room where cigars and Hookah pipes were available. ProV hated smoke so he was happy that his older friends said "no thanks" to the tobacco offers. The smell reminded ProV of the locker room at Augusta when he played in the Masters. Just a hint of cigar aroma.

With his imagination in full bloom, he remembered back to 2033 and the Augusta members sitting around in green jackets. He remembered how much he had coveted one of those tailored symbols of sainthood in the game of golf.

Now that a few hours had passed, ProV was laughing and confessing his sins from the fifth hole—"Integrity"—where each player had played alone. "That's when I realized I was just as bad as Dubs," he said, confessing his sins with a smile.

Lucas wanted to know, "So what did you really make there?"

"Okay," ProV said, counting with his fingers. "I think a nine?"

"Have you counted a penalty for looking too long for your drive? Didn't you say you looked for five minutes?"

He shook his head and said, "Okay, eleven! It feels so good to come clean!"

Wright and Lucas laughed so hard they almost spilled their coffee. "My so-called seventy-nine was with a fictional double bogey on that hole, so if we count the eleven, that takes me to 84," said ProV with a smile and shake of the head.

Then, turning serious, Lucas said, "When you finally realize the chief of sinners is in the mirror, the whole world opens up to wisdom and salvation."[225]

R.W. knew the time was slipping away and said his goodnights. ProV and Lucas found their way back to the Dormie House. A good eight hours of sleep with the windows cracked open would leave them ready for tomorrow's new memories.

[225] 1 Timothy 1:15-16 "Christ Jesus came into the world to save sinners, and I am the worst of them all."

CHAPTER 2
Monday Mulligans

It was Monday morning. Six o'clock. Lucas and ProV were wide awake, full already of the sea breezes and smell of the ocean. The sun had been peeking up well before five. Lucas had gone down to the beach for a walk. The planned four-mile walk had turned into six when he became so enamored with the views and the scenery and his prayerful thoughts that he was three miles away when he realized it was time to turn back. ProV had opted to sit on the porch with coffee and ponder everything from the day before. Was this a dream? Must be.

Lucas returned at 6:50, exhausted but exhilarated, and off they went to the clubhouse to see what this Thursday morning group was all about. They called themselves the Monday Mulligans: Men of a Second Chance.

At the same time every Monday in the bar at Hokmah, some of the wisest men in the world gathered to listen. Typically, those who attended were smart enough to keep quiet. Wisdom knows to stay quiet. Every week the teacher was someone worth hearing. Lady Wisdom was a favorite. She often came to teach the old boys from her many books.

Questions were appropriate, not loudmouthed answers.

The bar was quickly filling up. It was a men's group, except for Hollie, Lady Wisdom and one sweet older widow, Anna[226], who served the coffee and pastries. The presence of the women assured that the group stayed away from too much locker room humor.

Lucas saw Hollie and asked, "Who is teaching today?"

"Golf or God?" Hollie asked.

"Well, I didn't know there was a choice."

"Sure, it's one of the genius aspects to this morning. It starts at seven. After some opening conversation and introduction of newbies, the first agenda item is a ten-minute golf lesson. Then someone leads a study on wisdom. No homework required."

"Okay."

Lucas recognized several faces from yesterday. Forty or so men. Half were recognizable figures from the game of golf. The rest were, like ProV and Lucas, just simple men trying to find a golf swing or a better life.

Byron Nelson was sitting comfortably, dipping a tea bag into hot water, smiling.

Two balding gentlemen talked quietly in a corner table. Ben Hogan was with Larry Nelson, who had started to play golf at age twenty-one with the help of Hogan's book on the *Five Fundamentals*. No coffee for Ben. Caffeine did not help his personal battle with nervous four footers. Ben was using a fork to show Larry something about the grip. Larry was in the Hall of Fame, but he was still in awe of Hogan's grip.

Payne Stewart was hard to recognize since he was not dressed for golf. No fashionable hat or knickers. He was busy passing out bracelets. ProV asked R.W., "Who are the guys talking to Payne?"

"Oh. Bruce Leitzke. Won a lot of tournaments without playing much. Spent more time coaching little league baseball than playing golf. And his brother-in-law, Jerry Pate. He won a US Open when he was young. And their friend Bill Rogers from Texas, who won the Open at Royal St. Georges back in eighty-one."

[226] Luke 2:36 "Anna, a prophet, was also there..."

"You mean 1881?" said ProV, who had never heard of any of them.

"No, he's old but not that old! Nineteen-eighty-one. Just about seventy-five years ago. Seems like yesterday. Bill quit early to get off the road and spend more time with family. More to life than golf," said R.W. "You'd learn a lot hanging around those guys."

Bernhard Langer was sitting comfortably, chatting with Nicodemus, hard to recognize under a golf visor. "Nick, your study last week on being 'born again' sent chills up my spine. Thanks again!" Larry Moody came in late to sit with Bernhard and Nick.

Wright was the emcee for the morning. He banged on a coffee cup to get the meeting started. The custom was for the whole group to recite their theme verse together each Monday. He led them in a loud voice, "Blessed is the man whose bogeys the Lord does not count against him. Psalm 32:2." Amens were heard all around.

"Any first-timers?" Introductions were always short and sweet.

Bill Rogers jumped to his feet. "I am so excited to welcome for the first time one of my oldest and dearest friends," he said in his Texas drawl. "Y'all know Ben Crenshaw." Ben had just walked in late and tipped his cap with a friendly smile. Many of his old friends stood up to hug and welcome the two-time Masters winner.

When no one else responded, Wright spoke up. "I'd like to introduce two first-timers. We played Hokmah yesterday. Lucas Friend will beat you every day with his fourteen shots. Be careful. If I remember this right, he has two kids and six grandchildren, one of whom is trying to play pro golf."

He turned to ProV. "Paul Player is from California. He has a nickname which says it all. ProV can golf his ball. And after yesterday, he is on his way. He is single with two kids back home. Welcome these guys. They will play Segullah today and be gone."

Polite welcomes and quiet handclaps followed the introductions.

"Okay, men," said Wright, "I saw some of your golf swings this week. I've heard it said you should 'See it, feel it, trust it.'[227] But I saw some of

[227] David L. Cook, Golf's Sacred Journey (1st Zondervan Edition 2009)

your swings and I am not sure they can all be trusted. Some of you need a brand new swing, so listen up." Hogan didn't seem to get the joke.

The golf teacher for the day was Wally Armstrong, who stood without introduction. Everybody knew Wally.

Although he had specialized in teaching kids, the truth was that his ideas for children worked for adults too. Wally should have been intimidated to teach golf in a room with Byron Nelson and Ben Hogan, but he was as cool as the back side of a pillow.

He called Lucas to the front and handed him a Hula Hoop to demonstrate the circle of the golf swing. Lucas thoroughly enjoyed being the student. Wally's theme for the morning was "balance." He gave some tips on how to keep your balance and the importance of footwork in the swing.

After ten minutes and coffee refills, Wright stood up again. "Thanks, Wally," he said with a smile. "Our speaker today is rather new to Hokmah. He moved here just two years ago. Please welcome Paul Tentmaker."

Just like Wally, everyone knew Paul. R.W. took a seat with Lucas and ProV.

"Well, men, and ladies as well," giving a nod to Lady Wisdom, Anna and Hollie, "as most of you know, I am retired and basically just hanging out around this clubhouse most of the day with guys like you. I haven't played golf in ages. Thinking about it is good enough for me. You could say *'I have fought a good fight, I have finished my course, I have kept the faith.'*" [228]

This left ProV wondering where he had heard that before. Everyone smiled.

Tentmaker went on, "I visited this place for years but came here permanently just two years ago. There is a freedom to speak here I was unaccustomed to. Speaking my mind got me in a lot of trouble once upon a time. I have rented a house down by the first hole on Segullah, just a short walk from here. *'I welcome all who wish to visit, and do what*

[228] 2 Timothy 4:7 (KJV)

I can to boldly proclaim the Kingdom of God and teach about the Lord Jesus Christ. And no one tries to stop me.'" [229]

R.W. whispered to Lucas, "I go see Paul at least once a week. We spend a couple of hours just talking. Mostly I listen."

Lucas quickly figured out who this guy was and smiled.

"My subject this morning, just like Wally's, is *balance.* But not golf—life. Work. Play. Worship. How can we balance these three important parts of life?"

ProV was all ears, sipping his fourth cup of coffee since he awoke at 5:00.

"Let's start with work."

"Most humans spend forty-plus hours working every week. A few sluggards do not work, or they pretend to work. Some are cursed, and I use that word on purpose, by having so much money they don't really need to work. Many more work way too much."

Lucas thought about his father who did just that. He was a farmer, and it seemed like the work was never done. Sheep, cattle, plus crops. And equipment always needed to be fixed. He worked at least a hundred hours a week.

Tentmaker continued, "As for me, even though most people would describe me as a preacher, I never accepted money for helping people. I made my own living, and if I went somewhere to preach or teach, I paid my own way with the money I earned. No one could ever accuse me of being in the preachin' business for money. I worked with my hands."

ProV admired that. He had never articulated it, but one of his main hang-ups was TV preachers using God to get rich. He presumed it was all a scam. Lucas was the first authentic man of faith he'd ever known who wasn't making money off a religious gig. He had discounted every single Christian man he had ever known by the fact they made money from their faith.

"Okay, so the first box is work," Tentmaker said.

"The second box is play. Kids live for this one. Boys especially live

[229] Acts 28:30-31

and die for anything with a ball. And typically, in every culture, one day out of seven is dedicated to play. Saturdays are the play day."

Sundays too, thought Lucas.

"For us older folk with no athletic ability, hiking and anything outdoors counts for play. And of course, this is where golf comes in. For most people, golf is a weekend event. Saturday with friends. The occasional open competition or tournament somewhere. Most men are just adult boys. Their desire to play is a lifelong obsession."

ProV whispered to R.W., "We saw Mr. Hogan on the range this morning. No one even knows how old he is now. He's still playing."

"Exactly," said R.W. "Still trying to get better. Indeed, he was on the course last night as we had dinner. Dusk time is when he sneaks out. Usually no one but him and a caddie who is sworn to secrecy. He loves to play, and cannot even tell you why."

ProV and Lucas looked at each other and shared a smile, knowing they were little boys at heart.

"But now the third and last box—worship," said Tentmaker. "Most people never think about this one."

He's right about that, thought ProV.

"But even atheists worship something or someone. Sadly, many people worship their family, or a romantic relationship. Wife or girlfriend. Husband or boyfriend. That never really works out," said the wise man. ProV had been down that path.

"Worshipping money is another obvious mistake. The thirteenth hole has some victims of that disease," said Paul. Lucas thought about most of his friends on Wall Street.

"Some people worship their own kids. Easy to do. It sounds okay but always fails. For many centuries, people have worshipped creation itself. The moon and sun gods are too many to count."

ProV's face showed puzzlement.

Tentmaker raised his voice so all could hear clearly: "Worship is for God. *Only*."

"So, there you go. Work. Play. Worship. 'WPW,' I call it. But here's what has happened to mess up all this." He pulled out three matchboxes—each titled with a magic marker: Work was black with black matches. Play was red with red matches. Worship was white with white matches.

Hollie was smiling over her hot coffee with triple milk. She never grew tired of listening to Paul Tentmaker, even though he was not the most eloquent speaker. She had helped him write his letters, teaching things that most people never think about.

"First, for some kids especially, play can become worship." He dumped all the matches out of the boxes. He took some red matches from play and put them into the worship box.

"This reminds me of one of my cousins who worshipped golf. He would sit in church on Sunday while the pastor was preaching and be counting up in his mind how many putts he had on Saturday, and what he could have shot if only he hadn't lost that ball on sixteen. He worshipped golf when he should have been just playing golf."

ProV's brain could not resist thinking, *That's me. I used to skip school to go play golf. My parents thought I was in class but I was at the golf course. I didn't even graduate with my class due to skipping school my senior year. I had to go to summer school so I could play college golf.*

Tentmaker continued: "The flip side of this play box is also sad. If your play becomes work, you will be miserable." He filled the work box with a few red sticks.

"This explains why many golf pros hate golf. They start to play as kids because it is a game. They play the game they love, even worship. Then they excel and the money is so attractive, they decide to be a 'professional.' The game becomes work. And almost immediately, angst and misery set in. The simmering anger festers. They hate four-foot putts, or left-to-right wind, or six irons, or hotels, or early tee times, or dogleg rights, or fast food—whatever was their own special downfall. Eventually they end up as a club pro selling golf balls and giving lessons to people who will never get better. They started to *play* golf—now they go to *work*."

This was ringing ProV's bell. He well remembered his miserable days of professional golf.

"So, play needs to be play. Not worship. Not work."

Hollie smiled. Although she was only known as a caddie, almost nobody except her father and brother knew she loved to still play the game. On many summer evenings, they would walk nine holes at 10 p.m. The sun would never really go down completely in late June. No one kept score. Midnight finishes were common. They enjoyed each other's company.

The Trinity loved to play.

Tentmaker continued. "But now about work. Modern man typically turns work into worship."

He poured some black work matches into the white worship box. "How else can you explain the fact that some people work eighty hours a week? How can you explain the incredible pride which causes people to tell some stranger on a plane what they do for work. They ask, 'So what do you do?' just to open the door to talk about their own work.

"They worship their work. They are usually good at it. But if you took it away from them, they would have no identity."

This one hit Lucas. This was him in his younger days on Wall Street, when he could converse about takeovers and commodities and derivatives and millions. Thankfully, his failures in a financial crash had saved him from his ego, pride and workaholism.

Tentmaker said, "And for a few people, work is actually play. Not many, thankfully."

He took a few black work matches and put them into the play box. "They never take it seriously. They are perfectly happy to put in a few hours every week, not proud of their work, but just playing with those forty or so hours. They make enough to survive and pay off their credit cards each month. These are usually single men. Not many women put up with such characters."

That explained ProV's first divorce, at least partially.

"So work should be work. Not worship. Not play."

Tentmaker paused. "Finally, now for worship. It is really sad when worship turns into work. This is the dilemma for more than a few clergymen. They love God and all that goes with it. Church. Singing.

Preaching. Bible study. They love it so much they decide to make the worship of God a full-time profession—their work."

Tentmaker poured white worship matches into the black work box.

"The joy of Sunday worship and more becomes a week-long slog. The sermons that come easy at first turn into Saturday night meltdowns. The devotional hour in the early morning has turned into a ritualistic worship killer instead of a worship experience. He is now a professional holy man. Not a nice picture, usually. The Pharisees and Sadducees fall in this category, of course, and I know this better than anyone since I was a Pharisee of Pharisees."

From the back of the room came a huge "Amen!" from Nicodemus, shaking his head and knowing he had been guilty on that one.

Anna was quietly filling up coffee cups as the room got still with listening ears.

"So, let me finish this WPW sermonette. I would also say most people who go to church on a Sunday are just playing at the worship."

He poured red play matches into the white worship box. "They are not really worshipping. At a typical old style Scottish church, the rituals have taken over. And of course, in your country"—he looked at Lucas— "these modern so-called worshippers raise their hands and claim to give God their everything when in fact God gets almost nothing except a few dollars in the offering and an hour on Sundays. The so-called worship time on Sunday is nothing but a musical play time. With a good so-called worship band, it is just an excuse to dance like it's Saturday night for a few minutes on Sunday morning."

ProV was not a church goer. None of this made much sense to him. But Lucas knew exactly what Paul was saying. And knew he was guilty of weak dancing on Sundays. "So, worship should be worship. Not work. Not play."

"To summarize, leave time in your life to play. Golf is a *game*. Just *play* like you were ten years old again. Not worship. Not work. And remember, this game is so great you can play into old age."

ProV nodded and sipped his coffee again.

"As for work, *'Whatever you do, work as unto the Lord.'* [230] Work is not playtime. But it also is not to be worshipped. Balance is the key."

Lucas remembered how happy he was to be retired and out of the Wall Street rat race where the rats always won.

"And *worship* God alone. Not the game of golf. Not your work. Not even your wife or kids. A balanced person can see God on the tenth green as easily as he sees him in the Tenth Commandment. A balanced person can see God in the workplace as much as in the sanctuary. A balanced person can worship God alone all day, every day. In short, worshipping the wrong people or things will make you what I call an 'utter fool.' [231] Worship is not a Sunday event. Not a song to sing. It is way bigger and better than just a church event."

Tentmaker offered a prayer and sat down. Wright stood back up to offer an amen and a benediction. He cleared his throat.

"Guys, I had this conversation with Paul here a long time ago. He saved my life. I was a religious workaholic who played golf just to soothe my nerves and supposedly get away from all the pressures. I spent sixty hours at work, another thirty hours doing religious obligations imposed on me by the Church of Scotland, not to mention the voice of my mother telling me to be a 'good boy' and my father telling me to 'work harder.' Golf was my outlet from the pressure of those days. And then, one fine day, I came to Hokmah. I met many of the people you see today. I sat in this same bar. I talked to this same man," he said, pointing to Tentmaker. "Worship, work, play. All one life."

Wright reached over, grabbed all three boxes and emptied them onto the table, taking his hands to mix all the red, white and black matches into a random pile.

"I like to say I am 'mixed up.' Work feels like play, and play feels like worship, and worship brings it all together, with God in the center."

Lucas was nodding. Hollie was smiling. ProV was understanding.

[230] Colossians 3:23

[231] Romans 1:21-22 "Yes, they knew God, but they wouldn't worship Him as God... Claiming to be wise, they instead became utter fools."

CHAPTER 3

No Scorecard

As the meeting was breaking up, Hollie wandered over to Lucas, who was busy with Wally talking about the circle of the golf swing. "Lucas," she said, "you picked a good day to be here. Wally's circle and Tentmaker's message on WPW."

"Yes, Hollie. I needed both," said Lucas, who was just happy to be there.

"Now, let's find ProV and talk about today's adventure," she said.

They found him chatting with Payne Stewart and Bernhard Langer, putting on a wristband that said "WWJD." Nicodemus was listening in like a proud papa, knowing that his story had been used for centuries to bring new life to weary souls.

Hollie waited patiently and then motioned ProV to come over. She said, "The course today is called Segullah, or in English, 'the Treasure.' Let me explain. There are multiple treasures on this course. Indeed, it is a bit of a multi-faceted treasure hunt. The first treasure leads to another and so on until finally, you may find the ultimate treasure."

ProV was already in hyper mode thinking about the hidden treasure, secretly hoping it was some sort of financial bonus. He could use some debt relief.

But Hollie settled that abruptly. "When the word 'treasure' is mentioned, our minds always go to money. Things. Never ideas. Never thoughts. Never relationships. Never people. For example, long ago an angel spoke to Mary about the reality of her son. The holy book says she 'treasured' these things in her heart.[232] The love of a mother can be a treasure."

This mother talk didn't much help ProV. Sure, his mother loved him but she also drank too much and never stood up for him when his father yelled at him every day. His grandmother Addie had saved the day more than once.

Hollie said, "We are on the tee in fifty minutes."

Lucas nodded and said he would meet her on the range. ProV moved to the back of the room to meet Crenshaw, hoping for a quick putting lesson. He had not noticed that Ben's teacher, Harvey Penick, was sitting quietly with Ben. "Harvey, what an honor. I read all your books." The old man smiled. Ben said goodbye with a quick lesson: "Loosen your grip."

ProV saw Hogan as he was leaving. "Mr. Hogan, will you be hitting balls today?" The man known as the "Hawk" gave ProV the stare he had hoped to avoid. It was the gaze of a man who had just heard the dumbest question ever.

"Yes sir, that's what I do," Hogan answered.

ProV walked out with Wright, who said his goodbyes.

"So will we see you again?"

"Not today, ProV," Wright said. "I've got work to do. Looks like they need me to escort some lost soul around Hokmah today. But whether you see me again is up to you now. Yahweh has done everything he needs to show you the way back. Now it's up to you."

[232] Luke 2:19 (NIV)

He smiled, hugged ProV, and off he went into the cool Orkney morning.

So today was just Lucas and ProV, the perfect two-ball with the best caddies in the world.

As they stretched and warmed up on the range, Lucas and ProV discussed the idea that golf with a caddie is heavenly.

"Just something about the whole caddie experience," said ProV.

Lucas agreed. "Oh, yeah, the trolley or pull cart gets hard. Mine turns over at least once a nine. And buggy golf, as the Scots call it, takes away the rhythm of a round."

ProV chimed in as he was hitting wedges to a nearby flag, "And what could be worse than 'cart path only' on rainy days. Not to mention the sheer ugliness of concrete on a golf course."

Hollie was listening in as she cleaned clubs. *Concrete on a golf course. What could be more sacrilegious*, she thought to herself in holy disgust.

The walk to the first tee was just two minutes from the small range for Segullah. Three elderly men, all with perfectly behaved border collies, were chatting on the tee when they arrived. Daniel, Job and Noah got together at least once a week to walk and talk. The Lord loved to listen to what they had to say.[233]

The starter greeted the pilgrims with, "Welcome, gentlemen, to Segullah, and ladies too," giving a nod to Hollie. "My name is Noah."

Hollie hugged and shook hands with Noah like they had been friends forever. He seemed to be a typical Scotsman, way more in love with his canine friend than his wife or children or playing companions. As Noah began his opening speech for the pilgrims, the dog yawned. She had heard it all before. She was still damp after a morning romp near the beach.

"No scorecards today. No holes with names. Each hole yesterday was uniquely intriguing and brilliant, worthy of being a signature hole. The whole point here today is that there exists no scorecard, no par or bogey, nothing. Each hole has a simple tee marker. A fairway.

[233] Malachi 3:16 "Then those who feared the Lord spoke to each other, and the Lord listened to what they said."

Rough and bunkers. Water on many holes. A flag and a hole on perfect greens."

ProV was multitasking, listening to Noah while he petted all of the friendly creatures with wagging tails. He did better with dogs than his family.

"You will love this course but you may not remember a lot about it at the end of the day. With no scorecard, you will not make a single bogey today. Just enjoy the day without worrying about pencils and numbers," finished Noah.

"Sounds good to me. Bogey-free golf? Why didn't someone back home think about this?" said ProV, glancing at Lucas.

"Good luck with the Treasure," said Noah as he sent the two-ball with caddies off into the Orkney summer breezes. Noah left to walk the beach with Daniel and Job.

"So, Hollie," asked Lucas, "I presume that was the original Noah?"

"Of course," she said, "You should know by now this place is full of characters. And honestly, none are more authentic than that old man. He saved his family and, by doing so, the entire human race.[234] He is your original grandpa. But despite his great accomplishment he still feels like a failure, mostly because he got drunk and depressed after the boat landed on dry ground, not to mention the fact his children and grandchildren turned out to be worse sinners than the people he condemned."

ProV had never given Noah much thought.

Hollie went on. "This island was under water for several centuries after the great Noah flood. Hard to imagine when you see how beautiful and perfect this links is now. But sure enough, it was destroyed once upon a time like the rest of the world. It was under ice for a few hundred years."

ProV was curious. "Under ice?"

"Indeed. And we were so happy when Noah agreed to join us a few years ago. He learned to play golf after he arrived here and has never

[234] Hebrews 11:7 "It was by faith that Noah built a large boat to save his family from the flood."

made a bogey. He only plays this Segullah course, so he's never held a scorecard in his hand. He loves to say that not only has God declared him free and righteous from all sin, he is also free from all bogeys!"

ProV uttered words that would have been impossible just three days ago: "I agree. Keeping score is a bad idea."

The front nine at Segullah was pure joy and delight. Scenic. Challenging. Pure links golf. The ball bouncing just the way it should. Humps and bumps aplenty. More good breaks than bad ones. The "good guy" inside all golfers showed up repeatedly. It was the perfect challenge.

As they arrived at the long ninth hole, the rain from an ominous black cloud came pelting down, "Just like in the days of Noah," laughed Hollie.

They all dove into a small wooden shelter. It had been behind the ninth green for centuries. The "Shed of Tears," as they called it, could tell a lot of stories. It was more than two miles from the clubhouse. The front nine had come and gone in a ninety-minute exhilarating blur of casual golf, walking and talking.

Hollie had spent many hours in the shed. She went there often by herself, just to think and look out over the North Sea. Or just cry. Hollie wept more than anyone ever knew, although she was usually alone when it happened. Just like Jesus, she wept. For her beloved Orkney.[235] For her friends.[236] For the world.[237]

She was not really alone, of course. The Voice that spoke through her to ProV in the cathedral was always there with Hollie in the shed. She knew the *"wisdom in the sand."* She knew the *"treasure in the darkness."* The Voice never left her. It was the eternal Voice of the Father and she merely repeated what He said. The shed was a sanctuary for her. A holy place.

Lucas realized the raindrops offered him an opportunity to chat with Hollie for a few special moments.

[235] Luke 19:41

[236] John 11:35

[237] Luke 22:44

"So, tell me Hollie. You've caddied for a lot of people. Anyone stand out on the top of your list?"

Hollie hesitated. Her ageless mind was awhirl with possible answers. The list was endless. Presidents and Prime Ministers. She once had Churchill and Roosevelt and Stalin in the same group. They had snuck off to the Orkney Islands to try to stop a world war. Stalin had been in the group for the first few holes. He cheated all day. Churchill hit a weak slice, to be expected. Roosevelt took special pleasure in just being able to walk the course. He seemed to know that polio was about to end his days on a golf course. He was a good putter who credited a lesson from Bobby Jones in 1924.

A couple of popes came to mind. No one knew that any pope actually played golf. It was a Vatican secret.

But her mind quickly skipped to one of the first bags she ever carried. The original richest man in the world, Job, was also the greatest player in his era.

"Lucas, sit down. This could take a while." She smiled as she remembered that special day. ProV was listening too. The shed had a self-serve coffee and hot chocolate machine and a refrigerator stocked with simple drinks. Hot chocolate made a great companion for a good story from Hollie. It was still raining creepy cats and dirty dogs.

"Lucas, you've heard of Job?" asked Hollie.

"Sure, we saw the ol' guy yesterday. Right?"

"Correct. He was behind the Integrity hole with his three pals. My first time around the course with him was a real memory. Job was a legendary golfer," she said. "But he was more. He was a genius, with an IQ over one hundred and seventy. He inherited wealth from his father but then he had made all the right moves and investments. His home was on a nearby island which he owned, called Uz. He was handsome. He married a beautiful woman who gave him ten amazing children: seven sons and three daughters who all adored him."

Lucas sipped his hot chocolate as the rain lightened slightly.

"But then," continued Hollie, "his wife and all ten children were lost in a horrible accident at sea, not far from here actually. While he was in mourning, pirates came and stole all his possessions. In the stress of it all, he lost his health. Indeed, he lost everything. He had to flee his island, which is when he appeared here on the Isle of Mashal. He and three of his friends came here hoping for answers, or at least some relief."

Hollie looked out over the sea to the lighthouse as she continued with Job's story.

"Job had quit playing golf but he knew that a walk around here might be part of his therapy. I was assigned to Job's bag, of course, and off we went. He was still physically weak but his golf talent was something. We played this Segullah course with no scorecard, just a slow walk and casual talk to find consolation for his soul. Job was amazing that day. He made the golf look easy. We never spoke of his tragedy. He needed my presence, even silence, not advice. His three friends did not play golf. They just walked with us in silence."[238]

"Job was so exhausted after those nine holes that we stopped into this same shed to grab some refreshment and rest. His three friends decided this would be a good time to tell their theories of what he must have done wrong to cause a just God to take away all his family and possessions and health. They all offered plausible reasons for his collapse, thinking they were helping their friend.

"But Job did not take their advice well; he got upset and walked out onto the nearby beach. I heard him speaking to his Creator. He was eloquently defending himself. He was innocent of all the charges of his three friends, he told his Maker. How dare they accuse him, a man who was *'blameless – a man of complete integrity.'*[239]

"And to be fair, Job was indeed as righteous as a human could be. Not perfect. But he had been on the right side his whole life, including in his relationship with God. He knew God intimately. Yahweh was not theory for him. He was real. Those other three amigos were on the right side with God, too, but not like Job. They were just God fans, not

[238] Job 2:13 "No one said a word to Job, for they saw that his suffering was too great for words."

[239] Job 1:1

God followers. They were full of theology but not full of God. Like some professors of theology, they know all *about* God, but they do not actually *know* Him.

"So, I followed Job down to the beach and made a suggestion for him. Be still. And listen for the Voice of Yahweh. And sure enough, the Voice was loud and clear. As soon as Job quieted his own spirit, Yahweh spoke:

> *Who but God goes up to heaven and comes back down? Who holds the wind in his fists? Who wraps up the oceans in his cloak? Who has created the whole wide world? What is his name? And his son's name? Tell me if you know.*[240]

"God Himself was cross examining Job, who looked up to the heavens as an eagle and a hawk came soaring by, just as the Voice bellowed,

> *Is it your wisdom that makes the hawk soar and spread its wings toward the south? Is it your command that the eagle rises to the heights to make its nest?'*[241]

"Job then mumbled an honest confession, speaking directly to his friend Yahweh, an unseen but awesome presence on the scene," continued Hollie.

> *I know that you can do anything and no one can stop you. You asked, "who is this that questions my wisdom with such ignorance?" It is I—and I was talking about things I knew nothing about, things far too wonderful for me. You said, "Listen and I will speak! I have some questions for you, and you must answer them." I had only heard about you before, but now I have seen you with my own eyes. I take back everything I said, and I sit in dust and ashes to show my repentance.*[242]

"Tears of thankfulness for God's forgiveness filled Job's eyes.

[240] Proverbs 30:4

[241] Job 39:26

[242] Job 42:2-6

"I then reminded Job of one last duty. His three friends now needed the same forgiveness he had received. So, Job stopped on the beach and spent a full five minutes praying for Eli, B.D. and Zeke. Job prayed for his friends with loud wailing and weeping.[243] And of course, the Lord heard those prayers and answered them."

ProV asked a logical question. "How did this story end?"

"He started all over again, and within twenty years, he was on top again. Everything restored. He passed Yahweh's test. And of course, he now knew that God is sovereign – that he was not responsible for his great successes after all. When you actually see God, as Job did, it changes everything from a 'me' perspective to a 'thee' perspective. It can be explained quite well by the words of King David, spoken many centuries later.

> *"Yours, O Lord, is the greatness, the power, the glory, the victory, and the majesty. Everything in the heavens and on earth is yours, O Lord, and this is your Kingdom. We adore you as the one who is over all things. Wealth and honor come from you alone, for you rule over everything. Power and might are in your hand, and at your discretion people are made great and given strength."*[244]

"And by the way, after that great day here on Segullah, Job never kept score again. His golf game was better than ever but the score, either good or bad, just didn't matter. He hangs around now on the fifth hole at Hokmah and here at Segullah as well. He comes out almost every Monday just to walk and talk with his friends Noah and Daniel. They are on a whole other level. They all spend a lot of time praying for their friends and family."[245]

ProV then remembered a comment from Lucas on the plane coming to Scotland. Lucas had told him he had been praying for him. He

[243] Job 42:9-10 "When Job prayed for his friends, the Lord restored his fortunes."

[244] 1 Chronicles 29: 11-12

[245] Ezekiel 14:14-23

had been unmoved by those prayers. He had mumbled something like, "Hope it helps me make a few putts." But now he knew, prayers for friends are life changing for both.

CHAPTER 4
The Voice Will Guide You

The clouds rolled away and a beautiful blue sky announced the beginning of the back nine. The happy twosome had sat in the shelter long enough, listening to Hollie's story about Job and his friends.

"Okay, Hollie, let's go back to the beginning," Lucas said. "I am really curious. Have I been here before? Is it possible I was here twelve years ago and just don't remember? I had nearly forgotten Hokmah. I definitely had forgotten how to get here. But if I played Segullah the last time, I have zero memory."

"Well, Mr. Friend," she said with affection as she pulled the cover off his driver, "I surely cannot tell you what you remember. But I can tell you this: You know how they say the Masters only starts on the last nine holes? Same here. It is now time to start seeking that treasure."

ProV was glad to hear the good news that a treasure was waiting for them. The words from the cathedral were still ringing in his ears: ***"There's a wisdom in the sand. There's a treasure in the darkness."***

"Stop and listen for just a moment. Do not forget that valuable treasures are always hidden—often in a safety box or some other dark place. No one keeps precious jewels in the sunshine where anyone can snatch them. And so it is with God. His treasures are in the darkness[246] or the unseen. But," she stopped to show a holy smile, "they are not hidden *from* you. They are hidden *for* you. So now, just play golf. The Voice will guide you through this."

The tenth hole was "headed home." Indeed, it was time to go home.

With the help of Mr. T and Hollie, the back nine was pure joy. The wind had laid down for them. No scores. No bogeys. The only hole to remember was a hole-in-one by ProV on the tricky thirteenth hole.

Ten through twelve were played into the gentle breeze, then thirteen turned across toward the ocean with the lighthouse as a backdrop in the sea. It was a short hole, and ProV was coming off some pleasant but mediocre golf, by his standards. He struck a nine iron into the cross wind and landed his ball at the front right edge of the green. It covered the burn fronting the putting surface and curled up a slope toward the back left pin. When it disappeared, all of heaven and earth rejoiced.

Lucas jumped in the air. ProV threw his club into the stratosphere. Hollie and Mr. T became cheerleaders. The joy of that one shot lasted all the way to the sixteenth tee, as they laughed and walked and hit their shots freely. The fourteenth and fifteenth holes were a blur of fun. Even the search for a treasure was forgotten in the exhilaration of the "one." A rainbow appeared. God Himself wanted to join the celebration.

Lucas had a good question: "If you're not keeping score, does a hole-in-one count?"

That drew laughter and debate all around. Of course, ProV would be counting this ace, his fourteenth such miracle. It even topped his ace on the sixteenth at Augusta in a practice round in 2033, playing with Jordan Spieth.

The friendly discussion continued as they approached the sixteenth tee. Abraham was there to greet everyone. Had he heard about the ace and come out to congratulate ProV?

[246] Isaiah 45:3 "And I will give you treasures hidden in the darkness—secret riches. I will do this so you may know that I am the Lord, the God of Israel, the one who calls you by name."

"No, I often greet people on this tee," he said. "You will find your first treasure here. I will walk with you."

This was a big moment. "So, Hollie," whispered ProV, "why Abraham?"

"Do you remember what he said? He is a friend of God."

ProV was still confused.

Lucas and ProV hit nice, manageable tee balls on this beautiful seaside two-shot hole which scorecards would call a par four. Despite his nice swing, Lucas's ball toppled slowly into a fairway bunker on its last roll. Nothing about the hole or situation would indicate a treasure was in play. The Voice from the cathedral was faintly ringing in ProV's ears: ***"There's a wisdom in the sand. There's a treasure in the darkness."***

Lucas had to chop the ball out backward to the fairway. Then he played a difficult four hybrid to a green surrounded by more sand. He caught the ball perfectly. But the wind held it up and the ball plugged in a deep bunker short of the green.

ProV hit a shot that was aesthetically even better than his hole-in-one. His pure six iron stopped just six feet away from perfection.

The walk to the green was serene. The sounds and smells of the sea on the left were all around. Abraham walked the fairway with the pilgrims and chatted amiably with his new friend. "So, ProV, who's your best friend?"

"Good question, sir. I wasn't sure a week ago, but it must be Lucas," said ProV without much thought. Abraham merely said, "You will always need friends."

Lucas's ball was buried so deep in the sand that even Hollie had trouble locating it. He took three swipes to extricate the ball from prison and finally picked it up and came out of the bunker a beaten man.

Meanwhile, ProV nicely rolled in his putt, saying with a smile, "I like this hole." Then he turned to Hollie and asked, "Where's this great treasure you promised me? I hope it was more than that birdie."

"ProV, let's sit for a minute or two," she replied. She led the pair over to a comfortable bench near the sea's edge. "It's picture time."

Abraham asked for ProV's camera phone. "Okay, ProV, time to smile. Time for you guys to act like tourists," said Abraham, getting into position for the perfect picture of the two friends. The shutter snapped three times with the famous lighthouse in the background. He showed the pictures to the twosome and smiled. "So, ProV, you've found your first treasure."

As they say in Scotland, ProV was a "wee niggle" slow to get it.

Abraham grinned and said, "You're hugging your treasure. His name is Lucas."

Lucas was stunned as well. He had never thought friendship could be so priceless. Abraham pulled up a chair for a chat with the boys.

"Guys, most men live their whole life without a true friend. Just lots of acquaintances, hanging around the edges. But never a real friend."

Hollie heard Abraham and put an exclamation point on the conversation. "Even God Himself said you were his best friend."[247]

ProV and Lucas looked at each other and tears began to well.

"Finding God almost always means finding a friend on earth first. Almost every testimony you've ever heard says somewhere, 'I had a friend...' [248], usually at work or the golf course or the neighborhood. ProV, in your case, your testimony will always include, 'I had a friend[249] who took me to Scotland!'"

ProV was stunned with this new idea.

His treasure had brought him to Scotland. To Dornoch. To the Orkneys. To Hokmah. And now, this treasure was showing him new life.

Lucas the treasure said, "ProV, I still love that old verse—written by Paul the Tentmaker, by the way, who you met this morning—*'Only Luke is with me.'*[250] And that describes how I feel about you, bro. I am with you, no matter what."

Paul Player and Lucas Friend hugged each other as true friends. "Phileo come to life!" said Hollie. Abraham smiled like a proud papa.

Hollie said, "Let's go guys. We are not finished."

[247] 2 Chronicles 20:7 "...your friend Abraham."

[248] Proverbs 27:17 "As iron sharpens iron, so a friend sharpens a friend"

[249] John 15:13 "There is no greater love than to lay down one's life for one's friends."

[250] 2 Timothy 4:11

CHAPTER 5
Adam's Eve

The thirty-yard walk to the seventeenth tee was inspiring. The sky seemed bluer. The grass seemed greener. Maybe it was the pilgrims' tears coloring the landscape.

The seventeenth hole was reputedly the most beautiful hole on the entire thirty-six-hole property. Hollie and Mr. T had hinted that such a hole awaited them, but words could not have prepared them.

With no scorecard, it appeared to be 160 yards—all carry over the rocks of the North Sea. This was originally called Adam's Hole by the caddies. The Creator had built the seventeenth hole long ago in the beginning and loved it. In fact, it was the first hole built on the property. But as time moved on the Creator had decided He could do better. As God said in the garden after looking at His creation Adam, "I can do better." And sure enough, the most beautiful creature in the world came forth: a woman. God's best idea ever.

Shortly after creation, God re-did the seventeenth as well, and after the re-do, the caddies renamed the hole "Adam's Eve." A second treasure would be found on this seaside gem.

On the tee was a poet known as King Lemuel. No one was sure if he was a real king or not. For many golfers in more modern times, only Arnold Palmer deserved "the King" title. But Proverbs had ended with a chapter by this King Lemuel, so he must have been seen as a great thinker of his day.

Hollie suggested the two friends stop, take five minutes and listen to the King read his Proverb. By now, the boys from California knew enough to just do whatever Hollie suggested.

"Good morning, Hollie. What a grand day to see you again with new friends."

"Aye it is, King. Could you spare five minutes for a Proverb for us?"

"Of course. I've been quoting it now for about four thousand years!"

Lucas and ProV sat down in comfortable chairs. Adam was there to provide drinks. He had wandered over from the first tee at Hokmah where his duties for the day were done. "Not much happening on a Monday at Hokmah," said the original golf course superintendent. "It's our version of a Sabbath here."

The King began: *"The sayings of King Lemuel contain this message, which his mother taught him."*[251] He looked up and smiled, adding, "I had a wonderful and wise mother."

Lucas also remembered how good his mother had been. ProV had no such memories.

The King continued, reciting words he had been speaking for thousands of years:

> *O my son, O son of my womb, O son of my vows, do not waste your strength on women, on those who ruin kings.*
>
> *It is not for kings, O Lemuel, to guzzle wine.*
>
> *Rulers should not crave alcohol.*
>
> *For if they drink, they may forget the law and not give justice to the oppressed.*
>
> *Alcohol is for the dying, and wine for those in bitter distress.*
>
> *Let them drink to forget their poverty and remember their troubles no more.*[252]

He paused and said, "A quick reminder of what you learned yesterday: Wild women and alcohol are a bad combination."

[251] Proverbs 31:1

[252] Proverbs 31:2-7

ProV didn't need Lemuel to explain that one.

The King continued:

Speak up for those who cannot speak for themselves; ensure justice for those being crushed.

Yes, speak up for the poor and helpless, and see that they get justice."[253]

ProV had not thought much about that one. He had spent his life taking care of himself first. Leftover five-dollar bills went to the poor if he passed a Salvation Army kettle.

"Now we come to the real essence of my proverb," the King said. Hollie and Mr. T stood to the side, listening as if it was their first time there.

Who can find a virtuous and capable wife?

She is more precious than rubies.

Her husband can trust her, and she will greatly enrich his life.

She brings him good, not harm, all the days of her life....[254]

As the King continued to recite Proverbs 31, Lucas started to quietly weep, thinking of his beloved Angelina. They had been married for forty-two years. It was pure bliss for most of the days. They had met in college. She had been a high school teacher for thirty years. She loved Jesus more than Lucas, which was a good thing since Jesus taught her to forgive a lot. She was now just a memory that brought an odd combination of joy and sorrow to his heart when he thought of her. She was a "woman who feared the Lord."

The King found his way to the ending:

There are many virtuous and capable women in the world, but you surpass them all!

Charm is deceptive, and beauty does not last; but a woman who fears the Lord will be greatly praised.

[253] Proverbs 31:8-9

[254] Proverbs 31:10-12

Reward her for all she has done.
Let her deeds publicly declare her praise.[255]

ProV's emotions were just the opposite. He didn't have a wife. He had two ex-wives. Both had been, when he thought about it, huge disappointments. Quarrels[256] were the norm. But now, in the light of a day only Hokmah could bring him, he realized that Mary Ann, wife number one, was still his "wife." His second marriage merely showed him what he had thrown away when he left Mary Ann and the children at age thirty-four.

Looking back, Mary Ann had been virtuous and understanding.[257] She was beautiful. Why would any man leave a gorgeous homecoming queen for an ordinary and nasty woman with no talents other than a few tricks in the bedroom? ProV was weeping with his friend Lucas but they were tears of regret, not joy. He had blown it.

Hollie brought the golfers back to the golf, "Thanks, King, but we have another treasure to find."

She handed Lucas his five hybrid. It was either a good six or a bad five, and she figured this shot would be on the toe or heel since he was trying to swing through tears. But somehow the ball flew sweet and true and high, landing just fifteen feet behind the hole. He smiled and wondered if Angelina had anything to do with that shot.

Mr. T handed ProV a six iron with a thumbs up which meant, "Should be perfect, sir." ProV was still weeping inside, thinking about how he had blown his marriage. He half shanked the ball into a right front bunker. The six iron was flipped back to Mr. T, who by now was very familiar with the ebbs and flows of Paul Player's game and life. His treasure and friend was on the green and he was now in the sand. His hole-in-one and new-found treasure were distant memories already.

[255] Proverbs 31:29-31

[256] Proverbs 27:15-16 "A quarrelsome wife is as annoying as constant dripping on a rainy day. Stopping her complaints is like trying to stop the wind or trying to hold something with greased hands."

[257] Proverbs 19:14 "Only the Lord can give an understanding wife."

ProV's thoughts of his treasure only reminded him that another treasure had gone wrong. He needed more than a friend—he needed a lover. He wanted Mary Ann. All these thoughts possessed him fully as he climbed into the bunker. He eventually sank a five-footer for what yesterday would have been called a double bogey.

But for Lucas, this hole was like a dream come true. Lemuel had reminded him of his dear wife. Was she the treasure he had forgotten?

He trickled the downhill putt into the hole and handed his putter to Hollie, who pointed behind the green, where a simple man wearing all gray—slacks, sweater, tweed cap—was standing.

He shouted to Lucas, "The man who finds a wife finds a treasure, and he receives favor from the Lord."[258]

Lucas smiled back as he walked over and nodded agreement to the old man, who seemed familiar. "Do I know you?"

"We met long ago. At your wedding. See if you remember this." He recited:

> *You have captured my heart,* ***my treasure, my bride.*** *You hold it hostage with one glance of your eyes, with a single jewel of your necklace. Your love delights me,* ***my treasure, my bride...*** *You are my private garden,* ***my treasure, my bride,*** *a secluded spring, a hidden fountain.*[259]

The old man had paused to emphasize the word "treasure" each time. He continued,

> *I have entered my garden,* ***my treasure, my bride!*** *I slept, but my heart was awake, when I heard my lover knocking and calling: "Open to me,* ***my treasure,*** *my darling, my dove, my perfect one."*[260]

As he spoke, Lucas realized that the man speaking was Father Michael, his pastor back in 2011. Forty-five years ago, Lucas considered

[258] Proverbs 18:22

[259] Song of Songs 4:9-12

[260] Song of Songs 5:1-2

the pastor to be strange because he talked and preached all the time about the beauty of marriage as a symbol of the relationship God wants with his people. He had performed the marriage ceremony at an Episcopal church in Fresno. As a young man, Lucas found him boring and hard to understand. Now, though, he made perfect sense.

Memories of this beloved treasure, Angelina, came flooding back into Lucas's heart. The word "my" got his attention, too. Angelina was not just a treasure, she was Lucas's treasure. His very own.

"So tell me," Lucas stumbled, "Father Michael, can you explain why she had to leave so early?" She had been gone now for more than a decade, passing away from a brain aneurysm at age sixty, way too young, just after Lucas's first trip to Hokmah.

"I have no perfect answer for that, dear friend. But I can tell you that your loss is only temporary. Surely these last two days have proven that life is eternal. Remember what God said to Ezekiel?"

Lucas shook his head "no." Father Michael quoted:

> *Son of man, with one blow I will take away* ***your dearest treasure.*** *Yet you must not show any sorrow at her death. Do not weep; let there be no tears. Groan silently, but let there be no wailing at her grave.*[261]

Lucas now saw that God Himself will sometimes take away "your dearest treasure."

"Perhaps it is the only way he can show us what a treasure we possess?" the priest said. "We only know the eternal value of a gift when we lose it."

ProV saw Lucas weeping and came over to hug his friend. He had tears as well.

But the old pastor was not done with surprises. He pointed to his right where the sandy beach was just fifty steps away. There was a path to the beach, surrounded by pinkish sedum, purple Russian sage and brightly colored cosmos plants. Walking toward Lucas was his beloved Angelina.

[261] Ezekiel 24:16-17

His treasure. His bride. More lovely than ever.

She was about sixty, just as when she died. She wore a white dress that reminded him of their wedding day. No shoes. Sand between her toes. A flower in her brown hair.

Lucas ran to her. But as he drew near, she disappeared into the foggy mist. Lucas screamed, "Angie, come back! Don't leave!" But it was too late. She was gone.

But he had found his treasure. Her departure did not change the facts. *She was my treasure*, thought Lucas. He would see her again. Soon.

Hollie was there beside him, a perfect comforter. She was made for moments like this. Lucas buried his head into her shoulder and wailed just like he did twelve years ago at his lover's bedside. But somehow, this time it was different.

Back then he had merely hoped. A pastor had uttered all the expected funeral words about a better place and her final healing. But it felt like empty words of positive thinking.

Now he knew. He would see her again.

"So, Hollie, where did she go?" said Lucas, who was limp with emotion.

"Listen carefully. Can you hear the choir?" Sure enough, the sounds of bag pipes and an organ accompanied a heavenly choir in the air. The song was Beulah Land.[262]

"O Beulah Land, sweet Beulah Land!
"As on thy highest mount I stand,
"I look away across the sea
"Where mansions are prepared for me
"And view the shining glory shore
"My heaven, my home forever more."

Hollie took his hand. "There's no time to explain it all right now. Beulah Land is not Heaven, but a land between Heaven and Earth."

"You mean like Purgatory?" Lucas asked.

[262] Edgar P. Stites and John R. Sweney, *Beulah Land* (1876)

"No," Hollie smiled. "It's just a place on the journey. It can be right here in this world. You remember you had a great-grandmother named Beulah?"

"Sure."

"Well, the word is only found once in the Bible[263] and it literally means 'marriage.' God wants to be married to his people. Isaiah tells us that the people of God would no longer be destitute and lonely. They would be married to God. He would be their lover. Their savior. Their redeemer. Their provider. Their husband. God wants to be more than a judge. More than a father. More than a friend. God wants to be your lover."

This was overwhelming for Lucas.

Holly continued, "The notion of Beulah Land was made famous by John Bunyan in 1678 in *The Pilgrim's Progress*.[264] Bunyan described Beulah Land as the land just before Heaven. You can see Heaven from there. You can almost smell it."

Hollie's comments caused Lucas to look out over the ocean, to see what he could see, or smell, or feel.

"There is this idea, deeply embedded in *The Pilgrim's Progress*, that just as Beulah Land is on the borders of Heaven, so marriage is on the borders of Heaven. Not everyone has to be married to find God, obviously, but the relationship of marriage is given to us as the perfect metaphor, leading us to Heaven."

"Hollie, are you telling me Angie has gone to Beulah Land? She is on the borders of Heaven, waiting for me?"

"No, you may be misunderstanding. *You* are the one living in Beulah Land, on the borders of Heaven. It is meant to be on this earth. Your

[263] Isaiah 62:4-5 (NIV) "But you will be called Hephzibah ('my delight is in her') and your land Beulah ('married'). As a young man marries a young woman, so will your Builder marry you; as a bridegroom rejoices over his bride, so will your God rejoice over you."

[264] "The air was sweet and pleasant, and their way lay directly through it. Here they heard continually the singing of the birds, and saw every day new flowers appear on the earth... Here they were within sight of the City they were going to..." John Bunyan, *The Pilgrim's Progress: From this World, to That Which is to Come*. (Philadelphia; Chicago: S.I. Bell 1891).

marriage to Angie was just a foretaste of your marriage to Jesus Himself."

This was more than Lucas could fathom at this moment. It would take time for this deep wisdom to sink to the bottom of his spirit.

ProV had found his treasure in his friend Lucas.

And Lucas had found his treasure in his Angelina.

They walked the path to the eighteenth and final tee, wondering what possible treasure could top this?

CHAPTER 6

The Final Hole

The once great Job was back to act like a "starter" for the final hole. A small sign said: *"Welcome to the Valley of the Shadow of Death."*[265]

It was long and difficult and always played in a gloomy darkness, even at mid-day. It was the same darkness that comes to Orkney at midnight in the summer. You could see, but just barely. The fog had rolled in. The mist was a brooding and black cloud like an umbrella, blocking the sunlight.

Near the tee were several older ladies, sitting quietly in sweaters, a circle of saints looking out over the ocean view.

Job introduced them all, starting with Lettie Cowman: "This sweet lady was a missionary in Japan. She's not a golfer. She's too busy writing, but she loves this place."

He went on to explain that Lettie had suffered the untimely death of her husband. Tragedy had chased her for many years.

Lettie introduced the other ladies there, all of whom had suffered a similar fate. They were huddled together, shivering with a cool breeze that seemed to come out of nowhere.

[265] Psalm 23:4 (KJV) "Yea, though I walk through the valley of the shadow of death, I will fear no evil."

"We are all here to comfort each other. We have all suffered great loss, but you will notice a peace and contentedness," said Lettie. "Remarkable women, each one."

"Emily lost a four-year-old boy to a brain tumor," Lettie introduced each lady. "Katy never totally recovered from her son dying in a car wreck at age eighteen. The lady in the wheelchair is Jennie, homecoming queen in Alabama before a stroke left her paralyzed. Carla's husband left her with nothing but bills and two teenage kids who followed their dad out the door soon thereafter. Amy was an amazing missionary in India who spent her last decade bedridden with illness."

As the pilgrims moved to the tee box, ProV asked, "So how are they all smiling?"

Hollie assured, "We are here to find out."

On the tee was another smaller sign, a quote from one of Lettie's books. Her words came from the depth of a soul who had suffered much:

God permits trouble to pursue us,
as though He were indifferent to its overwhelming pressure,
that we may be brought to the end of ourselves,
and led to discover the treasures of darkness,
the immeasurable gains of tribulation.[266]

Hollie pointed to the words and said, "This was not in the Bible, but it would have been if Job had written it." She was serious. *"The treasures of darkness."*[267]

Lucas had the honors after his wonderful three on the previous hole. Neither golfer could see their drives, but off they walked into the mist, following two caddies whom they trusted completely. No one even mentioned how long this hole might be.

They found their golf balls, both in light rough to the left side near the sea. Hollie and Mr. T stood waiting with the golf bags. The green ahead was nowhere in sight. Nearby was Job, who had followed them

[266] Mrs Charles E. Cowman, *Streams in the Desert* (Cowman Publications, 1925), January 23rd.

[267] Isaiah 45:3

down the dark fairway. Now that they could see him up close, they realized he was the oldest man they had ever seen. But his age was not slowing him down.

Hollie smiled and playfully kidded Job, "So, old man. Are ya coming out of retirement today?"

He laughed at that one. He was walking with a wooden shafted old Scottish club, called a "cleek," for a cane. "Good morning. I can't play anymore but this old club still makes a good stick for walking."

Lucas said, "Hollie tells us you were quite the player back in the day. Is that true?"

He was too humble to agree. He just said, "The game was so different then. We played with a featherie ball that made almost every hole what you would call a par five. This hole would be a par seven in my day."

ProV had heard Job was rich. He still hoped to find some of that kind of "treasure." Friends and wives are nice, but he still had debt collectors back home.

"So, Job," he said, "this final hole has some sort of treasure too?"

"Of course, ProV. You found your best treasure in your friend Lucas." He paused, then added, "And you are lucky. With friends like mine you never need enemies." He chuckled about Zeke, B.D. and Eli.

"But actually, to get serious for a moment, all of what I learned about wisdom came from my suffering, not my success. Here is what I wrote long ago and still believe today.

God alone understands the way to wisdom;

He knows where it can be found, for he looks throughout the whole earth and sees everything under the heavens.

He decided how hard the winds should blow and how much rain should fall. He made the laws for the rain and laid out a path for the lightning.

Then he saw wisdom and evaluated it. He set it in place and examined it thoroughly.

And this is what he says to all humanity: "The fear of the Lord is true wisdom; to forsake evil is real understanding."[268]

[268] Job 28:23-28

ProV and Lucas both hit their second shots into the darkness with Job's words ringing in their ears. Hollie would have to find these balls. And sure enough, she did. Both shots had curled left and ended on the beach, luckily found since the tide was out.

As Job was walking away, Lucas and ProV stood near their golf balls on the murky beach, with all the smells and sounds and breeze of the sea.

Hollie stood back to let all of Job's words sink in. His trials and tribulations—his suffering—had been worth it all. He had come to know the Almighty. Instead of leading him away from God, Job's suffering led him into the arms of his loving heavenly Father.

ProV was assessing his lie on the beach when it happened, clear as a bell. The cathedral Voice said, ***"There's a wisdom in the sand, there's a treasure in the darkness."*** Just like two days ago in Dornoch, ProV turned to see whose voice this could be. And sure enough, this time it was Hollie, standing just six feet away. She repeated the words, but this time she used his name, ***"Paul Player, there's a wisdom in the sand, there's a treasure in the darkness."***

ProV stared at her and listened. "ProV, it is time for you to know something. Good times and prosperity never lead anyone to the deep and awesome presence of God. It is always some form of suffering."

ProV wanted to be sure he heard this right. "Always?"

"Yes, ProV, always," said the voice of wisdom. "Play away, gentlemen, and let's see what we can find." Hollie and the faithful Mr. T handed middle irons to Lucas and ProV, pointing to a lighter cloud in the sky. Both players did their best, sending their third shots toward the cloud. ProV and Lucas found they were both still in the left rough but safely on the golf course with wedges in hand for a fourth shot. The flag was finally visible, flapping in a steady and dark breeze.

Hollie advised center of the green, but ProV could not resist going for the pin, tucked behind the deepest bunker on the course. And sure enough, the ball seemed to hit a breezy wall and buried, again, in the sand. Lucas did the same.

"Both balls are under that sand somewhere," Hollie said. She found both balls, declared an "unplayable lie" for both and invited the boys to do the best they could on the green. "I would have quit golf if it was this hard," said a truly exhausted seventy-two-year-old Lucas.

Mr. T handed ProV his putter. His forty-footer seemed to vanish into the dark then disappeared in the hole for one final glorious amen. Lucas was not so lucky, three-putting from the same spot for at least an eight that no one was counting.

Both players embraced, found Hollie and Mr. T for final hugs, and started the ceremony of putting balls and tees, markers and gloves back into their golf bags.

As they did, Hollie placed a hand on ProV's hand and said, "Not quite done. Just like you dug that ball out of the sand in the bunker, you need to think about doing the same with your life. Go back and do some digging. See what you find."

That sounded painful, but he knew Hollie was always right.

Hollie whispered to Lucas, "I think it's time to tell ProV some of your story." Lucas agreed with a nod.

CHAPTER 7
The Experience

"Follow me," said Hollie. They started the eighty-yard walk back toward the clubhouse. Halfway there was an old worn bench just made for the moment. A plaque on the bench said, "In memory of Horatio Spafford, beloved member of Hokmah Golf Club. It is well with his soul."

"Take a seat, men," Hollie said, pointing to the plaque. "We can talk about Horatio later. Right now, Lucas needs to tell you a story." She looked at ProV as she spoke.[269] ProV did as instructed, happy to be seated after another long walk around the course.

"ProV," Lucas began, "you would not know this because I don't talk about it. Ever. But you've heard me brag about my one big moment in golf, the 2018 US Amateur at Pebble Beach. It was glorious. And the thrill lasted for many months. Everywhere I went, the subject would come up. I had played in the US Am at Pebble. It made me feel so good.

"I was thirty-four and on top of the world, making money on Wall Street. We lived in Westchester, New York. I joined Winged Foot, which is what guys like me did. And when I wanted to go down to

[269] Horatio Spafford wrote "It Is Well with My Soul" a hymn penned after all four of his daughters died in an ocean liner tragedy in the 1870's.

Long Island and play golf, I had business partners who were members at Shinnecock Hills and Fishers Island."

ProV was listening. He had "ears to hear and eyes to see."[270]

"We were still riding high in March 2019. Angelina and I had a little boy. This was after being told we would never have kids. She insisted we name him Lucas Maxwell Friend, Jr. We called him simply Max.

"Then 2021. Max was diagnosed with a brain tumor. He was two. The world was fighting Corona Virus and now we were fighting an even worse disease, brain cancer. After two more years of pain and sorrow, he died. March 18, 2023."

Lucas paused to collect himself. "My dear wife went into a depression which lingered forever, really. Max should be thirty-five years old. Even now I think he should be with me on this trip."

"I am so sorry, man. I never knew this."

"He was the joy of my life," Lucas began, his voice choking on tears. He struggled to continue. "What I miss most is just holding him on my lap. Reading bedtime stories...."

ProV was looking straight ahead, trying not to weep.

"Right before Christmas in 2022, the doctors told us the end was near, but we were not ready for it. Nothing can prepare you for the death of your only son."

ProV put his hand on his friend's shoulder.

"Then, the stock market crash in October 2023 hit my firm hard. I had made investments personally which were aggressive and bold, or so I thought. Turns out it was stupid. In fact, Max's death made me temporarily insane for a while. I did some things honest men won't do. I lost my job, then was criminally prosecuted. I went to a federal prison for two years."

"What?" ProV blurted. "If that is true, how did you ever get back on Wall Street?"

"Well, we won the appeal of my case. Even though I had spent two full years in prison, my record was expunged. I was eligible to work

[270] Proverbs 20:12

again, and someone took a chance, I should say second chance, on a forty-year-old depressed financial wizard. I got a mulligan.

"Let's finish this story at the clubhouse," said Lucas as raindrops started to fall gently.

The pilgrims and caddies arrived at the back entrance and Hollie led them into a small bar on the bottom floor, overlooking the North Sea. "Sit here for a while, guys," she said. "Finish your story, Lucas. Mr. T and I will take your bags back to the valet for delivery to your car. Take your time."

ProV and Lucas sat at the bar, their backs to the window and the sea. Cana the bartender was there again. "Good afternoon, gentlemen. Can I get you anything?"

"Cana, I suppose no one should leave without one tiny sip of your famous wine," said the normally teetotaling Lucas.

"Good choice, sir. And could I also recommend our daily bread?"

They nodded thanks, and Lucas continued. "So, ProV, let me finish this story. It won't take long. As it happened, the psychiatrist I was seeing suggested that religion helps certain people. She was not religious herself, but she was smart enough to suggest it when all else failed. And with me, all else was failing. Angie was still depressed. Max had died. Her crooked husband had gone to prison. Who can blame her?"

Cana brought the wine and a small loaf of bread, saying, "We save the best for last."[271]

Lucas continued. "But, I did not just decide to believe in God or some brand of religion." He paused to let his words sink in. "I had an *experience*."

"Such as?"

"Ever heard of Pascal?"

"Nope."

"Well, he was a famous French mathematician and philosopher. On November twenty-third, in 1654, at ten-thirty at night, he had an experience that lasted two hours. He called it 'fire.' He was immediately

[271] John 2:10

transformed. He spoke of it widely and went from being a very respected scientist and genius to being dismissed as a fool, all because he experienced God. He met Jesus Christ that night. Most people never have such an experience."[272]

Lucas took a sip of the wine. He was a teetotaler, but combined with the tasty bread, he sensed this was the holiest communion he had ever experienced, sharing his story with his friend.

"ProV, I too experienced the Holy. I was sitting in the bar at the Dornoch Castle Hotel. I came to celebrate winning the appeal of my case. It was my first trip to Dornoch. Angelina had stayed home, still depressed. I read Pascal's story in some sort of pamphlet I had randomly found. I went to my room at ten o'clock, turned out the light and at ten-thirty the same experience of Pascal became my experience. Fire! God entered my heart! Jesus Christ! I walked across to the Dornoch Cathedral and sat there on fire for two hours."

Lucas looked squarely into ProV's teary eyes: "When I got home, before I could even say a word, Angie said, 'What's wrong with you?' I said, 'What do you mean?' She said, 'You're smiling. You haven't smiled since the day Max died.'

"The good news for me was that Angie told me she had a similar experience on the exact same night. She was nervous about what to say to me when I got home, so when I showed up smiling it was the happiest moment of her life, or so she said."

ProV nodded like he understood.

"So, my friend, our suffering and sorrows led Angie and me both to the arms of a Christ who suffered but now comforts."

He sipped the Cana wine. He ate the Orkney bread. He did it in remembrance of his Savior who suffered to give him life.

"Our sufferings became a treasure because we let them bring us to

[272] *"Monday, 23 November, 1654: From about half past ten in the evening until half past midnight. Fire. 'God of Abraham, God of Isaac, God of Jacob,' not of philosophers and scholars. Certainty, certainty, heartfelt joy, peace. God of Jesus Christ."* Keith Ward, *Pascal's Fire: Scientific Faith and Religious Understanding*, (Oxford, Oneworld Publications, 2006).

God. You could do the same if you can find your pain. It is there. Let your pain lead you to Him. To quote our friend Hollie, 'There's a treasure in the darkness,'" said Lucas with a sincere smile. They sat in silence for three minutes. ProV didn't know what to say.

Hollie returned and said, "Guys, one more experience. Turn around."

As ProV and Lucas swiveled around, the room was suddenly filled with people who could be seen but not heard. How did they get there? Was this a mirage? Anything was possible by now.

ProV knew every person there. But it seemed as if they could not see ProV or Lucas or Hollie. Hollie said in a gentle voice, "ProV, it's time to let go of the pain and sorrow. Let God use it."

ProV saw his mother, just twenty-five, and was reminded she had seldom held him. She was on the phone, telling her friend Lucy, "I should have never had kids. Nothing but a pain." She was clearly referring to her troublesome and active five-year-old son, Paul.

ProV instinctively knew this "friend" Lucy was part of his mom's troubles. She was unhappy and wanted everyone else to be unhappy, too. His mom, after one too many, had once told little Paul Junior, "You remind me of your useless father."

He saw his father, sitting in a corner, nursing a straight vodka. He remembered Paul Senior had pushed and sometimes even physically shoved him to play better golf. His father's hopes for glory were all on the shoulders of a young Paul, whose swing was better than his scores for a long time.

He saw Sally, his first true love in the tenth grade. She was just sixteen, innocently looking out the window at the sea. He thought she was the one for sure until her family moved away. When he heard she had been killed in a car wreck in Los Angeles, he decided that day God either did not exist, or if He did, He was a really nasty dude. He wanted nothing to do with such a creature.

He saw three young men hanging around the bar. They were his three friends on the mini tours. Norman, Charlie and Fred all had died in three separate tragedies. A suicide. Drunk driving. Cancer. Suffering just proved God is not there. That was ProV's thought at the time.

And then ProV saw a little boy, perhaps five years old, sitting at his desk in the first grade in an elementary school in Paradise, California. It was 2018 and a black smoke was filling the room. And then a school bus full of children, that same black smoke filling his lungs.

He vividly remembered that even though he had survived the tragic forest fire, his heart was never the same. He never felt safe again. Other children had died. His parents had not seemed to care that much. They seemed more worried about their stuff than their son. Why did he not die? He had no answers. The question came into his brain almost every week since he was five.

Where was God in all the death and destruction?

Hollie was softly speaking into ProV's ear, "Embrace the suffering. Faith begins where logic ends. The mystery of God's way is that He takes suffering and redeems us all. He sent his son to die. At age thirty-three. Seemed way too soon, don't you think? He never even had time to get 'wise' like we've discussed. He had to suffer and die, and thankfully be risen... and now we suffer with him." Hollie paused to let her words sink into ProV's soul.

"In fact, my best times are at the Shed of Tears, praying with Jesus for people like you."

"Thank you, Hollie. You need to know—I *do* believe," said ProV before he could even think much about the words coming out of his mouth. A huge smile came across Hollie's face.

"I know," she said. "But there is one more bonus treasure. Go shower, pack your bags and come back here. We will have lunch ready and then you can hit the road."

ProV and Lucas were emotionally done, both refreshed and exhausted.

They returned to their rooms for a quick shower, with hot water from the ceiling and enough water pressure to make the skin turn red. Neither one wanted to leave Hokmah, but it was time.

The bags were packed quickly and returned to the clubhouse. One final treasure awaited.

CHAPTER 8
Malachi's Treasure

Hollie was waiting outside the clubhouse entrance. She said her good-byes with hugs and just said, "Now, go to lunch. Two men will meet you there with one last treasure."

Hollie wiped away a happy tear as she left her two pilgrims. No doubt about it. ProV had made progress. His smile was giving him away.

ProV and Lucas were happy to know that suffering would not be their final treasure.

The clubhouse doors opened and they marched into the same pub they had entered the day before. Epaphras was there again to greet them. Was it just yesterday when they walked in and saw Hogan in the locker room? It felt like ten years ago.

The host's name was Pascal, a handsome Frenchman, who sure enough reminded them of Jean Van de Velde, the man who had once been famous for losing a tournament he could not lose.

"Is this the guy in the fire you were telling me about?" asked ProV, who by now could not be surprised by anything or anyone.

"I don't know," said Lucas. "He always said he wanted to be a humble servant in God's kingdom."

Pascal led them to a corner table where two elderly gentlemen stood with a smile. One was Moses. He had been at the Mulligan group that morning to hear Paul. He had been sitting quietly in the rear and neither ProV or Lucas had noticed him until Wright introduced them as they were headed out the door. Moses stood to greet the tired pilgrims. "Good afternoon, men. Let me introduce you to my friend Malachi."

ProV and Lucas shook hands with Malachi and took seats facing the sea and the eighteenth green at Hokmah. The rain was dribbling again through the shadows and sunshine. "Showers of blessings is what I'd call them," said Malachi with a smile.

"So I hope your game this morning was exhilarating. I actually went out with Wally for a playing lesson until the rains came," said Moses, who was 120 when he died and looked every bit of it even now. He was dressed in golf attire instead of the outfit of a desert nomad. "I think I found something this morning on my backswing that may help me."

Moses was unaware that Wally had whispered to Hollie as they left the morning gathering, "Don't tell him I said this, but Moses might be the worst golfer I have ever tried to help. He is trying to shoot his age when he left the earth. One-twenty. He can't seem to get there. No one wants to play with him."

Moses's excitement about the treasure of a better backswing continued: "Hollie has promised to take me out next week and help me shoot my age from the super senior tees."

ProV couldn't help thinking, *How can bad golfers love golf so much? And who would ever think Moses would love golf?*

Moses now got down to the business of food, "So, what do you guys want for lunch? They literally can cook up anything." Malachi could not resist a bad joke. "Anything but manna and quail."

Lucas laughed. Moses had heard it too often. ProV looked confused and had no idea what they meant. He asked, "So, help me out, is manna some sort of Orkney specialty?"

Now they all three laughed out loud at ProV's expense. Moses replied, "There's a book I wrote, ProV. It's called Exodus. The story is all there. It is a sequel to Genesis, you could say."

Lucas offered to help ProV find a good copy. But Moses beat him to the punch, pulled out a Bible, signed the inside cover and held it up for ProV to see. "There you go. An author's copy might be worth something someday."

Lucas was shaking his head and smiling. ProV wondered if this might be the final treasure—and then quickly speculated on whether it might sell for a few million dollars. If he could authenticate it.

Moses could read the poor man's mind. "ProV, there is one final treasure you need to know about," he said as he opened the autographed book. "It is not the book, but it is *in* the book."

But first, Pascal took everyone's order. There was no menu. You could order anything you wanted at The Loaves and Fishes Bar and Grill. Every day.

They all ordered, and as they waited, Moses continued.

He opened the book. The pages fell open to Deuteronomy. Moses read words he had written long ago:

> *For you are a holy people, who belong to the Lord your God. Of all the people on earth, the Lord your God has chosen you to be his own special treasure.*[273]
>
> *You have been set apart as holy to the Lord your God, and he has chosen you from all the nations of the earth to be his own special treasure.*[274]
>
> *The Lord has declared today that you are his people, his own special treasure, just as he promised, and that you must obey all his commands.*[275]

[273] Deuteronomy 7:6

[274] Deuteronomy 14:2

[275] Deuteronomy 26:18

He emphasized "special treasure" all three times.

"Notice any words there in all three sentences?" asked Moses, who was born and raised in the palaces of Egypt and then led millions of his own people, the Jews, through the desert for forty years.

"His own special treasure?" ProV guessed the obvious.

"Exactly. Let me remind you, everything I wrote down was, literally, what God told me. I was merely a word processor for God's edicts. The Hebrew word for treasure is Segullah."

ProV was listening intently. He knew the course they had just played without keeping score was indeed a treasure.

The patriarch continued, "Perhaps you recall the seventeenth hole yesterday, the Love hole? Remember hesed, God's lovingkindness? There's no English way to explain it. We who deserve nothing receive everything."

"Our people, Israel, lived sadly in ignorance about all that. I wrote it down and explained it every day, but still, the people had a bad self-image. They were the '*treasure of God*,' but they couldn't believe it.

"As for me, I was a selfish man for eighty years. I was a murderer. I was living for myself. But I finally believed God's *hesed* was real for me."

Moses looked into ProV's eyes, and said, "You, Paul Player, are the treasure of God. He would literally do anything for you. In fact, He did it already when he came to earth as a man to die on a cross and pay the penalty for all your sins. But you must believe it. It won't happen inside you until you truly believe you are God's treasure."

"I do believe in Jesus. It's me I am not sure about," said ProV in a wonderful moment of honesty. He wanted to say more but could find no words.

Malachi broke the silence. "Two thousand years after Moses, and four hundred years before the days of the Savior, I heard the same voice."

He turned the pages on the book Moses had handed him. "I wrote a little book too. I am no Moses. But I did hear the same voice. And God promised me the same thing I tell you today. *You* are God's special treasure. You don't need to worry any longer about seeking a treasure. God is seeking you. You are His treasure."

He then read from the book:

> *They will be my people...they will be my own special treasure. I will spare them as a father spares an obedient child.*[276]

The room was now quiet, just as God seemed to be for four hundred years after Malachi's vision.

Malachi said, "My vision ended with a promise that a prophet would come along who would *'turn the hearts of fathers to their children and the hearts of children to their fathers.'*[277] Hollie had decided these should be the final words of the Old Testament."

ProV looked somewhat confused, but Malachi continued, "So, let me suggest, ProV, that when you get home, go find your father if he is still living. Is he alive?"

"I have not seen him in ten years. But yes. I am sure he's alive."

"Go find him. You will discover that you were more of a treasure to him than you ever believed. Paul Sr. may not have been very good at the fathering thing, as you well know. But trust me, you were his treasure. That's why he wanted so badly for you to succeed. And why he was so hurt when you didn't meet his ridiculous expectations."

ProV hadn't seen his dad in more than ten years. Their last encounter was a fist fight in the parking lot after his aunt's funeral. Paul Sr. said something negative about ProV's mother and instincts took over. He had punched his father and bloodied his nose. The fight was over before it started, but the memory had lasted a decade.

Malachi continued, "But none of this makes sense unless you first know this: *You* are the treasure of your heavenly Father!"

The food had come. One last fabulous Middle Eastern meal at Hokmah. The conversation turned lighter as Moses and Malachi asked what the boys thought about the golf course—favorite holes and favorite shots of the day.

[276] Malachi 3:17

[277] Malachi 4:6

Moses advised they write down whatever they remember because, "Honestly, the times here are so amazing that you will forget some wonderful moments."[278]

The "last supper" was finally completed. It was now 2:30 p.m., and they needed to try to catch the three o'clock Listening Ferry, then the five o'clock ferry back to Kirkwall and the eight o'clock ferry back to Scrabster, then the ninety-minute drive back to Dornoch. The rental car was packed and ready to go.

Moses and Malachi said their goodbyes, looking into ProV's passenger window to offer one last revelation. Malachi said, "Oh, by the way, the prophet who turns the hearts of fathers toward children and vice versa? You met him as you came in yesterday. Remember that John fellow out by the highway?"

They both nodded and ProV said, "Yes, of course."

"That's him. Be sure to say something as you leave."

"Thank you so much."

Lucas pulled out of the car park, quickly found the Listening Ferry with Mr. Z, back through Yahweh's Gate, waving goodbye to the gatekeeper Shallum, and onto the Narrow Way.

At the intersection to the main road, sure enough, John was there. ProV rolled down his window for a brief thank you, but John was not up for friendly banter. He was all business, very direct. "ProV, go find your father when you get home," said the same man who looked like he may have never had a bath or haircut. "He will be looking for you."

"My dad will be looking for me? Are you sure? Our last meeting was a fight in a parking lot ten years ago."

John just said, "Give him a chance. He loves you, man."

ProV rolled up his window, shaking his head at the strangest thing he had heard yet.

They arrived at the Pierowall ferry just in time. ProV was no longer nervous about missing the ferry—or anything really. He would have

[278] Deuteronomy 6:8 "Tie them to your hands and wear then on your forehead as reminders."

been fine to be stuck on Westray for another day or more. The nerves of locating Hokmah were gone. And so was his burden of sin. His burden of guilt. Hope was breathing in his soul for the first time. He was transformed like a caterpillar to a butterfly. He was free. He was also curious about how his father would find him.

The 5:00 p.m. ferry to Kirkwall left on time, as usual. The pilgrims settled into comfortable swivel chairs, and both got out journals to write down remembrances of the days at Hokmah. They would follow Moses's advice: Remember.

For Lucas, the second time was better than the first. The thrill of transformation in a friend is one of life's sweet pleasures, even better than the change in one's own life. Leading ProV to Hokmah and God was now the highlight of his life. He had paid a huge price and it had been worth every penny.

Both men went on the deck of the ferry to experience the sights and sounds and smells of traveling on a boat through the Orkney Islands. The sun was shining. The sky was Carolina blue. "Was that a dream?" asked ProV, still numb from the experience.

Lucas shook his head and said, "I am honestly not sure."

At 6:45 p.m., the ferry pulled into Kirkwall. Lucas drove the car out into the Orkney sunshine. A line of six pedestrians and four cars waited patiently to get back on the ferry for a northbound return. The steeple of the magnificent 900-year-old St. Magnus Cathedral dominated the city skyline. *I wonder if St. Magnus ever made it to Hokmah*? Lucas thought to himself.

Pulling out of the ferry, ProV saw the two monks they had met just two days ago, and shouted to Lucas, "Stop! There are the two monks!"

Lucas hit the brakes, made a U-turn and pulled up next to the two brown robed men. Sure enough, it was Father Stephen and Brother Victor—or was it the other way around, thought Lucas.

ProV smiled and greeted the holy men, not sure what to call them. He settled on, "Gentlemen, we made it back alive. Good to see you."

"Ah, I knew you would. We prayed for you. We are headed back to Papa Stronsay. Did you find your golf course?" said the older man.

ProV didn't wait for Lucas to answer. He was ready. "Indeed we did. Most amazing two days of my life. Changed everything, I hope."

"Wonderful. What did you find?" The holy men seemed genuinely interested.

ProV pondered the question, knowing many more people would make that inquiry when he tried to tell the story. Finally, he settled on the obvious: "We found a wisdom in the sand. We found a treasure in the darkness."

He smiled, hoping the monks would understand. Instead, the look on their faces left ProV pretty sure they were clueless on this one. The monks had not experienced the Voice in the cathedral. Maybe even these holy men needed an *experience* with Hollie and all her friends at Hokmah.

The older monk spoke for them both when he simply said, "God is good," smiling as he noticed people getting on the ferry. "Now it looks like we need to go. Can we hope to see you on our island someday?"

"For sure. And one last time, remind me. What's the name of your order?"

"Sons of the Most Holy Redeemer," said the smiling monk.

"I like that. Me too," said ProV with a grin that might never leave his face. "I too am a Son of the Most Holy Redeemer."

Lucas put the car into gear and off they went. His pilgrim had made progress for sure.

He was on his way.

A Son of the Most Holy Redeemer.

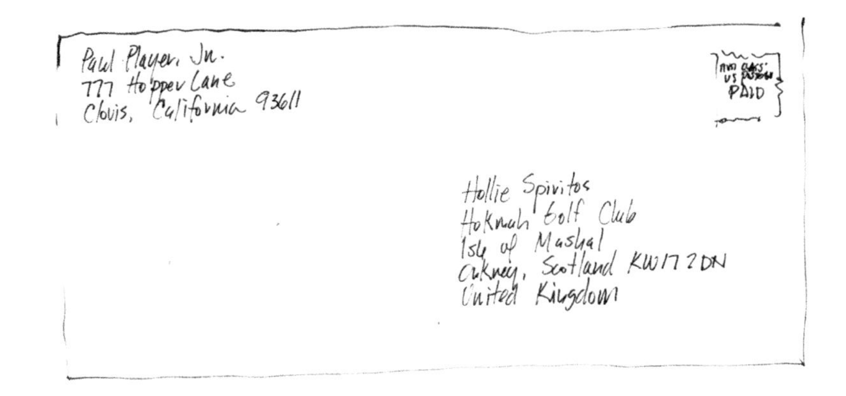

Postscript 2068

Dear Hollie,

I am sure you remember me. I will certainly never forget you and my two-day experience at Hokmah twelve years ago.

I hope to return in August. This letter will explain what has happened since we met.

First, an update on my father.

When I got home to California, it took me only three days to find him. He was working at a driving range, fitting people with golf clubs, and believe it or not, he was leading an AA group for alcoholic golfers near Oakland. They met in the bar of an old public goat ranch and driving range called Stewart's Links. He was sober.

I tracked him down at a 7:00 a.m. coffee-and-donuts AA meeting and walked in without any warning. I was nervous, of course. He was sitting on a stool upfront, speaking to twenty or so people about one of the "Twelve Steps." He stopped when he saw me come in a side door. He stared at me, and then broke down and cried for three full minutes. One of the young guys near the front walked up to embrace him as he wept.

He regained his composure and introduced me: "Hey, folks, see this handsome young man? That's my boy. He played in the Masters a few years ago and is the greatest golfer I have ever seen. I am not the only Paul Player on this planet. Welcome Paul Jr."

The small crowd of repentant drunks and druggies stood and gave me a standing ovation. Half of them came over and hugged me like I was a brother. One old guy with wretched coffee breath whispered, "The old man's been talking about you a lot lately."

Dad and I hugged and wept. Whatever agenda they had for this meeting was gone.

That's the moment I knew for sure Hokmah had not been a dream. I had wondered if the whole experience might have been some sort of hallucination.

Dad's first words after the meeting were, "Son, I should have found you earlier. About a month ago, I had a dream. It was all about you. Some sort of angel-like person showed up on my back porch where I drink coffee every morning. This person said, 'Paul, you have a *treasure* you don't seem to know about.' I told the angel, 'Great, because I have a lot of bills to pay. Where is this treasure?' He said, "It's not money, it's something better. You have a son. He is named after you. Paul Jr. is a special treasure. Go find him.' I haven't told anyone about that dream. I just didn't know what to do. But here you are. Then you come walking back into my life. Son, I am so sorry. Can you forgive me? I deserve nothing. But I need you to forgive me."

I said, "Of course, Dad, I forgive you. And I love you."

Hollie, I had never even thought those words, let alone voiced them. "I love you."

So our reunion was more than we could have ever planned. I suppose I need to thank you or Malachi or John the Baptist or someone for showing up to speak to my dad.

Second, there is my wife, Mary Ann. She had never remarried, so I knew, thanks to you and Lucas, that she should be a priority. I had hurt her in so many ways. No one could have been more selfish than me while we were married.

She refused all my phone calls for several weeks when we got back from Scotland. When I finally got through, she coldly said, "Call me when you catch up on the child support."

I called Lucas and asked his advice. My bank account had $239. He told me to sell my golf clubs and my beloved vintage 1966 Mustang convertible. I did. It took every penny to pay her the $12,000 arrearages in child support. I had never done anything unselfish like that in my whole life. Mary Ann saw some light. I wrote her letters. She read them. I told her about Lucas. I told her Dad and I were reconciled, going to AA and church. The fool who went to Scotland to play golf was gone, replaced by God's special treasure.

I prayed I could have "hesed" love for Mary Ann. And then God gave her a gift. He gave her "hesed" for me. She started to love me again, only this time it was God's love, not just some romantic misty feeling like we had in college. Agape and hesed replaced eros.

I deserved nothing, but Mary Ann gave me everything. Just like God.

So, after six months of "dating," she was convinced. Player's Progress was real.

Mary Ann and I returned to Dornoch eleven years ago, in August 2057. We got remarried in the Dornoch Cathedral. Pastor Fairweather was over ninety years old and still kicking. He agreed to marry us. His two sons, Luke and Timmy, were the witnesses, along with their wives and children. What a blessing. We said our vows on the exact spot where I heard you say, ***"There's a wisdom in the sand. There's a treasure in the darkness."***

We honeymooned at the Dornoch Castle Hotel. I arranged for the same room, 203, where I had stayed and begun to read about the connection between links golf and God. I finally told Mary Ann the full story of Hokmah. I had not been able to do it before we married. It was just too much. Who would believe it? A caddie named Hollie, plus Ben Hogan, Byron Nelson, Jack Nicklaus, and on and on until you get to Job and Moses and Abraham, not to mention Jesus Himself on the mountaintop.

And then the treasure named Lucas. On our honeymoon trip in 2057 to Dornoch, I didn't complain but I experienced a lot of leg and lower back pain. We soon found it was CKD—chronic kidney disease.

Doctors told me I needed a new kidney. It was difficult to find a donor. Lucas secretly went for a test and discovered he was a perfect match.

My friend gave me his kidney.

The doctors said Lucas's age, 73 at the time, was a small risk factor, but with his history of no smoking or alcohol abuse and no diabetes, it should be fine. Even his previous heart attack had done no damage to his healthy kidney.

We were all laughing that part of Lucas would be inside me! I joked with him that I should hit more fairways and greens with his kidney. And be wiser as well.

But then all the possible complications came true. Lucas never left the hospital. His heart stopped during surgery and he died the next day, his heart damaged beyond repair. He died on Christmas Eve, 2057. He knew the risk. He told me before we both went under the anesthesia, "ProV, I will see you soon. I am not giving you my life, just a kidney, so don't make this a bigger deal than it is."

I never spoke to him again. My treasure was gone. He died for me.[279] I woke up from surgery with a new kidney and dead friend. I know I don't need to quote Proverbs to you, but I found a verse which says the *"seeds of good deeds become a tree of life; a wise person wins friends."*[280] I have had a strong sense now for many years that Lucas was a seed planted in the ground and now, a tree of life has grown in me. His life changed mine.

I imagine Lucas was reunited with Angelina, just like at Hokmah, with a huge smile on his face. He passed through Beulah Land to find her alive and well.

I lost my treasure on the same day Lucas was reunited with his treasure.

Sorry, this is longer than I planned.

But last, the treasure of suffering and sorrow has also been granted to me since I last saw you. Not just my own illness and Lucas. That

[279] John 15:13 "There is no greater love than to lay down one's life for one's friends."

[280] Proverbs 11:30

would have been enough. But Dad died about a year after our reunion. He suffered a lot. I told him all about Hokmah. He believed me. And it helped him to understand his own suffering. He used it to counsel with the guys at his AA meetings.

And when I got sick with the kidney, I lost my job. But the blessing was that even though my income was eventually cut in half, my new part-time job working at a pro shop doubled my time with my family, including the children who needed me. I repaired my relationships with Lindy and Paul III ("Trey"). I even walked Lindy down the aisle when she married a nice young man who is too smart to play golf. Both of my children have found wonderful life partners.

And then the heartache of our first grandchild. Paul Player IV went to heaven after only one week on earth. How could this be? But again, the suffering of losing his first and only son led Trey to seek the love of Jesus for himself.

He was a skeptic on my stories about Hokmah. But when his son died, after a few months he finally believed for himself. He realized Jesus Himself was a man of sorrows, dying on the cross for all of us.

And now, my dear Mary Ann has breast cancer. The prognosis is uncertain. She is in remission, thank God. The good news is she now has a new husband, one who will take care of her night and day. Hesed!

Last, some golf news. I started playing golf again six years ago at age 49. I didn't touch a club for five years after Hokmah. Mary Ann is the one who said I should play again. Now that was hesed love.

In the back of my mind, I thought maybe the Senior Tour would be possible. Insanity attacks a lot of 49-year-old former college and mini-tour players. You forget that the same people who beat you at twenty-five are still around to beat you at fifty. Only those guys have been playing and practicing and working out in gyms every day since then, instead of selling golf balls, smoking, drinking and going to divorce court.

But I came to my senses, signed up for the US Senior Amateur last summer and, guess what, not only qualified but won!

A USGA champion. All thanks to Lucas and the things you showed me at Hokmah one fine day in the Orkney Islands in 2056.

Please give my regards and thanks to Mr. T. He says more with his silence than anyone I know says with words.

And of course, I am sure Mr. Wright is still swinging a sweet stick. Give him my regards and tell him I hope we play when I arrive in August. I sometimes laugh out loud thinking about Deadend and Mocker. What a pair!

I will be bringing a young man named Timothy. He needs a lot of help and Hollie, I can't think of anyone better than you to help him. Someday I will bring Trey. He is still busy with a wife and beautiful twin daughters who need him right now.

And by the way, as you know, I was the guest of Lucas on the last trip. He gave his all to take me there. I now realize the trip to Hokmah will cost me everything. I am finally ready to give it all.

Your special treasure,

Paul ProV Player, Jr.

Paul "ProV" Player, Jr.

Acknowledgments

Thank you, my dear *Sue*. You are on the top of the list. Do you remember ten years ago when we were walking on a beach in Florida? With fear and trembling I gave you the outline of *Player's Progress*. The search for Wisdom. The study of Proverbs. The journey of two friends into a world of bizarre characters. You said something like, "I like it." You did not realize the power of those words. I returned to the condo and wrote the first paragraph, starting with two pilgrims looking down a narrow road, hoping to find the greatest golf course in the world. So, Sue, thanks for saying, "I like it." I am just sorry it took ten years to get here. And once again, I hope you like it!

Thank you, *Pete Bronson*. I would not think to publish a book without your skillful editing and publishing advice. Your gift for writing is apparent, but you also have a passion for golf and God. Thank you, Pete, for protecting me from myself – once again. And thank you as well for recommending *Craig Ramsdell* for the design and *Jane Wenning* for proofreading. www.chilidogpress.com

Thank you *Laura Hopper, Ken Hopper* and *Adele Hopper.* As you well know, my friend *Jeff Hopper* (your husband and son) was supposed to be a major contributor to the final editing team. He had a draft in his "inbox" when he went to heaven last year. I now imagine that Jeff is on Hokmah's 18th green, with Hollie Spiritos on his bag, finishing the greatest day of his life with a closing birdie and a rainbow. Since I cannot thank Jeff personally, I thank you instead for sharing him with so many people like me.

Thank you, *Alicia Samuel*. This book could not have happened without your painstaking work on the footnotes and more. We pray for you now as you prepare in Singapore to be a missionary in your beloved homeland, India.

Huge thanks, *Carter Quina*. I wanted illustrations to be a prominent part of the book, just like *The Pilgrim's Progress* in 1678. You were right under my nose in our Friday morning Bible study at Steelwood Country Club in Alabama. Finding you was like getting Tom Brady in the 7th round of the NFL draft. You told me you could do it. And you did! Thank you for giving your talent and imagination to the readers.

Thank you, *Chad Crouch*. I would never undertake any creative project without your support and help. The cover finally came together thanks to your talent, using one of Carter's photos from the Orkney Islands. Your wise counsel on the website and all things creative has been essential. www.Cre8tivegroup.com.

Thank you, *Tom Heilbron* and *Steve Forrest*. You guys were also a vital part of the artistic team. Tom, you drew the first draft of Hokmah's 18-hole layout and made the course come alive – then suggested a call to renowned golf course architect Steve Forrest for help with the scorecard. Steve, thanks for the scorecard and your editing suggestions. www.hillsforrestsmith.com

Thank you to *Orkney friends*. I needed true Orcadians to help me accurately describe life in the Orkney Islands. Thanks to *Foster* and *Jean Wright* for your gracious hospitality and advice, sitting in your living room on the isle of Westray. Thank you, *Brother Dominic* at Golgotha Monastery. You hosted Carter and me on Papa Stronsay on September 25, 2021, a day we will never forget. You answered questions I didn't even know existed. Thanks also to *Tom* and *Rhonda Mui*r, expert storytellers from Kirkwall. I am hoping that *Player's Progress* might join your list of favorite fantasies from the Orkney Islands.

Thanks to *Royal Dornoch Golf Club* and *Brora Golf Club*, my two favorite courses in the world. I cannot overstate the influence on this book of the sensational linksland of Royal Dornoch and Brora.

In Dornoch, special thanks to *Neil Hampton* for sound advice and encouragement. Thanks to my Christian brother and champion golfer *Alex McDonald* and *Claire*. And thanks to the entire *Fairns family*, which includes my pastor in Dornoch, *Grant*, wife *Kirsty*, grandmother *Barrie* (whose edits were essential), plus sons *Luke* and *Timmy* who accompanied me around the Struie course.

Special thanks to *Rev. Dr. Susan Brown,* former pastor at the famous Dornoch Cathedral and chaplain to the Queen when she comes to Scotland (now that's impressive). You allowed me to borrow your timeless spiritual advice written into Royal Dornoch's Course Guide.

In the lovely village of Brora, thanks especially to club President *Andy Stewart* and my main golf combatant *David "Titch" Roberts*. Our games at Brora, contested for a valuable one pound, always seem to go the 18th hole. While Royal Dornoch is the more famous venue (currently ranked consensus #4 in the world), Brora is just as much fun and a worthy little brother. Many of the holes at Hokmah were developed with the perfect turf of Brora in mind.

Thanks to Brora's Sunday evening worshippers at *Fisherman's Hall.* Sue and I cherish our weekly evenings with you, singing old hymns and listening to the beautiful brogue of local preachers. And finally, to our friends in Brora the *Barbertons* (great neighbors) and the *Durbans* (perfect landlords).

Thank you, *John Oswalt*. You are a true biblical scholar. I texted you way too often, looking for just the right Hebrew words to describe concepts from Proverbs. You always responded with patience and lovingkindness. Hokmah. Segullah. Hesed. And more. Even though you are way too smart to play golf, you helped write a book for golfers!

Thanks, *Terry Faris,* for your wisdom and knowledge of the Greek New Testament. Your insight into love and wisdom, especially the "logos" of John One, was an education for me.

Thanks to the men who gather weekly at *Keene Trace Golf Club* in Kentucky and *Steelwood Country Club* in Alabama. Your valuable feedback over many months improved the book. You are the model for the Monday Mulligan group at Hokmah.

Thanks to the entire leadership at *LinksPlayers International.* You always make me feel like part of the team. *Jeff Cranford, Marty Jacobus, Dennis Darville, Randy Wolff, Drew Hamilton, Dereck Wong,* and *Lewis Greer* encouraged me all the way. www.linksplayers.com

Thank you, *Chris Tiegreen*, for your professional editing advice and encouragement. Thanks as well to *Wayne Jacobsen.* You will see some of your wise handiwork in the final edition. Thanks also to authors *Steve Flairty* and *Todd Wright* for helpful comments.

Thanks to the talented people from the world of golf for taking the time to read enough of the manuscript to offer compliments. *Bill Rogers, Larry Nelson, Ted Scott, David Cook, Wally Armstrong, Randy Wolff, Sophia Popov, Tracy Hanson, Jim Hiskey* and *Pete Hiskey*. I have been blessed to know you all. We are connected by golf and God.

To anyone I've missed: My apologies and gratitude.

Tim Philpot lives on a golf course in Loxley, Alabama with his wife, Sue, and their best friend, a shorkie named Birdie Bea. Tim has retired from a career as a lawyer, senator and judge. He now writes and tells stories to anyone who will listen. He has spoken in 67 countries but prefers now to stay home in Alabama, except for several weeks each summer in Brora and Dornoch in the highlands of Scotland. For more information, go to www.timphilpot.com or www.playersprogess.com.

Printed in Great Britain
by Amazon